Casework for a Broken Heaven

A Novel

20250907

www.harwoodjones.com

ISBN: 978-1-0696985-6-8

Preamble

THE ACCORD OF CLAIM AND DIVISION

A Celestial Covenant for Post-Mortal Adjudication and Claim Resolution

Let it be declared and recorded, that upon the cessation of Open Hostilities between the Celestial and Infernal Principalities, a mutual covenant of non-intervention, non-duplication, and partitioned sovereignty was proposed, negotiated, and codified into eternal metaphysical law by the undersigned Powers.

The terms herein bind all functionaries, agents, ministers, and powers acting under Heaven and Hell, and shall remain in effect until the reappearance of the Original Authority or the end of all process, whichever occurs first.

This Covenant, executed and declared celestial law, unassailable and indivisible, fully and eternally accepted and empowered,

By and between:

The Divine Powers of Heaven

("**Heaven**")

- and -

The Infernal Powers of Hell

("**Hell**")

(Collectively referred to as the "**Principal Powers**")

With Observational Ratification by:

The Office of Purgatory

("**Purgatory**")

WHEREAS the unchecked contest for dominion over mortal souls has led to vast spiritual devastation, metaphysical instability, and the endangerment of Earth and its inhabitants through doctrinal escalation and ethereal breach;

AND WHEREAS both Principal Powers, in recognition of the catastrophic potential of preemptive soul intervention, unauthorized damnation, or unilateral ascension, acknowledge the need for mutual restraint in matters of post-mortal claim;

AND WHEREAS the Principal Powers recognize the necessity of a unified routing mechanism by which souls shall be automatically conveyed to their rightful post-mortal destination absent dispute or anomaly;

AND WHEREAS the Parties declare their mutual intention to de-escalate the metaphysical arms race;

AND WHEREAS reaffirming that no realm shall infringe upon the sovereign jurisdiction of another through force, deception, or spiritual manipulation, and that post-mortal peace is to be secured with the least distortion of divine intent or mortal dignity;

AND WHEREAS the Parties urge the cooperation of all subordinate dominions and emissaries in adherence to this framework, and in pursuit of the shared aim of cosmic stability;

AND WHEREAS recalling the spirit of the Seventh Sphere Declaration and the Infernal Compact of Restraint, wherein both realms first expressed intent to cease the ungoverned seizure of mortal souls across disputed thresholds;

AND WHEREAS desiring to strengthen inter-realm trust, mitigate the frequency of tether ruptures, and limit the weaponization of divine or infernal intervention against human autonomy;

AND WHEREAS the Authority of Purgatory, in its custodial and redhibitory capacity, has affirmed the necessity of a ratified covenant to limit the theater of spiritual conflict and preserve inter-realm equilibrium;

AND WHEREAS this Accord is intended as a framework of primary legal principles governing jurisdiction, claim resolution, operative conduct, and metaphysical sovereignty, with the understanding that operational details, procedural mechanisms, technical definitions, and specific inter-party obligations shall be codified in such Annexes, Schedules, and Appendices as may be appended hereto from time to time;

NOW THEREFORE, the Principal Powers, with the ratifying and witnessing presence of the Purgatorial Authority, and in recognition of these eternal truths and operational necessities, do hereby enact this Accord of Claim and Division as the supreme governing covenant of post-mortal jurisdiction, to be interpreted in accordance with its Articles and subject to expansion through duly ratified Annexes, Schedules, and Appendices as may be adopted from time to time.

Article I.   Definitions

1) **Accord**: This Covenant, including all articles, annexes, and ratified interpretations.
2) **Agent**: Any functionary empowered to act on behalf of a Principal Power.
3) **Claim**: The act of asserting rightful custody over a Soul.
4) **Jurisdiction**: The recognized authority of a realm to process and house Souls within its

domain.

5) **Party**: Any signatory or ratifying body to this Accord.

6) **Protocol**: The automated routing mechanism for uncontested Soul transference.

7) **Soul**: The incorporeal essence of a mortal being, subject to post-mortem adjudication.

Article II.   Jurisdictional Boundaries

1) Heaven shall have exclusive jurisdiction over Souls deemed righteous, redeemed, or saved by grace.

2) Hell shall have exclusive jurisdiction over Souls deemed damned or irredeemable.

3) Purgatory shall serve as a neutral holding realm for Souls undergoing purification or awaiting final adjudication.

Article III.   The Protocol

1) As an essential component to negotiated peace, the Principal Powers have established an independent sorting power for the management of the post-mortal continuum and this Accord (the "**Protocol**"). The Protocol shall operate independently and remain neutral, unaligned with either Principal Power Its function shall be the reception, triage, and routing of incoming Souls in accordance with tether integrity, ruling clarity, and Protocol eligibility.

2) The Protocol shall serve as the default mechanism for the immediate, automatic routing of Souls to their ordained destination, as determined by the Judgment Record at time of

death.

3) The Protocol shall apply to all Souls for whom the tether is intact, ruling uncontested, and record complete.

Article IV.   Routing Criteria

1) Heaven shall receive all Souls marked for grace.
2) Hell shall receive all Souls marked for damnation.
3) Purgatory shall receive all Souls marked for cleansing, delay, or incomplete ruling.

Article V.   Operatives

1) Each Party is hereby vested with the sovereign and exclusive right to designate, commission, and deploy operatives ("**Agents**") for the execution of post-mortal duties, investigations, claims processing, field adjudication, enforcement, or spiritual retrieval, as determined by internal protocols and jurisdictional mandates.

2) An Agent duly appointed under this section shall act with full legal, metaphysical, and procedural authority in the name of their designating Party. Such appointment shall be deemed binding and operative upon inscription of the Agent's name and function in the Ledger of Appointment maintained by their respective Authority.

3) All Parties covenant to recognize, honour, and not impede the lawful function of an Agent acting within their assigned jurisdiction and scope. Each Agent's seal, signet, or authorization

mark shall constitute prima facie evidence of valid appointment and operative status under this Accord. Such identifiers shall be honored as conclusive evidence of operational status unless credibly challenged through formal complaint before the Council.

4) Agents shall remain subject to recall, revocation, or limitation at the sole discretion of the designating Party, provided such action is recorded and certified in the Ledger of Appointment. No Party may revoke or alter the status of another Party's Agent.

5) While deployed, an Agent shall not be considered a representative of any other Party save their own, and shall be immune from hostile metaphysical interference, unlawful confinement, or conscriptive invocation by opposing jurisdictions. Agents may be questioned or summoned only under trirealm accord or explicit multilateral agreement. Any attempt to detain or compel an Agent absent Council sanction shall be deemed unlawful metaphysical interference and may trigger sanction under Article VIII.

6) In the event of Protocol failure, alignment and transfer of a Soul may be referred to a certified Agent for manual transfer. Unresolved cases may be manually investigated and transferred by Purgatory, or in exceptional circumstances, escalated to the Council (as hereinafter defined) for review.

7) All Agents must possess valid credentials,

visible identifiers, and clear delegation.

8) All miracles, interventions, or ascensions must be logged with timestamp and origin tag.

9) Repeated failure to log shall be treated as dereliction and reviewed by the Party's compliance authority, and may, at the discretion of the compliance authority or upon cross-party petition, be escalated to the Council for formal review and possible sanction.

Article VI.   Non-Interference

1) Heaven shall not obstruct, delay, or reverse and lawful transfer initiated by Hell.

2) Hell shall not obstruct, delay, or reverse and lawful transfer initiated by Heaven.

3) Indirect influence shall not constitute interference unless proven before the Council.

4) Unauthorized entry into another realm's domain shall be deemed a breach and subject to sanction.

Article VII.   Non-Allocation

1) In the event that Protocol fails to signal a clear allocation of any Soul post-mortem (a "**Grey Soul**"), any Party's Agent may advance a claim to that Soul prior to Protocol clearance.

2) If a claim is advanced on a Grey Soul and determined to be inconsistent with Protocol allocation, the offending Agent forfeits Accord protection and is subject to immediate countermeasures.

Article VIII. Tri-Realm Council

1) A Tri-Realm Council (the "**Council**") shall be established, composed of one appointed Representative from each of the Parties, each vested with full deliberative authority by their respective realms. The Council shall function as the administrative and adjudicative body governing the enforcement, interpretation, and compliance of this Accord.
2) Council decisions require a unanimous vote unless otherwise specified. Each Representative shall hold one vote.
3) The Council shall convene each century in the Purgatorial Neutral Interstice, or sooner upon formal petition by any Party. All sessions shall be recorded, transcribed, and sealed within the Tripartite Codex, with summaries made available to each Party's Archive.
4) The Council shall possess the following powers:
    a. To hear and resolve disputes arising from contested Soul claims;
    b. To impose penalties, suspensions, censures, or corrective mandates on any Party or Agent;
    c. To authorize and receive regular compliance audits conducted by the Office of Purgatory;
    d. To issue binding clarifications, interpretations, and procedural guidance on articles or clauses of the Accord when ambiguity or conflict arises between Principle Powers; and
    e. To issue emergency protocols to suspend

or override routing operations pending investigation.

Article IX.   Role of Purgatory

1) With respect to this Accord, Purgatory shall:
   a. maintain an independent archive of judgment records;
   b. oversee the impartial execution of the Protocol in the event of instability between the Principal Powers; and
   c. Provide an Appellate Court for independent review of Council decisions. Decisions of Purgatorial Appellate Court are final and binding and not subject to further Appeal.

Article X.   Autonomy

1) Nothing in this Accord shall prevent any Party from furthering its own interests, realm management, or doctrinal framework, provided such actions do not interfere with this Accord, or the routing or judgment of souls.
2) Parties may collaborate on peaceful metaphysical innovation, subject to Council approval and oversight.

Article XI.   General Terms

1) This Accord shall constitute the governing framework for all post-mortal processes.
2) In the event of contradiction between this Accord and any annex, schedule, appendix, or ratified instrument, the text of this Accord shall govern. Annexes may supplement or clarify but

shall not nullify any core provision herein unless explicitly amended by unanimous consent.

3) Any amendments shall require unanimous approval by all Parties.

4) The Accord shall signed in triplicate and shall be registered in the official and binding Archives of Heaven, Hell, and Purgatory.

5) This Accord may not be altered except as herein provided.

IN WITNESS WHEREOF the undersigned, duly authorized, have signed this Accord.

DONE in triplicate, at the Nexus of Realms.

Archangel of Judgment, Representative of Heaven

Prince of Contingency, First Strategist of the Pit, Representative of Hell

Custodian of the Middle Ascent, Representative of Purgatory

CASE FILE: AMIRA PELL

"Tell me again. What was wrong about him?"

She didn't flinch. That was the first thing that marked her. Most do when they start to realize what's happening.

"He just wasn't the same," she said. "He was never the same."

We sat across a plain wooden table in a neat little apartment on Briar Glen Crescent, east end Hamilton. The kind of building where no one leaves, just gets quieter. Not dirty. Just paused. Like time had stopped returning calls.

No ticking clocks. No fridge hum. No breath.

"War does that to a man," I said.

"No." She looked out the window, down at the empty street. Grey neighbourhood. Black graffiti. A car left too long, stripped piece by piece. A rusted city works bin leaned into the sidewalk. One of the ones that still says "Ward 3" in faded stencil.

"His hands were wrong," she said.

I waited.

"Too small. Wrong side for the fork. He kissed different."

The past crept into her eyes like spilled ink.

"I met him at a pool hall. Loud friends. Bold with me. I liked it." She laughed — dry, quiet. "Until then, I was just a girl. Then, suddenly, I was a woman."

Her name was Amira Pell. Forty-one. Hands folded.

Hair pinned. Eyes too still.

The quiet thickened.

I gave her a nudge. "The hands."

She looked back at me. "He was good with a cue. Won a little money. Spent it on me. He showed me how to shoot. Wrapped around me. His hand over mine. I looked at it and thought…" A flicker of a smile. "Well, it's not ladylike to say what I thought."

I smiled. Crooked, but real.

"How old was he when he left?"

"Nineteen. We were just married. I said I'd wait."

"And when did he come back?"

"Four years later. Twenty-three. But it wasn't him."

I'd heard that before. Always the same tone—quiet, certain, unprovable.

"Still. You stayed together."

"Fifteen years." A pause. "He was kind. Made coffee. Sat with me when I cried. But it was like… he was copying someone who used to love me."

I took the note. Not because I believed her—just needed her to believe I did.

"Anything out of character?"

She thought. "He used to write me letters from the front. Little drawings in the margins. Doodles of our future." Her fingers whitened at the knuckles. "After he came back, he never wrote anything again."

I let that hang.

"And then?"

"He just…" Her voice thinned.

"Give me a little more detail. What day was it. What was he wearing."

She drew a breath. "Five years ago. Sunday. We'd just come back from church. Brown jacket—sleeve torn inside. White shirt. Blue tie. The one with the dog on it. I gave him that tie."

A bitter laugh. "I hated that tie."

"Go on."

"We came home. He didn't take off his shoes. I was going to say something, but…I don't know."

"What did you do?"

"I made lunch. Beef barley soup. He said he wanted it because…"

"Think of the kitchen," I said, softer. "The smell."

She closed her eyes. "Toast. Oven heat. The window open a crack."

She opened them again. "He said he needed air. And then I never saw him again."

"So you waited."

"Yes."

"For five years."

"Yes."

I closed the notebook. "That's the thing about grief. It needs proof. But it settles for ritual."

The bedroom air had forgotten how to breathe. Curtains drawn. Carpet stiff with time. A hush like dust settling on things meant to be touched.

She stood beside me as I opened the door.

There she was. Curled beside the bed. Kneeling, as if she'd started to pray and never stood back up. The body didn't look like her anymore. Sunken. Shrunken. Skin paper-thin over bone. Clavicle sharp as a broken prayer. The nightgown slipped from one shoulder. A teacup lay beside her hand, cracked but unbroken.

She didn't scream. Just looked.

"Oh," she said. Then, "I thought I'd catch it in time."

Not numb. Just past resistance.

"Didn't want the hospitals," she said. "They don't heal—just manage."

Her hand swept across a floodplain of magazines and herbal mugs. Medical paranoia turned into ritual.

"My sister pushed chemo. Didn't know what they put in those drugs."

She looked at the corpse like it was a draft she'd rewritten too many times.

"I thought if I stayed clean, stayed good, stayed faithful… maybe something holy would notice."

"And when it didn't?"

She didn't answer. Just looked at the body like it was a bad copy.

"It wasn't the cancer," she said. "It was the lie. The one I couldn't tell myself."

I walked to the dresser. Opened the bottom drawer. Pulled out the uniform I'd placed there.

Held it out.

"This was his."

She didn't move.

"The man who left," I said. "Not the one who came back."

She stepped forward. Touched the sleeve. Just her fingertips.

"He would've stayed," she said.

And that was it. Not proof. Just belief. A fiction strong enough to unstick a soul.

I didn't argue. Didn't correct her. You don't debate a tether. You cut it, or you ease it loose.

I didn't watch her dust. That part's not mine.

But the air softened. The silence exhaled. Whatever passed left its shame behind.

Precinct.

Case file 24:16. Location: Hamilton, Ontario. Type: Grief Loop. Disposition: Resolved.

"You're late," Mara said without looking up.

"Time's a mortal problem."

She slid a folder across the desk. "This one's flagged."

"Because I walked a soul out of her own grief spiral?"

"Because you signed in red ink. Again."

"Only pen I had."

"Hell uses red ink."

"We're not Hell. Yet."

She made a noise that could've been a laugh. Or a prayer

for patience. With Mara, the difference is theological.

"Wing status?"

Let the ruined edges show. Half-singed, half-forgotten. "Consider it self-evident."

"Same time tomorrow?"

"If the world doesn't end."

"It never ends," she said. "Just files itself deeper."

Almost done. Almost.

But the case itched. Not her. Him.

The tie. The letters. The hands that didn't fit.

I hadn't believed her. Still didn't. But something wasn't clean. The echo let go too easy. Like I'd used the right lie to unlock the wrong door.

So I checked.

Bad habit. Can't let go.

Military rolls. Resurrection anomalies. Hell-forged interference flags. Transit logs.

The precinct lights hummed overhead, that soft, too-bright glow they say mimics starlight. It doesn't. Starlight forgets. These lights don't. They etch you. Coffee went cold beside me, cup after cup—bitter stuff brewed in sanctified machines, holy in name only. Room's the same as always—desks too wide, chairs too straight, shelves that rearrange themselves when you're not looking. The kind of order that isn't clean, just inevitable.

Then—buried in a war with too many dead and too few names—I found it.

KIA.

Processed. Logged. Closed. And then—nothing.

No return file. No resurrection variance. No clearance.

No body came back.

Just a man in a brown jacket. No records, no remains. A hole too clean for rot—like judgment passed through and took the ash with it. If it's Hell's hand, it's been trained not to leave fingerprints. I told myself it was coincidence. That the dead leave gaps. That she filled one. But the jacket still smelled like a funeral someone got up and walked away from. And some lies sit too comfortably to be yours.

I sat with that a while.

Then stood.

Then filed a focused pull—Arthur Pell. Death processed, closed, but no return file. Just a name sealed in protocol and a hole where the body should be.

Probably nothing.

Bad habit.

But some things just don't want to die.

CASE FILE: JONATHAN MERCER

The air in the precinct was dry with memory. The kind that settles into old wings and stays.

I was tired in the bones, not the body. You learn the difference when time stops asking permission.

Mara didn't look up. She never did. Just slid the case file across the desk like a prophecy she was done believing in.

"You know I don't do Tuesdays," I said.

"It's Thursday," she said.

"Then I definitely don't do Thursdays."

The precinct never changed. Paper towers. Devotionals yellowed at the corners. That stink of sanctity faded to bureaucracy and back again.

Mara looked the same too—quiet, wings bound tight, humming nothing. Once she sang psalms between dispatches. Now she typed like she wanted Heaven to feel it.

"Flagged case," she said, tapping the folder.

I picked it up. Red stamp. *No-Show Ascension*. One of ours. Soul marked for Heaven. Never arrived.

"Jonathan Mercer," she said without being asked. "Fifty-eight. Cardiac arrest in his Bay Street office. Entry registered, no arrival. Echo-space confirmed."

"Of course I am."

She jerked her thumb behind me.

"And not alone."

I turned.

He sat on the bench like he was waiting for his first miracle. Robes clean. Scroll clipped. Wings—small, tidy, preened for inspection.

Bright eyes. Bright smile. No idea.

"Looks like a ringing hymn—before the congregation drags it down to a dirge," I muttered.

"This is Chandler," Mara said. "Your partner."

"No."

"Yes."

"Did I sin?"

"Daily. But this isn't punishment. It's policy."

"That *is* punishment."

"Sir! It's an honour. I've read all your incident reports. *The Loaves-and-Fishes Misclassification Review*— absolutely seminal. And to be placed in Threshold Division, under your command…"

"Waste of an audit," I said.

"They teach it in Ethics and Resource Management."

"It was divine overproduction. They docked my pay."

He straightened his collar. "Still—your record speaks for itself, Sael."

Mara winced. She knows how I feel about my old name.

I gave him a look. "Don't call me that."

I opened the file. Mercer's name. Death details. Attached: echo-space imprint. No ascension. No demonic interference. Just… absence.

I turned back to Mara. "What type of space?"

She shrugged. "You'll see." Then, with that glint of cruelty she saves for me: "And if you need a pen—he's got three."

"Of course he does."

I closed the folder. Looked at the boy. He was still smiling. God help him.

"Rule one," I said. "You don't talk unless I ask. Rule two. If I don't ask, assume I already hate the answer."

"Yes, sir!" he chirped.

God help *me*.

I turned to Mara. "If I don't come back, burn the file."

"You'll come back," she said. "You're too stubborn to die."

The precinct door groaned open behind me. We stepped out. One of us lit from within. The other trailing ash.

The descent hits like it always does. A brazier upended and you're falling. No hallelujah chorus. Just a *shift*. The kind of wrong you feel behind your eyes. One blink you're in the corridor outside dispatch; next blink you're nowhere at all—surrounded by concrete and shame.

We came down just outside the visitation room where he was waiting. Mr. Stuck. Needing me to unstick him— the soul janitor.

No smells. Not in echo-space. Scent's too real—too mortal. It doesn't get stuck here. What's left is just sight and sound, stripped and suspended.

I folded back into flesh like something worn, not discarded—like a coat that still fit, barely. Late fifties, maybe older if the light was cruel. Solid build, earned from too many fights I didn't start but had to finish. Hair salt-and-pepper, silver heavy at the temples. Beard trimmed short—silver, not styled, just maintained. Face like a weather map—creases where storms had been. Brow furrowed, eyes pale and sharp, the kind that stopped offering comfort a long time ago. Shirt rumpled. Trench coat scorched at the hem. Tie hanging like a noose someone had second thoughts about. Basically me, minus the wings and judgment. Honestly, I preferred it that way.

Not that it matters. You don't get to choose. Your earthside appearance is either God's jest or Satan's mockery.

I look behind me just to see how bad it is.

It's worse.

Chandler looked like he stepped out of a stained-glass window and onto a recruitment poster. Shiny blond hair swept back like he styles it between miracles. Buttoned white shirt, crisp collar, vest—a vest, for God's sake. Slacks like he's still interviewing for sainthood. Little shoulder bag strapped crosswise, like he's carrying communion wafers or field notes on salvation. Not a wrinkle in sight.

He even smells like hope. Or he *would* if smell were allowed in here.

I grunt. "You look like a recruitment poster."

He beams. "Thanks!"

"Wasn't a compliment."

On the other side of the glass is the visitation room. Or the idea of one. Two plastic chairs. A narrow table. Smudged glass that divided nothing from nothing.

Faded paint, faint scuff marks, cheap tile that remembered more than it should. A door in the corner that wouldn't open. Not locked—just indifferent.

A clock ticked, but the hands didn't move. That was normal.

Chandler let out a quiet breath, taking it all in like a first-timer. I didn't turn. Just said, "Welcome to nowhere."

"This is limbo?" he asked. "I thought it'd be… darker. Less waiting room, more reckoning."

"He's not going to Purgatory. He's ours—just doesn't know it yet."

He blinked. "Is this Earth?"

I shrugged. Tapped the table. "It thinks it's Earth. Close enough for the stuck."

"But he was marked for Heaven. Shouldn't that mean—"

"Don't quote doctrine at me. You know how many Heaven-bound we've found stuck in loops like this?"

"Isn't that a breach? I thought the *Accord*—"

"The *Accord* doesn't fix people. It just says we get ours, they get theirs. Doesn't say how, or when, or whether they walk in or get dragged. We guide them to grace. Hell hunts them for guilt. And the humans? They stall. They hide. They build entire echo-rooms out of shame. It all takes time."

"Seems messy for a sacred covenant."

"It's not sacred. It's scaffolding. Keeps the war polite."

"But it says—"

"It says a lot. So does scripture. You'll learn: the system

doesn't break loud. It just misfiles quiet."

He crouched, ran a hand along the chair without touching it. "No dust."

"There wouldn't be." I pointed at the window. "You see anything out there?"

He turned, looked through the smudged pane. Beyond it: a corridor that didn't quite resolve. Walls, maybe. A shape. But no edges. No door.

"I don't... I can't tell what's outside."

"Because there's nothing," I said. "This place only builds what the lie needs to survive. No extra walls. No exits."

He looked shaken. Good.

I walked in. The acoustics had that padded hush. Like the air didn't want to carry your voice too far in case it told the truth. Chandler followed, footsteps too light, posture too tall.

The door clicked shut behind us. A heavy, metal, final sound.

Took a chair.

Chandler stood beside me, a schoolboy pretending to be a man. The room made him look even cleaner.

I waved him back. Looked at the case sitting across me.

Mid-30s, maybe younger if you didn't look at the weight in his shoulders. Messy brown hair. Slumped posture. Pale knuckles gripping the edge of the table. Dressed in inmate beige. His name tag read *D. Mercer.* He stared at the door like if he waited long enough, someone would walk through.

They wouldn't.

After a long breath, I got things started. "Daniel?"

A flicker. Not a full response, but a blink. The kind people do when they've been underwater too long and someone cracks the surface above them.

"You're waiting," I said.

He nodded.

"For your father?"

Another nod. This one tighter. Defensive.

I nodded back. Mirroring. Always mirror, at first.

"What's he like?"

Daniel looked my way. Eyes grey, but muddied. Fogged over by something that didn't want to clear.

"He doesn't come," he said.

"That's not what I asked."

"He's…" he trailed off. Couldn't say. Didn't want to.

I'd seen the posture. The weight in the shoulders that said he wouldn't go easy. Like he'd holed up inside and locked the door behind him.

Alright. Back to basics.

"Daniel, my name is Sal. This is my partner Chandler. We're here to help."

Chandler placed a business card on the metal table. It read, in gleaming embossed script:

Chandler

Field Liaison – Threshold Division

License #3247-HC

Celestial Investigations

I stared at it. Of course he had cards. Of course they were embossed. And of course he listed the address like anyone makes it out of Saturn's veil without three clearances and a choir.

Threshold Division. Sounds like someone named it before the job existed. I still call it the precinct. Old habit — from when my beat had alleys, not altars. Never liked a cubicle. Doesn't matter how high they move mine.

"Subtle," I said. "You left out your halo polishing rates."

Daniel was holding up the card. "You're detectives?"

"Something like that."

"What's happened. Does this have anything to do with my father?"

I nodded. "We're trying to find him. Maybe you can help us."

"Okay. Sure."

Took out my notepad. "Trying to get a sense of him. Maybe you can describe him for me?"

"Well…he works a lot. Criminal defence lawyer. You probably know that."

"Yep."

"So he's not never home. He's just not…there."

He was slipping back down into his hole. Hardening. I waved my hand in front of Daniel's face, dismissing the subject.

"Forget about work. We all know lawyers are workaholics. He's no exception. What about hobbies?"

He blinked. Refocused.

"He likes games. Scrabble. Trivial Pursuit."

"Alright. Tell me about that. Something good."

He sat a little straighter. Thought back. "I beat him on popular culture."

"That's good. When was that?"

"Hmm… I was…fifteen? Sixteen? We were at the lake. I was winning. But there was a horse fly in the screen porch. They really hurt. He was asking the question, but I was nervous. I was watching the little nasty buzzing our heads. I had a rolled-up newspaper in my hand. Swatting. I got it, but I also destroyed the game. I thought I was in trouble, but he just laughed." He smiled, remembering.

I scribbled: *Good at Trivial Pursuit.* Then to him, "You must have been smart."

He sighed. "Oh, I don't know. Just a good memory."

"What about school. Good marks?"

"Pretty good. Until I…" He faded.

I pressed. "Trouble at school?"

His head dropped. "I didn't fit in so well. I was nervous, I guess. Just a bit shy. And my father, he expected. You know…"

"He expected you to become a lawyer?"

"No. I mean, maybe. He just had high expectations. You know, for a good future. Like him."

I waited. Patience. The only trick I got most times.

"I stopped going to class. Hung out. Back door. Friends who weren't quite friends. Just folks who didn't care too much. Didn't ask too much."

"What about your father?"

He didn't like that. Squirming in the chair. Looking at me, suspicious. "What does this have to do with anything? What do you guys want? And where's my father?" His eyes drifted back to the door.

I sighed. Dragged a hand down my face. The surface was cracking. Not the truth—the set dressing.

The light in the room tilted—just a shade. Not wrong. Just... rehearsed. The hum of the ceiling bulb shifted, like it remembered a different version of this day. The table felt warmer. The door, more possible.

Daniel's fingers relaxed on the edge of the metal.

He was slipping back into the good part. The part where his father still might walk through that door.

And if I didn't grab the thread now, I'd lose him to it.

"Daniel, your father's missing and we need your help."

The eyes swung back sharp. Got him.

"Look, we know you dropped out of school and your dad hit the roof when he found out. But we have to talk about it, because we believe that they way he reacted might be key to finding him. Like, what he's like when he's angry or upset. Not that we blame him." I added quickly. "If my son sabotaged his future, I don't know what I'd do."

He nodded.

"He has a temper."

"Don't we all," I said. "Tell me about it."

Daniel's fingers drummed once. Then stopped.

"He told me I could come home when I wasn't a

disgrace."

No inflection. Just fact.

I nodded like that was normal. Like I'd heard worse. I had.

"So where'd you go?"

"Places. Couch to couch. Guys who didn't ask questions."

"How old were you now?"

"Eighteen."

"You working?"

"No. Not then. Just… kept moving."

The room was holding still now. The light had stopped tilting. That was good. For now.

"Wasn't eating much," he added. "Too proud to ask."

That fit. Pride was the last thing to go. Right before the begging started.

He looked up, guarded. "Then someone told me my mom was trying to find me. Asking around."

"Good sign, right?"

"No. I got pissed." His jaw clenched, like the anger still lived in there somewhere. "She left. She doesn't get to come back in like it's nothing."

I didn't say anything. Let the silence gnaw at it.

Eventually he filled it.

"I went to see my sister. Figured if Mom had reached her, maybe she knew something. Maybe she'd help."

He paused. Swallowed. "Asked for money."

"Did she give you any?"

"A little," he said. "Told me to come home."

"Did you?"

He shook his head. "No. Took the money. Not the rest."

"Was it your father's money?"

A beat. Then: "Yeah."

"So he was trying?"

Another beat. "Yes."

"Maybe not hard enough?"

He winced. That one hit bone. "Maybe."

I gave it space. Let the room hold the next question.

"What else *could* he have done?"

He blinked hard. The walls were closing in. "Nothing."

The lie came out flat, with weight behind it. The kind that cracks foundations.

"He wanted you to come home."

That one didn't land.

He didn't answer. Just stared down at his hands like they might say it for him.

That was the truth, then. The silence. The not-knowing. That's where it hurt.

Had to be careful now. Shifted off the gas. Didn't push.

"Alright. Daniel, I need to ask you about the charges."

He straightened slightly. Swallowed again. "Okay."

"You've been charged with—"

"Double homicide."

I nodded. "Tell me what happened."

Daniel didn't lift his eyes when he began. Just spoke to the table like it was the only thing that hadn't betrayed him.

"There was this bar," he said. "Didn't even have a name. Just a flickering sign and a door that stuck in the cold. We used to huddle there on the weekends. Me, some of the guys. Arthur."

The name came with weight. Not fear, exactly. But memory that made him flinch inside.

"Arthur was... loud. You could hear him before you saw him. Big coat, shiny teeth, always tossing bills around like they grew in his glove compartment. He wasn't serious. Not real mob or anything. But he played like he was. Enough that guys like me hung around, hoping some of it might stick."

His jaw flexed. A muscle memory, maybe.

"I ran errands. Not drugs, not exactly. Just favours. Calls, drop-offs. He liked to make it feel official. Said I had the look—quiet, forgettable. Said that was a skill."

A pause. A breath.

"I bought a gun."

He didn't look at me. Just said it like confession should come without eye contact.

"Didn't buy it to use. Just... he made it sound like it mattered. Like carrying meant you were someone."

The next part didn't come fast. It dragged out like it didn't want to be named.

"That night outside the bar—it was raining. Not dramatic, just wet enough to make your socks cold.

Arthur was already drunk. He picked a fight. Not with me. With these guys—locals, I think. Rough types, but not his circle. He said something, they said something worse. I wasn't paying attention. Was leaning against the wall, trying to light a wet cigarette."

His hand lifted, miming the lighter. It shook a little.

"First shot sounded like a tire backfiring. Then screaming. Then nothing."

He swallowed hard. "They were on the ground. Two of them. Heads twisted the wrong way. Blood on the sidewalk. Arthur was gone. Just gone."

He finally looked up at me.

"I don't even remember dropping the gun. But it was there. They found it in the alley. My prints all over."

His mouth twisted like he wanted to spit the taste out.

"That's when I called my father."

I didn't speak. Just waited. You can't pull truth out of a man like a tooth. You have to let it loosen.

Daniel's jaw worked like it was chewing glass.

"I called him," he said. "Didn't expect anything. Just… didn't know who else."

His voice had gone small—the kind people use when they're standing outside a memory they're scared to walk back into.

"He didn't answer. Not right away. It was two days later. The waiting room. I was in the jumpsuit already. Wrists cuffed. One of the guards gave me a nod and said, 'Lawyer's here.' And I thought maybe—just maybe—he'd come."

He swallowed. His hands were flat on the table now,

pressed tight like he needed the metal to ground him.

"He walked in like a stranger. Suit perfect. Tie straight. No briefcase. Just him."

I didn't move. Didn't blink. The room was still.

"I said, 'Dad.' He said, 'Daniel.' Just like that. No... no anger. No softness either. Like it was a name he'd borrowed for the occasion."

"What did you ask him?"

Daniel shook his head slowly. "Didn't have to. I thought maybe he'd offer. I thought he'd say it before I asked. But he didn't. Just stood there. Said he'd spoken with duty counsel. Said I'd get a fair trial."

The next words came harder. Thicker.

"I said, 'You're not representing me?' And he said... he said he couldn't. Said it wouldn't be right. Conflict of interest."

His voice cracked.

"But it wasn't that. I knew it. He wasn't saying he couldn't. He was saying he *wouldn't*. And I saw it—in his eyes. He looked at me like... like I was already guilty. Like I'd wasted his name just by calling it."

He blinked fast. Once. Twice.

"He hated me," Daniel said. "He wouldn't say it. But it was in the silence. In the fact that he left. Didn't argue. Didn't explain. Just turned and walked out."

I let it land. Didn't rush to fill the space.

He didn't cry. Not out loud. Just let his breath tremble once and held it down like a secret.

I watched him fold in on himself. Not slumped. Just...

smaller. Like a man trying to disappear without moving.

"I see," I said. Voice low. Flat. Not sympathy—*recognition*. "That's the thing, Daniel. That kind of hate? It leaves a shadow. Doesn't matter how clean the man keeps his record. You can smell it on his absence."

He didn't look at me. But he didn't look away either.

"You didn't ask for a miracle," I went on. "You called your father. You asked for help. And he came into that room, saw the boy he raised, and chose to leave. Not because he couldn't defend you—but because he didn't want to."

Daniel's throat tightened. Just once.

"He didn't just let you go to trial. He let you drown. Watched you sink and called it justice."

His jaw clenched. A flicker in the knuckles, white against skin.

"He failed you. That's what you're not saying. You remember it from both sides. From the seat in the jumpsuit, and the one in the suit. That's why it won't come clean."

I leaned back, just a little. Gave him room to breathe it.

"When a father stops loving his son," I said, "something breaks. And it doesn't break clean."

Daniel's mouth opened. Closed. When he spoke, it came slow.

"He didn't come to the trial."

Quiet. Absolute.

"Didn't call. Didn't write. Didn't check if I'd been sentenced, or if I was still breathing. Nothing. Like I was a case he'd recused himself from in spirit too."

He looked up now. Not at me — through me. Somewhere far. Somewhere *after*.

"I used to think maybe he was ashamed. That he couldn't face what I'd become."

A pause.

"But that's not it."

Another.

"He didn't *miss* me. He was *relieved*. Like I'd been a burden lifted. Like he could finally move on. Be the man he wanted to be without the weight of my wreckage chained to his name."

The words hit the air like stones dropped in water — one by one, then ripples.

"I think he thought about defending me. I think he really stood in that room and weighed it. And he chose no. Not for law or integrity. But because... he looked at me, and saw everything he hated in himself."

He took a breath that didn't steady him.

"That's what he did with the pain. He buried it in me. Walked out. Shut the door. And never once turned back."

Daniel went quiet. Not because he was done — but because there was nothing left to bleed.

The air in the room shifted. Like breath held too long. Like walls that weren't built to carry the weight of truth. The hum of the ceiling light faltered. Not flickered — *stammered*. The kind of noise that means something old is coming loose. Behind Daniel, the door — the one he'd stared at so long — shivered. It didn't open. Just became... uncertain.

He looked toward it, slowly.

"He always walked out," he whispered.

And the light bent with him. Just slightly. Like the memory was leaning toward collapse.

I didn't move. Didn't speak. Just watched.

The metal table was warm now. Too warm. Like a fever under steel.

Daniel's cuffs were gone. At some point, they'd vanished. Or maybe they never were.

He reached for the card Chandler left. Read it again. Like he was seeing it for the first time.

"You're not here for me," he said. "Are you."

"No," I said. "I'm here for the man who built this room."

Daniel—no. *Jonathan*—looked up at me like a man caught haunting the wrong life.

And now the room stopped pretending.

The walls buckled, just slightly—edges bleeding into shadow. The chairs dissolved into suggestion. The hum flattened to silence. The table warped under his hands like heat rising off asphalt—reality bending where the truth had finally landed.

He looked around, dazed. "What is this?"

"A loop," I said. "You built it. To wait. To pretend."

"For what?"

"For him," I said. "For your son."

His throat moved. "But I didn't—he was guilty—he had a gun—"

"You didn't hate him because he was guilty," I said.

"You hated him because he wasn't *you*. Because he failed in a way you couldn't fix. And that terrified you."

He opened his mouth, but no sound came.

"You stood in that room, in that suit, and you chose silence. You told yourself it was the ethical thing. But it wasn't. You just didn't want the jury to see *you* on that side of the table."

"I was scared," he finally said. "I didn't know how to love him anymore."

"And so you didn't."

The light fractured — like truth through broken glass.

"I tried to move on," he said. "I really did. Cases. Clients. I built my life again. But it never — he was always —" He faltered. "Too late to apologize?"

"Maybe," I said. "But not too late to tell the truth."

He looked toward the door again. It was open now.

Not wide. Just enough.

He didn't move.

"I didn't mean to make this," he said.

"No one ever does."

He looked down at his hands — older now. No longer Daniel's. The weight of time returning to them.

"What happens next?"

I stood.

"That's not up to me," I said. "But this room won't hold you anymore."

He nodded once. A gesture of someone finally hearing a sentence that had been waiting too long.

Jonathan Mercer stood. Not proud. Just ready.

And he walked out the door.

Back at the precinct, the lights hummed like Heaven preferred silence to memory. The walls didn't echo here. Just absorbed. Everything was built to listen, not answer. Today, we bordered one of those folds in the city where time coiled inward and the alleys forgot their exits.

I dropped the file on my desk. The edges were already curling, like it wanted to finish rotting before I logged it.

Chandler was waiting, trying to look busy with an empty clipboard.

I slid the file his way.

"Tag it, log it, and file the metaphysical variance form under Subtype G—False Construct, Self-Originating. You remember where that one goes?"

He blinked. "The green cabinet?"

"No," I said. "The *other* green cabinet."

"Oh. Right." He took the file like it was humming. Maybe it was.

I left him to it and walked down the corridor. Mara's desk was lit like always—soft and orderly, like God still checked her work.

She didn't look up when I set the cup down.

"I already had one," she said.

"You'll want this one more."

She took it. Sipped. Didn't thank me. That wasn't how Mara worked.

She flipped a page in the ledger. "Took you long enough."

"Room didn't want to let go."

She snorted. "I could've handled it in half the time."

"That why you sent me?"

She gave a ghost of a smile. "I didn't say it would've worked."

I turned to go.

"Sal."

I looked back.

"You'll file it clean?"

"I always do."

"Mm." She went back to her pages. "Try not to write poetry in the margins this time."

"Don't flatter yourself," I said. "It wasn't poetry. It was a haiku about divine negligence."

"You misspelled 'negligence.'"

"Intentional. To symbolize moral collapse."

She snorted. "Symbolism doesn't file."

Back at the desk, Chandler had done the job. Logged, tagged, even initialed. He looked up as I passed.

"Can I ask something?"

"You just did."

He ignored that. "Why didn't he go to Hell?"

I sat.

"Because Hell," I said, "would've made it easier."

CASE FILE: CHARLIE GUNN

Coffee's always better when there's no crisis. Still tastes like burnt compromise, but at least you've got time to sip between disasters. That's the difference.

Chandler sat across from me, sleeves rolled, shirt still white. Not a wrinkle in sight. He was reading off a scroll that had no right to be that long unless it was scripture, which it wasn't. I couldn't tell if it bored him or if he was just determined to look busy.

Mara moved past behind him, balancing a tray of data slips and case fragments like she was auditioning for sainthood. She didn't interrupt. She never does. But her eyes flicked to me, and I gave the smallest nod. She set the tray down at her desk. No words. That's how it works.

"Anything new?" Chandler asked, eyes still skimming.

"Define new," I said. "Or define anything. I'm open."

He smiled. It was the kind of smile that still believed this was a job, not a penance.

"I was just saying," he started, "tether density's way up this quarter—"

"Don't quote stats before coffee," I said. "You'll start believing them."

He opened his mouth to reply.

That's when the light changed.

It didn't flicker. It didn't brighten. It just… *shifted*. Like the spectrum slid sideways and left the shadows lagging. The room held its shape, but the angles stretched where they shouldn't.

Mara straightened. Chandler froze. The scroll rolled itself shut like it had decided this wasn't the moment.

I stood up. Not out of respect. Just reflex.

He didn't enter. He *arrived*.

Camael doesn't need doors. His presence presses into a space like judgment that found your address. He stood near the viewport—no footsteps, no flare—just there, as if the precinct had remembered him into being.

His robe was clean, but not new. Gold, faded to memory. His face looked younger than it should, which always made it worse. His eyes were silver—flat, endless, and old enough to have watched the ink dry on the *Accord* itself.

He didn't speak for a breath. We gave it to him.

Then:

"Situation exceeds threshold. Protocol intervention has failed. Clause Seven is now active."

Chandler blinked. "Clause Seven? That's… a grey case, right?" He added, a beat too late: "Director?"

Camael didn't blink. "Clause Seven doesn't wait. First to touch owns the consequences. Name: Charlie Gunn. Four deaths. One clean ascension. Location: intersection of Dundas and Keele. Immediate dispatch authorized. Full discretionary authority confirmed."

Chandler stood slowly. "What's the risk classification?"

"Contested. Devil en route."

Mara didn't move. Just one glance to me. She knew what that meant.

Camael turned. His voice was still flat. But this time, there was something underneath it. Something that sounded like old law breaking open.

"If she touches first, and she's wrong... respond accordingly."

And then he was gone.

No flash. No wind. Just the snap of absence—like the room let go of a breath it hadn't realized it was holding.

I finished my coffee. Cold now.

"Let's go," I said.

The first thing I noticed was the silence.

It wasn't the kind of quiet you recognize. Not the echo left by sirens. Or the breath held after a scream. Not even the hush that follows violence. This was *judgment* silence. The kind that sits in a space like a sealed envelope—waiting to be opened. Waiting to be read aloud. The kind that says: *You will answer for what happened here. One way or another.*

Shattered glass spread across the intersection in a wide radial fan—like light trying to remember how to be holy. The bus sprawled in the middle of the street like a fresh metal carcass. A cruiser idled at the far curb, door still ajar, front seat empty. Blood on the windshield—dark, arterial, spattered wide. Old enough to dry.

Time wasn't holding steady here.

I stepped through the ripple.

Everything warped.

Overlaying the physical wreckage were two celestial echoes—stitched like broken transparencies over the world. First: the bus, still upright, clean. Interior lit too brightly, the white of hospital corridors, antiseptic and soft-edged. But the aisle stretched wrong—too long, too many seats, and a hallway at the end that never should've been there. Fluorescent lights buzzed like they were praying in tongues.

Charlie Gunn's echo.

It wasn't a memory. It wasn't a loop. It was belief. Reconstructed. Sanitized. Still holding.

The second overlay was tighter. Just across the street. It clung to the crash site like a stain.

Bill Jones—husband, 43, teacher, Heaven-marked but tethered—stood beside the wreckage of a silver sedan that no longer existed. He was looping: opening the passenger side door, reaching in, then freezing. Over and over. His mouth moved, but no sound came. Each reset started a little later. A little more broken.

Chandler came through behind me, tight-lipped. His shoulders were already tense. "I've got four D.O.D. tags in the precinct file," he said, scrolling through a light-slate. "One confirmed Protocol transition—the wife. One DT—the husband. One pending—bus driver's soul hasn't been logged yet. And one—"

"Grey," I finished. I already knew which.

Chandler glanced over at Bill's loop, jaw clenched. "He's stuck. We should help him. That's a clean mark."

"He can wait," I said.

"What? He's—"

"I said, *he can wait.*"

My voice was low but fixed. Chandler closed his mouth, but not the look in his eyes.

Charlie sat two rows back in the phantom bus-hallway,

hands folded like he was waiting for his name to be called. His clothes were the same ones he'd died in—soaked in blood from someone else's throat. But his posture was calm. Peaceful, almost. He looked around like he still expected to be congratulated.

Chandler checked the slate. "Schizophrenic. Off meds. Believed the driver was a demon. Stabbed him in the neck. Bus veered into traffic—killed a married couple. Police shot him at the scene."

"That's the story," I said. "But truth isn't what's written."

I stepped close.

"Mr. Gunn."

He turned toward me slowly. No surprise in his face. Just awareness. He knew he wasn't alive. But he hadn't accepted what that meant.

"I'm Sal. He's Chandler. This isn't a trick. We're here to review your case."

He nodded once. Not with trust or fear. Just… attention.

"Do you remember what happened?"

Charlie blinked slowly. "Did you see it?" he asked. "The second face? It was under his. Every time he smiled, the corners pulled wrong."

Chandler was standing just outside the bus. Possibly in the hospital hallway. "He's delusional. You know that."

"Maybe," I said. "Maybe not."

I'd seen souls damned for ignoring evil. And I'd seen monsters forgiven because they struck true, even blindly.

Chandler stiffened behind me. I could feel his judgment

building like static.

I crouched, slow. Kept my voice neutral.

"I believe you," I said. "But belief isn't the question here. You acted. Four people died. Three of them were not the driver."

"I didn't mean for —"

"I know."

"I was saving them."

That part was softer. But it wasn't guilt. It was conviction. He still thought he was right.

That was the problem.

Charlie's metaphysical weight didn't tip. He hadn't surrendered to remorse. He hadn't rejected it either. He thought he'd done something holy. Or something *true*. That made him dangerous to both sides.

"I need you to stay here," I said. "You'll see things. You'll hear things. That doesn't mean they're false. It just means this place isn't done deciding what to be yet."

He stared past me, eyes narrow. "You think I'm crazy."

"I think you're dead," I said. "And we have to figure out what that means."

I stepped away.

Chandler moved beside me, quiet now. Reading my restraint, but not yet understanding it.

"Murder and double involuntary manslaughter. He's Hell-bound," he said, voice low. "Isn't he?"

"I don't know," I said. "And I'm not guessing."

I looked back once more at Charlie. He was humming

now. Something tuneless. Something calm.

Heaven's process is forensic. We don't guess. We name. We wait. And sometimes, we lose.

That's when she arrived.

Smoke didn't herald her. Fire didn't follow. Just that feeling—like someone else had breathed in your place. A shimmer parted on the far side of the echo-space, and Enebris stepped through like it was her office door and we were late to the meeting.

She was young. Or looked it. Twenty-something, by Earthbound measures. Auburn hair tied half-back like she'd been working, not dressing for effect. Slacks, tall boots, black blouse with one button wrong. No ornament. No sigil. Just precision. Everything about her looked unfinished on purpose—just enough to imply you weren't worth dressing up for.

She carried a small black notebook in one hand, flipping it open and closed with her thumb. Not reading. Just the motion. *Snap. Pause. Snap.* A tic. Repetitive. *Measured.* Like punctuation.

"Hello, Sal," she said. Voice smooth. Unaccented. *Corporate clarity.* "Protocol's slow today."

I didn't answer. Didn't need to. I already knew the type.

There's a class of Hell agent they've started training young. No smoke and mirrors. No glee. No overt sadism. Just efficiency. Clinical posture. There was no war left to fight—just files to win.

They don't seduce. They *disarm*. You lower your blade because they didn't bring theirs out loud. They walk into your silence, and they leave with your dead.

I'd seen three of her kind before. One I talked down. One I outpaced. One I shot through the back of the head before she could say "ours."

I shifted my weight. Loosened my coat. Didn't draw. But my hand knew where the gun was.

Chandler moved instinctively beside me. Too fast. Too stiff.

"You have no standing here," he said, sharp.

She didn't even glance at him.

Walked slow, a spiral path around Charlie's flickering echo. Every step purposeful. She wasn't closing distance. She was *taking measurements*.

Snap. Pause. Snap.

Charlie looked up at her, confused. Not scared. Curious, even. She gave him the smallest nod—like a sales rep about to offer a trial period.

"You're early," I said, flat.

She smiled. Not warmth. Just teeth.

"I was in the neighbourhood," she said. "Thought I'd check the variance."

"Clause Seven is still active. No standing claim."

She stopped. Closed the notebook.

"That's not what I see," she said. "He saw evil. He murdered. That's not madness. That's Hell's virtue."

"He saw *a* thing," I said. "We haven't confirmed what."

"You're stalling."

I didn't flinch. Didn't argue, either. That's what she wanted. Debate gives shape to her kind. Make it a courtroom and they always think they've won. So I kept my voice low.

"And if you're wrong?"

She tilted her head, faintest twitch of a smile—like I'd asked whether two and two still made four.

"Then I lose the file."

I shook my head.

"No. You lose the protection of the *Accord*."

That landed. Not hard. But clean.

"Clause Seven doesn't pardon wrong guesses," I said. "You mark him without right, and I'm authorized."

A pause. Not long. Just enough for the air to go tight.

"Tell me, Sal—what box does he fit in on *your* form?"

"You give me time with him," I said. "We find out."

A breath.

Charlie looked up.

His eyes weren't confused. Not now. Just *tired*—the kind of tired that sinks behind your ribs when no one believes you, and you start to wonder if you imagined the whole thing just to make the world make sense.

"I didn't mean to kill them," he said quietly. "Just the one. Just the one who wasn't supposed to be here."

He looked at me.

"You saw it too. Didn't you."

I didn't answer.

Because she was already moving.

She didn't lunge. She just stepped past me—smooth, deliberate—as if the verdict had already been filed and she was simply collecting the evidence. One hand lifted. No weapon. No flourish. Just fingers outstretched, like she was checking a forehead for fever.

The moment her fingers touched his temple, the air *snapped*. Not sound. Something higher. A wrongness in the bones of the place. Light twisted. The corridor rippled, flickered, went white. She jerked back. Her hand smoked at the fingertips. She staggered once—just once—then steadied herself. The look in her eyes wasn't pain. It was failure.

I drew.

No warning. No pause. No ritual. Just one clean motion.

The shot caught her just above the sternum.

No blood. No body. Just light—fractured, silent— spilling outward like something ancient unraveling under glass. She collapsed. Like a marionette whose strings had been cut. And then she vanished.

I holstered the weapon.

Stepped forward.

The echo-space held steady now. The hallway still too long, but quiet. Charlie sat where he had been— watching. He didn't speak.

Neither did Chandler.

I looked at the place where she'd fallen. Nothing left. Not even ash.

"You misread," I said to the air. "He wasn't yours."

I stepped to Charlie.

His eyes were wide. Still watching. Still unsure. Maybe still seeing that second face.

I placed my hand gently on his head.

This time, no break. No recoil.

Just stillness.

Claim accepted.

Chandler stood a pace behind me. Voice low. "She touched first."

"She did."

"And you just… shot her."

"That's the *Accord*," I said. "You touch, you better be right."

Then we went to sort out the husband.

Still looping. But we had time to sort him out.

Nothing in Heaven stays put—not even the buildings. You can get lost. It's like putting something down and your wife "puts it where it belongs," whether you agree or not. There's a system. You just don't understand it. And she won't explain.

Today the precinct squatted near one of those apertures where law thins and consequence leaks through. No signage. Just clean lines, angled sharp enough to bleed.

Back at the precinct, the light was normal again. No shimmer. No weight. Just the steady glow of a ward that doesn't blink. The Seventh Sphere keeps its rhythm, even when the rest of Heaven holds its breath.

Chandler was pacing. Thinking out loud. "So… Clause Seven's like a loophole," he said. "No rules. Just whoever gets there first."

Mara didn't look up from her desk.

"*Accord* breach. Retaliation cleared."

Then she turned slightly, not quite facing him.

"It's not a loophole," she said. "It's necessary. And the most dangerous clause in the system."

She tapped her temple once — sharp.

"Don't they teach anything in school anymore?"

Chandler stopped pacing. Winced. Sat down across from me again, slower this time. Tie crooked. Shoulders tight.

"Either side can claim," he said, quieter now. "If they're right."

I sipped my coffee. Cold. Still better than it had any right to be.

"If they're wrong—"

"They're fair game," I said. "That's the *Accord*."

He nodded, slower this time. Less sure.

"What happens if both sides are wrong?"

Mara didn't look up. "Then the system fails."

He blinked.

"And what happens then?"

I closed my eyes.

"It doesn't."

I pushed the case log over to him. He stared down at it.

Case File: Charlie Gunn. Clause Seven. Disposition: Claimed. Incident: Contained.

"We don't make the rules," I said.

"Just clean up after whoever who break them."

CASE FILE: CHAD PARKER

The King's Anchor, Dundas Street West, Toronto. 2:03 a.m.

Low ceilings. Brick walls. One cracked mirror behind the bar, reflecting nothing worth saving. Crumpled napkins on every table like discarded apologies. Half-melted ice clung to the bottom of glasses no one was coming back for. A TV above the bar flickered with muted sports highlights no one watched. The smell was old wood, citrus cleaner, and something underneath — like a memory left too long in a locked room.

I stepped in first. Chandler followed, shoes too clean for this floor.

The bartender looked up, didn't blink. Balding. White rag over one shoulder like a surrender flag. He clocked me in a second, then nodded past me toward the slump at the bar.

"Third time this week," he said. "Never learns."

Chad Parker was hunched over a double of something brown, head lowered like the weight of it might crack his spine. The coat he wore hung uneven — black wool, boxy in the shoulders, cinched wrong at the waist, as if he'd taken something built for someone else and dared it to fit him. It didn't. Neither did he.

His frame was angular in the wrong ways. Hips too narrow, chest too flat, arms too long for a body that still clung to some ghost of softness. His bones didn't match his posture. His neck was corded, jaw squared but drawn tight — like the male shape had pushed up through years of repression and took the surface by force. It didn't look natural. It looked like a mask torn halfway off.

Hair shorn close, not stylish—just short. Practical. Ugly. Done in a mirror without care or ceremony. No makeup. No earrings. But the remnants showed: faint piercings in both lobes, a slight discolouration on the upper lip where something had once been bleached away.

The face was the worst part. Not for its horror, but its indecision. Chin too sharp for the cheeks. Eyes hooded but wide-set, shaped for expressions that no longer came. The features never settled—caught between man and woman, beauty and blankness. All of it misaligned.

A face that made people look away without knowing why.

His hands were large, calloused. One clutched the glass like it was leverage. The other spun a delicate silver ring on his pinky—too loose now. It slid. Slipped. Resisted. Kept circling back, like something haunted.

Nothing about him was whole. He looked like someone who had clawed his way out of a false life but hadn't found a true one waiting. The transition wasn't beautiful. It was violent. A soul breaking its cage and finding the wreckage still breathing.

He was talking, but not to anyone in particular. The kind of talking that had too much past in it. Too much self-loathing soaked in stale whiskey.

"Whole damn life, and worth nothing," he muttered. "No point. Not one. Did what I was supposed to. Worked. Married. Tried. Tried again. Built something, they said. Made something of myself. Bullshit."

He swirled the glass but didn't drink.

"Still ended up alone. Still ended up here. Can't sleep.

And I hate waking up."

He laughed, short and bitter. No amusement in it.

"Fifty goddamn years. Paid the bills. Sat through family dinners. Watched people talk like I wasn't in the room. Thought if I kept going, it would start to feel real."

Shot back the drink, smacked the glass down on the bar, and waved for another.

"Just wanted something to make it stop."

He glanced up at the mirror. Didn't like what he saw. Looked away.

I looked to Chandler. He caught the cue. Straightened his tie like he was walking into a chapel, not a bar.

"Let me," he said.

"Be my guest." I leaned back against the wall, arms crossed. "Let's see what they teach in year one."

Chandler approached slow, posture immaculate, voice soft. The kind of soft that makes people flinch harder.

"Chad Parker?" he asked. "You're not in trouble. But you didn't move on. That's not a judgment. It's just the scan."

Chad didn't turn. Just raised the empty glass to his lips, swallowed, and let it fall back to the counter.

"I don't need help," he said.

Chandler tried again. "You're what we call a delayed transcendent. It happens. Something got stuck. Sometimes it's love. Sometimes it's identity."

That got a reaction. Chad turned—slowly—and looked Chandler dead in the eye. His face was flushed. Eyes bleary, but burning.

"Identity?" Chad said. "Who the hell are you to tell me who I am?"

Chandler didn't step back. "No. I'm here to tell you you're more than what you settled for."

Chad laughed once. It was a jagged thing. Then he stood—abrupt, swaying, but solid enough to throw the punch.

It hit Chandler clean across the cheek.

He stumbled. Recovered. Blinked the surprise out of his eyes and raised his hands—not to fight, but to hold the space.

Then he looked at me.

"Sal?"

I pushed off the wall.

"Yeah," I said. "That's enough goodwill for one night."

I stepped forward. Not quickly. Not with hesitation. Just with the certainty of something overdue.

Chad turned to face me, fists still half-raised, stance all bluff and booze. He tried to square up. I didn't give him the chance.

First blow went to the ribs—flat knuckles, sharp and low. Took the wind. Second was an elbow across the jaw—not enough to break it, just enough to make his knees forget whose side they were on. He stumbled. I caught his coat and drove him back against the bar, hard enough to make the bottles clink.

He swung wild. I let it miss. Then answered with a palm to the chest and a sweep at the knee.

Down he went.

Wood cracked beneath him.

He gasped once—more shock than pain. Sat there breathing like the floor had stolen something from him.

Blood on his lip. One eye starting to swell.

"Don't," I said. Quiet.

He looked up, dazed.

"You're not fighting me," I told him. "You're just losing loud."

Chad tried to speak, but nothing came. Just a tremble. Just the beginning of the thing he'd spent years drinking not to say.

Good.

The belligerence was gone. What was left might finally be worth saving.

After a beat I hauled Chad up and put him on the barstool again. Rough, but not unkindly. Chad slumped, knuckles scraped, breath coming hard through the side of his mouth. His coat hung looser now, off one shoulder. Sweat darkened the collar. His cheek had started to swell. The ring on his pinky had stopped spinning.

Chandler leaned against the bar, one hand to his jaw, working it like he wasn't sure if something had cracked. He winced, then smiled anyway.

Chad glanced over. "Sorry," he muttered.

Chandler shook his head. "You hit hard. It's okay."

Chad let out a noise—part breath, part laugh, part shame. Then he raised a hand and gestured toward the bartender. "One more," he said. "On me."

I caught the barkeep's eye. Shook my head.

The bartender nodded, wiped the same section of counter for the fifth time.

Chad noticed. "What — no more pity rounds?"

"No," I said. "No more numbing it."

He scoffed, looked away.

I stepped closer, leaned on the bar beside him.

"I get it," I said. "You're angry."

He didn't answer.

"Why?"

He turned slowly, and for a moment his eyes met mine — not with defiance, but fatigue. Then the anger rushed in behind it like a tide.

"Why?" he snapped. "*Look at me.*"

He shoved back from the bar, staggered half upright, arms wide.

"You ever have a dream where you're in the wrong house? Not scary, just wrong? You don't know how you got there, nothing's where it should be, the walls are the wrong colour, and people keep calling you by a name that *isn't yours*?"

He dragged his hands down his face.

"Now I wake up in this bar, looking like this." He motioned to himself with loathing. "Broad shoulders, busted face, voice like gravel — *who the hell is this?*"

He rubbed at his face, eyes closed. The tension never left his jaw.

"My name is Lily," he said, quieter now, but not softer.

I didn't blink. Just filed the name in silence. People name themselves in all kinds of ways. This one had two — neither of them sitting right.

"Lily Parker. Vice president. Heritage Real Estate Group. People respect me, or pretend to. I've won awards. I have goddamn staff."

A snort. Not amusement. Just air venting bitterness.

"I'm not charming. But I am clean. Sharp. Put-together. I wear heels that cut into my feet. My face was never good enough, but I learned the angles. Smiled from the side. Photographed well if I tilted just right."

He smiled but it came out bitter and cruel without any joy.

"I dress for boardrooms. Hold eye contact just long enough without threatening anybody. Make rich men nervous."

He looked up, and now his eyes were wet. Not crying. Just worn thin.

"And now you tell me — *what's wrong?*"

I let it sit.

Chad sank back into himself. Just stared at his hands, thumbs twitching.

The silence held.

"You're not trapped," Chandler said. Voice steady, soft — but not shrinking. "You're dead."

Chad's head lifted. No surprise in it. No urgency. Just the slow recognition of something he already knew.

"Yeah," he said. "I figured."

But then he laughed — bitter, wet. "Didn't think it'd be a

bar, though. Thought maybe clouds. Choirs. Maybe just black." He looked around. "Not this."

"No one does," Chandler said.

Chad rubbed his jaw, winced where the swelling had come up. "You telling me this is the afterlife?"

"No," Chandler said gently. "This is the echo. What's left when something doesn't finish right."

Chad let that sit. Then snorted. "So this is what I get? A shitty rerun of the worst version of myself?"

"It's not a punishment," Chandler said.

"No?" Chad looked up, anger rising. "You think this is *mercy*? I die and wake up in a stranger's body with my own voice gone sideways and my name wiped off the wall?"

Chandler didn't move. "You're not a stranger. You're just unfinished."

Chad scoffed. "You two here to fix me, then? Is that it? Slap a sticker on my soul and push me through the gate?"

"We're here to help you *see*," Chandler said. "That's all. What you do with it — that's yours."

Another pause. The anger hit its edge and didn't have anywhere left to go.

Chad looked down again. Palmed the glass like he still expected it to be full. It wasn't.

A breath.

"Okay," he said. Quiet.

Another.

"What do I have to do?"

I stepped in again, calm as ash.

"Let's talk about life," I said. "Figure it out."

Chad looked up. No pushback this time. Just that shell-shocked stillness you only get after the third wave breaks and you're still breathing.

"Tell me about you," I said. "Not the version you built. The real you. The broken parts you don't talk about. Usually it's somewhere in there."

He exhaled like the words stung on the way out.

"You want the worst of me?" he said. "Fine."

He looked around, then back at us.

"This is Hell," he muttered. Half-laugh. "Admit it."

He paused. Swallowed.

"It's not, right?"

"No," I said.

He nodded slowly. "Just feels like it sometimes."

A beat.

"There's a lot of shitty things about being me." He ran a hand through his hair, short and rough. "But the one that got me fired, divorced, blacklisted from three Christmas parties? It's the temper."

I let him keep going.

"Controlled in public. I can play the part. But in private? I blow."

He flexed his hands like something in them still wanted to clench.

"Once shattered a glass trophy at an industry gala. They'd just introduced me as 'Lily Parker, a powerful *female* executive.' I smiled. Took the award. Got to the green room. Smashed it against the sink."

Chandler said nothing. Just listened.

"Fired an assistant once for calling me 'ma'am' instead of 'Ms.'" He shrugged. "She cried. I still didn't rehire her."

He picked at the edge of a coaster.

"Tried anger management. Lasted two sessions. Therapist fired *me.* Said I was 'reluctant to process interpersonal triggers.'" He laughed again. "Yeah, no shit."

He looked at me sideways.

"You sure this isn't Hell?"

"Yeah," I said. "Because in Hell, no one asks if it is."

Chad didn't answer right away. Just sat there with the shame laid out in pieces.

But nothing there to stick. No pivot point. No hinge. Just wreckage. Common, predictable. Human.

I waited a beat. Then: "What else?"

Chad laughed again, but it came out hollow. "You want the highlight reel?"

He didn't wait for an answer.

"Alcohol," he said. "Not every day, but enough."

His voice slowed, like the shame had to push through thicker air.

"Three stints in recovery. First stint, I lied through intake. Second, I slept with the guy running the group. Third—I didn't even finish. Just stopped going. Told myself I'd earned the relapse."

He traced a wet ring on the bar with one finger.

"Kept a bottle in my office safe. Told myself it was for clients. It wasn't."

A pause. A memory.

"Once left a client dinner in the middle of the main course just to drink in my car. Sat there with a thermos and a breath mint and cried into the steering wheel."

He shook his head.

"Came back in like nothing happened. Closed the deal."

Chandler looked away, respectfully.

I didn't.

"That it?" I said.

Chad breathed hard through his nose. "It should be."

But it wasn't.

And we both knew it.

I didn't speak. Didn't shift. Just let the weight stay there.

Chad exhaled like he was inventorying rot.

"First marriage — Peter Elgin. Met in university. Married too fast. Divorced five years later."

He rubbed the side of his face. "He wanted a wife. I gave him a rival."

Said it clean. Like a verdict already filed.

"Second marriage — Alan Brower. Corporate lawyer. Suave. Cold. Didn't like being outperformed."

Chad gave a tight laugh. "Didn't stop me."

But something in his tone curled inward — not out of pride, and not out of regret, but like a door he didn't want fully open.

A beat.

"He cheated. I drank. We both pretended. Then he left. That one, I didn't fight."

Didn't fight—but that edge in his voice said there was someone he *had.*

"Kid?" I asked.

"Marcus."

Chad stared down at his hands.

"He said I never hugged him. Only managed him. Cut ties at eighteen. Didn't even block me. Just disappeared."

He drummed his fingers once on the bar.

"No screaming. No scene. Just absence."

Then he added—without thinking—"*She said it wouldn't stick.*"

He caught himself. Blinked. Swallowed it down.

Just damage. Until now. A live wire in the ash. He didn't mean to say it. That was the point. Not Marcus. Not the boy who left. Not Peter. Not Alan. Not after any of them.

"You're getting closer," I said. "But that's not the tether."

Chad frowned.

He didn't push back. But he didn't offer anything either. Not yet.

But I had it.

I let the silence turn. Not tense. Just patient.

"That was the lock," I said. "Not the name. Not the love.

The failure to hold it."

Chad flinched like I'd repeated a slur.

I kept my voice low. "Who's she?"

"No one," he said. Too fast. Too clean.

I said nothing.

He stared straight ahead.

"Old friend," he muttered.

Still lying.

"Didn't sound like it."

He shook his head. "You don't get it."

"I don't have to," I said. "You do."

He swallowed. Voice tightened.

"Lucy."

Just the name.

Like he hadn't said it out loud in years.

The one who saw through him. The one who said it wouldn't stick — not because it was false, but because it was unfinished. And he hated her for being right.

"Lucy Wilson," he added. "Scottish — urban design. Righteous pain in the ass."

His hand twitched toward the empty glass. Stopped short.

"She used to laugh like it hurt — like something cracked inside her when it got too loud."

A long breath.

"We were close. Long time. But not like that."

"You sure?" I asked.

Chad looked at me, eyes glassy but fierce.

"I'm not gay," he said.

"You don't have to be."

"I told her that."

"And?"

"She waited." His voice went thin. "Too long."

I didn't say anything.

Chad went on.

"Final night was here. This bar. We were both drunk. I think she wanted to end it right. She told me —"

His mouth tightened.

"'I gave up waiting.' That's what she said."

"What did you say?"

"I asked what it meant."

He didn't stop it now.

"She said it meant she kissed someone else. And she liked it. And she wanted me to stop her."

A long pause.

"She'd kissed me once. Before. I froze. Didn't speak to her for a week."

"And that night?" I asked.

"She tried again."

He looked down.

"And I hit her."

No flinch. No drama. Just the truth.

"She left. Bar banned me for months. Never saw her again."

He covered his face with one hand.

"I thought I was protecting something. I don't even know what."

His voice cracked.

"And I ruined the only good thing I ever had."

I didn't argue.

Didn't call him Chad. Didn't call him Lily. Didn't need to.

"Doesn't matter who you were," I said. "You needed love. You turned it away. And now you think you deserve the emptiness that followed."

He didn't answer. Just sat there. Breathing like he wasn't sure he wanted to anymore.

I didn't wait.

Something tilted. The air stilled—like the room was holding its breath. Then the echo bent. Not with spectacle. Just inevitability. The air thickened. Shadows held still. Glasses on the bar stopped refracting light like they should. The world became *intentional*.

Then: movement.

The bartender—unchanged, but wrong. His eyes too knowing. Patrons at the far tables—figures now, not people. Ghosts dressed as drunks. Watching. Not judging. Just *witnessing*.

Chad stiffened.

"What is this?" he said. Voice low. Threatening.

He looked around. Saw the faces. Felt the stage.

"You think I'm doing this? Here? Like this?"

"No one's stopping you," I said. "But you don't get to hide either."

"This isn't real."

"No," I said. "But it's true."

He turned to leave the stool. Found his legs heavy.

Then she stepped into the scene.

Lucy.

She didn't glow. Nothing supernatural. Just presence—solid and impossible. Chad's eyes caught it first: that rare, exact ache for someone who saw you whole, before the fracture. Same coat. Hair still tied back. The sharpness hadn't dulled—just learned how to carry its own years.

She walked slowly. Past the bar. Past the watching faces. Past his shame.

He didn't breathe.

"Don't," he whispered. "Not here."

But she didn't stop.

And the body he wore began to change.

Not into Lily. Not back into anything. Just... *toward himself*.

The coat started to fit. The angles of his shoulders settled. His jaw didn't sharpen—it clarified. His hands stopped trembling.

It didn't land as beautiful. It didn't signal gender, but it held—settled—like the body finally matched the soul's blueprint.

Lucy stood in front of him now. One step away.

"You don't have to be afraid," she said.

Chad clenched his fists. "I'm not—"

"You are," I said.

He looked down. "This body doesn't deserve her."

That's the voice that kept him from her. The one that said broken things don't get to ask for grace.

Lucy reached out.

He flinched.

She touched his chest. Light. Two fingers. Right over the place that still believed it didn't deserve to be touched.

"I waited," she said.

"I know," he said.

"Do you?"

He shook his head. Not a no. Just too much.

"You hit me," she said. No accusation. Just history.

He looked at her.

"I hated myself," he said. "Not you."

Then—something gave. He leaned forward. Just a little.

Lucy stepped in. Kissed him. It wasn't passionate. It wasn't tragic. It was just real.

The bartender didn't look away. Neither did the ghosts. And Chad—finally, fully—stayed. He didn't flinch or flee. He let it happen. Let her lips meet his. Let the moment hold him. Then—a shimmer. No glow. No detonation. Just a ripple, the kind you get when sun beats on stone. And his form—clarified.

Chad.

Not a plea. Not a concession. Just truth.

Then — he exhaled.

And disappeared.

Dust, soft and slow.

No applause. No music. Just stillness.

What stayed behind wasn't him. Just the echo, settling back into silence.

Precinct. 4:11 a.m.

The office lights buzzed like they always did — flickering slightly in the corner near the intake desk. Scroll cases stacked higher than regulations allowed. Coffee stale in the carafe. Ghost of printer toner in the vents.

Mara was at her terminal, as always. She didn't look up when we came in. Just said:

"Case flagged for variance. Echo held longer than projection."

"Yeah," I said. "He was stubborn."

She tapped a key. "Disposition?"

"Resolved," I said.

She nodded once, didn't ask how. That's what I liked about Mara. She only asked questions when she already knew the answers.

I moved to my desk. Sat. Opened the log.

Chandler stood a moment longer, coat still buttoned. Hands in the pockets like he was holding something that hadn't finished cooling.

He looked at me—eyes steady, but something skewed. Like I'd stepped out of the frame.

"Are we allowed to do that?" he asked. "Alter the echo?"

I didn't look up.

"I didn't ask," I said.

He nodded. Sat across from me. Winced slightly, still nursing the jaw.

"I think I liked it better when I just handed out scrolls," he muttered.

"Then you should've stayed upstairs," I said.

Mara coughed once. A dry, knowing sound.

Chandler sighed.

I finished typing.

Case File: Parker, Chad (formerly Lily). Status: Delayed Transcendent. Tether: Emotional rupture—unacknowledged identity and suppressed love.

Disposition: Resolved via Echo Intervention. Dust confirmed.

I sat back. Looked at the name one last time.

Then closed the file.

Another page. Another silence.

Morning still hadn't come.

CASE FILE: PETER MORALES

I came in early. Or late. Hard to tell in a place where time doesn't pass—it waits.

The precinct shifts, but I know the feel of it: pressure without source, light without warmth, walls that don't echo when you walk. It's always clean, always quiet, and never still. You get used to that. Or you leave. I passed a sanctum I didn't recognize—spiral steps down into nothing, still lit. Someone must've filed something dangerous.

Down the corridor, I spotted Arrin at her post. She's not a receptionist—not really. More like a celestial intake node pretending to have a personality. But she liked me, for some reason.

"Sal," she called, eyes already scanning a scroll that wasn't unrolling. "You're behind."

"I'm eternal," I said. "I can't be late."

She snorted. "Tell that to Central. You've got a thread waiting. Do I want it?"

"No."

Then she smiled. "But you're getting it."

My office was where it always is—today. Third corridor, fifth aperture, just past the litigation vaults. A soft pull in the chest tells you when you're close.

Mara was already inside. Standing near the glyph-shelf, back to the door. Wings furled, robe loose, reading the room like a priest before absolution.

Chandler was at the side table, posture immaculate,

fingers folded like a catechism. His eyes lit when I walked in. "Morning," he said, earnest.

"Don't oversell it," I said. "Still time for it to get worse."

Then I saw the file.

Manila parchment with a tight weave of radiant cord, resting in a cradle of judgment glass. Thin smoke rising from it—not fire, just friction. Red thread. Tripled. I didn't have to touch it. I already knew.

"Grey," I said.

Chandler stood. "That's—real?"

Mara turned. "Unfortunately."

"They let us handle grey work now?" he asked.

"They let me," I said. "You're just here to ask questions and hope I answer them."

Chandler looked between us. "I thought the *Accord*—"

"—doesn't cover this," Mara cut in. "Grey files exist in the silence between clauses."

Chandler's brow knit. "But we're immortal. I mean—are you saying something could actually…?"

I stared at the thread. "You won't die," I said. Then paused. "But don't get shot. Or flayed. Or ruptured, or inverted, or broken across a soul-axis."

He swallowed. "How long would I be out?"

"Hard to say," Mara said. "Time's funny in recovery."

"And if they eradicated me?"

I shrugged. "Hell wouldn't dare. Too many of us still hold grudges."

He looked pale. "So… this is fine."

"It's fine," I said. "Just stay behind me. And if you see something with teeth smiling at you—don't smile back."

The world hit like a weight. Cold pavement. Dry air. Car exhaust clinging to the edges of the wind. Earth has a gravity Heaven doesn't—pulls different. Downward. Inward. Mortal.

My feet hit the sidewalk harder than I meant to. The coat hung heavier. Breath came slow, and the old ache in my right knee flared like it remembered a stairwell I never fell down. This body isn't real, but it remembers being worn. Enough years in the field and even grace collects scar tissue.

Beside me, Chandler stretched like he hadn't noticed the shift. Shoulders square. Eyes wide. He looked like he'd slept, prayed, and hydrated. Perky.

He adjusted the strap of his bag and scanned the building. "Hospice Saint-Jude," he read from the sign. "Charitable, bilingual, licensed for thirty-five beds, six palliative specialists on staff—"

"Save the brochure," I muttered. "We're not here for the architecture."

The front walk was lined with manicured hedges and a single broken streetlight. Someone inside had put up autumn decorations—cornstalks tied to the handrails, a grinning gourd lodged beside the planter, cheerful in the wrong season.

The door was unlocked. Always is, in places like this. We walked in.

Receptionist didn't look up. People moved past us like we weren't fully present. That's how it goes—half the time, they see you. Other half, they forget you were ever there. Memory blur. Minds smoothing out what doesn't fit. We pass for plainclothes. Cops, maybe. Social workers on a bad day. Someone nodded at us. We nodded back.

The corridor was too bright, too beige, too quiet. Clean tile, scrubbed baseboards, that faint antiseptic hush that always makes me want to cough just to hear a sound. We didn't check the chart. We didn't need to. We felt the pull. Down the left wing. Second room from the end. That's where the echo had taken hold.

I rolled my shoulders, felt the pistol weight under the coat. Standard issue for grey assignments—burnished, blunt, metaphysically unpleasant. I hadn't drawn mine in decades. Didn't like carrying it now.

Chandler wore his holstered high, tight against the ribs. He'd practised for this. A thousand clean draws on phantom targets. Crisp aim. Flawless form. No blood on his hands. Not yet.

We stopped outside the door. The room beyond was quiet. Lights off. Curtains drawn. But beneath it— layered like breath over glass—was the echo. Thin, harmonic, just a shade misaligned with real time. You learn to feel it before you see it. This was where Peter Morales died. This was where he hadn't left.

I looked at Chandler.

He nodded, too fast. He didn't know yet. But he would.

No need to spook him early. Just get in. Get the tether undone. And get out. Before trouble arrives.

I opened the door.

The room inside was still. Too still.

The real-world layer checked out: linoleum floor, steel bed frame, walls painted that institutional beige they reserve for endings. A cross above the headboard. Tray table with a half-finished cup of water—meniscus flat as glass. But the echo sat on top of it like held breath, frozen mid-exhale. Not dramatic. These things rarely are. Just… present, like a second exposure. No extra light. No extra sound. Just the dissonance of a note that doesn't end when it should.

I stepped forward. The world noticed. Shadows staggered out of sync. Temperature recalibrated. The air thickened—not with warmth, but with weight. Meaning held, not spoken. We were in.

Peter Morales sat upright in the bed. Not the man they buried. Not the wreck left behind at the end. This was how he still saw himself. Sixty, maybe. Trim. Clean-shaven. Wearing the hospital gown like it meant something. Hands folded, blanket pristine. He wasn't praying. Wasn't breathing. Wasn't distracted. He was waiting. Entirely. That's how you know you've got an echo—when time forgets what comes next and just loops the tension.

Chandler hung back, eyes scanning the corners. He adjusted to echo-space faster than most. Might've been the training. Might've been the faith. Might've been the way he still thought the world could be parsed into right and wrong if you just looked hard enough.

I gave the room one more sweep. Light didn't flicker. Air didn't bite. No pressure in the walls. No scent of sulfur or heat, no warping in the corners, no weight in the light. Nothing watching us. We were alone. For now.

I didn't relax. Just moved forward.

Peter Morales sat in the bed. Upright. Calm. Too calm. The kind of calm that's bought, not born.

"Peter Morales," I said.

He blinked. Focused. No panic. No surprise.

"Yes," he said. Voice calm, polite. "That's me."

I nodded. "You died."

He nodded back. "I know."

That made it worse. If he knew he was dead, and still hadn't moved on, then something in him wasn't tangled—it was *buried*. I circled the bed, slow. Let the silence stretch.

"Catholic?" I asked.

Peter nodded. "Cradle. Mass every Sunday. Fell off for a while in the seventies. Came back strong."

"Last rites performed?"

"Yes. Priest came in the night before. My daughter arranged it."

"Confession. Anointing of the Sick. Viaticum?" He nodded at each like a catechism drill.

"Yes. All of it."

Behind me, Chandler shifted. "Wait," he said quietly. "If he had Last Rites, wouldn't that mean…?"

I held up a hand. Not to stop him. Just to hold the thought in place long enough to examine it.

Peter's jaw tightened. Just a flick. A tic. I saw it. That's where the lie lives—small and practised. You don't need brimstone. Just hesitation.

"You're stuck," I said to Peter. "Which means something

didn't take."

Peter shook his head. "No. I did everything right. I confessed everything. I made peace."

"You made *some* peace," I said. "But peace isn't the same as truth."

Chandler frowned. "He's lucid. He remembers dying. Doesn't that mean he's ready?"

"No," I said. "It means he's aware."

I looked back to Peter. "Stuck isn't punishment. It's unfinished. Something tethered you — something strong enough to anchor an echo in the living world. And I'm betting it's not confusion. It's choice."

Peter swallowed.

I stepped closer. "I'm not here to judge you. I'm here to get you unstuck. But that only works if you *give me all of it*. If something was held back during Confession — intentionally or not — it *matters*."

The echo hummed underfoot. A low harmonic, barely there, like a violin string someone forgot to pluck. I didn't look at Chandler. Didn't need to. I could feel the clock ticking. I stayed standing.

He needed to look up at me. "I need you to walk me through it," I said. "Start wherever you like. But be precise."

Peter adjusted his blanket like it mattered. "What's the point? You already said I'm stuck. Doesn't that mean it's... too late?"

"No," I said. "It means you didn't finish the story."

"I told the priest everything."

"Tell me."

He started clean. Too clean. Birth in '54. Parochial school. Scholarship. Government recruitment.

"Linguistics support," he said. I let him say it. Let the euphemism rot in the air between us.

Then: civilian life. Teaching. Coaching. Marriage. Parish work. The arc of redemption.

"I know I'm not a saint," he said. "But I tried. I tried harder than most."

He said it like it bought something.

"You were in active service during the Cold War," I said.

He nodded.

"Classified operations?"

"Some."

"Did you ever kill anyone?"

Pause.

Then: "No direct action. I was support."

Not a lie. But not the truth.

Chandler stood at the window, eyes on the half-drawn curtain. "You've lived a good life," he said gently. "What matters now is grace. That's still on offer."

Peter's eyes flicked toward him. Something softened. "I know," he said. "That's what I want."

I stepped in closer. Dropped my voice. "What's the thing you didn't tell your daughter?"

He blinked.

"I—what?"

"You said she arranged the priest. But you didn't say goodbye. Why not?"

"I—" He faltered, just for a second.

"I didn't want her to see me like that."

"That's not it," I said. "Try again."

He stared at the blanket.

"I was tired."

"That's not it either."

The hum beneath us tightened. The room began to itch around the edges. The echo didn't like being pressed.

"You're very good at lying," I said.

Peter looked up, wounded. "I'm not lying to you."

"You are," I said. "But you believe it's justified."

Chandler moved closer. "Sir—Peter—you're not being judged. We're not here to punish you. This isn't some celestial trap."

Peter's mouth twitched.

"You think if you say it, you'll be rejected. You think it's the *one thing* grace won't cover."

"No," he said too quickly.

I circled again.

"You told your priest everything. Except the part you never told anyone."

He flinched. There. A crack.

But then it closed.

"I served. I came home. I did good work. I raised a family. I led a clean life for forty years."

"I believe you," I said. "But none of that is what's keeping you here."

The air thickened. The echo was coiling tighter, not unraveling.

Chandler looked at me. "How much time do we have?"

None.

The light in the corner folded in on itself. No crack. No flare. Just a shift—like someone flipped the room inside out and stitched it back without checking the seams.

He was already there. Leaning in the doorway like he'd been invited. Early twenties, maybe. Impeccable posture. Charcoal suit cut sharp as doctrine. Not a wrinkle out of place. And that smile. Just… delighted. Like this was his favourite part of the job. His eyes didn't blink. They reset—like a command line rerun behind polished glass.

"Well," he said, spreading his hands. "For a moment, I thought you might manage it. But no—*this* is better."

Chandler tensed beside me. One hand near his coat, not drawing yet.

"Identify," I said, flat.

He tilted his head like he was posing for a portrait. "Caedmon," he said. "Field Acquisition, Lower Division. Tag authority 9-Eleven. Jurisdictional claim pending, but soon to be resolved."

"You need to leave," I lied. "Check your paperwork. Protocol hasn't lapsed. The soul's still in play." He was young. Maybe the bluff would work.

It didn't.

He smiled wider. "Please—the paperwork's fine. Triple checked. We don't make mistakes."

Peter turned toward the voice, blinking. "Who—?"

Caedmon didn't even glance at him. "Don't worry," he said lightly. "You know me already. Just haven't admitted it."

He walked into the room like it belonged to him.

Chandler stepped forward, tense. "You're not authorized to speak until jurisdiction is confirmed."

Caedmon laughed. "Oh, sunshine. That's adorable."

I moved between them. Slow. Measured.

"Peter," I said, eyes on the devil. "This is your last breath. And it's not yours unless you spend it."

Peter looked panicked now. "I told you—I'm not hiding anything—"

"You are," Caedmon said, turning finally. "And you've done it for so long you don't even feel the weight of it."

Peter froze. The room shifted again. Not visibly. But the echo-space stuttered—like memory trying to overwrite itself. The past trying to assert itself. Truth clawing toward the surface.

Caedmon stepped closer to Peter's bed. "Shall I say it for you?"

Caedmon didn't wait for permission. He turned to Peter and said, with surgical cheer: "You tortured a man to death in Marrakesh, 1981. You knew he was innocent. You lied on the report. You called it acceptable loss."

Peter's mouth opened. No words. No denial. Just collapse. Like something inside him gave out.

"You didn't confess it," Caedmon continued. "Not to your wife. Not to your daughter. Not to your priest."

He knelt—squat, easy—face level with Peter's. "You carried it like it was penance. But it wasn't. It was pride."

Peter shook his head. "I—I didn't mean to—"

"Yes you did," Caedmon said, still smiling. "And you knew it. That's why you never spoke it aloud. Because you knew once it had a name, it couldn't be washed away with service hours and soup kitchens."

A flare of light—not warm or bright. Final. A symbol burned itself into Peter's chest—no fire, just finality. Then a sound: not a scream, just the soft click of a verdict sealing shut. Mark of claim. It was done.

Peter *snapped.* He lurched forward. Grabbed Caedmon's collar. Dragged him halfway across the bed. "NO!" he shouted. "I want grace—I want *God!* I want *out!*" He threw a punch that cracked against the devil's cheekbone.

Blood—not red, not liquid—splashed the wall behind him like shadow smeared on glass.

Caedmon laughed. "Oh, I like this part," he said, eyes gleaming. He hit back—fast, open-palmed, enough force to knock Peter off the bed.

Peter hit the floor and rose like an animal. No dignity. Just panic. Fight. Desperation. The echo-space trembled, peeling at the edges. One of the curtain rods fell into a layer of unreality and vanished. Peter grabbed the tray-table. Swung it like a weapon. Connected.

Caedmon staggered. Grinned wider. "Keep going," he whispered. "You're making this easy."

Chandler raised his gun. Didn't fire. Couldn't. He stood frozen, weapon half-drawn, eyes locked on the blur of limbs and flailing redemption. "This isn't right," he whispered.

"It's not," I said.

Peter got one more blow in. A real one. Broke something in Caedmon's face.

The devil's head snapped to the side. And then, with impossible calm, Caedmon grabbed Peter by the throat. Lifted him. "Time's up," he said. And he *dragged* him through the tear. Peter screamed. It wasn't the sound of pain. It was loss. It was hope being strangled into silence. It was a man still begging for salvation while falling the other way.

And then it was quiet. No echo. No light. Just the empty room. And the cup of water, still undisturbed.

I holstered my gun.

Didn't look at Chandler.

"Time to go."

Back in the precinct, time didn't resume — it just… waited in grief. Chandler walked three paces behind me. Didn't look up. Didn't make a sound. His robe still gleamed. But the shine looked thinner now. Like it had seen itself reflected in the wrong mirror.

I stepped into the office.

Mara didn't ask. Just stood at the shelf, tracing an unreadable sigil into the glass with the tip of her finger.

Chandler lingered in the threshold. Still holding the weight like he thought he had to name it before he could put it down. He didn't. He wouldn't. Not yet.

I sat. Reached for the case thread. It burned faintly as I touched it — residue of judgment, not heat. Let it unfurl. Let it log.

Case Log – PM-0666 Name: Morales, Peter

Disposition: Claimed Classification: Grey File

Tether Type: Withheld confession (unresolved mortal sin)

Intervention Outcome: Failed

Notes: Subject retained conscious will at time of death. Received sacraments without full disclosure. Echo formed around false absolution. Hellfield Agent Caedmon arrived prior to tether resolution. Claim was lawfully executed under Article 9.11. No Accord breach. Attempted resistance noted.

Status: Closed.

I sat back. Didn't speak. Didn't move. Just let the silence say what I wouldn't.

Across the room, Chandler lowered himself into the chair like it might judge him for standing. His voice, when it came, was small. Broken-glass soft. "We could've saved him."

"No," I said.

He waited. I didn't elaborate. He needed to learn which losses teach. And which ones *warn*.

CASE FILE: DUARTE CARVALHO

Sometimes I get lucky. Or careful. Resolve the stuck in one go. But most of the time, it doesn't work like that. People don't break clean—they knot. Layer on layer, pain wrapped in pride wrapped in silence, until you can't find the start of it. And then they die. After decades tangled in their own contradictions, we're meant to walk in and untie the whole thing with one gesture. But we don't do gestures.

We do truth.

Friction.

Blood on the stone.

The columbarium sat clean and square at the edge of the lawn, where the cemetery ran out of room and started pretending to be peace. Rows of black granite niches. Polished. Unblemished. A place for tidy sorrows. Two fake bouquets to either side, their colours too bright to trust. No one else in sight.

I stepped forward. Chandler stayed back, eyes scanning the walls like he was reading names off a list that hadn't been updated.

"You sure this is the right site?" he asked.

"Site's fine," I said.

We approached the wall. Third row from the bottom. Duarte Carvalho. 1949–2024. A narrow brass cross next to the name. No quote. Just dates. Like someone was afraid to lie.

Chandler reached out, fingers hovering near the engraved plate.

"Properly sealed," he murmured. "Blessed ground. Recorded interment. Protocol's clean."

"Then why's he still here?"

Chandler hesitated.

Behind us, the air folded. A flicker—not quite light, not quite shadow. Duarte leaning against an angel headstone ten paces away, looking at us like we owed him an apology. He wore a windbreaker zipped to the throat, grey slacks, scuffed shoes. Civilian clothes. The kind you wear when no one's coming to see you. His face was sharp, angular. Portuguese working-class proud. Lines like someone had carved his stubbornness in early and let time deepen it.

"You showed," he said, not to either of us. "Bit late."

I nodded. "Name's Sal. This is Chandler."

He didn't look at us. Just nodded toward the wall.

"You ever watch your own funeral?" he asked. "I don't recommend it."

"What happened?" Chandler said.

"They came late. Wrecked the whole thing." Priest tried to keep going, but—" He snorted. "Portuguese." As if that explained everything.

"You were never finished," I said.

He looked at me. Not surprised—just relieved someone finally said it.

Chandler stepped forward, silent but sure. From the inner pocket of his coat, he pulled a small glass phial. Holy water. Mortal-blessed, not celestial. He shook a few drops onto his fingers and touched them to his brow, then traced the sign of the cross in the air over the niche. Not theatrical. Practised.

"In the waters of baptism, Duarte Carvalho died with Christ and rose with him to new life," he said, voice steady. "May he now share with him eternal glory."

He reached into the coat again—pulled a folded square of white cloth, smoothed it over one palm like it meant something.

"Into your hands, O merciful God, we commend your servant Duarte. Acknowledge him as sheep of your own fold, a sinner of your own redeeming."

The cadence shifted—more than Mass now. Something older, off-registry. Protocol layering under liturgy.

"Let the name be spoken where the silence ends. Let the life be recorded where no witness fails. Let him go, let him rise, let him rest."

A breath. A pause. He made the sign of the cross once more—this time over the brass plaque. No light stirred. No wind. No shift of grace.

The stone stayed stone.

Chandler stepped back. Folded the cloth. Palmed the phial. Nothing in his face but confusion softened by habit. His fingers twitched—just once. Like a note struck wrong. He looked at the phial as if it might answer him back.

"That should have held."

"It didn't," I said.

He looked at me. I looked at Duarte.

Still leaning on the angel headstone ten paces back. Still watching like the whole show had proved his point.

"Thanks," he said. Voice dry, cut with sarcasm. "Really

moving."

Then sharper: "I don't need a rite. I need a reckoning."

He nodded at the plaque.

"They buried the body, sure. But they didn't give a damn about *me*."

"What happened here?" I asked.

"Disrespect is what happened!" He stepped forward. Words came like a runaway engine—too fast, no brakes. Started counting on his fingers. "First, Elisa hires a priest I don't know—couldn't even speak Portuguese. Couldn't even say my name right. Second, cremation. Not what I wanted. Third, my corrupt brother has the nerve to show up after all he's done…"

"Okay. Okay." I held up a hand. "If you want our help, we need to start at the beginning."

"The beginning? Where the hell's the beginning."

We hadn't even started, and already I had a headache.

"Your parents," I said. "They were first-generation?"

He nodded. "Mamãe and Papai came over in the sixties, looking for a better life. No education, no family money. Just work ethic. That's how I was raised. Never asked for a goddamn thing."

Chandler winced. "Maybe let's not take the Lord's name in—"

"Sorry. Yes, of course." Duarte crossed himself. "But still."

I pushed him on. "You were raised in Portugal?"

"Until thirteen. Then we came here. Brownstone off Lansdowne. You know the kind—cracked stucco, three locks on the door. Grew up working with my dad. Commercial cleaning, mats, overnight shifts while other kids slept."

"Did that work pay off?"

He laughed once. No humour in it.

"Not for me."

"Why?"

"Because everything was always about Filipe."

He spit the name like it tasted rotten.

"I'm the oldest. I stayed. Helped build the business. Didn't go to school, didn't complain. Elisa too—she married Frank, moved to Mississauga. But Filipe?" He shook his head. "Born here. Baby of the family. Private school. Med school. Never touched a mop in his life."

Chandler looked confused. "So what happened to the business?"

Duarte didn't blink.

"My father died. Quiet. No will."

"And your mother?"

"Had one drawn up after. Left it all to Filipe."

"Why?"

He opened his mouth, closed it again. When he finally answered, the words came out slow.

"Said he had the education. Said he could 'grow it right.' Said I'd already had my chance."

"You challenged it."

"Damn right I did. Took it to court. Elisa backed me— swore an affidavit, said I built it too. Said it was ours.

Me and Papai. Not Filipe's to inherit like some damn trophy."

"You win?"

"Course not."

He turned to the plaque.

"She didn't just take the business. She took the story. Made him the heir. Made me the mistake."

"I heard you did pretty well for yourself," I said.

He shrugged, but the pride showed anyway.

"Started my own company. Cleaning and mats, just like Papai taught me. Leona helped get it off the ground — real backbone, that woman. We raised three kids. All decent. All still talking to each other. Imagine that."

"Elisa?"

He hesitated. "Five kids. Married Frank. Canadian. Loud. You've met the type."

Chandler gave a polite cough. "Catholic funeral, yes?"

"Of course." Then, quickly: "Though not like it mattered."

I nodded. "Let's come back to the funeral."

He stiffened. Not grief. Fury with nowhere to go.

"Cremated," he said flatly. "Not what I wanted, but it was easier. Cancer had taken too much already. I'd planned everything. Wrote a letter to be read. Leona arranged the whole thing — hired the priest, booked the spot. Family was supposed to come early."

"But they didn't."

"No."

The word landed like a bruise.

"Filipe shows up with his whole flock—late. No warning. Struts in like he owns the Mass."

"And?"

"I told them to leave."

"And?"

He paused. Longer this time. Then:

"I was already dead."

I waited.

"But I said it anyway. Loud. Inside. I stood at the back of that chapel and screamed at him to get out."

"And he heard you?"

"Didn't flinch. But Elisa did. Her kids started crying. Frank started shouting. The priest tried to keep going, but something was off."

He looked at me now. Eyes sharp, voice low.

"Something came through. Not a voice. Not mine. Just— anger. Heavy. Like incense gone sour."

"The spiritual equivalent of a broken radio signal," I said. "A soul demanding authorship. Forcing its name back into the script."

"Whatever it was, it infected the whole damn service. Like rage passed hand to hand. No one could say the right words. The priest fumbled the name. Elisa got up to fix it, and Frank stopped her."

"And then?"

"He hit someone. Got hit back. Don't know who started what. But when it ended, Frank's arm was broken, the priest was gone, and I was still in the box."

"No rites."

"No ending."

"No release."

"No point," he said bitterly. "No one heard me when I was alive. Guess I got louder after."

I'd heard enough grief to know when it calcified. When the echo needed evidence.

So I went looking for it.

The Archive wasn't part of the precinct. Not really. It sat further back — behind protocol, behind prayer — where the echoes go when no one's listening anymore. It didn't organize knowledge. It let it accumulate. Shelves bent inward. Scrolls leaned like they remembered being opened once, long ago, by someone who thought the past could be corrected. Time didn't flow here. It folded. Names repeated. Witnesses doubled back. Files you'd sworn were resolved reappeared under different dates, asking different questions.

You don't discover anything in the Archive. You arrive where you started, and read it again for the first time.

Chandler hovered at the threshold, arms folded.

"You're really filing him?" he asked.

"No. I'm reading him."

"You're building a case, not closing a soul."

"Same thing," I said. "Closure needs witness."

I found the drawer marked C. Pulled three folios:

- **Will of Sofia Carvalho**: business transferred in full to Filipe. No mention of Duarte.

- **Civil claim filed 2007**: **Carvalho** v. **Carvalho**. Probate challenge.

- **Affidavit by Elisa Mendes née Carvalho**: support for Duarte's role in founding the company. Loyalty, but too late.

I laid them out on the long table beneath a skylight stained by time and something older.

The judgment had been final. The Will held. Duarte lost, on paper and in court.

I reached for the funeral transcript next. Diocese copy. Half-complete.

> The liturgical header was there: *Mass of Christian Burial: Duarte Carvalho.*
>
> First reading: *Psalm 23.*
>
> ~~Homily:~~
>
> Eulogy: not delivered.
>
> Commendation: *Disruption in service. Ceremony discontinued. Priest discharged.*
>
> No mention of the letter.

"Chandler," I said. "There's no record of Duarte's words. Not the letter. Not the eulogy. He was erased."

Chandler looked at the crossed-out eulogy. "This isn't procedure anymore, is it?"

I closed the file.

"We're going to get Eliza and Leona to finish this thing properly."

"And Filipe?"

"Him too. But he doesn't get to speak."

Chandler made the call from a quiet hallway outside the archive. He paced while it rang, voice rehearsed, collar straight.

"Hello, Mrs. Carvalho? My name is Daniel Chandler. I'm with the diocesan office handling funeral reconciliations—yes, with the Catholic Church."

He nodded into the air, listening.

"There was a small irregularity recorded in your husband's file. Nothing serious, I assure you. Just a missing Commendation rite. The formal commendation was never performed—yes, that's the final prayer before interment. The Church takes such things very seriously."

He waited. Smiled.

"Of course. We'd like to offer a brief resolution service. Very small. No audience. Just presence and prayer. Would you be willing to attend?"

A pause.

Chandler mouthed *yes* to me.

"She says she visits regularly," he whispered, covering the mic.

Then back into the phone: "Wonderful. Would Saturday afternoon work?"

He confirmed the time, said thank you, and hung up with reverence in his spine.

"She's in."

Two seconds later, and with a little help from Mara, Elisa's phone — tucked inside a purse three cities away — lit up and called Leona.

Leona was in her kitchen. Quiet. Boiling water for tea. She picked up without checking.

"Elisa? I didn't expect—"

She frowned. No voice on the other end.

But she spoke anyway.

"Hey, looks like you just pocket dialed me. Strange, because I was jus thinking about you. Someone from the Church called. Said they're doing a little Commendation for Duarte. You remember the priest had to leave? Well, it never got finished. They're correcting it. Anyway, thought you might want to come. It's this Saturday. Give me a shout."

Meanwhile, I took the letter to Filipe.

His house was white brick and glass, the kind of architecture that looks like it cost more than you. He opened the door wearing a fitted shirt and a look that had outlived several apologies.

"Yes?" he said.

I handed him the envelope.

"This was recovered during a diocesan review. It's marked for public reading. We believe it was intended for your brother's funeral. It never reached the lectern."

He turned it over. Read the handwriting. Froze.

"I don't know who you are," he said. "But this is—"

He stopped himself.

"Thank you," he said, too fast. Then, quieter: "This was

never meant to be public."

"Good night," I said.

The columbarium hadn't changed. Same polished rows. Same cold, stone reverence pretending to be peace. But something in the air had shifted. Not just weather — *weather remembers*. This was pressure. The kind that builds behind words unsaid.

They pulled up together in a silver Corolla that had seen better years. Didn't idle. Just parked hard against the curb and cut the engine like mercy was expensive. Gravel crunched under the tires. Doors opened slow.

Chandler stood at the gravesite, vaguely Roman Catholic — hands folded, back straight, as if he'd stepped out of a liturgy.

I watched from across the green.

Leona stepped out first — coat black, neat, collar turned up against the rain. She moved like someone who still kept appointments. Like grief, for her, had an order to it. The umbrella stayed closed in her hand. She didn't bother. Just looked once at the clouds, accepted what was coming, and moved.

Elisa followed. No umbrella either. Brown trench, buttoned wrong. One hand clutched her purse like it might float. The other held the envelope. She didn't look up.

They didn't speak.

Filipe came last. Of course he did. He hadn't read Duarte's letter — just handed it to Elisa like it might burn if he held it too long. The girls had told him about the Commendation. So he came. Present enough to count.

Distant enough not to matter.

Elisa opened the envelope. Inside, two sheets, creased from too much waiting. She looked at Leona, who put a gentle hand on her arm. She looked at Filipe, who just gave a small nod.

She inhaled, once, like she was stepping into cold water.

Her hands trembled, but her voice didn't break.

"I wasn't the best man. I was proud. I was sharp-tongued. I held grudges. I loved my family like a hammer loves a nail—loud, rough, and with the expectation they'd hold. I didn't have your beauty, Elisa. I didn't have Filipe's chances. All I had was my hands and my heart. Papai taught me how to work. Mamãe gave me music and a belief in myself. I gave what I had. Every day. I stayed when others left. I built something.

"Leona, you are better than I deserved. You did right by me, and right by ours. I love you. Matheus, Ana, and little Rosa — listen to your mother. She knows better than you. I love you.

"You don't have to like me. But you do have to listen. Just this once. Because I'm lying here on my deathbed, thinking about my life, and here's what I think: I'm okay with this. I'm proud of what I've left behind. What I did — it mattered. Maybe not because of me. Maybe despite me. But still good. And that, I hope, is what stays.

"So say my name. Love it, curse it, spit it if you must. But say it.

"Because it mattered.

"I wasn't a perfect man. But I built something good. Say that much."

She folded the letter. Looked at the plaque like it had finally heard her.

Chandler stepped forward. "Let the silence end," he said softly. "Let the name be known."

He opened the rite book with quiet hands, fingers reverent, movements practised. His voice, when it came, was soft—but not uncertain. "In sure and certain hope," he began, "we commend this soul to the mercy beyond merit…"

The first drop of rain hit the stone.

The wind shifted. I felt it before I saw him.

Duarte stood beside me—quiet, present, no echo of pain now. Just the shape a man leaves when he's said enough. He watched Elisa fold the letter. Listened as Chandler gave the rite its due. Looked at Filipe, long and level. Didn't speak. Didn't forgive. But he nodded.

"Took me a whole life to be heard," he said. "Took them ten minutes to do it right."

The rain picked up, steady now. No music. No trumpet. Just the sound of water on stone.

And Duarte—gone.

Just absence where a wound used to be.

Not peace. Not grace. Just a name, finally said.

Sometimes that's enough.

I looked at the plaque one last time. Niche 7-C.

Finally closed.

CASE FILE: ARTHUR PELL

Heaven keeps everything. Catalogues it. But that doesn't mean it sees. Some things fall quiet. Slip past. Wait. That's where we come in.

It was waiting on my desk when I returned. No shimmer. No sealburst.

Just a name: Arthur Pell.

Not red for Hell. Not gold for Heaven. No judgement embossed. No tether code logged. Just a file. Loose documents, archived in several places, like they mattered once. Not flagged. Just creased, corded, soft at the corners from too many unhurried hands.

I didn't touch it right away. Let it sit.

Precinct light doesn't cast shadows unless it wants to. That night, it wanted to. My desk floated in a sallow cone while everything beyond it slipped toward unreality. Filing alcoves. Empty chairs. A cup half-drunk by someone who didn't return. You start to notice the ambient absences, this long into the work.

I poured the coffee anyway. It had cooled. Of course it had. Heaven's machines don't keep warmth. They just offer what's owed.

But the file wasn't cold. Not yet. The cord on the file was red. Not Hell red. Not the ceremonial scarlet of judgment writ. Just faded department twine, the kind used when no one expects the folder to be opened again.

But I had asked. Asked for the full mortal record. Birth to death. Identity trace, career index, variance tags. It had taken seven days to process and none of that time felt wasted, which was strange. Usually, you make a request like that and wait so long you forget what guilt drove you to file it. But this one… this one came quick.

I pulled the cord. It gave with a whisper, like breath leaving a confession.

Opened the file. Edges yellowed. Pages uneven. Some typed. Some copied. Some handwritten, like the bureaucracy hadn't agreed yet what century to believe in.

First page: birth record. London, Ontario. 1981. Parents: Linda and Joseph Pell. Weight: 6 pounds, 11 ounces. A smudged footprint. Left heel. Ink faded. Real.

Next: school files. C-pluses. Track team. Some mention of shoplifting gum in grade eight — no charges.

Flipped. Minor note in the margin aught my eye: *"Quiet. Respectful. Doesn't cause trouble."*

The next page started with a photo. It was the kind they used to take in recruiting offices, back before image filters and symmetry algorithms. Just a boy, really. Not soft, but unfinished — like the world hadn't finished carving him yet. Buzzed hair, ears a little too wide, collar buttoned all the way up.

The form beneath it was standard. Enlistment, Canadian Armed Forces. Signed 2001. Tank squadron. Loader position requested. Evaluation: *"Cooperative. Shows aptitude for confined-space logistics. Resilient under simulated fire. Likely to follow chain of command under stress."*

The pages that followed were dry. Station logs. Deployment orders. Transfer notes. Each stamped, each dated, each confident that Arthur Pell had been, and had gone, and had served. None of them knew how the story ended. Just that it did.

Then came the incident report.

JULY 19, 2006 — OPERATIONAL THEATRE: IRAQ — SOUTH QUADRANT *At 14:26 local, Unit encountered IED-initiated RPG attack at rural intersection. Enemy fire targeted convoy midline. Vehicle ID 41A3-C sustained internal breach. RPG entered lower hull, detonated at crew level. All crew members listed as KIA. No recoverable remains. Burn radius compromised biometric scan protocols. Visual ID impossible. Field commander, Lt. O'Hara, attempted extraction. Succumbed to secondary shrapnel wound. Deceased en route to medivac. KIA Confirmed: Arthur Pell (Loader, Position 2A). Remains: None.*

That should've been the end of him. No resurrection variance. No flagged interference. Just the clean, quiet closure that comes when a man is burned into paperwork.

Except two months later, he bought a car in Ontario.

I leaned back in the chair. Heaven's chairs aren't built for comfort. They're built for posture, for record-straightening and penance filing. My spine ached. It always does when the air thickens with heat and blood and no one else reacts.

Two months.

I flipped forward.

A tax record from the CRA. Employment claim: Used car dealership, Hamilton. Date: September 12, 2006. Driver's license renewal. Social insurance number reactivated. Same name. Same birthdate. Not a single question raised. Because the file was closed.

That's the trick of it. If a soul's been marked dead and Heaven agrees, nobody checks the street corners to see if the corpse is getting groceries.

And then came the mortgage. Briar Glen Crescent. Same unit Amira Pell had died in. Purchase finalized October 4, 2006. Joint ownership. No note on return. No explanation. No resurrection tag. It was as if Arthur had simply paused for breath, then resumed his life at a different pace.

I reached the bottom of the stack and found a printed web trace — mortal-side metadata scrubbed into the file by someone with clearance I didn't recognize.

SOURCE: Amira Pell (spousal record) Online forum participation, 2009–2019. Flagged phrases: *"Holistic disarmament," "sovereign ritual," "the veiled mandate."*

Engagement with content labelled: anti-institutional, semi-theological, borderline paranoid. Primary associations: spiritually-inflected conspiracy networks, illness denialism, post-sovereign theological theory.

The report didn't judge her. But it didn't believe her either. That made two of us. Or maybe one and a half.

That's when the itch returned. I flipped back through the record. Noted the gaps. No primary care visits. No insurance activity. No contact with DND veterans services. No registered next-of-kin beside Amira. For fifteen years, Arthur Pell lived in Ontario with no living history and no dying proof.

And we let him.

I checked for celestial tags. Metadata. Anything. Sometimes even closed files leave a shadow. Nothing. No resurrection. No procedural notes. Just a file marked CLOSED and a man who didn't stay dead.

I closed the file. Not with finality or reverence. Just enough pressure to remind it that it wasn't finished.

The lights hadn't changed. Heaven's precinct runs on a kind of breathless constancy—rooms that forget you until you're needed again.

I stood. Let the ache settle in my knees. Let the paper dust cling to my fingers. The kind of dust that remembers who was here last.

I could've filed a request. Could've passed it to Mara. Could've waited for signs and seals and the slow trickle of celestial sanction. But I already knew what they'd say. The file was closed. And if something was still walking in Arthur Pell's skin, it wasn't our problem—unless it made itself one.

I looked once more at the empty seat across from mine. The chair Chandler used when he still thought belief was enough. The one Mara passed without pause. No one ever really fills it. We work alone here. Just at different desks.

I thought about involving them. Then didn't.

Best not to drag Chandler into my hunches. Best to leave Mara clean. Or whatever she is now.

Going off-script shouldn't be their burden.

Not that I'm barred from walking the lower halls. I go where I like. But this wasn't my role anymore. We manage DTs. Departures. Not metaphysical breaches.

No partner. No writ. Just curiosity. And a case that wasn't one.

Purgatory doesn't announce itself.

It's not a gate or a tunnel or a threshold of judgment. It's a hallway that forgets to end. It's descent without declaration. One corridor too far and the walls start to yellow, like parchment left in the sun too long. The light gets greasy. Doors stay shut longer. And nothing echoes the same way twice.

No guards. No checkpoints. Just a feeling—like gravity is asking questions.

I walked slow. The way you do when you're not expected and don't want to be.

The angelic office in Purgatory is worse than you think. Not cruel. Just tired. Filing alcoves with no central map. Pale stone scored with numbers that don't follow each other. Everything smells like chalk and regret. You can tell they tried, once. That someone meant for this place to stay sacred. But meaning leaks.

I turned left at a prayer that had been reclassified as inadmissible testimony and down past the Redemption Appeals corridor, which hasn't seen a success in a century. There was a tea stain on the wall near the transfer desk. Familiar. Same one as last time.

Laziel's desk looked the same. It looked like it had survived being condemned just long enough to be promoted by default. A single drawer, jammed shut. Three stacks of files arranged not by alphabet, but by the likelihood they'd be asked for. A cracked terminal sat to one side, wired into something not visible and not strictly Accord-approved. The machine hummed in a tone that felt like it wanted you to leave.

Laz didn't look up.

"You smell like old law and bad decisions," he said.

His voice was dry, scratched at the edges, like it had

been ironed flat one too many times.

"Must be Tuesday."

I didn't sit.

He gestured vaguely toward a battered wooden crate beside the desk. "I know you're not here officially. If you were, I'd have heard the shouting."

"I need a look."

"Everyone does."

He clicked something on the terminal. A soft whir. The lights flickered once.

"This is off-ledger," I said.

"No," he replied. "This is under the ledger. There's a difference."

He leaned back, steepled his fingers. Wore no robe. Just a shirt that might've been white once and sleeves rolled to the elbow, stained with ink in the way that says he files by feel.

"What is it?"

"Arthur Pell," I said.

That made him pause. "Ascendance?"

"Maybe. Maybe not. I don't need to prove anything. Just need a way in."

He exhaled slowly, like the name tasted of unfinished sentences.

"You brought a query ID?" I shook my head.

"I brought a name. And I know it walked out of a blown-open tank."

Laz closed his eyes. Pressed one finger against the

terminal's side. The screen blinked once — no colour, just greyscale figures in motion. Lines of code like veins.

"You know what the internet is, Sal?"

I didn't answer.

He smiled. Not warm. Just the kind you give a child holding a lit match. "It's the last mortal miracle no one knows how to classify. Built on belief, on repetition. It remembers faster than Heaven forgets. It's not divine, but it's not entirely not."

"Just show me what he touched."

Laz started typing. Not fast. Just sure.

"You'll owe me," he said.

"I already do."

"No. This time it counts."

He didn't look up. Just nodded toward the crate again.

"Sit. This'll take a while."

I sat. The wood creaked.

Somewhere behind the wall, a soul was crying. Faint. Familiar. Like sorrow on repeat.

The screen resolved slowly. This wasn't Heaven's machine. It didn't obey. It leaked.

At first, just a still frame. A group photo. Midwest setting — trees thin and scrubbed, the kind that don't weep when burned. A dozen people, most of them white, most of them smiling too broadly. Camouflage jackets. Denim. Bad facial hair. Mismatched flags behind them.

And there he was. Front right. Different name on the caption. But it was him. Older. Not aged. Just hardened.

The soft edges Arthur Pell had worn—the cautious boy, the tentative husband, the silent driver—were all gone. What sat in this image wore the same face, but tighter. Like it had been pulled over something meaner.

"That him?" Laz asked.

I didn't speak. Just nodded once.

He brought up the metadata.

>Username: **Melvin Stokes.**

>Alias Index: **None recognized by Accord.**

>Location tags: **Northern Michigan. Rural county.**

>Associated Group: *New Clarion Order.*

No file. No origin trace. Not even a flagged variance. I could've gone back, pulled records. Asked for oversight. But there'd be nothing waiting. You can't pull what never existed.

Click.

The manifesto loaded. PDF. Twelve pages. Garish font. Typing like a sermon, delivered in heatstroke. First line read: *"America has been turned against God, and God has sent us to turn her back."* The paragraphs got worse. I scanned them like a coroner might scan bones. Looking for the fracture, not the life. Phrases like: *"Martial law must be declared." "We do not negotiate with rot." "Those who will not leave must be removed. Those who will not kneel must be corrected." "JFK was a cleansing. We were there."*

Laz raised an eyebrow. "Bold."

"Not bold," I said. "Untouchable."

Forums, broadcasts, encrypted threads—the group was layered. Not wide-reaching, but far from marginal.

They'd been recruiting for years. Rural cells. Disappearances. Threats no one had time to investigate.

The photos were worse. Rallies. Training. Books handed out with verses that never came from scripture but were bound in leather anyway. And always him — Melvin — centre frame. Smiling. But not Arthur's smile. Like someone had practised his grin so long the edges broke.

"He's not hiding," Laz said. "He's marketing."

I leaned closer.

Not at the man. At the space around him. Because something was wrong. There *was* a trace — subtle, scorched at the metaphysical edges. Not celestial. Demonic. But dulled, like it had been filtered through flesh too long. He wasn't echoing death. He was masking it. The digital signature didn't hesitate. No stutter, no spiritual resistance. The image flowed clean — too clean. Most resurrections leak doubt, slip somewhere under scrutiny. This didn't. This wasn't someone trying to pass as human. It was something convinced it had the right.

"He didn't slip protocol," I said. "He acts like it doesn't exist."

Laz turned. "You sure?"

"Look at his eyes."

He did.

"Dead man walking," Laz said softly. "But I'm not sure which part died."

We kept scrolling.

Another image. A map. Supply chain notes. Locations marked with symbols I recognized — not from Heaven's archives, but from old interdiction logs. Half-legible glyphs used by Hell when they were trying to seed belief systems through violence. Most had failed. But this one hadn't. It was growing.

"Your boy's got a plan," Laz said.

"He's not mine."

"You opened his file."

I didn't argue. I just stared at the latest post. A countdown. *'CLARITY COMES IN NINE DAYS.'*

I stood.

Laz didn't stop me. Just slid a data slip across the desk. Burned to mortal format. Illegal to transmit.

"That's a felony."

"Not if you don't show anyone," he said.

I took it. Turned back toward the hallway. The descent didn't feel as far this time. The weight had already caught up.

Arthur Pell was dead. But something wearing his smile was counting down—and Heaven hadn't noticed the clock.

But I had.

The bridge that joins Michigan to itself is called the Mackinac Bridge—five miles long, strung like a prayer across the straits. A miracle of engineering. Or delusion. Depends who you ask. They built it to say the state was one. That the Upper Peninsula wasn't an afterthought. But you can't bind north to south with steel and span and call it settled. The bridge holds. The divide doesn't.

South Michigan has cities — Flint, Detroit, Grand Rapids. Unfinished revolutions and busted economies. Old factories turned artist enclaves. Brick towns held together by stubbornness and drive-thrus. You don't go there to vanish. You go there to be seen, or to be changed.

North is something else.

I stood outside a gas station off Highway 123, just past Trout Lake. Restaurant attached. Deer skull above the door, rifle bolt screwed into the lock plate like someone ran out of decorative options and said: hell, this'll do.

Sky was low. Cloud cover like wet canvas. Cold trying to claw under the collar. Not snowing yet, but the wind was rehearsing.

Cottagers were long gone for the season. What was left were the lifers — the born-here, die-here types who fished when it wasn't hunting season and hunted when it wasn't Sunday. Independence wasn't a virtue up here. It was assumed. You weren't expected to call for help. You were expected to *be* help. If something bad happened, folks might ask what *you* did to deserve it.

Every truck in the parking lot had a rifle rack. Most probably had something less legal under the seat. Up here, the right to carry wasn't a debate. It was a birthright. And they didn't just have Michigan flags — they had Upper Peninsula flags. Yellow and black, like warning tape that someone turned into pride.

Melvin Stokes had chosen well.

He didn't go to a hideout. He went somewhere that didn't want to know.

The bell over the door didn't ring so much as *surrender.* One of those faded brass chimes with a half-bent clapper, like it had given up keeping time a decade ago. Inside, the place smelled like burnt coffee, fryer oil, and old linoleum that had lost its shine sometime around Reagan.

Red vinyl booths lined the windows—cracked at the seams, foam showing through like bones. Tables were faux-marble laminate, dulled by thousands of elbows and a few bored knives. A napkin dispenser on every one, plus ketchup bottles that hadn't been full since morning. A wall-mounted jukebox blinked in the corner, too proud to admit it didn't work.

Truckers made up most of the crowd. Heavy coats. Mud on boots. Big shoulders hunched over eggs and meat. Conversation stayed low, slow. The kind of quiet that didn't mean peace—just routine. A voice shouted from the kitchen—could've been orders, could've been anger. Nobody flinched.

The waitress looked like she'd been carved from one of the stools and given a nameplate. Late fifties, maybe older. Hair held back in a loose bun. Sneakers with the soles going soft. Lines on her face like she'd spent her life squinting into someone else's nonsense.

I took the counter. Easier to talk there.

She came over with a pad she didn't need and a pen that didn't write. "Coffee?"

"Yeah."

Poured without asking how I took it. She knew how I took it—black, burnt, and not worth complaining about.

I set the photo on the counter. One of the older prints, before Melvin had started smiling with confidence. Back when he still looked like Arthur. Edges curled. No caption.

"You seen him?"

She didn't look long. "Nope."

"Sure?"

"Sure."

Tone like she was done before we'd begun.

I waited. Let the silence do what it does best—test for weakness.

Nothing.

"Name might be different. Goes by Stokes. Part of the New Clarion Order."

That got her. Just a flicker—eyelid pause. Not recognition. Recoil.

"Don't know them," she said.

"You *heard* of them."

"I've heard of a lot of things. Don't mean I want to talk about 'em."

Her eyes flicked to the trucker crowd. Then back to me. Harder now.

"Look," she said, "I don't know who you think you're gonna find, but folks around here don't appreciate the way the rest of the country tells stories about us. Makes it sound like anyone north of the bridge is a gun-toting cultist just waitin' to start a war."

"That not true?"

"Doesn't mean we like the headline."

Fair.

"Most people come up here looking for New Clarion," she went on, "they're either cops or gawkers. Either way, you're not getting help."

"I'm neither."

That got me a look.

I shrugged. "Maybe I'm a sympathizer."

She didn't laugh. Didn't scoff. Just reached under the counter and slid a printed slip across the laminate. The bill. For the coffee. Like the conversation never happened.

Then she turned. Walked back toward the register without another word.

I tried two more stops that afternoon.

First was a bait-and-tackle shop with a freezer full of nightcrawlers and a help desk staffed by someone who looked like he *hunted* for solitude. He said he didn't know Stokes. Didn't know Clarion. Didn't care. The only thing he believed in was the price of diesel and the lie that this winter might be mild.

Second was a hardware store that smelled like rust and regret. It had a bulletin board covered in job ads, prayer chains, and hand-scrawled warnings about a cougar that probably didn't exist. The woman behind the counter offered me a smile made of duct tape and suspicion. She looked at the photo like it might curse her and said she didn't recognize the face. Said it too fast.

Both times, I stayed polite. Didn't push.

But the third place—

That's where it changed.

It was a diner again, though this one pretended harder. Cleaner windows. Local art on the walls—birch trees and lighthouses and Jesus in a hunting vest. The kind of place that wanted to convince you nothing bad had ever happened here.

I took a booth. Ordered nothing.

Waitress didn't ask why. She had the look of someone who didn't care if you ate so long as you paid.

I tried again.

Same photo. Same name. Same calm.

"Looking for someone," I said. "Might be in the area. Goes by Stokes."

She didn't answer.

Didn't have to.

Someone else had heard me.

I caught it in the mirror behind the counter — a man three booths back. Face like it had been pressed into leather and left to cure, neck red from work and weather. He looked up too slow. Too interested. I didn't acknowledge it. Didn't need to.

The waitress handed me a napkin without a word. Noticed her hand trembled just a little.

That was enough.

I left a bill for nothing and walked out slow.

They were waiting by the dumpsters.

Three of them. Not organized. No plan. Just enough rage to fill the gaps..

First swing caught me in the ribs. Second took the wind. The third — I blocked that one. Not well, but enough to stay upright.

"No questions," one of them hissed. "No cops, no crawlers, no feds."

"I'm not—"

Fist to the stomach. Hard. Not trained. Just committed.

I dropped to one knee. Caught breath. Tasted metal.

"You think this is your business?" the biggest one growled. "Go back where you came from."

That's when I smiled. Just a little.

"You're not hiding *him*," I said. "You're hiding what *he's doing*."

That froze the small one. Just for a second. The big one didn't freeze. He kicked me in the side and they ran. Left me coughing on pavement that hadn't been washed since summer.

I stayed there for a moment. Let the sky tilt. Could've called for help. Could've used the card. Didn't. Instead, I reached into my coat. Pulled out the photo. Still there. Still intact.

"Melvin," I muttered. "You're getting sloppy."

Because someone knew him. And someone was scared.

Which meant I wasn't just close. I was *seen*.

The ascent scrapes more than skin. Pain doesn't follow you through. Not the mortal kind. My ribs stopped aching the moment I crossed.

But Mara saw it. She didn't see the bruises. She saw what they meant. Paused mid-step as I passed. Looked like she might speak. Thought better of it. Just watched me like you watch someone try to carry something they shouldn't. She knew it wasn't casework.

She knew better than to ask.

The precinct held still around me. Hallways forget you once you're through. Lights dim in recognition. Doors part like they regret it.

Heaven's archive isn't for the curious. It's for the marked. Not all files live here. Only the ones that leave residue — truth heavy enough to stick. I hadn't come for their names. I'd come for their signatures. Each man who struck me, I let tag himself. A brush of soul against soul. Not mercy. Not restraint. Just identification. I was marking them. They just thought they were hurting me.

I approached the drawer and placed my hand to the seal. Three pulses answered — no warmth, no pulse. Just recognition, old and absolute.

Drawers opened. Recognition isn't warmth. It's gravity. The archive doesn't invite. It claims.

File 1: RICHARD ELI MARSH

Sault Ste. Marie. Forestry dropout. Failed upward into rage. No convictions. Two sealed interventions. Lives with mother. Believes in purity through rewilding. Practises minor ritual fasting.

Note: *Initial soul tether unstable. High metaphysical conductivity. Susceptible to ideologic resonance.*

File 2: JACOB RANDLE SMITH

Newberry. Honourably discharged, dishonourably remembered. Service record flagged. Seven unfiled complaints. Self-identifies as "tempered steel." Prays aloud before every violent act.

Note: *Fragmented doctrinal uptake. Intermittent prophetic* *episodes.*

File 3: PETER THOMAS KROLL

Whitefish Bay. Age 19.

Incest flag. Lost sister to overdose. Choirboy turned zealot.

Note: *One attempted suicide. Continued suicidal ideation.*

Recurrent notations about Clarion. No reference to Melvin, but the shape of him was there—like rot behind wallpaper. All three files bore the same burn-marked sigil. But strangely, neither celestial nor infernal. Accord-adjacent. Algorithmic. Built of recursion and oath-script. The kind that isn't spoken—but believed. I touched it. It flexed. Spiraled. Whatever this was, it believed harder than they did.

I heard him before I saw him. No footsteps. No breath. Just presence—that hum the precinct allows when it still believes in someone.

"Thought I'd find you down here," Chandler said.

I didn't look up. Still watching the sigil spiral in on itself like it was trying to remember its own name.

"No reason for you to be here," I said.

He ignored that. Walked a little closer. Robes straight, expression uncertain—like maybe he'd rehearsed this in his head and didn't like how it was going.

"What is it?" he asked. "What're you pulling?"

"Nothing official."

"That's what worries me."

He stepped around to see the drawer. Three open files.

All with the same stink. None with a clearance stamp.

Chandler's face tightened. "This isn't ours."

"It is now."

"You traced them," he said slowly. "Off-ledger. No active file. No tether."

"They jumped me."

"That doesn't make them ours."

"It makes them mine."

He stepped closer. Read the files. Caught the shape of it.

"You think they're damned?"

"No," I said. "I think they're being used."

He frowned. "Used by who?"

I didn't answer right away. Not because I didn't know — because I didn't know how to say it without sounding like I'd already decided.

"There's someone behind them. A name that doesn't show up in any Accord registry. No variance. No death trace. Just a man who shouldn't exist, organizing boys who shouldn't matter."

"You're not saying they're possessed."

"Not them. Just the one they follow."

Chandler blinked. "Possession? Then it's not ours. That's exorcism jurisdiction—clerical. Tactical. They'll flag it for retrieval."

"No, they won't."

"Why not?"

"Because they don't know he exists."

That landed.

He stepped back. Hands at his sides. Like the robe had gotten heavier.

"We've got a backlog of stuck souls who still believe in Heaven," he said. "And you're chasing ghost files and martyrs-in-waiting."

"He's not just preaching death. He's selling it. Mass-market salvation, on a timer."

Chandler didn't argue. But he didn't agree, either.

"What do you want me to do?"

"Stay out of it."

"Can't."

I finally looked at him.

He held the stare.

"You'll need someone to remind you why we're not supposed to work alone."

I gave Chandler the outline. Melvin Stokes. No record. No death. No resurrection. Just *appears* in Northern Michigan a few months after Arthur Pell burns alive in a tank and starts recruiting. Group name: New Clarion Order. Recruitment method: fringe forums, encrypted threads, curated sermons. Message: salvation through clarity. Timer: ticking.

I left out the part about Purgatory. Laziel. The data slip. Didn't lie. Just stepped around it.

Time doesn't work the same up here. Earth's clock was already bleeding hours. I guessed five days left.

Chandler listened. No interruptions. No nods. Just quiet absorption, like he was translating it into something softer before deciding how much to hate it. When I finished, he didn't ask questions. He just said: "You think they're going to kill someone."

"Not someone," I said. "Anyone. That's not the point."

"Then what is?"

I opened the manifesto again. Turned it toward him. Let him read it.

After a few lines, he exhaled. "It's not the violence," he said. "It's the promise."

"Go on."

"This isn't just another militia group. It's not about revolution or replacement. It's about *reward*. They're not trying to change the world. They're trying to cash out of it."

He tapped the page.

"Heaven is earned through clarity. Clarity comes through sacrifice."

"That's not doctrine," he added. "That's debt. It's transactional theology."

I nodded slowly. "North American martyrdom."

"Exactly. A suicide bomber with a flag and a Facebook feed."

He paused. Eyes clouded for a moment. "Division's been struggling with cases like this. Not here. Overseas. They don't talk about it much."

"You mean Islamic martyr cells?"

"I mean the *consequences*. Heaven can't process half of them. The math's broken. Too much belief. Too little clarity."

He looked at me. "But this... this is tailored. Westernized. Commercialized. They've stripped out the discipline and left only the payout."

It made my skin itch. Deep. Quiet. Like something old was watching itself get reborn.

I had been trying to locate the bunker. The basement. The cabin where Clarion stockpiled bullets and belief.

"You're still looking for a cell," Chandler said behind me. "But there isn't one."

I didn't answer. Not yet.

"They don't meet," he said. "They connect. Message boards. Videos. PDFs full of scripture that never passed through Heaven. No compound. No chant. Just repetition."

"And Melvin?"

"Could be anywhere. Behind a screen. Doesn't matter. The body's irrelevant. The broadcast is what counts."

I let the drawer stay open. Watched the top files breathe.

"But if it's suicide theology," I said, "if he wants impact—he'll want control."

Chandler looked over. "You think he has someone ready."

"I think he's groomed someone. Someone primed. Someone devout."

I reached for the third file. Peter Thomas Kroll. Nineteen. Whitefish Bay. The quietest of the three, but the file read loud. *Suicide attempt. Persistent ideation.* No criminal record—but grief like a fuse.

Not the loudest voice.

Just the one most likely to *follow through.*

There was no quote. No timestamped vow. But Melvin's outline was there—thin and hidden, like mold behind a mirror.

"He's the one," I said. "Peter."

Chandler hesitated.

"You're sure?"

"No," I said. "But I believe it."

He didn't speak again.

Didn't have to.

The house sagged like it knew winter would finish what time started. White siding buckled in long strips. A plastic tarp flapped against one window where glass should've been. The porch steps leaned. A snow shovel lay snapped in two beside a drift that hadn't been cleared in days. Lake Superior waited a few klicks behind it—vast and grey and watching.

We arrived on the roadside. No driveway, just ruts and gravel. Snow crusted underfoot. The kind that stays past when it should've melted. Cold enough to hurt, but not enough to numb.

Trucks whooshed past behind us—one every few seconds. Each blast of wind felt like punctuation. Like the world was counting down and didn't care what the sentence said.

Peter opened the door before we knocked. Hoodie zipped to the throat. Nineteen. Gaunt in a way that wasn't about food. Eyes wide but not frightened. He looked like someone who hadn't slept well in a year and stopped caring six months ago. Something settled in his posture—readiness, not peace. He wore a zipped hoodie, loose jeans, no shoes. His hands didn't fidget.

He took me in.

"You were at the diner."

I didn't answer.

He gave a half-smile that didn't touch his eyes. "Guess you didn't like getting jumped."

"You're Peter Kroll," Chandler said.

Peter's gaze shifted. "I know who I am." A flicker of calculation. "You're cops?"

"No," I said.

"Sure. You've got that thing—you look like you're pretending not to judge people."

Chandler stepped forward, collar high, breath fogging sharp in the cold. Vest straight, shoes too clean for the porch. "Peter, we came because you're in danger. What you're planning—"

"I'm not doing anything wrong."

"Not yet," I said.

Peter looked past us. The highway behind. The flat rhythm of the world continuing. Trucks groaning over asphalt, wind pushing roadside weeds like they still believed in direction.

"You came to stop me," he said.

Chandler's voice was soft. "We came to help you."

Peter smiled. It wasn't cruel. It wasn't kind. It was finished.

"I don't need help. I've already been chosen."

"By who?" I asked.

He didn't answer.

Chandler stepped forward, close now, just at the edge of the porch.

"Peter, suicide is not clarity. It's not sacrifice. It's despair dressed as obedience. You die like that—there's no tether left to catch. There's no mercy."

Peter looked at him, and for the first time, something flickered.

"You think I care about your Heaven?" he said. "That gate's closed. Locked behind cowards and compromise."

"Then what do you believe in?" I asked.

He smiled, small and certain. "A Heaven you can *force* open. One built for those who bleed for it."

"And who pays the price?"

"I do," Peter said. "Gladly. I'm not afraid to burn."

Chandler looked stricken. Not with fear. With sorrow. "You think that's faith. It's not. It's surrender to nothing."

"It's not nothing. It's truth. And I'm not alone."

I stepped in then. His eyes snapped to mine.

"You've met him."

He didn't flinch.

"Melvin Stokes," I said. "You've seen him. Not just online."

"I don't know who that is."

Still no flinch—but something behind the eyes. A ripple.

"He's close," I said. "Too close to risk broadcasting from miles away. If he's trusting you to die for him, he'll want to be near enough to make sure you do it."

"I don't know what you're talking about."

"Sure you do."

I let silence stretch. Trucks passed again. One every six seconds.

"Where's the vest?" I asked. "You have it already?"

Peter flinched—just barely.

"You've got instructions," I said. "Given in person. That's why we're here."

"Get off my porch."

"He didn't trust you to download a vest. He handed it to you. Maybe not here, but close."

Peter stared. Breath shallow. Cold burning in the pink of his nose. "You can't stop it."

"Why?" I said. "Because the broadcast's ready? Because the script's locked in?"

He didn't answer.

Chandler stepped in. "Peter, whatever he promised you—whatever salvation he sold you—it's counterfeit. Suicide isn't obedience. It isn't sacrifice. It's void. It severs the tether. You die like that, and there's nothing left to claim."

Peter's voice cracked. "You don't get to tell me what Heaven looks like."

"Neither does he," I said.

Peter's lips parted—almost a reply. But the trucks kept coming. One. Two. The beat in the silence.

He stared at us. Belligerent. Proud. "You'll never find him. He's off the grid. Places your city cars wouldn't even—"

His voice hitched. Just for a breath. Like his mouth caught up to what his pride had leaked.

His right hand twitched—not much, just a thumb grazing the seam of his hoodie like it itched. But it lingered. Pressed. Shifted slightly inward. The kind of movement that meant weight. Not nervous habit. Intention.

He had something under the fabric. And now I knew where.

I stepped up the pressure.

"He didn't send you the vest. He didn't mail it. He walked it in. Because he doesn't trust anyone else to carry clarity but you. Maybe, doesn't even trust you."

"He trusts—" Peter started, then stopped. Too late.

I stepped forward. Closed the space between us. Let my voice drop, not loud but heavy. "Where?" I said. "Where did he hand you the vest? Don't lie. You didn't get it in the mail. He brought it. He put it in your hands. So where?"

Peter backed up. "I didn't say—"

"Yes you did."

He shook his head.

"Not here," I said. "Not your house. Too exposed. He needed somewhere quiet. Somewhere close enough to make a run if things went sideways. Out past the ridge.

Off the grid. Where city cars can't get."

"I didn't—"

"There's only one access road west of here that matches. It dead-ends into a fire trail above the lake. The kind of place a chimney would still be standing, even if the roof's caved in."

Peter went still. All breath. His fingers twitched again. Like the belief was fraying—and the grip was what held it together. Then he said, too fast, too loud, "You don't get it—if you stop him, it all falls apart."

His voice cracked on *falls*. The certainty was gone. All that was left was fear dressed like defiance.

His hand moved. Quick.

Hoodie hem lifted. Gun came up—cheap, small-caliber, shaking in his grip.

Chandler shouted his name, but I was already moving.

No weapon drawn. Just motion.

I hit his wrist. Elbow. Disarmed in half a second. The gun clattered onto the porch and vanished into snow.

Peter gasped, stumbled, caught himself on the frame of the door. His eyes were wild now. Not with conviction. With loss.

"You don't understand," he said.

I stepped in. Shoulder turned. Fist tight.

One clean strike—jawline, hard left.

His head snapped. Knees buckled. Body dropped.

The porch groaned as he tipped off it.

Snow took him.

Peter lay crumpled at the foot of the porch, half in the snow, half on the threshold. No blood. No broken bones. Just out cold.

Chandler knelt beside him, checked his pulse, then opened one eyelid with two fingers. "He's breathing. Heart's steady. Nothing fractured. He'll wake with a headache and a decision."

I nodded, already moving.

Inside, the house was what you'd expect for a boy who'd lost too much and stopped pretending otherwise. One-bedroom. Smelled like mildew, cold sweat, and cloves — cheap incense clinging to wood that hadn't been cleaned properly in years. The floor sloped just enough to feel it. Radiator dead. Windows plastic-wrapped and stapled. Mattress on the floor, no frame.

The table near the kitchenette was covered in cigarette burns and off-brand energy drink cans. One still fizzed. Ash spilled over a cereal bowl. A cracked mug said *God Is Good* in blue cursive, but someone had scratched "At Lying" beneath it.

We moved room to room. No second occupant. No hidden basement. Just rot, paper, and static faith.

A bookshelf held two Bibles. One dog-eared and underlined. The other burned at the edges and taped back together.

In the hallway, faded pictures lined the wall. School photos. Backyard trampoline. Then — one different. A girl. Fifteen maybe. Auburn hair. Wide smile, but tired eyes. Someone had thumb-smudged her face like they were trying to erase guilt. Below it, a sticky note curled at the edges *Lucy. 1990–2013. Still waiting.*

We reached the back room. Here, the mess turned surgical. Notebooks stacked in precise towers. A GoPro case. Black gaffer tape. A hand mirror scabbed with fingerprints. Lines drawn in marker on the floor, not occult—just blocking.

And at the centre, a single manila folder.

No seal. No label. But it hummed, faint and wrong. Like something had been repeated too many times inside.

I opened it.

Chandler stood beside me, arms folded. He didn't speak until he read the first few lines. Then, "This isn't just a manifesto," he said. "It's a liturgy."

Divine Blood: The Right to Ascend; A Soldier's Covenant.

Typed pages. Numbered. Each with stage directions in parentheses. Lines for camera framing. Call-and-response cues. And Peter's script:

[CAMERA BLOCKING NOTES]

- (Camera locked. Chest-up frame. Eye contact unbroken.)

- (Room silent. Flat lighting. Minimal background texture.)

- (Begin with single breath. Centre body. Shoulders square. Deliver like testimony, not speech.)

[SCRIPT – PETER]

(looking directly into the lens)

"It doesn't matter who I am.

Or what my name is. What matters is the truth.

(Hold two-second pause. No blink.)

We are weak. We are broken. We are ruled by shadows in suits and screens.

We used to believe in something. We knew what sacrifice meant. We gave our lives to light the way.

[CAMERA BLOCKING: Slow zoom-in begins. Stop at collarbone.]

Now we kneel to new gods: Money. Pleasure. Compromise.

Nothing that lasts. Nothing that saves.

Once, we understood that death was not defeat. It was the price of eternity. But now —

Now we stay small. We eat dirt. We obey.

They tell us there is no Heaven. That it cannot be earned. They lie.

(Pause. Drop voice half-step. One slow breath.)

Heaven is real. Heaven is waiting. It belongs to those who take it.

This world is dust. A shadow. A test.

And the only thing that matters…is how you leave it.

[CAMERA BLOCKING: Cut to wide shot. Hands visible. Body centred in frame.]

If you believe in nothing, you will die for nothing.

But if you believe in truth —

and you give yourself to it —

then you will never die.

[CAMERA BLOCKING: Return to tight close-up. Just eyes. Just voice.]

We were told we were too weak to deserve clarity. But

clarity is earned through action.

(reads with rising conviction)

Read the manifesto.

NewClarionOrder.com.

There is no salvation without sacrifice.

(Soft inhale. Slow exhale. Eyes locked.)

You will not see my face again.

But I will show you the way.

[CAMERA BLOCKING – FINAL STAGE]

- (Final line: 3-second eye contact after delivery. Do not blink. No tears. No smile.)

- (Detonation is manual. Trigger on cue. Thumb pressure must be smooth. No hesitation.)

- (On blast: fade to white. Cut stream. Preload message board sequence.)

Chandler's hands clenched the fabric at his wrists. "He's not meant to survive this."

"No," I said. "He's meant to be believed."

He turned to the wall. Stared at a whiteboard Peter had half-erased but never finished.

A sketched floor plan. Entry angles. Sightlines. The letters MBN circled twice. A transmission time: 11:04 a.m.

Below it, just one word in red ink:

"Proof."

The fire trail narrowed after the ridge. Snow deeper

here. Untouched. Trees like black ribs overhead. The wind had gone still, but the cold was worse—thick, sunless, watching.

Chandler's voice was quiet but firm. "This is a possession. We call it in. Let the exorcism unit handle it."

"We don't have time," I said. "By the time they clear the paperwork, Peter's dead and the message is global."

He hesitated. Just a breath.

Then, "Then we contain."

I looked at him. "Might need to kill Arthur to contain this"

He didn't like that, but didn't say anything. Checked his gun like it would give him the answer.

We followed the ruts half a klick past where the plow had turned back. The car couldn't make it. We walked the rest.

Chandler said nothing. His shoulders were tight. His jaw hadn't unclenched since the folder.

The cabin came into view slow. Sagging. Twisted. Like it had been dropped here by mistake and never got around to leaving. Siding half-torn. One window patched with cardboard. Smoke from the chimney, thin and steady. Not warm. Just present.

I stopped forty yards out. Snow up to the ankles.

The door was ajar. Waiting. So much for surprise.

The cabin didn't look like it could hold heat, let alone doctrine. Roof slumped. Chimney cracked. The woodpile half-frozen in its own shadow. Smoke rose anyway—thin and slow, like it was trying to pretend someone was just cooking beans.

I turned to Chandler. "You stay here."

He blinked. "What?"

"Back behind the tree line. Call it in."

"No."

"If he comes out, I talk. If I die, you finish the job."

Chandler stiffened. "You want me to—"

"If there's anything left of Arthur, save it. If there's not, name what's inside and burn it. You know the forms."

He didn't answer.

He was young enough to believe in doing things clean. Old enough now to know it wouldn't be.

I turned back to the cabin and raised my voice.

"Stokes."

The door creaked open like it had been listening the whole time.

Melvin stepped into the frame. Arthur Pell's skin—but pulled wrong. Too tight across something that didn't know how to sit still. The lines didn't match the man. No fear in his face. He didn't speak. Just looked.

I kept my hands visible. Empty.

"Come outside."

A pause. A calculation. Then, slowly, he stepped forward. He was already wearing the vest. Not strapped tight—loose over the hoodie, as if it was a statement, not armor. One hand resting on the front. Thumb against the trigger cap.

Chandler shifted behind me. Snow crunched.

Melvin smiled.

"Disappointed?" I asked.

"A little," he said. "How did you find me?"

"Met your wife."

That caught him—not in surprise, but in interest. The smile didn't drop, but it refocused. A sharper edge.

"Amira," he said, like he was tasting the name for the first time in years. "She wasn't meant to last. She held longer than I thought."

"She died tangled in a lie."

"She died believing in one." He stepped forward—three slow paces. Twenty-five yards now. Still not close enough to kill, not without catching some of the blast ourselves. "There's a difference."

"She thought you came home from war."

"I did."

"Not as her husband."

Melvin stopped. The smile faltered—not cracked, just tilted. "And what did you tell her?"

"The truth."

He nodded once. Thoughtful. "You know, I was curious. What you'd say. What she'd believe. That's what this is, isn't it?" Another step. "Belief. Yours. Hers. Mine. The boy's. Same game, different stakes."

Chandler didn't move. Gun raised. I could hear his breath now—short, not panicked, just bracing. He was doing the math every second: wind, angle, range. What body part might detonate least.

Melvin's eyes never left mine. "Did she ascend?"

"She let go."

"Not what I asked."

I didn't answer.

He took another step. Twenty yards now. The trigger moved slightly in his hand — not a threat, just a reminder that it only took one.

"You think if you talk long enough, I'll give you something," he said.

"I think you want to be seen."

"By you?"

"By anyone."

He chuckled. "I've been broadcasting for years. You think this vest is the message? It's the punctuation."

"You're not even wearing your own name."

He grinned again — wide this time. "Neither are you."

Chandler shifted left — still outside the blast cone. Gun up. I could feel the strain in his silence. Wanting to intervene, not knowing how.

Melvin took another step. Fifteen yards.

I changed tack.

"We've got your martyr."

His smile faltered.

"Peter's done," I said. "Vest off. Script burned. He's alive. You lose."

Melvin's hand flexed on the trigger.

"You're lying."

I said nothing.

He took another step. The snow didn't even creak.

"You're bluffing."

I tilted my head. "You're not the only one who can see the future of this."

The rage wasn't loud. It came all at once, like heat off iron.

"He was ready."

"He was a boy."

"He believed."

"He believed in *you*."

Melvin stopped walking.

"He believed in something bigger than me," he said. Quiet now. "I was just the door."

"To what?" I asked.

He didn't answer.

Not right away.

Then: "You think this is about a vest. Or a name. Or a sermon. You're still working the old system. Calling it faith."

He stepped forward. Ten yards. Close enough to end this. Me. Him. Done.

"It's not faith anymore," he said. "It's protocol."

He said it like the word was sacred. Like doctrine had shifted and Heaven hadn't caught up.

He smiled, teeth bared. "You'll learn the word soon enough."

His hand flexed on the trigger. His lips parted, just slightly. Then—

The shot cracked the moment the sentence broke.

Melvin jerked. One step back. The vest shifted.

Then the second shot. Upper chest. He dropped to one knee.

I was already moving.

"Chandler!"

He was standing tall now, both hands on the weapon, face frozen—horrified but firm.

Melvin looked up. Bleeding. But still holding the trigger.

Still smiling.

"Too slow," he mouthed.

I reached him.

Dove.

Grabbed the vest, his wrist, the trigger housing.

Click.

Nothing.

A beat of silence so thin you could hear the blood cooling.

I stared at the trigger. Wires. Thumb contact. Ready. But something hadn't completed the circuit.

Melvin coughed like a curse. "Damn battery," was all he managed before crumpling.

I ripped the trigger from his hand.

Chandler dropped the weapon and ran toward us.

Melvin lay prone, eyes dilatated, still. Jaw slackening. Something inside him starting to let go.

I reached into the coat.

Not for a weapon. For the ember. Not standard issue. Never was. You don't get one unless you've seen a Gate close from the wrong side and lived to report it. Unless you've held jurisdiction in your own blood and declared a rite while everything else burned. Mine was a shard of first-light glass, scorched black around the edge. Barely stable. A relic from before the Hosts split command. Before exorcism was codified. Before we stopped doing things alone.

I hadn't touched it in years. Kept it inside the coat, stitched beneath the lining. Hidden. A last resort. The kind of tool they let you keep only if they thought you'd never use it.

I knelt, cursing Chandler under my breath. Working against time to try to save Arthur's soul.

I held it in my palm like a verdict and said the words — not aloud, not with any sacred tone. Just enough to bind the space. Not to destroy him. To unseat the thief. If anything of Arthur was left, it deserved a door.

"I speak under sanction. Field Authority, Host-declared. This body is not yours."

Nothing moved. Not at first.

So I pressed the ember to the snow beside him, and the glyph caught. Quietly. Just a circle and a line — silent scripture, old as the first split. Enough to say: You are seen.

"Melvin Stokes," I said. "False bearer. Unauthorized spark. You have no right of occupancy. You are not Arthur Pell."

The body twitched.

I leaned close.

"Arthur—" I said the name slow, full, remembering every line of the man I'd known. "You were born July 11, 1958. Married once. Lost her twice. You liked burnt toast. Fought with your son over a Pontiac you couldn't fix. You had a scar under your left arm. You hated the sound of cellos."

Melvin's jaw flexed.

"If any part of you is still in there—remember it. Anchor to it. I can't pull you out unless you give me something."

No response. Just a flutter. A groan.

"Protocol demands clarity," I said. "So show it. If he's gone, then you stand revealed."

I stood and stepped back. Held the ember high and let it flare. Not flame. Just light—cold and exact. Truth without warmth.

"Last call," I said. "Reveal or be rendered."

Melvin screamed.

It wasn't a sound. Not fully. It was pressure—the kind that makes your teeth ache and your skin forget where it ends. A crack split across his lips like something ancient trying to remember how to shape syllables.

And then—just for a second—his eyes went brown. Arthur's brown.

But the scream tore out—and something tore with it. The glyph flared white, then black, then nothing. No ember. No line. Just a hollow scorch on the concrete, and a smell that didn't belong to anything born.

Melvin arched once, spine bending like a bow pulled too far—

Then—

He came apart. Not exploded. Undone. He came apart from the inside, like a name unsaid. No flame. No gore. No spectacle. Just erasure. As if Heaven had never written him. As if Hell refused to claim him. Nothing left but the stain of where a man once fought to matter.

I stayed kneeling.

"Arthur?" I asked the absence.

No answer. Not even silence. Whatever had been left of him—if anything had—was gone now. Unreachable. Or worse: never there.

I closed my fist over the cooling air and felt the echo pulse through my knuckles.

Something noticed. A pulse across the current. Not a response. A record. A mark. Something above—or below—had felt what I'd just done.

Footsteps behind me.

Chandler.

"What did you—" He stopped. Swallowed. "Sal… what did you do?"

I stood. Not taller. Just heavier.

"Something permanent."

UNFILED: ELIAS SHAW

Flight 217 from Montreal to Syracuse didn't make it.

The pilot tried to ride it in anyway—eyes on the runway, heart in his throat. It came in low, too low, skimming treetops with one engine coughing and the other already gone. The trees took the wings. The tarmac took the rest.

Now the wreckage lit the night like a false dawn—metal torn open, still smoking, bathing everything in a strobe of ambulance red and emergency white. Sirens wailed. Foam hissed. Floodlights sliced through clouds of dust and jet fuel, casting long shadows of first responders hauling stretchers, barking orders, dragging hoses through slurry and ash.

The forward fuselage had split on impact, cracking open like a ribcage. Most of the dead were already gone—protocol handled them fast, clean, efficient. That left fifty or so. Stuck. Hovering. Looping.

A high number, but not unheard of. Crashes do that. It's the suddenness. The weight. The unanswered prayers.

I stepped across the outer ring—yellow tape sagging in the heat, floodlights propped against torn fencing. Emergency services had carved their perimeter: generators, triage tarps, scattered oxygen tanks, and the kind of brisk shouting that never actually solves anything. The living didn't see me. Not really. A man in a coat they didn't remember arriving. That was fine. I wasn't there for them.

First thing you notice in a crash like this isn't the fire. It's the stillness. Not real stillness—emotional. The kind that hangs in the air between scream and silence, when no one's sure if they're supposed to survive.

And under that, always, the souls.

The first one was easy.

Middle seat, row twenty-three. Male, late twenties. The body had split wrong, torso and head at odds. His soul hovered a few feet away, trying to dial a phone that didn't exist anymore. Hands trembling, lips moving.

"It won't ring," he said. "It won't—why won't it—"

"Because you're not holding it," I said.

He looked at me. Not through. *At.* That was enough. The tether cracked. Not like glass—like guilt. He dusted.

I moved on.

Chandler followed, clipboard clenched like a prayerbook. His hair was still neat. His collar still buttoned. It made him look less human.

"What do I do?" he asked.

"Find the ones caught in memory. The loops. Speak their names if you know them. Use gentleness. If that fails, use rites."

"I only know three rites."

"That's two more than most."

He nodded, jaw tight. I could see the doctrine turning in him—page after page of standard procedure. He hadn't realized yet that the dead don't read policy. They only respond to what they can't deny. When it hits home.

Some souls ran. Others crawled. One woman tried to wake her own body—shaking it, sobbing, whispering apologies like they were currency. A teenager floated two feet above a seatback, lip pierced, shirt burnt, still texting. Another soul staggered through the cockpit wreck, repeating the last twenty seconds of descent on loop:

"Mayday mayday mayday — we're — "

"You're done," I said. "Let it end."

He did.

By the time we reached the central wreck, the triage tents were half-empty and the night had thickened. Smoke curled in streamers around the broken shell. The heat still pulsed from the frame like the last breath of something sanctified and broken.

And that's when the air changed.

Not sound. Not smell. Something under that. A texture shift. Like someone had turned the world one degree left of familiar.

I looked up.

And there she was.

Cyr stepped out of the smoke like the wreckage had summoned her by name.

No wings. No flare. No sulphur wind. No throne of judgment. Just stillness in boots. Her coat was charcoal — buttoned high, collar sharp, the kind of cut that remembered uniforms. Hair braided tight, looped once, coiled like habit not vanity. Her cheekbones looked carved, her eyes glacier-pale and patient in the way cold countries teach. She didn't move like someone walking through fire — she moved like the fire had learned to step aside.

"Cross-jurisdiction," she said — each syllable crisp,

vowels flat, the trace of an Eastern accent that didn't ask permission.

"I figured," I replied.

"Thirty-eight confirmed. More partials." She scanned the ruin like it was a ledger, not a loss. "You're running grief?"

"Loop and drift. You?"

"Guilt. Full suite."

"Usual division, then."

We didn't shake hands. There are things older than civility.

She moved past—heading toward the souls that wouldn't let go of their sins. I turned back toward the ones that wouldn't let go of their grief. Chandler stayed in the middle, blinking.

"You two—know each other?" he asked.

We both ignored him.

Time doesn't move properly in a crash zone. It pools. One moment stretched, another collapsed.

I found a girl sitting upright beside the emergency exit, soul unmoored but still holding her knees. She didn't speak. Just stared.

I sat beside her.

"Do you know where you are?"

She nodded. A lie.

"Do you know your name?"

She nodded again.

I didn't press. I just waited. A minute. Maybe three.

Finally, she said:

"I was supposed to make it. He said I would."

"Who?"

"The man next to me."

"Was he family?"

She shook her head. "No. Just kind."

I looked over. The seat was empty. The soul was gone. No signature. No echo.

Already passed.

I felt the tether release. She flickered. Then disappeared.

The work took over. It had to. Once you start talking, you start thinking. And no one assigned to this wants that. I moved through the field with my rites half-spoken and the rest implied. Names aren't always needed. Recognition is. Grief doesn't cling to language—it clings half-formed tears, to things unsaid, to brokenness held inside until the hooks were in.

I touched the shoulder of a man stuck in the loop of an apology. He mouthed it again and again—*I shouldn't have yelled. I should've stayed awake. I should've driven instead.* His tether was thin. Regret, not damnation.

I brushed it, gently. It let go like breath before sleep.

Across the flames, Cyr worked her side like a soldier pulling bullets—methodical, unsparing, untouched by the screams. She didn't kneel. Didn't console. Consolation implies mercy, and mercy slows the work. She read each soul like a dossier already stamped—just sorting what burned and what still begged. You could see it in the way she moved—quick, final, cold. The dead didn't confess. They were taken.

I watched her reach into a half-collapsed row of seats—hands precise—and stop in front of a man clawing at the floor like he could still drag himself out of the moment of impact. His soul hadn't detached cleanly. It recoiled—forward, back, over and over. Not memory. Panic.

"Shouldn't have taken the late flight," he muttered. "It's not my fault. How was I to know? She didn't—"

He saw Cyr and lunged, voice spiking into terror.

She didn't flinch. Just caught his hand mid-strike, and drove a black-handled blade into the chair behind him—deep enough that the impact echoed. He screamed. Phantom pain surged like the body remembered what the soul denied.

Not cruelty. Necessity. She pinned him like evidence.

"Envy," she reported. "Obsessive. Self-inflicted."

Not pity or condemnation. Just a column filled in.

The man thrashed once more, but the blade held. His legs kicked at the wreckage like he could still run. That was the truth of it—he wasn't repenting. He was fleeing.

She opened her coat. Drew a writ the colour of coagulated ink—no sigils, no halo, no hope. Just weight. Fixed it to his chest.

"You'll need that," she said. Flat. Uninterested. "It gets checked on arrival."

He convulsed once—twice—then buckled. His shape crumpled, edges folding, like the will had been vacuumed out. Not passed. Dragged down.

Descended.

No ritual. No peace.

Just enforcement, done fast as a pulled trigger.

She yanked the knife loose. It vanished into the folds of her coat like it had never been there.

Next.

Chandler was somewhere near the tail, trying to talk a young woman out of her own death.

"Ma'am, you're deceased," he kept saying. "If you'll allow me—"

She screamed. Not at him—through him. Her grief passed straight through his doctrine, shredded it, left ribbons of good intention flapping in the wind.

"I didn't mean to fall asleep," she wailed. "I was just tired. I didn't mean—he would've needed me—"

I stepped in.

"What was his name?" I asked.

She told me. Whispered it like a prayer she'd already lost faith in.

"He forgave you," I said.

"Before the impact. Before the fear. He forgave you."

Her tether snapped like thread pulled from old cloth.

Chandler just stared.

"She wasn't listening to me," he said.

"No," I said. "She was listening to the version of herself that never left the stove on."

The wind turned. Plastic. Gasoline. And beneath them, something older—no clear shape, no clear sorrow. Just silence, not yet named.

"How many does this make?" I asked, half to myself.

Cyr answered anyway.

"Thirty-nine. Forty, if the torso by the wing belongs to its head."

"You always round up?"

"Only in Hell."

I let the silence stretch. She didn't fill it.

We went back to work. No handoff. No nod. Just the rhythm of the dead, one soul at a time.

A man knelt beside a scorched briefcase, whispering numbers.

"Flight time was ninety-two minutes. I was in seat 14C. No window. Average cabin temp sixty-eight Fahrenheit. The wingspan was—"

"Stop."

He looked up. Confused. Not defiant—*distracted.*

"If I just reconstruct it…"

"You don't need to."

"But I might've missed something. If I replay the sequence—"

"You died. That was the last thing. Not the math."

His lips kept moving. But the tether had already loosened. Like he was *waiting* to be interrupted.

"Was there anyone?" he asked. "At the end?"

I looked at him. Not his sin. Not his stats. *Him.*

"You weren't alone," I said.

That did it.

He vanished—not like resolution. Like someone finally hit *pause*.

Chandler fell into step beside me, wide-eyed. Finally got the courage the speak what he was thinking. I didn't want to know. He told me anyway.

"She—she just stabbed him," he whispered. "That man in the row. Did you see? She pinned him to the chair. And then she—filed him. Like a record."

"She processed him," I said.

"That's processing?"

"Hell doesn't do grace," I said. "You get what you gave. They sort by sin."

"What kind of sin was that?"

"Doesn't matter."

"And she just knows?"

"That's her job. Seven categories. Same as always. Pride. Envy. Wrath. Sloth. Greed. Gluttony. Lust."

He stared at her, horrified.

"It's so wrong—no forgiveness. No second chances."

"Not her department. Not their model."

"Then what's the point?"

"The point is, she doesn't care what the point is. That's what makes her good at it."

***

The fire crews were wrapping.

The air had lost its colour. Ash swirled in patterns that meant nothing.

No sobs. No screams. Just cleanup and the start of paperwork.

Old guidelines and procedure rattled around in my head: *Disposition pending. Field agent present. Wait for the stillness.*

So I waited.

That's when I saw him.

No panic. No pleading with paramedics. No frantic movement at all. Just sitting on a wrecked fuselage. Staring into space. *Still.*

Didn't register right away. I wasn't really paying attention. Thought, maybe a paramedic taking a break, just like us. Or some lone survivor who walks away without the blood to prove they were part of it. It's not unknown.

But something about him kept me from moving on.

He wasn't looking at the wreckage. He was looking at me.

I walked over. Not fast. Just… recalibrated.

He didn't move. Didn't flinch. Just watched me approach like he'd been waiting for it—and was already disappointed. Up close, he looked about forty. Collar pressed flat. Clean-shaven. Dark jeans. One char mark at the hem like a fire had started and changed its mind.

That's when I saw what wasn't there.

No ID tag. No gear. No soot. No blink when the searchlight swept across him.

No blood.

And no breath.

I adjusted. Quietly. Shifted myself a half beat—out of time, into the place where souls start to bleed through. Not a full cross, just enough to touch the margins. If he was dead, he'd flinch. They always did. Even the brave ones. There's something about being seen from the inside that rattles them.

He didn't rattle.

I stepped in fully. That thin crackle through the air as my celestial presence declared itself. That's usually when they look up, startled. Ask if this is Heaven. Ask where their mother is. Or their child. Or their god.

He just smiled. Close his eyes and waited.

Then nothing.

The man just sat there like gravity as his smile faded. Not scared or angry. Just let down. Again.

I stepped forward, slow and casual, like I wasn't already cataloguing everything: posture, breath, eye focus, hand position. The usual reads.

I checked the passenger list. "You got a name?"

"Elias Shaw."

"Elias," I said, voice steady, "you remember what happened here?"

Souls usually start there. Story spills out. Confession by way of context. It's how you find the tether—what they're holding, what won't let go.

"I remember," he said.

"Good," I nodded. "So tell me how you got here."

He turned his head.

"It's not like that," he said.

Flat. Not defensive—just exhausted. Like someone used to explaining something even he doesn't understand.

I waited, but nothing followed. No unraveling. No crack in the voice.

Just a stone on still water.

My jaw twitched. "You're here, Elias. That's what matters. Something's holding—"

"Not your kind of thing," he said. "I'm not caught in grief. Or denial. Or confusion. I know what happened. I know I'm dead. I remember the moment of it. And I know I didn't move."

That stopped me.

Because he was right. This wasn't a loop. Wasn't a bleed. No grief pretending to be form.

He was whole.

And that made no sense at all.

"You waiting for something, Elias?" I was checking the flight manifest.

He didn't answer direct. Instead, he said, "You're not the first to come for me. But you're the first to ask."

The words didn't echo. They *landed*.

Voice dry, not cracked. Like he still had a throat to use.

I froze. Not because of the words. Because of what they implied.

"I'm the first to *ask*," I said. "What came before?"

He turned to me fully then. His eyes were dark. Not deep. Just final.

"Light. Voices. Orders. Pulls like undertow." He pauses.

Cold ran down my spine.

"Protocol," I said.

He nodded. "Whatever it was, it tried to move me. But it didn't take. It wasn't *right.*"

"How did you resist?"

"I didn't. It just moved on."

He looked down.

"I waited," he said. "And now you're here."

"Do you know what I am?" I asked.

He looked at me, and I knew he wasn't seeing me — he was seeing through me.

"I know what you're pretending not to be," he said. Then took out a cigarette. The pack was crushed, but he fished one free without ceremony. Lit it with a cheap red lighter. The kind you buy at a gas station for a dollar and never refill.

The flame was real.

So was the smoke.

And when he exhaled, it didn't vanish into echo-space. It clung. It curled around my coat like it remembered heat.

"You can't smoke here," I said, out of habit.

"I'm not here," he said.

But he was.

Because dead souls don't light cigarettes. They don't *flick* lighters. They don't stand in the middle of a cleanup zone acting like they're on break from a job that doesn't exist anymore. And they *damn sure* don't look you in the eye without flickering.

He wasn't looping.

Wasn't echoing.

Wasn't confused.

I've seen suicides who didn't know they were dead. Fire victims still screaming. Children waiting for mothers who had already crossed. Echoes trapped in bedrooms. Old men polishing doorknobs that don't open anymore. All of them flickered. All of them strained. All of them pulled on the tether.

But this man—this *still one*—stood like he had *no tether to pull*.

"You died here," I said, more to see what it did to him than for any confirmation.

He didn't react.

"Burned in the initial blast. ID's in my wallet. Back pocket."

I stared at him. "You remember."

"I remember all of it."

That isn't how it works. Souls forget. That's part of what keeps them stuck—some fragment of denial, some blind spot they can't admit. We help them see it, let go of it, pass through. But this one *knew*. I scanned him. Nothing in his outline matched. No aura tug. No trauma halo. No metaphysical bleed. He wasn't *present*, but he wasn't *absent* either. He was… *complete*.

Which should be good. Except it wasn't.

Because I couldn't feel the exit.

No Ascension pull. No damnation weight.

Just nothing.

Like the system *registered him as resolved.*

And he was still here.

"You shouldn't be here," I said slowly.

"Yep. I'm guessing that," he replied.

His tone wasn't smug. It was patient. Like a deadline that's already passed.

I looked around. The site was quiet again. No one glanced at us. Even the floodlights seemed to blur where he stood. Like the world was politely omitting him from the record.

"I was meant to go," Elias said. "But I didn't."

"Why not?"

He took a long drag and held it. Let the silence stretch out until the smoke curled from his nose like incense. He dropped the cigarette. Stomped it out. Nothing crunched. Nothing burned.

I read the manifest. Blank. No name. No cause. No ruling.

Elias Shaw didn't exist in the system.

But he was standing here. And he knew it.

So did I.

I stepped closer. Two fingers outstretched. Tether touch. Even the worst loops have a hook — a grief snag, a denial fragment, a place where the spirit's weight catches. But when my fingers brushed his outline, it passed through like smoke. No resistance. No connection. Just void. Nothing. Like dragging your hand through air that didn't care.

"Chandler."

He stepped forward quickly. Too quickly. Nervous.

"Rites," I said.

He nodded. Reached for the slim rite book he kept in his shoulder bag. The book was dog-eared, well-used. He flipped to the passage he knew best.

"Elias Shaw," he said, reading. He rushed too much, but the words were standard, so delivery shouldn't matter. "Your mortal life has ended. You are not among the lost. No longer are you bound by body or memory. You are seen. You are known. Ascend now and find your eternal resting place."

Nothing.

No flicker, no shudder, no shift in presence. Not even the subtle wind the air makes when something gives way.

I told him to repeat it in the old tongue — older phrasing, for stubborn cases. Chandler flipped. Made a worse botch of it. Sounded like they didn't teach Latin anymore.

Elias didn't blink.

Didn't even pretend to notice.

Chandler's jaw tightened. His free hand went to his hip, unfastened the clasp on the vial.

"Don't," I said.

He froze. "It's not a weapon."

"It's still a threat," I said. "He's not reacting because there's nothing *to* react."

Chandler stared at Elias. "Then what is he?"

I didn't answer.

And then—Cyr arrived.

Like she always does—without warning, like gravity made room and the moment agreed. She stepped across the field, black coat flawless, hair braided and tight. Her heels clicked like punctuation. No rush. No drama. Just control. She came to stand just beside me, chin high.

"You took your time," I muttered.

"You flagged it late," she said. "I assumed you had it handled."

"Still think that?"

She turned toward Elias, studied him like a forgery under a lamp.

"No flicker," she said.

"None."

She circled once—precise, not predatory. Measuring.

"Who are you?" she asked Elias.

"I'm the man who didn't go," he said.

She raised an eyebrow. "That's not an answer."

"It's the only one that matters."

"Not to me."

Then she tried *her* rites—quiet, exact, cold. Something mathematical in the cadence. Not speech. Calculation. Judgment.

It should have rearranged the air. Even the innocent feel it—like a charge in the lungs.

Still nothing.

She frowned. That was rare.

"Tether?"

"None."

"Loop?"

"Not even a gesture."

We both checked our lists.

Her ledger flicked open: blank. No disposition, no ruling, no divine authorization. Mine was worse—my record had no line for him at all. Not missing. *Omitted.*

"That's impossible," she said.

"Apparently not."

"You think he's a reject?"

"No. System reads him as complete. Just not processed."

Her brow furrowed, just slightly. Enough to count.

"I've seen fragments. Mutations. Constructed echoes. But this—this is full agency. It's like he made it out clean and then turned around."

She turned to Elias again.

"Who sent you?"

He didn't answer.

Cyr and I exchanged a glance. Not hostile. Just aligned in the way only shared failure can make you.

Then Chandler stepped in again. He looked paler than before. Tense. Hands shaking—not from fear, but from the kind of heartbreak he didn't know what to do with.

"I don't think he's angry," he said.

Cyr didn't respond. I didn't either.

Chandler reached into his coat pocket. Slowly.

Deliberately. And pulled out a small, worn object. A wooden bird, hand-carved, no paint. The kind of thing you carry not for protection, but to remember something soft. He walked toward Elias. Quietly. Without calling attention. And he handed it to him.

"This helped me," he said. "When I thought God had gone."

Elias looked down at it. Then took it. Held it in both hands. Thumb brushed the wing. No metaphysical wind. No halo ignition. No sudden rupture. But he closed his eyes. And breathed.

Not air—something quieter. Something older.

He didn't look calm. Didn't look free. But for the first time all night, something in the room felt real.

Cyr turned her head just slightly. Not approval. But curiosity.

I watched Elias cradle the bird like it weighed something. And for the first time, he looked like he might have belonged to someone once.

I waited a moment after Chandler stepped back. Elias still held the wooden bird, thumb absently running along the wing. He wasn't soothed. He wasn't comforted. He was *present*. That was the problem. I moved to sit on a jagged piece of fuselage across from him. The metal hissed faintly beneath my coat. Not hot—just reluctant to cool.

"I need you to think back," I said. Calm. Even.

Elias didn't object.

"Tell me the last thing you remember. Before the crash."

His eyes flicked toward the sky, but not in search of it.

"I woke up early. Coffee. No sugar. Apartment was cold. I remember a neighbour's dog barking—"

Not unusual. Not yet.

"Go on."

"I packed light. Just a carry-on. Flight to Syracuse for a client consult—nothing major. Family planning. Insurance investment. I'm an accountant."

"You enjoy it?" I asked.

"It pays the rent."

That sounded human.

Which is why it bothered me.

"What about people?" I asked. "Clients. Family."

"I help where I can," he said. "I try to make the numbers less frightening. Help people plan for what comes next."

"Retirement?" I asked.

"Death," he said. No irony.

Chandler shifted. His hand moved toward his shoulder bag, then stopped.

"That's a strange way to describe your work," I said.

"It's honest," Elias replied. "People think accounting is about money. But it's not. It's about order. Proportions. Preparing for the inevitable."

"And what do you prepare for?"

He hesitated.

"I don't know," he said finally. "I've never thought about that."

"Not even once?"

"I live alone. I work. I file on time. I keep my head down."

"Friends?"

"Colleagues."

"Close?"

He considered it like someone checking a ledger. "No."

"Family?"

"My parents are gone. No siblings. I send Christmas cards."

"Ever fall in love?"

That stopped him.

"I took someone to dinner once. We talked about interest rates. She never replied to my follow-up."

He wasn't joking. There wasn't even a trace of bitterness.

Cyr's voice slid in, low and surgical: "You're describing a life lived *correctly*. Not *actually*."

He looked up at her.

"Is there a difference?"

"Yes," she said.

But he didn't understand.

Not because he was lying.

Because he genuinely didn't know what was missing.

He blinked. Slowly. "I don't know what I'm supposed to feel."

Cyr didn't react. She adjusted her stance, just slightly, and began to trace a circle midair with two fingers — her method of detecting imprint. The air around Elias shimmered. Faint. Peripheral. Not enough for a full mark. But something *was* there. She didn't finish the symbol. Just lowered her hand.

"Say your full name," she said.

"Elias Shaw."

She looked to me. "Doesn't echo."

I felt it too. Names usually carry weight. Family, history, resonance. This one… evaporated on contact.

I leaned in. Changed tack.

"What about childhood?" I asked. "Your mother's name. Your father's?"

A pause.

"Margaret. James."

"Where did you grow up?"

"Upstate New York."

"Where?"

He opened his mouth.

Stopped.

"I… I remember her hands. She made bread every Sunday."

"You remember how it smelled?"

He blinked. No.

"She hummed when she kneaded the dough," he said.

I didn't press.

Cyr said what I wouldn't. "Are you sure those memories belong to you?"

Elias looked at her. Not offended. Just… puzzled.

"I don't know."

That hit deeper than I expected.

I stood again. Stepped into a slower orbit around him. I'd seen echoes with fractured memory. Souls caught in identity loops. Victims so shocked by death that the facts rearranged themselves.

But Elias wasn't rearranged.

He was *assembled*.

Too clean. Too coherent. Too present.

I tried the name again. "Elias Shaw."

This time I said it with weight. Like I expected the *Accord* to notice. Nothing happened. No pulse. No resistance.

Cyr looked at me. "He doesn't register as incomplete."

"Because he isn't," I said.

"He's not missing pieces," she said. "He's complete in the wrong direction." She tilted her head. "That's not residue. That's structure."

We all went quiet.

Elias hadn't moved. He just sat with that bird in his hands, as if the weight of it was the only thing keeping him tethered.

He looked up at me.

"I didn't fake this," he said.

"I believe you."

"I didn't steal anyone's life."

"We never said you did."

"But you're thinking it."

Cyr crossed her arms. "We're thinking it doesn't add up. That you're here without tether, memory without fracture, death without departure. That shouldn't be possible."

"Yet here I am."

"You shouldn't be able to *remain* here," I corrected. "Unless you're being held. Or sent. Or you're something the system doesn't recognize."

He looked at me. Something in his face had changed. Not expression. *Texture.* There was less of him behind his own eyes.

"What if I passed already?" he asked.

That hit hard.

Chandler straightened. Cyr didn't move. I exhaled.

"Passed?" I said.

"When the plane hit, I remember light," he murmured. "The press...out of my body. Weighlessness. And then... nothing. Not peace. Just... displacement. And silence."

He paused.

"In the plane, I was a man. In the screams. Before the crash. And then...this." He waved at himself. His eyes wandered as he considered. "It's like... something was waiting for me. A feeling. Like a client, or an accounting exercise." He looked around. "But I don't see any clients. And I don't remember what it was."

"What client?" Cyr asked.

He looked down at the bird. Shrugged.

No one moved.

Elias stood there, the bird in his hand. He looked at it, unsure if it had weight or memory. Looked at us—not for guidance. For confirmation.

He'd already decided.

Got up off the fusilage.

And started walking.

Not toward any glowing door. Just forward.

Through the wreckage field. Across the blacktop. Past the ruined engine. The floodlights didn't blink him out. The mist didn't blur his outline. He didn't flicker.

Because he wasn't like the others.

He didn't exist as a memory hanging onto place—he existed *in* place. In the world. Not bound to it, not detached from it.

And that was the worst part.

I watched the ground as he passed—expecting no footprints, the theatrical fade. But there were marks. Faint, almost imperceptible. Like dust shifting where no one's stepped. The light refracted just slightly around him. The world didn't reject him. He just… continued. The mortals rushed passed him, caught in their fleeting and passionate lives.

But he was there. Not in the exho space. In the mortal world.

And then he was past the boundary tape. Past the rescue perimeter. Out into the edge of the night, where the wind forgot to howl and even the ash held still.

Cyr's voice was quieter than usual.

"He's not stuck."

"No," I said. "He's settled."

Chandler sat on a slumped section of landing gear, elbows on knees, hands empty. He looked down at the scarred pavement like it might explain something.

"So what are we even supposed to call that?" he asked.

Cyr didn't respond. A single tap, screen turned away. No haste. No flair. Could've been a message. Could've been a mark. She didn't clarify. She never does.

Neither did I. He wasn't damned. He wasn't ascended. He didn't resist. He just… stayed.

But no one told him he could.

Crash team wrapping cables. Coroner units tagging the last of the recovered. Clerics reciting soft rites by the body bags—low enough not to spook the living, firm enough to carry the dead.

Souls were passing now. Smoothly. As they should.

Protocol was reasserting itself.

The air had shifted. Cleaner. Still not fresh. But ordinary. Survivors cleared. Witnesses debriefed. The last loop dissolved thirty yards from the wing tip—an old man who'd been waiting for his wife. She'd gone first. Took longer to convince him that she'd be waiting on the other side too.

I watched as the final glows faded. Souls passing. Untethering. Letting go.

It was working.

The crash was resolving.

But Elias wasn't there.

Cyr checked the final sweep. Her tablet glowed with jurisdictional lines, case codes, soul manifests. His name never reappeared.

Back at the precinct. The overhead lights buzzed like they knew they were being ignored.

Case ID: 3:17. Type: Multi-soul Breach. Location: Syracuse, USA. Flag: Dual-Agency Deployment.

I sat at my desk. Field journal open. Blank page waiting. Not moving.

There was a line I should have filled.

Disposition:

But there was no box for *walked away like he still partly belonged to the living.*

No code for *no tether, no flicker, no error — just presence.*

No ruling.

No case.

Just Elias Shaw. And the empty space he didn't leave behind.

I could write something. Label it deferred. Archive it as "pending resolution." But it would be a lie. And worse than that — it would be *neat.* And he wasn't.

The door opened soft.

Mara.

She crossed the room with her usual weight — controlled, unhurried, like she never walked unless she meant it.

She didn't ask.

Ceramic cup, chipped rim. No steam. Still warm.

She stood a moment longer. Watching the page. Watching me.

"You didn't file," she said.

"No."

She nodded—once. It didn't carry approval or worry. Just the bare shape of acknowledgment, clean and unreadable.

"You want to talk it?"

"No."

Another nod. That one quieter.

She stayed a breath longer—just long enough to carry some of the weight I hadn't admitted was there. Then, "You'll write the next one."

"I always do."

She left.

I sat alone in the flickering quiet. I could still file it. Something cleaner. Something that would pass inspection. *Case misfiled. Soul already processed. No ruling necessary.*

I hovered the pen again.

What would Cyr write? She had seen what I saw. Asked the same questions. Saw the same absence. She'd flagged worse—souls half-formed, faked rites, possessed grief loops. She catalogued, escalated, condemned. Surgical.

But this time?

She left.

No warning. No report shared. No request for joint ruling. Just silence.

Maybe she sent it straight to the highest sanction she could reach.

Or maybe—

Maybe she lied too.

The pen hovered above the page.

Then lowered.

And didn't write.

Elias Shaw. Not sent to condemn the world. But didn't save it either.

CASE FILE: MARYSIA ZIELIŃSKA

"You can't just not file it," he said.

His voice didn't tremble, but it wanted to.

I sat at the long table beneath a skylight stained by time and something older—a shadow of grief trapped in the glass. The light that came through was weak, sallow. It didn't illuminate so much as admit defeat.

The archive room didn't hum. It held its breath. No flicker. No flame. Just dust motes suspended like unsaid things, and cabinets that hadn't been opened since protocol still made sense.

The table was wood, old enough to creak like it remembered being a tree. Every inch of it was buried— casefiles, folios, scrolls with broken seals, reports typed on machines no one serviced anymore. Some pages curled at the edges, like they'd recoiled from what they held. Ink bled. Names faded. Judgments rendered in languages Heaven no longer spoke.

A few of the stacks had slumped to the floor, forming small, desperate towers around my chair. I didn't clear them. Didn't sort them. Just kept digging.

Three days in, maybe four. The smell of old paper had settled into my skin. I couldn't tell which cases were mine and which just wanted to be remembered.

Across from me, Chandler stood too straight, expression too clean for what he was holding. He held the casefile like it was still smoking. Elias Shaw. No verdict. No seal. No closure. Just a black folder bloated with silence.

I didn't look up. My eyes were deep in the back stacks— old records, pre-standardization, back when we still catalogued in duplicate and bound in thread.

"If I file it, it gets closed. If it gets closed, it stops being a question."

"That's not how this works," Chandler pressed. "There has to be a record."

"There will be," I lied.

I kept searching. Leafing through records so old that dust puffed every time I moved something.

"The assignment was just aiding DTs," Chandler said behind me. "It's done."

Delayed Transcendent. Straight from the academy glossaries. As if a clean phrase could unstick the dead.

I spoke about what mattered. Elias.

"You saw him," I said. "Not protocol. Not stuck."

"I saw a something unfinished," he said. "Or tampered with."

Infernal still didn't sit easy on his tongue.

I pulled a file from the stack. Parchment, not paper.

The tag in red: B-44/73-KR.

"This girl."

He peered down. Scanned the faded label. "It's a Kraków purgatory case. Logged centuries ago."

"Maybe. Maybe not," I said, pointing. "No containment field record. No anchor glyphs."

He took the parchment. Shook his head, disappointed.

"This is exactly why records need to be properly filed."

"No. That's why you shouldn't file if you can't record the truth. Look at the bottom."

I sat back. Wanted to see his reaction to test my hunch.

He saw it. "No release date."

"It's not our jurisdiction," he said. But I saw it. The recognition. No release isn't just sloppy record keeping.

"Then whose is it?" I pressed.

Silence.

I pushed the second record across the table. Fragment, really. The page was thin, brittle. Not filed with the other. Not even marked as related. Took me days to see the shape of it. The ink had bled slightly—but only on one side. Because it wasn't ink. It was scorched. Precise lettering burned into the fibre like a brand. Not human fire. Not Heaven's either. The kind of mark that doesn't glow—it judges.

A miscellaneous record of events in Kraków. And at the bottom, three words, seared clean: *She remembers. Still.*

Chandler's mouth tightened. "This is a Hell trace."

He stepped back from the desk like the scrap might bite. "If it's demonic, we're not supposed to touch it."

"She's not a soul under judgment," I said. "She's already dead. And still here."

He didn't answer.

"You felt it. The system's clean until it isn't. These are the cracks. Not loud enough to trigger an alert, but deep enough to sink a whole precinct if we miss them."

He exhaled. "You're chasing ghosts."

"This isn't haunting. It's retention."

I lifted the parchment file again. Held it out. He didn't take it.

"Even if you were right, that girl's been gone centuries," he said.

I looked at the scorched script again.

"She's still there."

That held him.

Then: "Where?"

I handed him the folder.

We landed outside the shell of a church, burned out in the Kraków fire of 1850. Dusk had sunk low, casting everything in a bruised light, slow and uncertain. No roof—just blackened ribs where beams once held up belief. The walls slouched inward, mortared by ash and stone, their edges softened by time. A stone arch, almost intact, marked where the entrance might once have been. It rose black and blistered, its curve defiant, holding up nothing. Wind caught in the frame but made no sound.

The churchyard was untended, veined with the remnants of an old cemetery. Headstones planted in the ground, like the dirt husks below. The path overgrown—knee-high weeds, crumbled gravel, brambles knotted with bone-white roots. We moved toward the arch.

Inside, light didn't fall—it settled. Grey and reluctant. The air held a scorched hush—thick with soot, too dense for echoes. Charred pews sagged where they hadn't fully collapsed. Paint flaked from icon niches, saints reduced to outlines and smoke shadows. A few fragments of stained glass clung to the apse—blood red and gold, fractured but still clinging.

The altar still stood—bare, cracked, scorched. No echoes. No looping. Just stillness.

"She's not here," Chandler said.

"She is."

And she was. She stepped out from behind the ruined pulpit like she'd never left. Maybe eleven. Small. Barefoot. Dress too thin for the air. Hair long—matted in places, tied with a frayed ribbon the colour of dried blood.

Her face was delicate, high cheekbones, eyes wide, but wrong in the symmetry. And her skin—smoothed over where it shouldn't be. Like the aftermath of third-degree burns, sealed too clean. Flesh rewritten.

"Name?" I asked.

She didn't blink.

"I had one," she said. "He said I might again."

Her voice was soft. Not dazed. Not broken. Measured.

Chandler stepped forward slowly. "Do you know who we are?"

She nodded. "You're not the first."

Chandler glanced at me.

"Who came before?" I asked.

"The pale man," she said.

She hopped up and perched herself on the edge of the altar, legs dangling off the side of the blackened stone, as if it were a garden wall or a fountain lip—not the burn-marked heart of a forgotten ruin.

I approached her—kept enough distance to be careful, but near enough to catch what stayed unsaid.

"What's your name?" I asked again.

"It's somewhere."

"Do you remember where?"

She looked down at her hands. Pale. Still. No dirt. No ash. No aging. "Underneath."

"Underneath what?"

"The fire."

She didn't mean the building.

I tried a different approach. "Do you remember your parents?"

She shook her head. "They didn't stay."

"What do you remember about the fire?"

"Screaming. Then breath. Then stillness."

I leaned in. "You remember dying?"

She shook her head. "I didn't die in that fire. I died later. In the other fire."

"Later when?"

"When the people burned me in the square."

Chandler recoiled like the words had struck flesh.

"Why'd they do that?" I said.

She looked down. Clammed.

I reached into the coat. Pulled the glyph set. Not Heaven's standard issue—mine. Old. Scarred. One or two still warm from the last time I tried to bend rules into redemption. I began the rite—not a full passage, but enough to trigger Protocol engagement. If there was still a clean tether in her, it would light. It would lift.

Nothing. The symbols burned faint, then sputtered. One even cracked.

But she didn't like that. Slipped away and down. Hid her body behind the altar. Just a pale face peeking out, staring at me with eyes too old for a child.

Chandler approached, body easy. "You don't have to be afraid. We're not hear to hurt you. We're just trying to help."

The girl didn't move.

"The people in the village, they didn't like you?"

Nod.

"Why not?"

"They didn't like the things the voice said. And the father couldn't fix me."

"What voice?"

"The one the pale man put in me."

"How?"

She touched her chest. "He said I'd stopped. So he made me keep going."

"While the fire was still burning?"

She nodded.

Chandler kept his voice soft, but it was taut beneath. "He put a voice inside you?"

She looked at him like it was obvious. "It didn't burn."

"And then?"

"After he fixed me, he just went into the fire. Everyone was dead, so I walked to the village. But the voice was talking. And they didn't like it. I tried to stop him. But he wouldn't listen."

She started the cry.

"Hey. It's okay. I'm sure you weren't bad. Maybe they just didn't understand. Did you tell them it wasn't you?"

She nodded, but her eyes remained downcast.

"What did he say? Can you tell me?"

She shook her head. "I don't want to."

Chandler took her hand. She didn't resist. "You don't have to speak," Chandler said, steady. "But if you do, we might find your name."

A beat. Two. Then, without turning, she whispered: *"hoc est meum."*

The words didn't belong to her voice. They rode it like a parasite — too old, too poised. Latin rendered with perfect cadence, wrong in the mouth of a child.

This is mine.

Chandler didn't flinch, but his body stilled with the shock.

"Okay," I said. "Then let's start there."

Chandler, recovering, asked, "And the voice talked like that? Did he say anything else?"

"Lots of things, but I don't remember them all."

He turned away. Circled the nave like he was trying to find an escape route. Not for himself — for her.

"Can we talk to the other voice?" I asked

"He's gone."

"Where?"

She didn't respond.

I waved to Chandler. *Get back over here.*

Chandler stopped pacing. Squatted, hands look on his calves. "Where did he go?" he asked.

"I don't know."

"How do you know he's gone?"

"At first, he was always shouting. But after we died, he just got quieter and quieter, and then one day I couldn't hear him anymore."

Chandler took a breath.

"Think about that girl," he said. "The one who died in the square. What was her name?"

She looked at him. Her little hand in his. Then—

A crack.

A flicker of something breaking loose.

"Marysia," she whispered. "You found my name!"

She smiled. Bright. Like it was a game we'd won. Two centuries dead in a ruined church, and she still found joy in being remembered. Like that was enough to make it right.

"Marysia," Chandler continued, "Normally, when someone dies, they are taken to Heaven. Someone comes to get them. Sometimes lights. Sometimes it's someone like us."

"Can I touch your wings?" she asked.

I blinked. We were still earthbound. No wings, no robes, no glory.

But Chandler didn't hesitate. "Sure," he said gently. "Go ahead."

Not a flare. A reveal. Quiet. Certain. Like truth stepping out from behind a veil.

Light folded into the air—subtle at first, then sharper. His back arched slightly as the wings emerged—not unfurled, just present. Clean arcs of light reaching forward. No flame. No force. Only form.

Marysia reached out, fingers trembling. Touched one.

No reaction. No recoil. Just the stillness of being allowed.

"Tell me what happened when you died."

"Nobody came. Not for a long time." She stroked Chandler's feathers with her soft fingers.

"So what did you do?"

A little shrug. "Mostly, I just waited." She indicated the ruin around us.

"Can you leave?"

She nodded. "But I don't like to."

"Why?"

"This is my home."

Shadows stretched long across the cracked tile, spilling over broken pews and creeping through the weeds that had claimed the nave. Dusk filtered in through the hollow rafters, soft and unhurried, like the ruin was being tucked in for the night.

"The pale man," I said.

Chandler took her hand again. "Marysia, did you ever see the man again? The one from the fire? The one with the voice?"

"I think so. But he didn't come. He just watched from

the door."

Chandler extricated himself from the girl, reassumed earthbound form, and we retreated to talk it out.

She wandered about the ruin, humming fragments of a hymn.

"Possession?" Chandler asked, low.

"Can't see it. Halo's clean."

"Not a ghost," he said, looking at her. "She can touch. Be touched."

No tether, no loop. No echo. But not alive either.

"Protocol can't touch her. Like Elias."

I didn't like being right.

"The other side found her burning in the church," Chandler said, "Flickering. Barely a thread left. And they—"

"They gave her company," I said.

"A demonic soul."

"Or part of one. A fragment. A tormented voice."

Chandler turned to me, eyes sharp now. Not angry. Wounded. "She was a child."

I didn't respond.

He said it again, quieter. "She was a child."

I was thinking it through. "She liminal. Then on the doorstep, a splice. It takes, but now she's speaking in Latin. Who knows what else. And in 1850 Kraków, with a church just having burned to the ground, her strangeness is not well received. They call a priest. Try an exorcism. When that doesn't work, they burn her at the stake."

Chandler recoiled like the words had struck flesh.

"Burned twice," he said. "First by accident. Then by faith."

I thought; maybe the people weren't wrong.

"She's prevented from passing on the first time by the splice. The second time, she's not mortal anymore. Protocol passes over."

Chandler called her over. Knelt and took her hands again.

"Do you want to leave? Come with us?"

I sucked in a breath through my teeth. "Don't."

But it was too late.

A pure longing filled her face as she smiled at him. "Yes. I'd like that very much."

Chandler held her hands a moment longer.

"Okay," he said softly. "Then let's try. You just have to let go. That's all. Take my hand, and we'll walk out together."

He meant it. Every line of him carried belief — shoulders set, wings bowed, posture simple and sure. A shepherd's stance, not a warrior's. The way a child would expect Heaven to look.

Marysia reached up. Slid her fingers between his. Her eyes closed.

Everything stilled.

"Marysia, daughter of Kraków," he intoned. "You are not forgotten. You are not condemned. You are not alone."

And the rite began.

He summoned it—not from books, but from himself. Breath remembered: mercy's names, the gates of return, the syllables angels keep in the hollow between stars. His eyes were shut now too. Trusting the rite. Trusting her.

The light pulsed once.

She rose a half-inch off the cracked stone.

And then it broke.

The light didn't fade. It *snapped*—as if some unseen blade had cut it down. Marysia jolted in place. Chandler staggered, like something punched the breath from him.

She hit the ground.

No thud. No sound.

Just a child kneeling where a soul should've lifted.

"No," Chandler said. "No, that should have—"

I started to speak. He cut me off.

"Something interfered," he said. "Maybe the tether's tangled. I can fix it—"

He tried again. Light thickened, winged presence swelling. "*Marysia, filia Cracoviensis,*" he whispered, voice scraped raw. "*Non es oblitus. Non condemnatus es. Non solum.*"

Nothing.

Her face changed.

Not rage. Not panic. Just that deep fatigue that doesn't ask for anything—not even rest.

"I told you," she said. "Nobody comes."

He knelt again, frantic now, hands bracketing her small shoulders.

"You *felt* it," he said. "You *started* to rise. I can try again. There's something in you. I *know* there is."

But Marysia only shook her head.

"It's okay," she said gently. "You tried."

He blinked fast, once, twice.

"I'm *not* giving up," he said.

"I did," she replied. "A long time ago."

And that broke him.

Wings retracted—folding not in pride, but retreat. Light waned. His hands dropped, useless. Darkness pooled in the nave.

Marysia walked back to the altar and climbed onto it, quiet as breath.

"I don't understand," he said.

"Hell's dabbling broke her soul," I said.

He didn't turn.

"She's not a demon," Chandler muttered. "She's Marysia."

"I know."

"But that *should* have worked."

I didn't argue.

Because it *should* have.

Instead, I walked to the altar, and sat down beside her.

"You don't want to go," I said.

"I do," she whispered. "I just can't."

Her head rested against my arm. Not like a daughter. Not like a soul. Just weight, small and steady. A presence that should not be.

And we sat like that, in a church no god had touched in centuries, watching light die slow across the rafters.

Precinct.

Log Entry: B-44/73-KR Disposition: Unresolved. Filed Under: Soul Integrity Compromise / Infernal (Suspected)

The ink resisted the page.

Some cases do that. Like the parchment remembers what it's recording. Doesn't want it said. I wrote it anyway.

Chandler stood at the window. He hadn't spoken since we left Kraków. No questions. No protest. Just the sound of his breath—measured, like a hymn he didn't believe in anymore.

"She wasn't contained," I said. "Wasn't protected. Just… used."

He nodded, barely.

I set the log aside.

Opened the record box from before our descent. Scanned for flagged purgatory cases—entries marked complete but missing a trace.

There were more. Not many.

Just enough to make it deliberate.

Human subjects. Child deaths. All with ambiguous grief entries. Each one marked Resolved by systems that shouldn't have accepted the data. Not failures. Not errors. Tests.

Chandler finally spoke. "Why would Hell do this?"

I closed the file.

"Hell's not breaking the system," I said. "They're replacing it."

CASE FILE: MAEVE LIN

This was one of those mornings. The kind that started grey and kept going.

Woke in the room that isn't warm. No clocks. No bed. Just the chair I never remember sitting in and the silence that waits for me to break it. The kind of silence that presses under your ribs—not comfort, just presence, like something remembering you're still here.

The walls hadn't changed. Still etched with script no one writes anymore. Still cracked where something holy left and never came back.

I thought about cleaning. Reordering the scrolls. Relighting the glyph-lamps. But you don't tidy a memory. You survive it.

Pulled on the coat. Brushed ash off the sleeves. Looked at the halo—still sitting there, gathering dust—and didn't pin it on. Again. I haven't worn it in a century, but I look at it every day. Like memory's a mirror I keep checking to see if it's still holds me.

Probably wouldn't fit anyway.

No food, of course—just a jug of water that reflects too much and satisfies nothing.

I took nothing with me.

I was sitting in the intake office nursing old coffee and older guilt when Mara came in wheeling a dolly stacked with three banker's boxes. No folder. No smile. Just the soft *thud* of institutional weight dropped into my lap.

"Don't look surprised they sent a whole graveyard," she said, levering the boxes down like penance. "You said full spectrum."

I grunted. "Yeah. Didn't think they'd take it literally."

Chandler looked up from the rites manual, halo already clipped neatly like he wanted it to register in every department. "Wait—this is your request? I thought you just wanted to check one file."

"Didn't say that," I muttered.

Truth was, I hadn't said much of anything. Just filled out the form, signed the line, and sent it upstairs like I thought the system wouldn't answer. It did. Should've known better. My hunches don't scream. They rot—slow, quiet, patient. I've learned to hate them. I follow them anyway. Too many people bleed when I don't.

They bleed when I do, too.

I tell myself the blood's better when it happens my way.

I'm probably wrong.

Chandler walked to the boxes and lifted the lid off the top one. Inside: records. Printed, stamped, yellow-edged. Some fresh. Others curled by time and filed by hands no longer assigned to this division.

Mara tapped the label: *Query 042-L: Non-return anomalies.*

The silence that followed wasn't empty. It was watching itself fill.

"Every death that matches your parameters," she said. "Confirmed deaths. No resurrection variance. No tether logged. No protocol flag. Earthbound presence reported post-resolution."

She looked at me then—no kindness in it, no cruelty either. Just that same measured gaze she gives when I ask for more than I'm ready to hold.

"Reassure me," I said. "Maybe it's just clerical error."

"Sure," she said. "And maybe God lost the receipts."

She nudged the top box with two fingers, like it might bite. Then her eyes tracked past me to the desk. To the paper drift. The files cracked open like autopsies mid-sentence. The three empty mugs, two sealed envelopes, and a scroll I hadn't dared unroll.

"You'd have a place to review this," she said, "if we ever sanctified the wreckage you call a desk."

"Don't touch anything," I said. "There's a system. I know where everything is."

"Sure," she called, walking away. "A system."

Chandler sat on the floor. Not collapsed. Just defeated by logistics. He had a folio spread across each thigh and three more balanced like a cathedral dome across his knees. One slipped. He caught it with a prayer and a grunt.

"This is insane," he said.

I didn't argue. Paper doesn't lie — but it doesn't confess either. It just waits for someone tired enough to see the pattern.

The first few files were noise.

A retired librarian who died in her sleep. No anomalies.

A sixteen-year-old who overdosed in a motel. Processed. Dusting confirmed.

An ice-fisherman found frozen with his radio still playing.

All standard. No loops. No return.

Then came the ones that itched.

File 22-408: A hospice worker declared dead by physician attestation. Time of death logged. No deathbed witnesses. No family. No disposition follow-up.

File 22-536: A man in cardiac arrest signs a DNR mid-seizure. His body disappears in transport.

File 22-603: "Declared deceased by request." No attending physician listed. No autopsy. No dusting. Just the checkbox marked: *"Exit granted by internal review."* I held that one a little longer.

Chandler leaned over. "How is that even a category?"

"It's not," I said.

We kept going. Something hollow had started in my gut—like the space between a breath and a scream.

Then I found her.

Maeve Lin. File 22-744 – T. R. N., RN, Vancouver BC. No cause of death. Just: *"Resuscitated following unconfirmed spiritual event. Visionary clarity reported. Subject redirected life purpose and now functions as Lead Death Coordinator at a Dignity Clinic. Volunteer rate: 200+ euthanasias supervised."*

Chandler frowned. "So… she had a near-death experience and became a nurse?"

"Backwards," I said.

The file included a quote she gave to a hospital debrief team: *"I didn't see a light. I became the light. It told me: go back. Help them choose. Let death be clean again."*

"That's not what people say when they come back. That's what something *else* says, when it wants to stay."

Chandler didn't catch the tremor in my voice. He was too busy nodding, like a seminarian defending mercy as a sacrament. In his world, easing death is holy work — clean, brave, kind. In mine, death still means something. Still hurts for a reason.

"I've heard of these places," he said. "Human-rights clinics. They do everything above-board. Assessment periods. Psych review. There's nothing illegal here."

"Didn't say illegal," I replied.

I wasn't talking about law. I was talking about death. The kind that should ache. The kind that should mean something. Chandler thought suffering was a design flaw. I knew better. Sometimes the agony is the only part that's honest.

I closed the file and tapped it against the desk.

"What'd you say then?"

I looked at the page one more time.

"I said it's time to go."

The clinic didn't look like a clinic. That was the point.

Frosted glass. Cedar panelling. Native landscaping arranged just wild enough to feel curated without feeling colonial. The mulch was fresh. The walkway swept. No birds, but wind chimes clicked under the overhang — soft, polite, antiseptic.

The parking lot was nearly empty. A few clean sedans tucked against the far edge like confessions no one wanted overheard. The snow had been cleared in tidy arcs. Someone cared how this place looked from above.

A bronze plaque near the entrance caught the morning

light:

DYING WITH DIGNITY

A National Charity for End-of-Life Autonomy

"Your Life, Your Choice"

I read it out loud. Flat. No emphasis. Just enough to let the words sit with their own weight.

Chandler gave me a look like I'd kicked a puppy in front of a Sunday school.

"Just saying," I said. "Looks like they forgot what life is and trademarked mercy."

He didn't take the bait. Just stood there with his hands folded in front of him, eyes on the path to the double doors like they were sacred. His halo badge was pinned and polished, catching light it didn't earn. His collar was still crisp. The leather wallet at his side embossed with the seal of his station.

"They help people," he said at last. "People who've already said goodbye."

"Goodbye," I echoed. "That what you think they're selling in there?"

He didn't answer. Didn't need to. He believed in mercy. Thought it could be institutionalized. Codified. Bottled and handed out at scheduled intervals. Clean death, gentle hands, no flinching. A hymn you could hum as your lungs stopped working.

Me? I'd seen death without its makeup. Heard it gurgle. Watched it crawl. Mercy wasn't clean. It was earned. And pain—real pain—wasn't a failure of the system. It was the only part that didn't lie.

Just inside the vestibule, a clear plastic stand offered

brochures in three languages. I reached in and took one.

The cover showed a woman on a sunlit porch, holding a mug with both hands. White sweater, silver hair. Alone, but peacefully so above the words, *"End Well."*

Inside, soft language. "We believe death is part of life. Our team of doctors, nurses, and trained volunteers are here to support you through your final transition with dignity, autonomy, and love. Our process is safe, compassionate, and always patient-centred. You do not have to suffer." Even the word *death* had been made lowercase, tucked behind flowers and funding. Back panel listed funding sources—charitable donations, partial provincial support, "special partnerships." Nothing metaphysical, of course. No side effects listed for the soul. Just silence, staged to look like peace.

Chandler put the pamphlet back.

"She's not hurting anyone." He didn't look at me when he said it.

"Maybe," I replied.

The inner doors clicked open.

Inside, everything was soft. Soft walls. Soft lighting. Soft footsteps on padded floors. Even the receptionist's voice was engineered not to carry. We were led down a hallway lined with framed affirmations—Margaret Atwood, Maya Angelou, policy excerpts, names I didn't recognize. One read: *"The right to a peaceful death is a fundamental aspect of individual autonomy."* Another, in bold serif: *"Assisted dying is a compassionate response to unbearable suffering."* There was a quote from a physician's open letter: *"This is not about choosing death. It is about reclaiming agency in how life ends."*

They weren't wrong. But truth can be weaponized, too.

The suite door was ajar. A nurse in grey-green scrubs stepped out, closed it gently, and nodded to us. "A procedure is in progress. You may observe from the gallery." Gallery. As if we were in an art museum.

We stepped into a small alcove — glass on one side, silence buttoned down like reverence. Inside the room, a woman lay in a reclining bed. Elderly. Thin. Calm. Her eyes were open, but not searching. A doctor sat nearby, reading from a checklist in a voice low enough to be mistaken for prayer. The nurse — our nurse — stood at the head of the bed, hand on the patient's shoulder. She didn't pulse with unnatural light. No wrongness visible.

A family stood gathered. No crying. No panic. Just stillness. The daughter held her mother's hand with both of hers, mouthing along to the words she already knew were coming. The boy clutched a knitted scarf like it meant something. They looked like they'd rehearsed this. Maybe they had.

Chandler whispered beside me. "Look at her. She's not afraid."

"That's the medications," I said.

He kept watching. "She's at peace. She's choosing this."

I turned. "You really think peace is the same thing as anesthesia?"

"She filled out the forms. Psychiatric clearance. Consent reviewed. No coercion. Every safeguard in place."

"No," I said. "Every comfort in place. That's worse."

His brow furrowed. "You don't believe in mercy?"

"I don't believe in *mechanized* mercy." I tapped the glass. "That's a ritual in scrubs. A clean ending in a world too scared to suffer."

The nurse leaned in and whispered something. The woman smiled. The IV line began to drip.

"Maybe that's what she needed," Chandler said, quiet.

I looked away. "Then we built a world where death is easier than dignity."

He exhaled like the air hurt going out. "I think you're wrong."

"I hope I am," I said.

The line stopped dripping.

No fanfare. No pause. Just a soft tone from the monitor, and the doctor pressing a button like he was ending a song. A grief counsellor appeared from somewhere — professional blouse, clipboard, practised empathy. She offered tissues no one took. Said the patient's name like it was a benediction. Then led the family out the back way — *not* the door we came in. Different exit. One-way flow. Efficient. Like closing a curtain between scenes.

Inside the room, Maeve checked vitals that no longer changed. She didn't look rushed. Just ready. She removed the IV line. Straightened the sheets. Smoothed the woman's hair with tenderness. Another nurse came in with gloves and a fresh bedroll. Maeve nodded once, already prepping the space for the next name on the slate.

As the orderlies arrived to wheel the body away, we moved from the viewing lounge to the hallway — just far enough to be polite, just close enough to block the nurse between procedures.

I sat outside the suite, elbows on knees, coat open, watching the floor like it might offer a better version of the day. Chandler stood beside me, clipboard in hand, back straight like doctrine could hold up the walls.

Then it started.

A man shouted. A woman shrieked. Then heels. Then force.

The receptionist answered, smooth and trained, but not fast enough.

"You can't do this! She's not of sound mind!"

Another voice followed—booming, righteous: "We have the order. Signed by a judge. She's our daughter."

They stormed in—two people in their sixties, grief worn sharp. The man brandished a folded document like a weapon. The woman's voice outpaced her tears. Behind them, a younger man—suit jacket too small, tie crooked, face too set for someone that young. Family or lawyer. Probably both.

"She's sick," the mother said. "This is murder."

Staff moved. The receptionist stood. A man near the wall I hadn't noticed shifted—plainclothes, but not unarmed. Security, hiding in a brochure suit.

Maeve and the doctor stepped out into the hall, hands up, voice calm. He started reciting the process—intake forms, waiting periods, psychiatric evaluations. Paper shields.

It didn't matter.

The father shoved the paper at him like it was holy. The mother's hands trembled. Her sobs didn't. Chandler took half a step forward, unsure.

I stayed in my chair.

Then she appeared.

Early twenties. Pale. Thin. Eyes ringed in bruise-coloured fatigue. She moved like something already broken—upright, but cautious. Like surviving hadn't made anything better.

"Mom," she said, voice barely above breath. "I told you not to come."

"You don't mean this," her father snapped. "We're taking you home."

He reached for her.

Maeve moved faster. Stepped between them, arm raised—not hostile, just firm. The kind of motion that says *don't make this worse.*

But someone shoved. Not clear who. An IV stand caught it first, clattering sideways into the wall. A vase—glass, ornamental, unnecessary—hit the floor and exploded. Water and shards across tile. Voices overlapped. One staffer shouted for security. Another was already on the phone. The plainclothes guard stepped in, hand hovering over his belt but not drawing.

And through it all, the girl didn't scream.

She just looked down, watching the water spread like a secret spilled across tile.

Then they took her.

Court order raised like a torch. Her father gripping one arm, the legal boy the other. She didn't fight. Didn't speak. Just went limp in their hands like a verdict already passed.

Maeve didn't cry. Didn't argue. She followed them to the front doors. Watched until they disappeared. Then turned. Didn't go back in. She stepped around the corner toward the back lot—where the air still held the sharp, sweet edge of old smoke. A staff exit. A break room. Maybe a cigarette. Maybe just silence.

No one stopped her.

Maybe no one noticed.

But we did.

She was lighting a cigarette when we stepped out. No coat. Just scrubs and a cardigan, sleeves shoved to the elbow, forearms tense. The sky had that Canadian winter brightness — grey pretending to be white. A light that didn't land. Just hovered. The corner of the lot still held a city-planted pine with a placard that read VANCOUVER MUNICIPAL PARTNERSHIP.

She didn't look up.

"Nice of you to follow," she said. "You cops or press?"

"Neither," I said.

"Then I'm not really in the mood."

"You went out of your way for that girl."

She took a drag. "Doesn't matter now, does it?"

Chandler stepped forward. Palms open. Voice warm. "We saw what happened. We just want to talk."

She gave him a long look — tired, not hostile. "You here to tell me I did the wrong thing?"

"No," he said.

"Yes," I said.

She scoffed. "Figures."

Silence stretched. The cigarette burned. Behind us, a door clicked shut. No one came looking.

I broke it. "You believe in what you do."

"Of course I do."

"Tell me why."

She turned to face us. First time. Her eyes were red, but clear. No flicker. No loop. Just someone who'd stood too close to too many endings and started calling it kindness.

"You ever see someone beg to die?" she asked. "Not scream. Not cry. Just—ask? Please, I've done enough. Please, I want it to stop. Please, can I just go now?"

"Yes," I said. "But that's not permission."

"It should be."

Another drag. Smoke curled around her, not rising—just clinging.

"She tried to kill herself before," she said. "Three years ago. Pills. Her parents were abusing her. She told me during assessment. Said she wanted out. We gave her that option. Legal. Clean. Gentle."

"That's what this is to you?" I asked. "Gentle?"

"It's better than rope. Better than waking up with charcoal in your lungs and restraints on your wrists. We didn't force her to die. We gave her control."

Chandler looked at me. Eyes asking me not to push it.

I stepped in closer. "What about you?"

She blinked. "What about me?"

"You said she tried to die once. What about you?"

Something twitched behind her face.

I didn't stop. "Oregon. Barbiturates. You flatlined for

ninety-three seconds."

Silence.

"I read your quote," I said. "'I didn't see the light. I became the light.'"

I let it hang.

"That's not a survivor talking. That's a voice remembering."

She stared at me.

The cigarette trembled in her fingers—but not from cold.

Her eyes narrowed—not with anger, but recognition. Like something old had shifted behind them. Like her skin remembered a shape the world had pressed out of her.

She inhaled—slow, shallow—and I caught the flicker. It wasn't understanding. Wasn't suspicion. Just that fragile edge of knowing that bypasses logic.

"You're not police," she said. It didn't land like a question. And it wasn't a guess. More like the truth brushing the surface before either of us was ready to touch it.

"No," I said. "Worse." I didn't explain. That's how you break things.

She didn't run. That told me more than anything. She didn't know. But that didn't means she wasn't tampered. I didn't understand it, but I was getting a very bad feeling. And it was no celestial trigger going off. It was just old school intuition.

"I remember the hospital," she said. "The bright white. My hand strapped down. The monitor screaming when

I dropped off. Then… quiet."

Her voice softened—like a hymn remembered by someone who no longer sings.

"I wasn't floating. I wasn't falling. I was inside something. Warm. Infinite. And it spoke in my voice. It said: *Go back. Help them choose. Help them end well.*"

I nodded. "That's when you changed."

"I was reborn." Her voice sharpened. "I came back with purpose. With peace. You don't know what that's like—to help someone finally stop suffering and not feel guilty about it."

I watched her. Not the words—the weight beneath them. The certainty. The stillness in her body when she spoke, like the message had been waiting years for breath again. This wasn't possession. Wasn't suggestion. It was conviction, soldered to the soul.

"How many have you guided since then?" I asked.

She didn't blink. "Three hundred and twelve."

An exact count.

She wasn't lying. That was the problem.

I saw the realization sink in. Chandler's shoulders didn't tense, but it settled, like he'd been handed a new kind of weight to carry. She believed. But she believed in a way that was just off. Not just a believer. An imprint. A coded command. Or something more complicated even than that.

Chandler listened like he wanted to believe her. Like some part of him *did*. He glanced at me. Not for permission. Just to see if I *saw* it too.

I did. But not the thing he thought he saw.

I needed to press but couldn't use the celestial tools that might have made this easy. Transcendent reveal. Blinding light. Or just rip her from the mortal coil. None of those allowed with a human under the *Accord*. So, I resorted to old fashioned bullying.

"Let's stop pretending you're just a nurse with peace in your pocket."

Her jaw tightened. Her eyes didn't flare, didn't flash—just narrowed, like trying to focus through a pain she hadn't expected to feel.

"You think I'm dangerous," she said. Not loud. Just... wounded. "Because I helped them die well."

"No," I said. "I think you're not what you think you are."

She flinched.

Not at the accusation.

At the *doubt* it cracked open.

Her fingers twitched like she wanted another cigarette, or maybe just something to hold onto. Her breath hitched once—but she steadied it. Swallowed it.

"I am what I think I am," she said. Firmer now. Conviction settling like armour. "I've sat with the dying. Held their hands when no one else would. I didn't erase their pain—I gave them a choice. That's not cruelty. That's care."

She thought she was defending her calling.

But all I heard was a script that had written itself too clean.

I couldn't prove it, but I knew the truth.

But I was grasping at straws. Under the *Accord*, I *couldn't* take a living human into custody. Not only would that break about a dozen celestial laws, but it's also literally impossible for a celestial to breach the word codified in the *Accord*. But I knew what I knew. This thing in front of me was fully human—and something else too. I just couldn't prove it.

I barrelled forward anyway, pressing hard.

"You've mistaken the how and why. All of this," I said jabbing a finger at the clinic, "It's a lie."

She stepped back—not to run. Just to brace.

"Three hundred and twelve," she said again, quieter this time. "Every one of them chose. Every one of them *thanked* me."

Then, lower still, almost to herself: "Don't tell me I was wrong. Don't take that from me."

I reached into my coat and brushed the edge of the cuffs. Old tools. Older than her. Not ornamental. A covenant forged for what didn't belong.

I hadn't used them for decades. Mostly, they were a relic of my old days in Purgatory division. Back when I was just a rookie with too much faith and not enough preservation instinct, chasing down rogue souls that needed to be hauled in, jailed, and sentenced.

Would they even close? Would they burn? Or just hang there—open, inert, like trying to chain water? I didn't draw them. Just let the weight settle in my palm.

Wanting to use them wasn't the same as knowing I could. That was the problem.

She might not trip protocol. She might pass every scan. But something in her had already passed through the fire. And come back speaking peace.

Chandler stepped between us. "What are you doing?"

It was a lie, but I said it anyway, just to see what she would do. "Taking her in."

"Under what authority?"

"Same as yours."

"That's not what I asked." His voice rose now. "On what *grounds*?"

The nurse still hadn't moved. "I thought you guys said you weren't cops."

I ignored her. Stared down my well-meaning idiot partner.

"She's not harming anyone," he said.

"She's not *supposed* to be here."

"That's not a crime."

"It's a breach."

"It's a *life*," he snapped.

"You want to arrest me because I believe in what I do? Because I take the wrong and make it right?" I'm not guilty of anything." Her voice wasn't trembling. It was *clean*. "I'm here because I was *sent back*. Not because I clawed my way out. Not because I cheated some law of return. I heard it. Felt it. Whatever spoke to me was real—and I listened."

Chandler turned to her, voice gentling. "I'm sorry, miss. You haven't broken the law. You're not under arrest, and my partner is way out of line."

That last part was aimed at me. Hard. Clean.

I should've let it drop.

I didn't.

"She's a counterfeit," I said.

Both of them froze.

I didn't stop.

"Hell-forged. Folded into a mortal script. You just can't see the seam."

Maeve blinked, confused—but not afraid. She thought I meant corrupted. Misled. A metaphor for moral compromise.

Chandler knew better.

He stepped forward so fast the air shifted. Got in close.

"Sal, you are seriously crossing a line," he hissed. "You can't talk like that…around here."

"She doesn't know what it means," I said, more defensive than I intended.

"She alive," he said. "And you just accused her of being demonic."

"She *is* demonic. She just thinks she's a balm."

Chandler's hands balled into fists. He didn't throw one.

"This isn't our case."

"It should be."

"I won't be part of this."

"Three hundred and twelve souls passed under her hand."

"In peace."

"No," I said. "In sedation. Mercy without reckoning."

"Then maybe you've forgotten what mercy looks like."

He turned. Walked. Footsteps loud in the meltwater silence.

She turned to him. And for the first time, she looked grateful. Her shoulders squared. Pulse steady. Whatever doubt I'd cracked—it was gone. Burned off like morning frost under conviction.

I looked at her.

She looked back—proud, defiant. Thought I'd called her dangerous like some bitter old man warning the world about progress.

She'd already rewritten the story. I was just the villain in the footnotes.

I said nothing.

Didn't move. Didn't stop her.

She walked.

And I let her.

Not because I forgave her.

Because I couldn't prove a damn thing.

I stood alone in the parking lot. The cuffs still rested in my coat. No glow. No heat. Just weight—like a question with nowhere left to go.

The bar had no name. Just a flickering sign that used to say OPEN and now said PEN.

I sat at the corner of the counter nursing something that passed for whisky. The kind of place where no one asked questions. No hymns. No dispatches. No glow. Just the low murmur of a hockey game on mute and a bartender who looked like he'd never believed in Heaven anyway.

Mara slid onto the stool beside me like she'd always been there. She didn't speak. She didn't need to.

"You followed me," I said.

"You left a trail," she said. "Boxes out of order. Cuffs not checked back in. Chandler gone silent."

"Did he report me?"

"No."

"Will he?"

She shook her head. "Doesn't want to. But he's upset. Said you crossed a line."

"I probably did."

She glanced at my glass. "You look like someone who meant to drink less."

I didn't answer.

"She's not possessed," I said. "Not hostile. No infernal tether. And she's not lying."

Mara raised an eyebrow. "So what is she?"

"I don't know."

I turned the words over again in my mind. *Counterfeit. Folded into a mortal script.* I'd said it earlier, and it had felt too natural. Like it had been waiting for someone to name it.

She wasn't summoned. Didn't slip through. Didn't take a body.

Woven.

No seams. No residue. Not embedded — built in. A life so smooth it never even nudged the alarms.

I took another sip. It didn't help.

We'd never seen anything like it. No reports. No rumours. No doctrine. And that meant no protocol. No precedent. Just instinct, suspicion, and the weight of something old moving beneath the skin of the world.

If I was right, it wasn't just one nurse.

It was a method.

And the method worked.

"She said she came back with purpose," I said.

Mara didn't respond.

"No doctrine. No banner. Just peace," I said. "Peace as mandate."

Mara's eyes narrowed slightly, but she didn't press.

"She's not corrupted," I said. "She's convinced. That's what makes it dangerous."

I'd said *counterfeit*. It felt too easy.

But easy doesn't mean wrong.

She turned back to her drink. "What do you need me to do?"

"Nothing. Not yet."

"Sal." Her voice was low, but hard. I looked at her. "If you're going to war over this—if you break the *Accord* open—I need to know the rules of your side."

I stared into the bottom of my glass. At what was left.

"I don't know the rules," I said.

I finished the drink. Let the burn settle into the hollows of what used to be faith.

This wasn't the kind of case I was meant to take. Not assigned. Just something broken I stepped into because no one else did.

No sanction. No map. No backup.

Just a question no one asked —

— and an answer that might damn me.

The cuffs still rested in my coat. No glow. No heat.

Just weight.

Case File: Maeve Lin. Status: Unfiled. Reason: Insufficient proof. Flagged for surveillance.

CASE FILE: GERRY WILES

I got to the precinct early. Not to be productive — just to stop feeling like I was still sitting at that bar, trying to disappear through the bottom of a glass I knew wouldn't save me.

The scrolls were stacked wrong on the intake rail. Mara had realigned them. Chandler's chair was empty. So was the air. No morning light. No sanctified steam. Just silence — thick with the kind of disappointment that doesn't ask questions anymore.

He walked in late. No apology. No halo. Just doctrine in retreat.

I didn't look up.

"You accused her of being demonic," he said.

"No," I replied. "I said she was counterfeit."

"That's worse."

"No. It's different."

"She's alive," he said. "Human. And you treated her like a glitch."

"She was a glitch," I said. "Just not one the system could read."

He laughed once. Not because it was funny.

"You logged the case?"

"Flagged," I said. "Unresolved."

He stopped. "She's alive."

"I'm aware."

"You filed her."

"She's not what she thinks she is."

He moved closer. Not fast. Just the kind of deliberate that means: don't make me say this twice.

"You don't get to do that," he said. "We don't log living souls."

"I do when they preach peace without pain," I said. "When they're part of something that calls sedation salvation."

"They made a choice. Voluntary. Legal. Measured."

"No. They were offered silence. And they took it because it was easier than meaning."

"That's not protocol."

I met his eyes. "Neither is counterfeit humanity."

He stepped back like I'd drawn something. Not a weapon. A line.

"You've forgotten what we are," he said.

"No," I said. "I remember. That's why I know the shape of what we're not."

He stared harder. "You're drifting."

"Maybe."

"You used to work cases. Now you chase ghosts."

I set the mug down. "Maybe the rules stopped pointing north."

His voice dropped. "And you're the compass?"

"No," I said. "I'm what's left when the compass breaks."

"You used to follow procedure."

"And you still think belief is the answer."

His jaw tightened. "Of course I do. And I don't think I'm above it."

"No," I said. "You think it's still holy."

He looked at me like I'd blasphemed. Maybe I had. But not against God — just against the version that still answered prayers.

He stared a second longer. Then sat. Stiff. Cold. Everything but gone.

Mara didn't knock.

Didn't need to.

She moved like the precinct made room for her — a soft shift in presence, not arrival. A file tag in one hand. No tray. No coffee. Just weight.

She crossed the threshold, not in haste, not by accident. Just when the room had gone too still. Her timing wasn't coincidence — it never was. She wasn't there to deliver. She was there to cut the current before it sparked.

Without ceremony, she held the tag out.

"You have a drift error," she said. "Unclaimed soul from the Gunn file. Gerry Wiles. The driver. Never logged. No reappearance. No claim attempt. Nothing."

I stared at it. The tag glimmered once, then settled. Pale grey. No disposition ring. Just the imprint of a case that never closed and never made noise about it.

"We thought Protocol took him," I said.

"So did everyone," Mara replied. "Except the log. Which says nothing."

Chandler leaned forward. "Wait. That never got resolved?" He frowned. "Then where'd the soul go?"

Mara tapped the edge of the tag. A fresh glyph blinked, then projected a trace line—thin, faint, already fading.

"Last metaphysical ping was at the crash site. Weak. Incomplete. No tether signature. Just… bleed."

I picked up the tag. No temperature to it. Just that off-note sensation—like holding a breath that should've been released hours ago.

The tag sat between us. Still faintly warm, like it hadn't decided whether it belonged in this world or the next.

Chandler frowned. "Is it even possible for a soul to wander off from a death site?"

"That's your problem," Mara said, already turning. "I just file the slips."

I turned the tag over once, watching the glyph flicker.

"Elias did," I said.

She paused at the threshold.

"Oh—and if you're going back to the crash site?" she added, not looking at either of us. "Try not to kill anyone this time."

Then she was gone.

The tag sat between us.

Chandler didn't reach for it.

I did.

Back to Dundas and Keele.

Cold air hit hard—street-level, salt-sharp, laced with exhaust and melted grit. Snow in the gutters had gone grey at the edges. A garbage bin leaned against the light post like it had given up trying to stand straight. Across the street, a florist's sign blinked with one dying bulb. No echo overlay. No metaphysical residue stitched to the air. Just Toronto in winter: wet, scabbed over, forgetting each day in turn.

We stood on the median.

The crosswalk was clear, but the asphalt still bore the faint black arc of rubber from the crash. Faded, but there. The kind of mark that doesn't wash out. Just wears down.

I stepped to the edge of the intersection. Knee-high slush soaked the curb where plows hadn't reached. My coat caught the wind and twisted, directionless. Chandler stayed behind me, eyes scanning windows, bus shelters, rooftops. Not for signs—just for a reason to say we'd tried.

I moved slow. Back toward the point of impact.

Streetlamp. Fire hydrant. Still bent at the base, painted over once but not repaired. Bits of plastic and amber glass in the gutter—shards so ground down by boots and tires they looked like city mulch. One had blood on it. Dried, old. Maybe someone else's.

No tether. No glyphs. No bleed.

Just the ordinary wreckage of something that ended fast, caught a headline, and then didn't matter—except to those it broke.

Chandler crouched by a storm drain. Touched the lip with two fingers. They lit faintly—one syllable of a forgotten prayer.

"Nothing," he said. "If he was here, he didn't stay."

I didn't answer.

The air had gone too still. Not quiet—still. Like the block was holding breath. Like the cold had stopped being weather and started being witness.

Then I heard the click.

Not a weapon. Heels.

Measured. Confident. I turned.

Cyr.

Her presence hit first—like a cold verdict handed down in silence. Nonchalant. Viciously calm. She'd always been precise, but now there was something stripped away in the way she held herself. Like anger, tempered to edge and cooled in doctrine.

She stood on the far curb like she'd been sculpted there—one foot slightly forward, weight on her back heel, the kind of stillness that doesn't wait, just watches. The broken pedestrian signal behind her flickered between symbols, washing her silhouette in alternating green and red like judgment couldn't decide. Her coat high-collared, dark charcoal, no buttons visible—if there was a regulation-cut Hell military, she'd be it. Wind pressed it flush against her frame without lifting a single edge. The fabric looked too tailored to be mortal—cleaner than city air had a right to allow. She wore black gloves. Not for warmth. For control. No slush on her boots. No scuff on the soles. The heel clicks had been deliberate—announcement, not accident. Her hair was up, twisted and pinned like it had been there since morning without a single strand daring rebellion. Her mouth was neutral. Her eyes weren't.

She didn't blink.

"If it weren't for the *Accord*," she said, "I'd end this here."

No fire in it. Just the clean, mechanical certainty of someone still waiting for the paperwork to catch up to her judgment.

"You disintegrated an active embed," she said. "No writ. No chain of claim. No process."

She stepped forward. Not to confront—just to be closer when the knife dropped.

"He was ours."

I said nothing.

I'd already filed the report she hadn't read. She didn't know what he was. Just that I'd unmade it. That was enough.

"You didn't banish. You didn't bind. You *erased* him."

I still didn't answer.

The silence stretched. Chandler broke it.

"You don't get to threaten him," he said, voice sharper than usual. "He's operating under mandate. We're investigating a flagged drift."

Cyr didn't look at him.

"I don't need to threaten him," she said. "I'm reminding him the *Accord* isn't armor. It's delay."

Chandler took a step forward. "He's a celestial agent."

"Then he should act like one."

I turned my head just enough to see her clearly.

"No jurisdiction," I said. "Not here. Not on this case."

Her eyes didn't flicker. "That won't always be true."

I didn't smile.

"Then I'll enjoy the waiting."

We let the silence hang a little too long. Long enough to prove no one was backing down. Long enough for the job to start breathing again underneath the weight of it.

I crouched by the curb and touched the scorched glyph I'd found earlier. Old. Demonic. Gate trace.

Not hers. But familiar.

"You're not here for me," I said.

No reply.

"You're not here for Heaven either."

Still nothing.

"You're hunting," I said. "Something off-script. Something unsanctioned. And I'd guess this is your last good chance to find it before someone upstairs notices you failed."

Her head tilted, just slightly. That was as close as she got to a tell.

I stood.

"You're looking for Gerry Wiles."

That made her blink. Once. Slow. Calculated.

"You think saying his name gives you leverage?" she said.

"No," I said. "It gives me context."

"You don't have context."

"But I have a name," I said. "And if I've got that, it means you're behind."

She smiled without warmth. "You think this is a race."

"No," I said. "I think someone else already won."

Her mouth twitched, almost a grin, but her eyes stayed

sharp.

"You don't even know what he is," she said.

"Neither do you," I shot back.

That landed. Harder than she wanted it to.

Chandler stepped in, trying to cool the air that didn't want to be cooled.

"He's a drift error," he said. "Never logged. Soul disappeared after the Gunn incident. Last ping was here. Nothing since."

Cyr turned to him like she was looking at a window, not a person.

"How long have you been in the field?" she asked.

Chandler didn't answer.

"You're too clean," she said. "You think drift error means lost. It doesn't. It means untethered. It means look for a new door."

I cut in before she turned it into a lesson.

"Found residue. Gate signature. Demonic side. You tracked it here too."

She didn't deny it.

"You're late," I said.

"You're unqualified," she said.

"Maybe," I said. "But I'm still the one who found him."

I didn't wait for agreement.

"We're going," I said.

Cyr's eyes flicked sideways. Calculating. "We?"

"You've got access through the demonic side. I've got a

drift-tag Heaven still recognizes. You want the soul. I want the file closed."

She studied me. Not with suspicion—with appraisal. Like she was weighing materials for a job. Seeing if the cracks lined up well enough to use.

"You'll never come back clean," she said.

"Wasn't planning to."

Behind me, Chandler stiffened. His breath hit the air like it wanted to argue before he did.

"You're going with *her*?" he asked. Stunned.

"She's the only one who wants this solved."

I didn't add that he didn't. That he was afraid of where it went. That he still thought procedure could carry the weight of rot.

"Better the devil I know."

Cyr made a sound—half breath, half approval.

Chandler stepped forward. Hands at his sides, fists just starting to close.

"This isn't your call."

"I just made it."

"You don't have clearance for this."

"I've got precedent."

"You're breaching protocol."

"Then call it a detour."

His voice dropped. "I'll report it."

I turned to face him fully.

"Do it," I said. "But if we're lucky, you'll never have to."

He looked at me like he didn't know who I was anymore. Like the person he'd signed on to learn from had stepped out of his own shape.

That hurt. A little.

Cyr, still watching both of us, smiled. Just slightly. Just enough to say she was enjoying herself without needing to explain why.

"I'm starting to like him," she said.

"Don't," I replied.

"Too late."

I stepped off the curb. She matched my pace without being asked, heels marking steps like a signature. No slush touched her boots. No one heard who she didn't want to hear. We moved in silence that didn't ask permission—just cut a path through the city like we'd filed a claim on consequence.

Chandler didn't follow.

He didn't raise his voice. Didn't plead. Just stayed rooted there—white-knuckled, collar crooked, still hoping the system would notice the rupture and seal it shut.

I didn't look back.

He still believed in the work.

I was already past belief.

We didn't go through the front.

There is no front. Not for Purgatory.

Just backdoors, misfiled slips, forgotten stairwells that don't show up on celestial maps. You don't request access. You remember where it used to be and hope the rust hasn't sealed it shut.

We were going in on the demonic side. Intake level.

That's where the dirty work gets done — where justice doesn't mean judgment, just containment. No mercy. No flame. Just paperwork and time. Souls too damaged, too tangled, or too dangerous for Heaven or Hell. They get processed, sentenced, and shelved. Do your years. Get wiped. Try again.

It's not damnation. It's not grace.

It's logistics.

Cyr led the way. Her celestial form took no care to dim. Nude, nonhuman, elegant, and indelibly wrong. Bare feet left no prints in the frozen muck. The concrete culvert swallowed light around her, as if ashamed. Platinum-white skin without warmth, shoulders bare, markings coiled down her spine — blasphemies in script no prophet ever spoke aloud. Where the snow clung to rebar and chain-link, it melted at her passing, not from heat but refusal. The hatch ahead was half-buried in ice, its paint sloughed in shapes too exact to be accidental. Glyphs, misread by the world but not by her. She reached it without hesitation. The lock was gone. Of course it was.

She knelt and pressed two fingers to the rusted seam.

The metal inhaled.

The hatch opened, inward.

Stale air rolled out — dry, chalked with old paper and colder than the wind outside. We stepped in.

The corridor wasn't straight. The walls sloped subtly, like they weren't sure whether they were structural or symbolic. Ceiling too low, floor too clean. Fluorescents hummed with bureaucratic guilt.

Cyr didn't speak. She walked like someone who'd been here before, but not recently — not as a witness, but as a consequence. Her bare feet made no sound, but the silence counted. Each step felt tallied — not echoing, but entered. The world kept record. It always had.

Purgatory is run by both sides, but staffed by neither's best. Young agents. Burnouts. Reassignments. No promotions. No honour. Just rotation. You get sent here because someone needs you out of the way — but not gone. Everyone thinks it's temporary.

It's not.

We passed through a gate that wasn't a gate — just a frame of blank metal with two punched holes where a nameplate used to be. I reached into the folds of my robe and drew out an old token: brass, worn thin, the emblem half-erased by time and disuse.

Cyr raised an eyebrow.

"Didn't know they still issued those."

"They don't," I said. "This one never got returned."

I slotted it into the wall.

The lock recognized something older than approval. The light turned green.

We stepped through.

The intake zone was colder than the hallway, but not physically. The air was thinner. Like meaning had been reduced to trace amounts.

Desks without names. Agents without rank. A filing

system that didn't store what you were—just what you *weren't allowed to be anymore.*

A soul screamed in one of the upper queues. No one looked up. Sound doesn't count as resistance unless it interrupts a process.

This was the demonic side of Purgatory. And unlike the angelic half, it worked.

No mercy here. No hesitation. No backlogged compassion bleeding through the walls. Just intake, routing, sentencing, reset. Efficient. Precise. Inhumane in the cleanest sense of the word.

The angelic side tried to *understand* its cases. To sift each knot of guilt and grief until something yielded.

This side didn't untangle.

It cut.

And I wasn't supposed to be here.

My token bought me entry, not shelter. Heaven's jurisdiction ends at the threshold. Inside, I'm not an agent—I'm an exception, walking under paperwork that's only binding until someone decides it isn't.

If I touch the wrong soul, interfere with a sentence, speak too long without a sanction stamp—the *Accord* lifts. Not permanently. Just long enough for someone to do something irreversible.

That's the moral clarity of this place.

No wrath. No chaos. Just procedure with teeth.

I could be hurt here. Killed, technically—though they don't call it that. They call it *reconstruction.* A polite word for disassembly, followed by decades of metaphysical audit and slow reassembly under celestial supervision.

It's happened before. Agents who stayed too long. Spoke too much. Forgot that neutrality isn't protection—it's consent.

No one said it. No one had to.

The floor already knew how to categorize me.

The signs were printed in three languages, none of them human. The glyphs above each checkpoint pulsed in narrow loops. No decoration. No doctrine. Just status.

Cyr moved through it like she still belonged. I followed. No one stopped us.

We passed an agent at a counter, sorting soul chits into hexagonal trays. He didn't have eyes. Just hollows. His badge was clipped directly to his skin. It read *LIAISON*. Nothing else.

He glanced up. Glanced away.

That was permission.

The queue ahead was slow-moving, but orderly. Souls shuffled forward in partial form—half-made bodies, half-forgotten faces. Some still mouthed the last words they'd said in life. Others were already muttering fragments of the life to come.

One repeated a birthday over and over. Another kept blinking like she was trying to wake up.

This wasn't punishment. This was delay, stretched taut enough to look like justice.

I felt it before I saw it.

One slot in the queue was... wrong.

A blur. A dissonance. A place where the line hesitated, blinked, and stuttered forward again like it didn't want to touch what was in it.

Cyr slowed beside me.

Her voice dropped.

"There."

She didn't have to point.

Even here, even drowned in demonic bureaucracy, Gerry Wiles stood out.

Not because he glowed.

Because he didn't.

He was *trying* to glitch right.

And failing.

His form stuttered — frame by frame. It wasn't a loop. Wasn't tether backlash. Just something off, like reality couldn't quite hold him. The queue around him hiccupped with each pulse. One soul behind him blinked, then lost her place entirely. The one ahead restarted her intake — name, age, method of death — then again, slower. A ripple passed through the line. Subtle, but widening.

Gerry's body wasn't coherent. His uniform phased in and out of alignment, collar offset from neck, buttons spiralling out of sequence. His skin flickered between sickly flesh and placeholder grey, like a template trying to fill itself in. His eyes were open, but unfocused. He mouthed phrases with no sound.

The system was trying to process him.

And it couldn't.

He wasn't just stuck.

He was corrupting intake.

Cyr moved forward two paces, slow, deliberate.

Nothing in her hands. Nothing needed. Just watching.

For a second, we just stood there. Watching him.

"He didn't log clean in your system either."

"Not Hell-bound. A signature with no origin, no destination. Doesn't input."

I let the silence stretch. Then, "Seen others?"

"Fragments. Glitches. Not like this."

I looked at her.

"You think it's connected?" I asked.

"I've seen drifted souls before," she said. "None like that."

"Because he's not a soul," I said.

She glanced sideways at me. "You're guessing."

"I'm confirming."

"If it's not," she said, "we're both wasting our lives on the same coincidence."

We stepped closer.

The floor under him had started to desync — no cracks, no fire. Just a widening dissonance — like the world was tuning away from him. A soft glitch in reality's checksum. The kind of error the system usually suppresses instantly. It was trying. It wasn't succeeding. The intake queue was starting to fail around him — small resets triggering one row up. A clerk frowned. Another tray jammed mid-sort.

"Get him out," I said.

Cyr didn't argue.

Steel floor. No glyphs. No mirrors. Just a single bench bolted to the wall and the smell of something sterilized so long ago it never left.

Gerry sat hunched, arms twitching out of sync with his breath. His face blurred at the edges—not shapeshifting, just failing to hold.

Cyr stood near the door, back straight. No claws bared. But her fingers flexed once. She was ready.

I crouched in front of him.

"Gerry Wiles."

His head lifted. Eyes dilated. Recognition—maybe.

"You burned the test," he said.

His voice doubled—two layers, one behind the other. Not loud or forced. Just truth losing structure on its way out.

"You knew he'd see," I said. "Charlie Gunn. You wanted him to act."

"I didn't choose the trigger," Gerry said. "I was placed. Conditions were correct. Resonance field logged. Outcome expected."

"You killed three people."

"I made one visible."

He looked at me like I'd shown up too late to stop what was already buried.

"You think we're deluded," he said. "We're not. We're designed."

His smile flickered, wrong. It stuttered through three expressions—faith, fear, certainty—before settling on none of them.

"You're not a soul," I said. "You're not demon. Not angel. So what are you?"

He didn't answer.

I leaned closer. "You're not tethered. You don't loop. You don't belong. What are you doing here?"

No answer. Just smiled. Three smiles, teeth chewing each other.

I shifted.

"You want a reset? I want a name," I said.

"They're coming for me," he said. "They monitor failed transitions. I'm overdue."

"Who's they?"

He smiled again. A better one this time. No glitch. Just confidence.

"You don't have a box for it yet."

Cyr stepped forward. Quiet.

"Is it Hell?"

"No," he said. "Hell still thinks you matter."

"Then Heaven?"

He laughed. Once. Dry.

"You're both centuries behind. Still thinking in two sides. Still sorting souls like it changes anything."

"Then what are you?" I asked.

"I'm next."

His body began to twitch again—more rhythm than spasm. Something inside him bracing. Somewhere, something had noticed he wasn't where he was supposed to be.

"You think the *Accord* binds me?" he said. "You think it applies?"

That was it.

Cyr moved.

One breath. No preamble. Her fingers touched his temple. No sound. No flash. Just that brief shimmer of interruption—like the moment before a system reboots. His body didn't fall. Didn't fade. It just stopped—wrong in a way you couldn't name.

Cyr stepped back. Reset posture. No expression.

I stood.

"You didn't need to do that," I said.

"He was about to breach containment."

"We were getting close."

"We were getting watched."

I stared at her.

"He was my witness."

She didn't blink.

"No," she said. "He was your warning. He wasn't just broken. He was formatted for something else— something no one trained us to name."

The precinct was quiet when I got back.

Not silent. Just quiet in that particular way only Heaven manages—where the stillness isn't peace, but waiting. A hallway that doesn't echo. A light that doesn't warm. A door you don't remember walking through.

Today the precinct anchored closer than usual to the

terraces of failed virtue. I could see their lines from the window—etched into the sky like regret set in marble. They don't usually drift this near. I guess someone thought we'd earned the reminder.

I stepped inside and the air felt... hesitant. Like the place didn't know whether to recognize me or redact me.

Mara was at her desk.

She didn't look up.

Just reached for a tray, shifted a few scrolls, made space that hadn't been there a moment before.

"Back early," she said.

"Didn't feel early."

She nodded like that counted. Like I'd filed my hours wrong and the penalty was silence.

I stood for a moment longer than I needed to.

"Chandler?" I asked.

She didn't answer right away.

"Not here," she said. Then, "He'll file something. When he's ready."

I moved past her. She didn't stop me.

At my desk, the chair had been moved slightly off-angle. Not disrespect. Just a quiet correction. I sat. Tried to begin.

The parchment sat ready—boxes unmarked, lines waiting for answers I didn't have.

A reset that wasn't mercy. A system built on reincarnation, not redemption.

Gerry wasn't trying to escape punishment—he was

trying to go back to work.

Heaven didn't catch it.

Hell didn't stop it.

And the *Accord*? He said it didn't apply.

And I believed him.

I stared at the page. Not because I had nothing to say — because I didn't know what would be done with it.

No category fit. No box wouldn't lie. I didn't trust the system to read it honestly.

Maybe I didn't trust myself to write it. Or maybe I did — and that was the problem.

"He said we're centuries behind."

I said it just to hear it in the air.

Mara didn't answer.

I didn't expect her to.

She stood eventually. Walked past my desk. Set a mug down—warm, but not hot. The kind of gesture that didn't register on official forms.

She didn't look at me when she said it:

"You shouldn't have gone with her."

I didn't reply.

She didn't wait.

"But you did."

Then she walked off.

No judgment. No report.

Just space—cleared quietly, like she knew I wasn't going anywhere.

And the parchment on the desk. Still blank. Still waiting for a case that couldn't be named.

CASE FILE: FRANK STEPHENS

Sometimes I can't go in. The clarity of the past can make the present feel like a lead vault, sealing you in.

There was a time when we knew who we were chasing. Back before the *Accord*. Back when Hell wore red and Heaven wore gold and neither side pretended the other had a point. Back when the dead stayed dead, and the ones who didn't were called miracles or monsters, not "misfiled." Now it's all subtler. More polite. We share doors. We whisper terms. And every week, Heaven feels a little less like sanctuary — more like surveillance.

All I needed was a minute by the Stair of First Entry — the one thing they haven't moved, because no one remembers who built it. Stone worn smooth by soles that never returned. No light, no guard, no inscription. Just the place you come through — if you come through clean.

I didn't make it two steps before the summons came.

No location listed. None needed. Camael never moves. Everything else just learns how to orbit.

I passed one of his assistants on the way in. She didn't speak. Just nodded — one hand hovering over the glyphboard, still transcribing a sentence she either hadn't finished or already knew the end of.

The walls along the last corridor shifted — no longer smooth, but scored with shallow grooves. Like something had tried to claw its way out of the walls.

Camael's door opened on its own.

He didn't stand. Didn't gesture. Just looked.

I stepped in. The door closed.

He didn't ask me to sit.

"You've been off-pattern," he said. Not even as accusation. Just as fact. "No writs filed for the last two entries. No confirmed tether. No standard logging language."

I let the silence stretch. Let him decide whether that was evasion or invitation.

"Collaboration with a Hell agent, unfiled."

He didn't say Cyr's name. That would mean admitting they let her operate.

"Metaphysical accusation against a living agent."

Still no names. But I could hear Maeve's voice—cut-glass and laughing.

"And language in your reports that could be interpreted as destabilizing the *Accord*."

That one landed soft. Because it wasn't a warning. It was a wedge.

Camael turned the page. Didn't look at me when he said, "This isn't punishment. It's observation. If you deviate again, you'll be removed from casework and reassigned precinct duties. Permanently."

I let that hang a second.

Then, "I filed what was true. If it looked like heresy, maybe the system's allergic to facts."

That earned a glance—sharp, brief, then gone.

"You think you're irreplaceable."

"No," I said. "I think I'm already replaced. I'm just the one still writing the reports."

Camael turned the page again.

Dismissal, like judgment: implied, not spoken.

I should've gone back to my desk. Filed something routine. Let the days go soft again.

But once you've seen the cracks, you don't unsee them. You trace them. And hope they split.

The boxes were where I left them — stacked in the intake annex under Query 042-L. Non-return anomalies. Confirmed deaths. No resurrection variance. No tether logged. No protocol flag. Earthbound presence reported post-resolution.

Low priority. Low visibility. Low probability of forgiveness if I got caught pulling them again.

I opened the first. The paper smelled like resignation — like it had been touched by too many hands that thought it would file itself. Names, dates, sites of death. Not recent. Not noisy. Clean deaths with long silences afterward.

One was a cardiac arrest in Thunder Bay. Wife swore he walked into the kitchen a week later. Another: drowning victim in '87, spotted on security footage two months post-funeral. Margins full of handwriting, most of it crossed out.

I flipped through three more. Possible tether. False ID. Suspected duplicate. All plausible. All boring. Nothing caught.

They stacked like apologies — neat rows of names that had already been forgiven. The kind of file you stop questioning if you want to keep your station.

I should've been satisfied. Probably.

Maybe I wasn't digging hard enough.

That's what did it. Not a scream. Just a splinter.

For deep research, you've got two options. You embed in Earth. Or you go down.

Not to Purgatory. To the Overflow.

I stepped back into the main precinct. Mara was already watching.

"Going to the Overflow," I said. Not loud. Just enough to make it real.

She didn't ask why. Just slid a tray aside and made a little space on the slate. Like she was already logging the time — like she'd been expecting it.

There's no signage on the way down. Just thinner air. And the sound stops echoing.

Cases don't start on desks like mine. Or Chandler's. Mara doles them out based on calligraphy no one teaches anymore. The files come from upstairs — administered by a cascade of titles: undersecretaries, assistant directors, and somewhere above them all, Camael, who runs Threshold. Threshold takes orders from Protocol. Or maybe not orders. Maybe just allocation — some system that sorts the dead like sealed envelopes, marked for Heaven, Hell, or Purgatory, based on criteria no one survives long enough to read.

Finished cases go to Archive: the celestial record, perfect and permanent.

But the Overflow isn't Archive.

It isn't part of Heaven.

It's where you put the files that don't close—but don't want to admit are still open. Every precinct has a backlog. Celestia just happens to have infinite space and infinite time to *get around to it.*

Unattended files trickle down like sediment. Leave one on your desk too long, and Mara cleans it off, tags it, shelves it. When the cabinets get full, they clear themselves. Down here.

Past Protocol. Past prayer.

Down here.

To the place where closure is presumed, not proven.

The Overflow wasn't built. It settled. A metaphysical residue of misfiled faith and quiet neglect.

The third ring. Beyond Earth, past echo-space and purgatory. The Overflow hovers like a fog of unresolve. A shared space—Heaven and Hell both have access, neither has dominion. All the rules apply. None of the certainty does.

Any celestial can descend to check old cases. But no one does. It just accumulates. Expands. Clutters.

Unresolved deaths without salvation, condemnation, or purgation. Files that don't scream, don't loop, don't flare. Just stall. Lives that should've resolved, but didn't. And someone hoped they'd fix themselves if left alone long enough.

The shelves sag. The cabinets lean.

Some boxes won't open unless you stop looking at them.

I didn't start with anything recent. Went back to the earliest tier, near the central sink where the light fails politely.

Found one. Marked low priority. Extremely old. Resolved. No notation. No date. No indication how, or by whom.

Resolved cases don't belong in the Overflow. They're supposed to be in the Archive, sealed, faded, sung over. Not here. Not leaking time.

I went to check it out. Opened the scroll. Reached in.

Nothing. No tether. No trace. No echo-space. Just a name and a death date that didn't connect to anything.

The kind of blank that makes you feel like you were never meant to ask.

I put it back. Found another. And another.

Same story. Resolved. But not filed where it should be. Like someone had been cleaning with a blindfold on.

System error?

Or system rot?

I shifted approach. Skipped the historical strata. Pulled something closer. Last hundred years or so.

Case was marked low priority. Expected to self-resolve.

It hadn't.

I took it.

The descent isn't marked. No gate. Just a hinge in the world, swinging the wrong way.

Then I was there—on Earth. 1925. Rammed into my body again—like forcing a snake into a balloon. Or something close enough. Boots on shale. Air wet in the lungs. Skin remembering how to ache. And the sound— You don't hear it. You *feel* it. The kind of sound that shakes your teeth loose and tries to fold you from the inside. A constant collapse, like judgment rendered in pressure and sound. Not a roar—an ongoing ruin. The Niagara river becoming punishment. Forever.

I stood near the bluff's edge, ground slick underfoot. Couldn't see the bottom. Didn't need to. Mist rose in curtains. Heavy but untouchable. The kind of mist that doesn't soak—it accuses. Hanging in the air like a threat.

The barrel came into view—a long wooden capsule, banded in steel, low to the water, bobbing with theatrical confidence. A trivial object batted around at breakneck speed in a world of chaotic power. Rushing headlong to the drop. And Frank inside—believing.

Bob, slide, tip, plunge into the mist. Gone. Then—

Snap.

Frank reappeared, fifty yards upstream. The launch point. Crude ramp of warped slats, bolted into limestone like someone thought permanence could be improvised.

He stood beside the barrel—grinning. Bare arms, rolled sleeves, chest out like a man posing for his own legend. Ducked in headfirst, confident. Like this was just another test run.

Someone—no face, no voice—lowered the lid, latched it down.

Then the barrel rolled. Slow at first. Tipped into the water like it had all the time in the world. The current took it with no ceremony. Grabbed. Spun. Slid. Took the plunge into the mist.

Frank didn't know he died at the bottom. He was still trying to prove something his bones couldn't argue anymore.

I tried to move toward the ramp. Didn't get far. The ground pulled strange—like crossing a memory that didn't recognize you. Fifty yards might as well have been a continent. I circled wide. Took the long way, until the slope let me climb.

The closer I got, the worse the sound became. Not louder. Just more *final*. Like the world was trying to end one square foot at a time, and this was where it started.

Then he was there. Already in motion—tightening a strap on the barrel, checking a seam like this was just maintenance before glory.

I called out anyway. "Frank." It broke apart mid-air. No resonance. No echo. Just mist swallowing syllables like they never mattered.

He looked up. Saw me. Waved. Said something. His mouth moved with confidence, but the roar took everything. Could've been a joke. Could've been a prayer. Didn't matter. I couldn't hear it.

He climbed into the barrel. Settled like he'd done it a million times. Which, maybe, he had.

Someone sealed the lid. I couldn't see who. Didn't matter. The loop didn't need help—it conjured silhouettes like stagehands.

The barrel rolled. Slid into the current. Vanished. Splash. Mist again. Same arc. Same violence.

Then he was back.

The same ramp. The grin. The confidence

I lifted my arm. Waved. Frank waved back. Grinned wider.

Reset.

I moved. Fast. Tried to reach him before he got in.

The moment my hand crossed the ramp—

blink.

I stood near the bluff's edge, ground slick underfoot.

Same position. Same mist. Same impossible distance.

I stepped back. Not far—just enough to let the loop breathe without me in it. Let the current play out the way he thought it needed to. I watched the cycle unfold three more times. Each identical. The strap. The nod. The wave. The plunge. Every detail locked. Like a ritual. Like the water needed him to believe it *wasn't* the end. He got faster at the prep. Like he'd been optimizing over iterations I couldn't see.

Every soul finds a script. Most read it. Some write in the margins. He carved his into the current. Didn't matter that it killed him. He wanted the last word. He wasn't mourning. Wasn't even remembering. This wasn't grief. Not guilt. This was proof. He'd rather die again than admit he already did.

I didn't speak. Didn't wave. I just watched.

You watch something long enough, and it starts glitching around the edges. This loop was tighter than most. But nothing stays perfect under repetition. Not even denial.

The fourth time I watched, the barrel hit the water at a slightly different angle. A dull *thunk* I hadn't heard before.

Fifth loop, the metal plate caught the light too soon— just a flash, but early. Like the sun remembered something Frank didn't.

Sixth, a ripple upstream. Too far ahead. The kind of disturbance that doesn't come from the world, but from memory trying to pre-load belief.

Then the dent. Left side. Low on the barrel. Visible for a second before the plunge. Gone the next round. Back again the one after.

That was the tell. The soul's subconscious can't loop perfectly. Not forever. Every fiction blinks—eventually.

It wasn't a scream. It wasn't a plea. It was a flaw.

And that was enough.

The loop was holding, but something underneath had started to slip—not because of me. Because even perfection cracks when you repeat it enough times. That was the grace built into ruin: it gets tired.

Frank climbed into that barrel again, rolled his sleeves, checked the seal. That same performance of control. Same breath before legacy. And then he vanished. Water. Mist. Noise. Reset. Barrel back at the ramp. Frank in place. Someone sealing the lid. But the rhythm had changed. Slightly. Like a musician missing the downbeat by a hair.

I waited. Let the next cycle run. And the next. And then I acted. Didn't shout. Didn't move toward him. Didn't try to touch the script. Instead, I found a scrap of material from the edge of the construct—not real wood, not real metal, just echo-shaped matter. Anything with surface tension would do.

I scratched the words in by hand. No stylus. No sigil. Just a line of truth he didn't have the right defenses for.

STEPHENS BROTHERS ENGINEERING

Then I nailed it to the side of the launch ramp. Slightly crooked. Not confrontational. Just there. Not a threat — just a fact.

I stepped back.

Frank was tightening the strap again. Shoulder muscles shifting under sunburned skin. Whistling something I couldn't hear. He didn't look up right away. He crouched. Checked the underplate. Ran his hand along the welded seam with pride. He was in it again — his masterpiece, his myth.

Then the head turned. Eyes found the plaque.

He froze. One hand still resting on the barrel. The other half-raised, like he'd forgotten what it was doing. I didn't move. Didn't breathe. Didn't interrupt. His eyes traced the letters. Not fast. Like each one required effort.

Then his mouth moved. No sound. But I didn't need it.

What?

He blinked. Turned to look behind him, as if someone else might explain it.

And then the world went soft at the edges. The ramp blurred. The water held still. The mist settled like a breath no one exhaled.

No sound.

No fall.

The barrel was gone. So was the current. And Frank —

Frank was standing in a new space.

I took a step. The world didn't blink me back. This one

wasn't sealed.

The grass was real. Bent under my boots. Held dew like it didn't know anything was wrong.

Porch light flickering. Slats whitewashed once, now peeled to grey. Columns on either side—one leaned slightly, like it forgot how to carry weight. A house built before electricity, then adapted. Like it learned to compromise with time.

A woman sat on the steps. Head in hands. His mother. Frank didn't move toward her. Didn't look at her. Inside the house, someone pacing. A radio low. Someone else praying, almost under their breath. A family trying to hold together a man already tilting toward his monument.

Frank stood at the top step. Arms crossed. Posture set.

This wasn't death. This was decision. The moment he committed.

1924.

Frank turned to me.

Didn't speak right away. Just looked.

"Frank Stephens?"

"That's me. You a reporter?"

"No."

"Then who sent you?"

"Call it follow-up."

He blinked once. His hands didn't move. One rested on his thigh. The other hovered slightly, not quite clenched.

"I'm not doing interviews," he said.

"This isn't one."

He shifted slightly, like the air had gotten heavier.

I waited.

"I'm not here to stop you," I said.

That got him.

He looked at me harder. "Then what?"

"My name is Sal. I just want to ask you some questions about the barrel."

He looked at me again. Thinking I was a competitor.

"I'm nowhere close to where you are, and won't be ready before you. I want you to make history. Show it can be done. I just want to understand the engineering."

That was enough to break the ice. He had time for someone who reinforced his belief.

"There's no anvil. Obviously," he said.

He stepped slightly to the side, as if giving a tour. A porch rail to his left. Grass flattened in a track toward a shed. The same kind of wear you'd see in places walked daily, without thinking.

"It's steel-banded," he went on. "Top and bottom. But the base plate's the difference. Curved. Not flat. Spreads the shock outward. Everyone gets that wrong. They think the water's soft."

"It's not," I said.

"It's worse than concrete," he said, like he was correcting a student. "Because concrete doesn't grab you after."

He was relaxed now. Almost proud.

"Base is reinforced with a lattice. Local smith helped me weld it. Hidden seam down the centre—intake plate for pressure equalization. You don't want too tight a seal or it'll crush your chest before you hit the water."

I nodded like I understood more than I did. Let him talk.

"Interior's layered. Foam and padding. Not straw. Not hay. That's theatre. This isn't theatre."

He glanced down the yard. Squinted slightly.

"I've done the math three times," he said. "I've tested ballast. I'll have about three seconds of flight. Then thirteen of chaos. After that—stillness. That's how I know it worked. Because I came out the other side."

I let that sit a moment.

"You remember the landing?"

He paused. Not long. But he noticed the question.

"I remember the quiet," he said.

"That's not the same."

"It's enough."

I didn't press it. Not yet.

"What about your brother?" I asked. "He used an anvil?"

He nodded once.

"Charles."

"Older or younger?"

"Older," he said. "By six years. Used to take me fishing down by Queenston. Taught me how to splice a line."

"Was it his idea to do the drop?"

"No," he said quickly. "No. That was mine. He didn't

even talk about it. Just did it."

"He told no one?"

"Left a note. Brief. Said it would make us known again. Said it was legacy."

Frank's voice flattened slightly.

"Did it?"

Frank didn't answer.

The house behind him creaked again. The pacing had stopped. The porch light flickered once, then held.

"I read about him," I said. "Tied himself to the weight."

Frank nodded. "Anvil punched straight through the base. Barrel split before it hit bottom."

"That was 1920?"

"Yes."

"You ever think he didn't mean to die?"

That hit something. His jaw set. He didn't answer.

I waited. He looked past me.

"You feel like he got forgotten?" I asked.

Frank's voice came low now. "You don't understand what it's like to watch someone disappear in public."

"No, I don't," I said. "But I do know what it looks like when someone tries to reverse it."

He stiffened. A breeze moved across the grass. Neither of us shifted.

"What about your mother?" I asked. "She's been out here with you the whole time?"

He turned slightly. She was still sitting on the steps.

Head in hands. Perfectly still.

"She prays," he said. "She said if I survived, it meant it wasn't cursed. That it was just a mistake."

"And did you?"

"I came back," he said. "No injury. No fracture. Just cold. Some bruising."

"But there's no record."

"I didn't need one," he said. "She saw me walk through the door."

"I'm not saying she didn't," I said. "I'm saying no one else did."

He didn't respond.

I stepped once more onto the porch. He didn't stop me. But his mother did.

"That's enough."

Her head lifted—slow. Not curious—someone remembering a part she was supposed to play. Her eyes were wrong. His eyes looked out of her face, and there was anger behind her eyes. Or fear.

"He's given you what he can," she said. "You've got your notes."

Voice wasn't raised. But it shut the space between us.

"I don't think I do," I said.

"You've got the math. What else is there?"

"The part that won't let him leave."

Her eyes didn't move. Didn't blink.

"Goodbye, Mr. Sal."

Frank didn't look at me. He turned toward the screen

door. Put one hand on the knob. Stopped.

"I remember quiet," he said again. "That's all."

Then he stepped inside. The door clicked shut.

I stood there for a moment longer. The grass didn't move. The wind held its breath.

Then I turned.

Time to check the records. Not the barrel. The aftermath.

Where belief twists into tether.

The precinct light was stable again. No shimmer. No weight. Just the steady glow of a ward that doesn't blink.

The Charles Stephen file was thick with metaphysical readings—arc structure, echo degradation, acceleration metrics. All of it pointing to one destination: Hell. Clean intake. No dispute.

But in the margin of a secondary report, someone had scrawled a comparison.

"Repeat signature. Copycat trajectory. See Frank S., 1925."

That was it. No tag. No elaboration. Just a footnote in someone else's damnation.

Mara passed behind me. Tray of fragment tags in her hands.

She didn't stop.

Just said, without looking, "You've got about twenty seconds."

Then walked on.

I didn't move.

Didn't need to.

The door opened on seventeen.

Chandler stepped in.

Shirt still pressed. Sleeves unrolled. Tie straight, like someone had retied it in the hallway out of spite.

He didn't speak. Just stood there. Like a witness summoned and not sworn.

I rolled the scroll closed. Set it flat.

"Don't hover," I said. "Either walk in or go file another report."

He stepped forward. Slowly. Deliberately. Like each foot had something to prove.

"Wasn't personal," he said.

"Sure felt like it."

"I didn't lie."

"Didn't say you did."

Chandler's jaw clenched. Just once. Then, "You broke protocol."

"And you went to Camael."

He didn't answer that.

I stood. Straightened my coat. Looked him over.

His eyes were tired. Not from sleep loss. From conflict. The kind you don't win, even if you're right.

He looked at me like I was two different people. One he respected. One he didn't know what to do with.

I looked at him like he'd finally grown up. And I hated

that it showed.

"You think I'm reckless," I said.

"I think you're better than this."

"And I think you're still polishing your halo."

That one landed. He looked away.

Silence held for a beat.

Then, "You find anything?" he asked.

"Maybe."

"Want help?"

"No."

He nodded like he expected that.

But he didn't leave.

We stood there a moment longer, two men orbiting different convictions and pretending it was proximity.

"You did the right thing," I said.

"I know," he said.

"I still don't like it."

"I don't either."

I picked up the scroll again.

"Close the door behind you," I said.

The door clicked shut.

Chandler stayed where he was, hands loose at his sides, like he was waiting to be dismissed or forgiven.

I didn't offer either.

He glanced at the scroll I'd unrolled again.

"What's the file?" he asked.

I didn't answer right away. Just slid it toward him.

He read. Saw the red tag. I saw the worried tightening of his jaw.

"Relax. I'm researching his brother. Died in 1925. Still stuck."

"Is this the Charles Stevens—" he started.

I nodded. "Went over Niagara Falls in 1920. Tied himself to an anvil."

"I've heard of it," Chandler said. "Famous case. Used in training lectures. What not to do."

"Younger brother built a better barrel. Same river. Tried to finish what his brother started."

"Legacy play?"

"Guilt play."

Chandler looked back at the scroll.

"Family was broke," I said. "Charles thought if he pulled it off, they'd be famous. Sponsors. Cash. A name people remembered. Frank was the one who pushed the story. Told Charles he could be the first man to go over and survive."

Chandler looked at me. "And then he didn't."

"Nope."

"And Frank carried it."

"Worse," I said. "He tried to fix it. Built a better barrel. Better pitch. Thought if he did it right, it would undo the wrong."

"Did he?"

"Not according to anyone but him."

Chandler moved closer to the scroll.

"This line here," he said, pointing. "Mother—living at time of event. Witnessed departure. Filed no claim. Gave one statement."

He read it out loud.

"I can't lose another."

I watched him read it twice.

"That's the tether," I said.

Chandler didn't argue.

"She saw Charles die," I said. "Then saw Frank leave. Thought it would happen again."

"And he internalized it."

"He didn't just internalize it," I said. "He built a barrel to prove her wrong."

Chandler looked up.

"But when it worked—if it worked—it didn't matter."

"No," I said. "Because her belief was stronger than the truth. And he loved her more than the record."

He was quiet.

I rolled the scroll back and tied it.

"If I can turn that belief," I said, "I think he'll come loose."

Chandler hesitated.

"You want me to come?"

I looked at him.

"If you don't come, you might miss the chance to report me."

He almost smiled.

Didn't.

We dropped in clean.

No tension in the air. No resistance on descent. No flare.

I had a feeling before we landed. Something was off.

The echo was gone.

No dissolve. No closure. Just absence—like someone took it and erased the outline.

Chandler took three steps forward. Then stopped.

"There's nothing here."

He wasn't wrong.

No grass. No porch. No house. No pacing inside. No flickering light. Just open space where a memory used to live. No colour. No sound. No weight. Nothing.

I scanned the ground. No burn marks. No residual tether fracture. No judgment curl. Nothing protocol.

Chandler crouched, ran a hand over the surface.

"Doesn't feel neutral," he said. "But it's not active either."

"Not enough signature," I said. "It didn't shut down. It lifted out."

He looked up at me. "You think he resolved?"

"After a hundred years stuck in freefall? No."

"But you got him past the drop."

"Not past the lie."

We split. I circled wide, tried to map the old position—

bluff line, launch ramp, porch. Traced a few steps where the bench would've been.

Nothing.

I went to where the tether should have ended. Knelt. Pressed a hand to the ground. There was something there. Not fire. Not energy. The shadow of a flare that never came. It left the air brittle — charged and sealed. Barely there. Impossible to dismiss.

Chandler walked over. Stopped beside me.

"You feel it too?" he asked.

"Almost."

"Demonic?"

I shook my head. "Not clean enough."

He didn't press.

I stood.

The air held still. Like it was trying not to speak.

Chandler looked around again, slower this time.

"No judgment trace. No call. No seal. You think it was —"

"I don't know what it was."

And that was true.

I didn't.

I didn't go back to the precinct.

Not yet.

Didn't bring Chandler.

Overflow doesn't like extra voices. It listens better when

you're quiet.

The descent was slower this time. Like the place was considering whether I still belonged. The light down there never sharpens. It just… accumulates. The deeper you go, the more it starts to feel like recollection dispersing into dust.

Frank's file wasn't where it should've been. Not under his name. Not tagged. Not among the other non-returns. I checked anyway. Three shelves over—spine cracked, re-bound in different thread. It hadn't been refiled. It had been moved.

I unrolled it slowly. One new line since I'd last touched it.

Status: Resolved.

No initials. No date. No closure note. No signature. No explanation. Just that word. Clean. Permanent.

Filed like the others in Overflow. Where no one looks.

I stared at it for a long time. Then rolled it back up. Didn't log anything. Didn't take it with me. I stood there a while longer. Then turned and walked out.

I didn't keep quarters for comfort. There was no bed. Just a window that didn't open, a wall that didn't remember, and a shelf where the Halo lived when I didn't.

Light fell through the ceiling, soft and straight. Heaven doesn't cast shadows unless it wants to.

I stood for a long time.

Marysia. Maeve. Elias. Melvin. Gerry.

And Frank.

It should've been any of the others. Elias, who couldn't resolve and didn't know why. Maeve, back from death with a mission and a taint I couldn't prove. Melvin, who possessed a soul to elimination. Marysia, a broken soul, like a failed test discarded. Gerry, running for purgatory to get a reset, claiming there were more than two sides. Each one marked the edge of something—a line I couldn't always name. But it was Frank who moved.

Frank, who couldn't resolve himself for a hundred years, then suddenly did when I was getting close. And closed files sitting in Overflow, like someone was tidying up the backlog without protocol, mercy, or judgment.

The silence of the room shifted. Not louder. Just more present, like the space remembered what I'd been avoiding. Camael's voice. Flat. Measured. He hadn't accused me. Not directly. Just listed the discrepancies and let them settle, like dust over a body no one had permission to name.

"If you deviate again, you'll be removed from

casework."

He hadn't meant it as threat. Not even judgment. Just outcome. Consequence dressed as procedure.

I crossed the floor. Reached the shelf. The Halo sat there, unchanged. Untarnished. Unworn.

Cold, as always. Smooth enough to look like mercy. But sharp enough to draw blood.

I didn't put it on. Just held it for a moment, wishing for a time that made sense. The one that wasn't coming back. Then left it behind.

Today the precinct squatted near the Vaults of First Abandonment. You could feel it in the floor—like standing above memory that didn't want to be found.

Inside, the ward glow held steady. No shimmer. No weight. The kind of calm that isn't comfort, just containment.

My desk was buried.

Three stacks. Not tall enough to threaten collapse—just enough to suggest someone cared about the optics. Each scroll tied with gold-threaded ribbon. Casefiles. Routine. Unurgent. The kind of death that resolves clean when someone bothers to listen.

It's easy to keep me busy. Just takes volume. The world dies fast—faster than we can sort. Protocol caught most. A clean system, for a while. But it didn't stop the Stuck. Too many deaths still fall sideways. The kinds that don't log smooth. That carry grief like inheritance. That don't answer when called. Heaven and Hell weren't built for this speed. We never have enough eyes or time. Just enough to pretend we're managing.

So the backlog grows.

And someone—maybe Mara, maybe not—decided I was better spent here. Quiet cases. No deviation. Just witness and move on.

I sat. Opened one.

Lapsed theologian. Rural Saskatchewan. Died alone. Echo formed around an unwritten sermon. Already flagged for minimal intervention—just needed a witness to nod and close it clean.

Second file.

Retired nurse. Halifax. Built a construct of the hospital wing she died in. Nothing stuck, no unresolved trauma, just habit. Tether type: Dissociative Loop. Resolution: Presence required. Standard detachment.

Third.

Clockmaker. Blind. Memory echo recreates sounds of ticking, stuck in an unfinished watch. Small grief. Small time.

All clean work. All worthy. All meant to keep me busy.

Mara passed by, tray in hand. She didn't pause.

"You know these aren't usually your kind of pulls," I said.

She set the tray down, still not looking at me. "You're cleared for Threshold Duty. These are all unresolveds below barrier level."

I flipped a ribboned scroll open and closed again. "Low-risk. Low-profile. Low chance of attracting attention."

"That's how I filed it."

"You file anything else lately?"

"Only what I'm given."

I watched her. She let me.

Then I nodded. No accusation. Just the obvious conclusion.

Someone wanted to keep me occupied.

It wasn't exile. Just redirection. A not-so-subtle reminder: I still had a desk. I still had work. And I was expected to stay in it.

I was halfway through the fourth file—fisherman, Quebec coast, believed the sea had a soul, couldn't let go of the waves—when the precinct changed temperature.

Not colder. Just stricter.

Camael arrived like he hadn't been watching the whole time. No announcement. No need. Heaven didn't clear his path; it yielded. The light around him flattened into obedience. He moved like a verdict that didn't need to raise its voice.

Behind him, she followed.

She wasn't deferent. And she wasn't tentative. She moved with the exact posture they teach when precision matters more than grace. Her robes were crisp—platinum, not white, not gold, but that perfect midpoint Heaven issues when it wants sheen without warmth. Her halo wasn't visible, but you could feel its permission in the air around her—newly earned, still sharp. Her hair was black and smooth, drawn back so tight it felt punitive. No wing flare. No aura. Just presence. Studied, restrained, pure.

Camael flowed past. Went to Chandler.

"This is Seraphine," he said. "Assigned active. You'll

support her."

She stood beside Camael with posture engineered for approval. Tall—five-nine or close to it. Lean, angular. Robes pale as frost and just as sharp—layered formal, nothing forgiving. Every line of her attire signalled order. Hair black and bound so tightly it looked structural. No makeup, no softness. The kind of beauty Heaven weaponizes. Not to seduce, but to discipline.

Her face was still. Not blank—composed. A discipline so intact it might as well have been prewritten. She held the grey file like it was liturgical. Not even clutched—presented. No hesitation, no strain. Just protocol in flesh. If Chandler was a hymn sung too earnestly, she was the procedural manual bound in leather and written in passive voice.

The kind of agent you promote quickly.

The kind of agent you send when you're tired of mess.

Chandler straightened like a cadet meeting inspection.

"Ritual martyrdom. No divine sanction," she said. "Ten planned. Five confirmed deceased. Protocol is incomplete. Window's still open."

Her voice landed like policy.

Chandler blinked. "Religious cult?"

"Not doctrinal. No named deity. But metaphysical structure is coherent. Belief is patterned."

She held up the file. "Protocol has not taken. They're waiting for something."

That caught my attention.

Camael barked the next words like a drill order.

"Hell will contest. Resolution window is closing.

Move."

Chandler looked at the file. Then at her. Then—too late—at me.

Seraphine didn't wait. She was gone—*descended*. No motion. No farewell. Just absence, shaped like purpose.

Chandler hesitated half a step. Then followed. His outline held for a breath longer than it should have—then unstitched, and fell inward.

I leaned back slightly in my chair, watched the future leave the room—efficient and fine-boned and impossible to love.

Camael lingered a moment longer. Not watching me. Just confirming the correction had taken root.

Then he was gone.

I stayed seated. Let the stillness settle. Let the weight of Heaven's intention cohere in the room. Three minutes. Maybe less.

Then I stood.

Mara didn't look up from her desk.

"Don't," she said.

It wasn't a warning. It wasn't a plea. Just the kind of word you use when the outcome's already certain—and the report's half-written.

I didn't answer.

Didn't request a writ. Didn't need one.

Heaven hadn't closed the aperture. Not yet.

The descent landed hard.

Thompson, Manitoba—administrative lungs of the North. Regional hub for RCMP command, medevac response, rail logistics, and whatever else Ottawa couldn't be bothered to staff properly past Winnipeg. Boxy buildings. Pale facades. Gravel shoulders turned to grey sludge. Still too much snowbank in May.

I stepped out onto Selkirk Avenue. The street was half-cleared at best—slush refrozen into rutted ice, dark with soot. Squad cars sat skewed across the intersection like dropped toys. No cordon. No visible command. Just confusion thick in the air—the kind you taste before you breathe.

One civilian lay facedown behind a dented green dumpster. Winter coat, wrong colour for any uniform. Unmoving. Might've been looking for cover. Might've been a body.

But further down the alley—just past the police lot fence—I caught movement.

A figure running.

Long coat, handmade. Not modern. Dark red with tasselled edges, the fabric thick as ritual. Soft-soled boots left no crunch in the frost. He moved with direction—not fleeing. *Departing.* I didn't get a look at his face. Just the glint of something hung around his neck—stone, not metal, swinging with weight that wasn't just physical. Then he was gone. Down the service lane. Into the treeline.

No one else seemed to notice. And I didn't have time to follow.

I moved forward to the pop and drag of gunfire—close. Semi-auto. Not clean. Sound cracked sideways down the alley between the detachment and the post office, bounced back in fragments. No coordinated volley, no trained pacing. Desperate, not tactical.

The RCMP detachment had taken the first hit. One front window punched out clean—the frame had buckled inward at the seam, warped like a lid forced open from the outside. Smoke curled from the eastern corner, slow and greasy. Burned insulation. A scorch mark traced upward from where something—pipe bomb, likely— had gone off low against the wall, just enough to crack the siding and blister the paint.

The sign above the entrance—RCMP THOMPSON DETACHMENT—hung crooked, chain half-snapped, the rest groaning in the wind. It hadn't decided whether to fall or keep pretending it belonged.

I stepped into the breach.

No one saw me. No one stopped me.

Celestials don't need permission, just timing.

Inside, the air carried that smell—concrete dust, hot brass, and expectation. No fire. No blood. Just the metallic cling of aftermath, heavy with things that never should've happened.

The front desk was overturned—metal legs twisted, paperwork soaked in someone's coffee and something darker. Frost crusted the inner panes where the window had blown out, and shards still glittered in the entry mat like a welcome turned warning.

Seraphine was already here.

Her coat wasn't regulation. It was worse. Tailored. Bone-white. Lapels stiff. No dirt, no creases, no memory of ever being touched. The kind of coat you wear to be obeyed, not warmed. Underneath: clerical shirt and collar, every edge straight. Her boots made no sound. Her steps left no trace. She didn't walk through the scene—she documented it.

She stood near the dispatch hallway, flanked by bullet-scored drywall. A filing cabinet behind her leaned open, punched through at the centre like someone had tested their marksmanship on municipal bureaucracy.

Chandler hovered beside her, trying not to look shaken. Trying not to look like he knew how late they were. His vest was still crisp. His cuffs still white. But his knuckles clutched the strap of his bag a little too tight.

"One left," Seraphine said, without turning.

Her voice was flat. Not cold—clinical. The tone of triage.

The soul was near the holding cells—kneeling. Young. Painted. Red smears on his face, hands wrapped in stolen ribbons, beads tied in his hair. No blood. Just symbols. Identity as declaration. Hadn't moved on.

The hallway to the cells flickered at the edge of protocol—half-light stuttered where metaphysics failed to reconcile the transition. Time didn't flow clean in scenes like this. It eddied. Stalled. Broke on itself like a record with no next track.

The other four?

Gone. But I felt it. Residue in the air. Not cold or hot. Just *drag*—a metaphysical skimming, like something too large had slipped out through a doorway not meant to open.

The gunfire started again—further inside the detachment.

Not warning shots. Panic, maybe. Or ritual.

"Sal?" Chandler's voice. "You followed?"

He looked like he didn't know whether to be grateful or terrified. Probably both.

Seraphine turned.

Her eyes flicked once over me. Not in recognition. In disapproval. Like I was a smudge on a clean page.

"You're not assigned," she said.

Neither of us blinked.

"Leave."

I didn't move.

She waited—exactly long enough to confirm it. Then turned from me as though I were the irrelevance.

"Chandler," she said. "Cover me. I'm going in."

He hesitated. His weight shifted—toward me, then toward her. The moral compass of a seminarian who hadn't yet realized Heaven wasn't magnetic.

I saved him the anguish.

"Go," I said.

He turned to me. Mouth partway open.

I cut him off with a look.

"You're not my shield," I said. "She needs you. I don't."

He swallowed hard, nodded once, and moved.

Seraphine had already drawn her sidearm. Black. Sleek. Clean grip. No inscription. No cross. Just silence rendered into threat. She moved with purpose into the interior of the detachment.

I followed, boots silent through the glass.

Because here's the truth they never wrote into the manuals: Bullets *can* hurt us.

They don't end us, not always. But they tear skin, shatter ribs, pierce lungs. Our vessels bleed. Our hands shake. If you rupture the container fast enough, clean enough, sometimes the spirit inside doesn't hold. The body isn't sacred. It's permitted. And permission can be revoked.

We moved through the detachment with mortal steps and borrowed breath, into the space where dying and doctrine had come to terms.

Past the intake counter, the hallway split—cells left, offices right. The sound was coming from the right. Drywall buckled under stray rounds. A corkboard split clean in two above an overturned coffee station. A fluorescent light fizzled on the ceiling, sparking where the casing had cracked from concussive force. I passed a constable slumped against the filing room door—eyes open, unseeing, chest caved inward. He didn't scream. He didn't breathe.

The main operations room was chaos.

Tables flipped. Radios crackling open-channel warnings that no one was left to receive.

One of the warriors had holed up behind a row of lockers near the northwest wall—rifle barrel twitching through the slats, trigger finger too steady for his age. Breath shallow. Not afraid. Focused. A second crouched behind the copier bay on the east side—late twenties, sleeves pushed up to the elbow. No weapon drawn. Blood on her forearm, but the skin beneath unbroken. She was whispering something low. Might've been a prayer. Might've been a countdown. A third was wedged between two filing cabinets along the rear wall—girl, maybe sixteen. A fourth stood nearest the hallway exit, behind an overturned desk—tall, narrow face, body vibrating with the effort not to move. A makeshift Molotov sat lit in his right hand, wick burning low but controlled. His left hand clenched a lighter like he hadn't decided whether this was his weapon or his offering.

And at the centre of it, the leader—fresh streaks of paint down her cheeks, one hand raised like she was calling judgment. No cover. No fear. Chanting.

Not Cree, not exactly. Rooted in syllables that predated compromise. Old vowels curled under her tongue, consonants shaped in the back of the throat where breath turned to stone. It wasn't melody. It wasn't incantation. The kind of sound that makes the world remember it was made by something other than words.

And then—

CRACK.

A single shot. Sharp. Police-side. Not celestial.

Her chest jerked. Just once.

A red bloom widened under her collarbone. No scream. No collapse. Just a soft breath pushed from her lungs like the wind had changed its mind.

She dropped forward.

The chant ended on her lips—half syllable, still forming.

"Clear shot," someone called from the far stairwell—RCMP, helmeted, rifle drawn.

On the far side, pinned deeper in the far corner, were the remaining RCMP. Three behind an overturned table. Tactical gear. Visors up. Mid-rank. One was clutching a radio but not transmitting. One dead, near the intake desk, half-shielded by a collapsed partition, blood smeared in an arc from a blind shot fired too early. Two more dug in by the inner hallway—backup squad, one with a shotgun braced to the wall, watching the dead constable with eyes that wouldn't stop blinking. The sixth—helmeted, rifle drawn—stood at the far stairwell, weapon still up, body language proud. He was the one who fired. Didn't lower his aim. Didn't apologize.

The room held its breath. Twelve metres by twenty, roughly. Fluorescent panels overhead, half of them shattered. Paper drifted in the air like memory caught in suspension.

And into this—the smoke, the bodies, the unfinished chant—Cyr arrived.

She didn't enter. She unfolded into the room—already inside by the time anyone realized she should have had to pass through a door. No fanfare. No smoke. Just her. Cut cheekbones. Hair swept in precise asymmetry. Red lips shaped for verdicts, not mercy. Her heels didn't click. They warned. Black suit, razor-perfect. Gloves already off.

Seraphine stiffened. Just slightly. A narrowing of the jaw. The temperature in the room didn't drop. But the possibility of survival tilted.

That's when it happened.

They didn't scream. Didn't shout. Just *moved*—fast, direct, feral.

The girl with the blade vaulted the table first, small frame coiled like a spring. The bone-handled knife flashed once—then disappeared into the throat of the officer with the radio. He gurgled, collapsed.

The second officer fired point-blank. Caught her low in the ribs, but not before she slammed the hilt into his jaw—broke teeth, split lip. She went down twisting, already dead before she hit the floor, but her momentum knocked him off balance and he fell with her.

At the same time, the youth behind the lockers rose and screamed—not words, just *fury*—and opened fire. His rounds sprayed wild, stitched chaos across the hallway entrance. Two constables there dropped immediately— one struck clean in the temple, the other taking a burst to the chest and spinning sideways into the wall. Another took a round to the thigh and fell screaming.

Return fire shredded the boy. Rounds ripped through his chest, shoulder, face—he dropped like a switch had been thrown.

Then the tall one threw the Molotov.

It arced over the tipped desk and shattered against the rear filing cabinets—igniting paper, spilled toner, something chemical that shouldn't have been exposed. Flame caught like it *wanted* to.

The fourth warrior—woman with blood on her arm— charged through it.

Clothes already smoking, face seared on one side, she hurled herself into the remaining officers. She managed one swing with a broken chair leg—caught a constable in the knee, brought him screaming to the ground— before gunfire took her apart. Three rounds, centre mass. She collapsed as if unstrung.

One of the wounded officers opened fire *after* she was already down—emptied the clip into her back. The clip ran dry with an empty *click* that sounded more afraid than necessary.

Then silence. Real, this time. Not the kind that waits. The kind that *follows*.

Six officers had been standing. Now one was dead. One maimed. The others bleeding in degrees that would mean something if they made it to triage.

Not a rebellion. Not a rescue. A rite. The final act in a language no one else had learned to read.

One of the wounded RCMP, the youngest—looked at the bodies, looked at his own shaking hands, and muttered under his breath like a prayer, "Jesus."

The dead woman's hand twitched. Just once.

No one holstered.

The surviving RCMP stayed crouched behind tables and debris, voices low, tight with adrenaline. One called for medical, another for backup. They didn't move to help the fallen yet—not out of cruelty, but calculation. They needed to know it was over.

"Clear?" someone asked.

No answer. Just the crackle of static and the shuffle of broken glass under careful boots.

In that space—the physical world stuttering back to procedure—the echo began to form.

Not visible to them. Not sensed. But present.

Layered just beneath their reality, like breath fogged against a mirror. Not quite aligned. The angles shifted. The lighting lost its source. Walls remembered things the living had forgotten.

It wasn't the world. It was the shape the soul gave it. Constructed. Partial. Imperfect. But real enough to bind.

The humans weren't here. They moved in the layer

above—adjacent, unaware. Separate.

I let it take me. Didn't resist.

And then I was in.

It began with the girl. The soul slipped loose—not in pain, not in peace. More like gravity finishing what it started. Her face rose with her, untouched by blood, eyes still half-lidded. She hovered inches above her corpse. No ascent. No descent. The tether curved sideways, trailing into a metaphysical space no doctrine defined.

Another followed.

Then another.

The fallen warriors surfaced one by one—silent, whole, waiting. Five in total. Each bearing the shape of who they were moments before—paint intact, weapons still carried in posture if not in hand.

Across the room, the body of the slain RCMP constable shimmered faintly. A soft hum rose in the stillness. The tether curled upward, narrow and clean. No struggle. No resistance. Just extraction. He lifted—his form folding outward, rising along a spiral none of the others could see. A single thread of gold cinched his core and drew him gently up. No delay. No doubt. *Protocol.*

One of the injured officers looked up from where he crouched, fingers bloodied on a tourniquet. He didn't see the passage. But something in him *felt* it. His breath hitched like he'd just missed the end of a sentence.

The Cree didn't move.

They sat. No signs, no sorrow. Just a posture that said: we're ready. As if they were waiting for their summons. And nothing came. No hum. No spiral. No draw. Just silence.

The girl who'd held the blade looked to the chanter. The one who'd thrown fire looked down at his own hands, still echoing with motion.

Then they became aware of us. Not with fear. Just *anticipation*.

The leader—her soul now risen, breathless but unbroken—stepped forward. She looks down out of respect. Her voice, when she spoke, did not echo. It simply *carried*.

"We're ready."

She wasn't pleading. She was reporting.

Cyr didn't blink. She took one step forward, heels slicing the edge of the metaphysical boundary like paper. "It's suicide," she said. "Clean Hell claim."

Seraphine didn't look at her.

She looked at the leader. Then at the others. Their wounds still visible. Their defiance still etched in their limbs like muscle memory refusing to fade.

"No," she said. "It's martyrdom. It isn't clean."

She was right. The claim was dangerous. And we all knew it.

Not just because it was contested. Because either direction was *possible*. That's what made it lethal.

Chandler stepped forward, hesitant.

"Permission to speak with the dead," he said—formally, like he still thought the rules mattered here.

Seraphine didn't turn. "Denied."

"I just want to ask—"

"I said no." Her tone was flat, but not cruel. Not now. "They're in a state of metaphysical tension. Observation risks distortion. If they see what they want in your face—"

"They're looking at us," I said.

She went still for half a beat.

Then, "*I'll* speak."

She stepped forward with poise carved from a doctrine no one could afford to write down. Her hands stayed at her sides. Her posture open, but not inviting. The dead watched her like children watching a teacher from a culture they didn't believe in.

Behind her, Cyr began to circle, her black dagger slipping between her fingers. Not exactly aggressive. Just *in motion*. Her steps formed a slow perimeter around the standoff, heels tapping the echo-boundary. Not quite in the way. Not quite out of it. Measuring.

She wasn't looking at the Cree. She was watching *us*. Waiting for a crack. A misstep. An opening to call foul.

I stayed where I was. But my thoughts moved. If it had been pure suicide—an act of self-annihilation without cause or metaphysical framing—Hell could have taken them before their bodies cooled. No trial. No debate. But martyrdom introduces *belief*. And belief complicates everything. They believed in something bigger— something sacred enough to make sacrifice feel like a path, not an end. That belief—misguided or not— created resonance. Enough to stall judgment. Enough to make a claim uncertain.

And that's what made it lethal.

Seraphine stepped closer, into their circle, but not within

reach. Her voice was steady, pitched just above silence — formal without being cold.

"My name is Seraphine," she said. "I am an Advanced Field Officer, engaged to operate within the Celestial Threshold Division of the Seventh Sphere. You are no longer living."

Every syllable landed with the weight of sanctioned clarity. The kind of introduction built to function across language, creed, and collapse. Issued like a warning label. Spoken like scripture. Meant to reassure the freshly dead that Heaven still remembered their names — even if it never learned how to pronounce them.

"You have reached a point of passage. This place is temporary. Transitional. What happens next is not punishment. It is processing. You are seen. You are known. Grace is available."

Cyr clicked her tongue — just once. Not loud. "Funny how often processing looks like forgetting."

The five remained silent, eyes downcast. They had fought. They had died. But they didn't look lost. They looked... unconvinced.

The leader frowned — not in anger, but in thought. She looked to her left, to the boy with the shredded chest. He gave a slow, uncertain nod. Then to the girl with the knife. Then to the fire-bearer.

The youngest, the one who'd crouched between filing cabinets, finally spoke.

"What do you mean, *grace*?"

Seraphine's face didn't change.

"Release from burden. Passage beyond pain. Mercy

without merit."

Cyr's voice slid in behind it, quiet but precise. "A lovely phrase. But false."

She took a step closer to the souls — not threatening, just *occupying*. The way a surgeon handles a wound.

"You," she said to the leader. "Name?"

"Shayenne," the woman replied.

"You orchestrated your deaths?"

"We made the sacrifice that was needed."

"You knew these men would kill you."

A pause.

"Death is the way of the warrior. We do not fear death."

"You did not act out of a lack of fear," Cyr said. "You acted out of a desire for death."

Another voice broke in — male, firm. The fire-bearer. "We did desire death. Our sacrifice was required as restoration of the Cree people's soul."

Before I could stop myself, I asked it too. "Required by who?"

Shayenne answered, eyes forward, voice resolute:

"White society has broken every covenant. The old treaties were lies. Assimilation was not survival — it was erasure. Only sacrifice can reclaim the land and call forth the ancestors."

The words didn't tremble. They didn't even rise. They *settled* — like ash, like history.

Cyr nodded once. Not in agreement. In completion.

She turned, addressing all of us now — Seraphine,

Chandler, me. "There can be no doubt," she said. "That intentionally killing oneself is a sin. The Sixth Commandment clearly states: 'You shall not murder'. Suicide is murder of the self. Under the *Accord*, judgment has been granted to agents of Heaven and Hell. And by all precedent, suicide was and is a mortal sin—nearly as grave as killing another."

Her gaze fell back on Shayenne. Sharp. Final.

"And here, you"—she pointed—"have done *both*."

Shayenne didn't move.

Cyr took one step closer.

"You chose death, and you chose murder. Answer plain. Do you repent your mortal sin?"

Shayenne raised her head. "No," she said. "We do not."

Cyr smiled, very slightly. "Noted." Then she turned to the killer who had opened fire on the RCMP. "Do you repent?"

He met her gaze. "No."

That was enough.

Cyr's hand raised. A seal burned into their skin. The writ appeared. Judgment, clean and lawful.

The souls of Shayenne and the boy who'd fired last dropped—slow, then sharp—as if gravity had remembered them. A touch of flame, but no time to scream.

And then—*silence*.

The remaining souls stood. They backed away—just half a step, but enough to break the circle. The warrior girl gasped. The youngest covered her mouth.

Shock.

Then horror.

Then—*realization.*

Seraphine stepped forward, voice hard as Scripture.

"Hell is *very* real."

She swept her gaze across them—eyes sharp, cold, desperate in a way she would never admit.

"If you wish to avoid it, *confess now.* Speak your sins. Denounce the lie. Repent, and your souls can still be taken up. This moment *can* be redeemed."

They stared.

She took another step.

"This is not a metaphor. You are on the brink of eternal damnation. You have seconds. Choose."

Chandler moved faster. He crossed the line like it burned him to stay still.

"Please," he said, breath ragged. "You didn't *mean* to die. You didn't mean to kill anyone. You were misled. You—"

He turned to the youngest, kneeling slightly to meet her eyes.

"You didn't want this."

"I did," she said quietly.

He shook his head. "You were lied to."

She hesitated. Her voice broke.

"We were... called."

"*Who?*" I demanded. Hard. *Who told you this would save you?*"

And then it broke. Not from one. From all of them.

"He walked with us—he said resurrection would not be as spirits, but as warriors."

"We would be the first to reclaim our true ancestral paradise."

"On the Great Plain."

Each phrase dropped like a drumbeat—practised. Remembered. Not fantasy. *Doctrine.*

"What's his name?" I demanded again.

"Wâsakâmaskwa. Burning Bear."

A name shaped like belief. Said without fear. Said like prophecy fulfilled.

Cyr started circling. Heels sharp. Rhythm slow. Like a dance she'd done before, always ending with a soul claimed and a sentence sealed.

One of the boys looked at her. Flinched. Not because he knew what she was. Because some part of him remembered the old language of predators.

I stepped forward and pulled out the cuffs. Pre-*Accord.* Not regulation. Still held trace glyphs from the Threshold Authority—back when we wrote law with presence, not paper.

I triplicated them.

Bound each boy in turn. Wrists together. Not tight. Just real.

"Chandler," I said. "Take them to Purgatory intake. Get a triage team. Flag their state as contested but incomplete."

He blinked. "Wait—Purgatory? I thought we don't—"

"Do it."

Seraphine's voice cracked like frost. "You don't have clearance."

"I do," I said. "And I just used it."

"This is irregular," she said. "These aren't lost. They're claimed."

"Two were claimed," I said. "The rest weren't. Each soul is unique. And martyrdom's messy. Sometimes it ends in Heaven."

"You don't get to make that call."

"I didn't. I just gave them a chance."

Cyr's heels stopped.

"No," she said. "They're mine."

"Not yet."

She stepped in front of one of them. The smallest. The one still bleeding through the echo. "You," she said, sweet as venom. "Do you admit your violence? Without remorse? Without repentance?"

The boy opened his mouth.

"Don't answer that," I snapped. "Not a word."

Cyr smiled without humour. "Souls can't lie."

"No," I said. "But they can keep their mouths shut."

I turned to the three of them. "Do not talk to this woman. Do not answer questions. Do not engage. Not until you reach Purgatory intake."

They stared at me, wide-eyed, half-real in the fading echo.

"We are trying to save your unworthy souls," I said.

"Whether you want it or not."

Chandler hesitated—just for a breath—then moved. Took the boys without looking back. No resistance. Just duty, sharp and clean.

That left me with Cyr.

She turned. Ink-black knife suddenly in her palm—no motion, no draw. Just there. Like it had always been waiting.

I didn't move. I knew what she was thinking. Her jurisdiction was clear. I'd broken the *Accord*—technically. Moved souls without consensus. Claimed a route outside the process. Worse: I'd interfered with her harvest. And she hadn't forgotten Melvin.

Neither had I.

Seraphine said nothing. Just stood there—platinum silence, hands folded like a sealed warrant. If she had sympathy, it was buried too deep to reach.

I met Cyr's gaze. Held it.

"You can kill me later," I said. "File it clean. Use the right seal. Make it poetic."

Her lips curled, but she didn't move.

"Right now," I said, "there's one soul left in the next room. Still metaphysically entangled. Still holding knowledge—about Burning Bear, a plan, and four souls who disappeared before we got here. And I'm guessing… without Protocol."

Her eyes narrowed. Calculating. Dangerous.

"There's more here than mercy or damnation," I pressed, "and you know it."

We stared at each other in silence.

Her hand coiled as if it itched.

After a beat, I added, "The way I see it? I'm more useful to Hell alive than in reconstruction."

The last soul had shaped his own prison beautifully.

We found him in the front room of the detachment—polished now, scrubbed clean of blood and fire, as if time had looped back to just before the breach. The floor was dry. The Plexi at the desk was uncracked. A kettle steamed faintly in the corner, untouched. The windows had repaired themselves, flawless panes framing the world he still believed in.

And outside it was perfect.

Golden grass rippled in rows like scripture sung low. The light was prairie light—sincere, unsuspicious. Far off, a herd moved in slow procession: bison, antlers high, breath misting in the dawn. The sky looked hand-washed and hung to dry. Everything gleamed with promise.

But the door was closed.

And he couldn't open it.

He paced with the steady rhythm of someone not ready to admit it yet. Who thinks maybe the timing is wrong, or the lock needs a second try, or salvation is just being delayed, not denied. Each time he reached the door, he tested it. A hand on the knob. A push. A pause. Then back again.

Not frantic. Not yet. But it was coming.

The plain was still out there, exactly as he dreamed it. He just wasn't invited.

Seraphine stepped forward. No sound from her boots. No shift in her face. Just movement—like a judgment arriving by courier. She raised one hand, not in threat, but invocation. The air around her stilled.

She said his name.

"Liam Littlebear."

The soul stopped mid-step.

I moved before the next syllable left her mouth.

"No."

She turned, slowly. Not startled—offended. "He's ready."

"He's useful."

Her eyes narrowed, lips still parted like the invocation hadn't finished vibrating in her throat. "You're delaying mercy."

"I'm delaying closure until we know who promised him that." I nodded toward the window. "That plain out there didn't come from nothing."

"This is heresy."

Cyr's voice, low, almost gentle.

"Claiming will be contested."

Seraphine froze. Just for a moment. Enough. Not in fear—in realization. No clean passage. No consensus. A grey file.

She lowered her hand.

Didn't bow. Didn't blink. Just stepped back.

"Liam."

He didn't answer right away. Just looked out the

window.

The glass was cracked. Not shattered—just one clean fracture line along the top right corner. Like the window wasn't sure whether to hold or break.

"You're dead," I said.

He nodded once. Not in shock. In confirmation.

"You can't get there from here."

That got him. He turned.

His paint had faded in places—around the jawline, across the throat—but enough remained to see what it meant. A declaration.

"I need to get there," he said. "That is the Great Plain. It belongs to my people. To me."

"Then talk to me. You came here with a plan. What was it?"

He didn't flinch.

"To seize the station," he said. "Declare the Land of the First Blood. Force recognition. Make the sacrifice public."

"How many of you?"

"Ten. All chosen. Anointed. Armed. Named."

"Named?"

He nodded again. "By the old rite. Not birth names. Purpose names."

"And before you left?"

"Three days," he said. "Fasting. Fire. We burned the band office. Bureaucratic betrayal. Then the church. A white man's god for a dead man's soul."

"And the rite?"

"Sunrise. On the ridge. Ash, feathers, paint. Names spoken aloud, then sealed."

"What did you carry?"

"Traditional blades. Hunting rifles. Whatever we had. Paint, not masks. No one hides when dying right."

"And you struck at dawn."

"Yes."

"Expected resistance?"

"Of course. The white men always resist."

"And you expected to die?"

"That was the point."

I let that hang a second.

"Why?"

He didn't hesitate.

"To restore honour. Not through conquest. Through sacrifice. To become what we were before they told us what we had to be."

I watched him.

He didn't blink. Didn't ask for approval.

"We reject their heaven," he said. "Their scripture. Their forgiveness."

"What do you believe happens next?"

He pointed, not to the sky, but toward the wall. "Resurrection. Not as spirits. As warriors. On the Great Plain. Our place. Our right. Native. Sovereign."

"Who's Wâsakâmaskwa?"

That word, finally, softened him. His eyes lowered. Not in shame. In reverence.

"Our chief. Our guide. He speaks to the ancestors. He's walked the fire and not burned. He told us the Plain would receive us."

"And you believe him."

"I saw it," Liam said. "I died, and I saw it. Fields without fences. Sky without wire. My brothers were taken."

"You didn't get in."

He looked away again. Toward the glass.

"No," he said. Quiet now. "But I will."

"What happened to your brothers?" I asked.

He turned his face back to me, but slower now. Like the number hurt.

"They made it," he said.

"Where?"

"To the Great Plain."

"Who took them?"

"Wâsakâmaskwa. And a spirit guide."

"Who?"

"I don't know."

"Try."

He searched the memory—not for truth, but for permission.

"An elder," he said finally. "Not from Cross Lake. He spoke like us. But not to us. Only to Wâsakâmaskwa."

"Describe him."

"Long coat. Not a parka. Not local. Hair was grey at the sides, but short. Eyes like… not white eyes. Just watching ones. Nothing behind them."

"You saw your brothers go to the Great Plain. How?"

"Wâsakâmaskwa and the elder took their hands. I saw the light of the plains," he said. "My brothers walked forward and the grass took them."

"Did it feel right?"

He looked at me then. Really looked.

"It felt like something we earned."

"Or something you were sold?"

That cracked it—just the edge. A flicker of unease.

I held the silence, let it widen.

"What happens," I said, "if the Great Plain is real—but you were led to the wrong one?"

He didn't flinch. Didn't look at me. Didn't say a word. Just turned back toward the window, slow and final. Like someone closing a door from the inside. Outside, the wind moved a scrap of police tape. One end had torn free. It fluttered. Then stilled.

I waited.

Nothing. No blink. No shift. Just the posture of someone who'd made a vow, and remembered it. He had shut the world again. Not to deceive me. To protect what remained. He didn't need proof. He had belief. And for now, that was stronger than truth.

Cyr appeared at Liam's side—one moment standing near me, the next behind his shoulder, angled slightly toward the window like they were just two people admiring the view.

"Do you remember how it happened?" she asked. Calm. Soft. No heat in it.

Liam didn't look at her. But his breath changed.

"I was inside," he said. "After the breach. We'd cleared the front. The sergeant raised his weapon."

"And?"

"I raised mine."

"Did you fire?"

He hesitated.

"No," he said. "I slipped. My foot caught on something. I—"

A short breath. "I fell. My finger was still on the trigger."

"And the gun went off."

He nodded.

"Where did it hit?"

He touched his stomach. "Left side. Above the hip."

"And you died?"

"I tried not to."

"But you did."

Silence.

She stepped around him now. Not in threat. In certainty. Her eyes scanning—not his body, but his guilt. His shame. His orientation to sin.

"Did you regret it?" she asked.

"Falling?"

"No. Dying."

He didn't answer.

Cyr studied his posture. His stillness. The quiet lack of remorse — not because he resisted it, but because it never occurred to him that it mattered. It wasn't about sin. Or penitence. Just the wreckage left behind by a sacred act misfired. She turned her head slightly toward me. Just enough for me to catch the look. Not doubt. Not sympathy. Calculation.

She stepped back.

"Well?" I asked.

Her answer was a whisper with the curve of a smile.

"He didn't kill. He didn't want to die. He doesn't regret it. And he's still sure he's right."

"So?"

She looked to Seraphine. Then back to me.

"I'm not dying on a guess."

Smart. One false claim, and Seraphine would freeze her into protocol for reconstruction. I wouldn't stop her. Cyr knew that.

She gave Liam a last glance — almost respectful. Then folded her hands behind her back.

"Not mine."

And just like that, Hell stepped away.

Leaving him to the window. To the pacing. To the plain.

Seraphine stepped forward again. No announcement. No invocation this time. Just movement. Executed like a ruling. She stopped precisely one pace from Liam. Measured her breath. Then spoke.

"Liam Littlebear," she said. "You are eligible for

ascension."

He didn't answer.

"You have died without malice. Without guilt. You have walked a path of meaning."

Nothing.

"I am here to receive you."

He looked at her. No fear. Just resistance dressed in reverence.

"You're not what I was promised," he said.

Seraphine blinked once.

"Come with me," she said. "You will be known. You will be restored."

He frowned. "To what?"

"To what you were before the fracture. Before the error."

"Before the treaties?" he asked. "Before the church? Before the schools?"

She froze.

Then, "To your true self."

"My self doesn't live in your Heaven."

She drew in a breath—not for herself, but for the doctrine she was about to recite.

"I am the truth," she said. "The way. The door opens only where grace is accepted."

He turned. Back to the window. Back to the plain that didn't want him either.

She stepped forward half a pace — too fast, too sharp. But the room didn't respond. There was no door. No aperture. No resonance. You can't enforce grace.

She lingered—just a beat too long. Something locked. Something unresolved. Then she pivoted and walked. Not fast. Not shaken. Just compact, like a decision compressing itself into motion. At the door, she stopped. Met my eyes. No fury. No scorn. Only the cold, administrative gaze of someone updating a record—permanently.

Liam stood exactly where he'd started—between a door that wouldn't open and a promise that had already taken his brothers. Still painted. Still pacing. Still waiting for a God who looked like him to arrive and say, "Well done." But Heaven didn't send someone like that. It sent me. And I couldn't give him what he needed. Only what was true.

So I let him be. Not because he was right. Because he wasn't ready to be wrong.

I turned away. It would hold for now—not repeating, not sealed. Just clinging to a truth too deeply rooted to break on its own.

"Liam," I said, just once.

He didn't turn.

Didn't nod.

Didn't ask.

Outside, the golden plain shimmered one last time. A trick of light. A promise without an oath.

Cross Lake smelled like cinder and thawing rot.

The band office had collapsed inward, its neutral siding scorched black, the sign above the doorway half-melted. Across from it, ditches brimmed with slush and ash runoff, the edges still smoking where insulation had caught late. Overhead, the power lines buzzed, faint but steady, like they were trying not to notice.

I stood in the shadow of the wreckage.

No sulfur. No sanctity. Just belief—dense, exact, and settled like ash. The fire wasn't his doing, not directly. But it had his voice. Doctrine doesn't stain the scene. It hands out matches and waits for kindling.

I crossed Kichi Sipi slowly. The church stood canted on the other side, roof partially collapsed, bell long gone. A hymn book lay facedown in the slush, pages blistered and curling like they couldn't hold doctrine anymore. Burned pews. Broken statue. Altar dusted with ash and unspoken conviction. Not a riot—ritual.

Wâsakâmaskwa hadn't stayed. He'd led them to Thompson, lit the vision, then vanished the moment Heaven responded. Not fear. Strategy. Leave the martyrs to ignite the prophecy. Keep the prophet untouched.

Past the school. Past the houses that hadn't opened their curtains since the fires. No signs. No questions. This was a town holding its breath.

But belief leaves trails. Not physical. Not forensic. Metaphysical drift—like gravity turned sideways.

I followed it.

At the treeline, I found the house.

It wasn't hidden. It wasn't marked. It was simply there—waiting.

The house sat at the edge of the treeline, where the road gave up trying to be paved. Modest. Two windows front-facing, one boarded. Birch siding warped near the base, weather-peeled at the corners. Shingles missing. No sign of wealth, no sign of abandonment either. Just a house. Still standing. Unburned.

Smoke lifted behind it—low, steady, domestic in scale but not in tone. Backyard fire. Purposeful. Someone tending it.

I stepped off pavement and onto gravel.

Then—click. Behind me.

I didn't draw.

"You're late," I said.

"I'm here," Cyr answered.

She came up even with me on the road, hands empty, coat still perfect. Her eyes flicked to the siding, the window, the slant of the eaves. Then the smoke.

"Band office and church were acts of war," she said. "This one's something else."

I nodded. "Doctrine's birthplace."

We listened. Fire crackling out back. No voices. No footsteps. No run.

"He knows we're here," I said.

"He's not stupid."

"No. Just cornered."

"That makes him worse."

Cyr didn't argue.

We both looked at the same house from two angles. Same enemy. Same doubt.

"I take the yard," I said.

She didn't answer right away. Then, "I don't follow

your lead."

"Wasn't a request."

Another beat. Then, "Fine. I'll take the north side."

It wasn't a plan. It was a ceasefire.

We moved.

I came around the east side of the house slow, boots crunching the frozen debris. No birds. No breath. Just the crackle of paper that had once held purpose.

He was crouched low over the pit. Jacket open, sleeves rolled. A blade tucked in the snow beside him — thin, ceremonial, the kind you don't use for anything but meaning. Smoke curled from the logs. Pages flared orange and died in bursts.

I saw handwriting. Latin script. Precise. Sharp. One line caught the light before curling inward:

First wave indoctrination complete. Four accepted. Contingency failure at celestial arrival —

He tossed another stack in. Didn't look back.

Then he did.

Wâsakâmaskwa turned like a man trying to measure how far conviction could carry him. He wasn't dressed for travel. But his eyes held calculation, not surrender. Still weighing exits.

Cyr stepped into view, one hand loose at her side. No weapon drawn. She didn't need one.

He saw her. And I saw the decision collapse in his eyes. He wasn't getting out. Still, he reached for the blade.

I stepped forward. "You know that won't help."

He hesitated. The handle shook in his hand. The fire

crackled beside him. Doctrine burned.

"You were expecting us," I said.

"It was possible."

Voice low. Not broken. Not angry. Just *caught*.

"Why here?" I asked. "Why Cross Lake?"

His eyes flicked to me. No defiance. No remorse. Just the exhaustion of someone who'd sold the lie too long to pretend it was still sacred.

"Because belief lives longer when it's already been betrayed," he said. "They don't resist salvation when they know the world never meant to save them."

I stepped once toward the fire. The smoke shifted.

"What were you offering?"

"What they wanted. What they needed. The Great Plain."

Cyr circled. "And how many believed it?"

He didn't flinch.

"It caught like wildfire," he said. "The ones who heard it—really heard it—walk taller now. They eat better. Sleep without fear. Die without shame."

His eyes flashed. Proud. Committed.

"I gave them something to live for and something to die into."

Cyr folded her arms. "That's not faith. That's programming."

He tilted his head, almost amused. "Same outcome. Cleaner process."

She didn't blink. "You bypassed judgment."

"I bypassed inefficiency."

I watched him. Not the fire. Not the knife. Him.

"You changed their deaths. What about their souls?"

"They were never yours to begin with."

Cyr stepped forward, tight with disgust. "You rerouted four. Where are they?"

He didn't answer.

"Who are you working for?" I pressed. "What are you?"

He just smiled.

Cyr stepped in, voice low but sharp. "You're not human. Not entirely."

He didn't move.

"You pass for human, but your soul is twisted. Tampered."

He smiled. Just slightly. "I'm what I need to be."

Her fists curled.

"So you admit it?"

His eyes shifted between us. Calm. Undamaged.

"I admit nothing."

He stepped once toward the fire.

"You can't touch me," he said. Calm, almost amused. "You don't even know what I am."

I raised the gun.

He didn't flinch. His eyes stayed level. The fire snapped behind him like punctuation, but his voice didn't change.

"I know what that is. It won't help you."

Cyr didn't move. She watched me, not him. She didn't raise a hand to stop me. That was all the permission I needed—or all the permission I wasn't going to get.

I held the gun steady. Sighted him centre mass. I could feel the moment tightening—not just between us, but inside the world itself. The *Accord* wasn't a law. It was a force. If he was protected, I wouldn't be able to fire. The gun would lock. The shot would fail. The moment would hold.

"You can't lie if you're dead," I said.

He smiled. Not a grin. A soft, confident curl of the mouth. Like the test had already failed.

"Then it's a good thing you can't kill me."

I pulled the trigger.

The shot rang out hard. A full-bodied crack that split the quiet open. The muzzle flash flared, and the recoil hit my arm—but the barrel lifted just before I fired. A reflex. A tremor. A recoil, not from the gun, but from the weight of what I was doing. Because in the space between breath and consequence, I knew. This wasn't an execution. It was murder. A kill outside mandate. Outside judgment. Outside mercy. And my body remembered it faster than my mind did.

The round struck high—through the shoulder, clean exit. It spun him sideways and dropped him to one knee.

He screamed.

It was not the sound of a believer. Not pain in reverence. Just pain.

Cyr stared at me across the fire. Not shocked. Just still. Watching something she hadn't expected.

"You shot him," she said.

"I could," I answered. I wasn't looking at her. I was looking at him.

Wâsakâmaskwa touched his shoulder. Stared at the blood on his hands like it had broken something open. His breath hitched. His mouth worked once. And then the look changed. Not to rage. To fear. The kind that wasn't performative. The kind that didn't care who was watching.

It wasn't the fear of death. It was the fear of what he would reveal after death.

Then he moved.

Didn't hesitate. Didn't pray. Didn't offer a final word. Just jammed the ceremonial blade held in his hand upward, under his chin, through soft flesh and hard resistance in one steady movement, angled not for the throat but for the brain. His body locked, shuddered. Legs gave. He crumpled beside the fire, one hand still twitching, the other wrapped around the hilt.

His eyes stayed open.

He was still breathing. And whatever had lived behind those eyes—whatever plan, whatever conviction, whatever chain of knowledge connected him to the shape of the thing we were chasing—it was gone.

Dead?

No.

Worse.

Unreachable.

I dropped to my knees beside him. Felt for a pulse. Still there. Weak, thready. But he wasn't seizing. He wasn't present either.

Cyr crouched beside me. Her expression unreadable.

"Frontal lobe's gone," I said.

"Brainstem's intact," she confirmed. "He'll live."

"But he won't talk."

She nodded once. "Not now. Maybe not ever."

We both looked down at him.

A living body. A soul still tethered.

And a mind turned to smoke.

The bar had no name. Just the same flickering sign—OPEN missing its O, PEN blinking like it wanted to quit.

The air was stale with cleaner that didn't clean and heat that couldn't quite hide the cold. Behind the counter, the bartender wiped the same spot with the same rag like he'd been doing it since the war. No questions. No dispatches. Just background noise and a muted hockey game limping through overtime.

I sat near the back, nursing a glass that tasted like someone's memory of whisky. The kind of drink that burned on the way down, not because it was strong, but because it had nothing left to offer.

Mara was already there. Same coat, same silence. She didn't speak. She didn't ask. She just sat opposite me, letting the quiet say what neither of us needed to.

"I didn't kill him," I said eventually.

She nodded once, barely.

"But you tried," she said.

"I missed."

"You flinched."

"I didn't know I could shoot."

"But you didn't kill him."

"Not for lack of trying."

She didn't smile. Just leaned back slightly and let that be enough.

The door opened. Cold air rolled in. No chime, no greeting. Just the soft, unmistakable drag of hesitation. I didn't turn. I didn't have to.

Chandler stood in the doorway. He didn't shine. Didn't loom. Just stood there — too composed to be at ease. The hair, the coat — still immaculate. But the posture betrayed something. Like the weight hadn't settled. Like shame hadn't found its shape yet.

He looked around like he didn't expect to be welcomed. Saw us. Hesitated. He could have left. Could have waited for the next official review. Could have passed the file to someone else and stayed clean.

But he didn't.

He walked in.

Stopped at the edge of our table. Didn't sit.

Mara didn't speak.

I didn't offer a chair.

He looked at me, then down at the floor, then back again.

"I told them," he said.

"I know."

"They assigned me to Seraphine."

"I know that too."

He stood there a second longer, like he thought there might be a test he still had to pass.

"You came anyway," I said.

He nodded.

"Sit down."

It wasn't an invitation. It was permission. Barely.

He took the seat.

None of us spoke for a while. The silence wasn't comfortable, but it wasn't cold either. Just the kind of quiet that hangs around when no one wants to be first to break it.

"They're stuck," Chandler said finally. "The Cree. The ones from the detachment. Heaven can't process them. System reads them as valid entries, but the tether logic breaks midstream."

"Too much belief," I said. "Too little doctrine."

"They're in angelic Purgatory for now. Holding pattern. No claims filed."

"Good," Mara said. "Maybe we can reach them before the system tries again."

Chandler nodded. "One of the processors said the metaphysics were... anomalous. Called it 'echo drift.' Like the field's expanding inside them instead of decaying."

"They're still hoping," I said.

"That's what scares me," he replied.

He looked at me more directly now. Not like he was waiting for judgment. Just like he wanted to understand if it had already happened.

"What happened in Cross Lake?" he asked.

I told him the outline.

A false shaman. A human soul that wasn't. That the *Accord* didn't stop me. A body that stayed breathing. A mind that didn't. And four missing souls, taken—God knows where. If God knows anymore.

No one answered.

Behind the counter, the bartender changed channels. No one noticed. No one objected. The screen flickered again. Another game, another team, another set of rules no one had time to explain.

Chandler turned his glass slowly, watching the way the ice melted around the edges.

"God knows," he said.

He didn't look at me when he said it.

"And he's watching over you."

I didn't move. Didn't speak.

"He saved your soul today."

I looked down at my hands. The glass. The scars beneath the skin. The part of me that hadn't pulled the trigger— not all the way.

And I let that be enough.

CASE FILE: RAYMOND BOIVIN – part 1

Montreal. Rue Des Ormeaux.

At the end of the street, where the sidewalk forgot to finish and the city's snowplows never quite reached, sat the house. A squat, rectangular thing — split-level 1980s suburban, built cheap and fast, like most of that stretch. No landscaping. No fence. Just a sloped patch of dead grass, now mostly gravel, and a narrow driveway that curled inward like an afterthought.

I landed at the end of the driveway. Gravel crunched beneath boots that hadn't been boots a moment earlier. I shrugged myself into my earthbound form — bones reknit, weight returned — and took a breath.

The air here was blue-collar cheap. Not the stink of catastrophe, but the quiet, permanent kind of smog — the kind that never made the news. There was a low metallic tang, like rusted tools left out in spring. Factory breath. Salt from old plow routes. The faint, stubborn staleness of smelted something — aluminum maybe, or paint thinner — still lingering from some shuttered plant a few blocks too close.

You didn't gag on it. You didn't name it. You just lived in it. The kind of air that taught your lungs to take what they were given.

The house itself was boarded up. Not neatly. Just enough to keep squatters out — plywood tacked across the front window, door chained from inside. The siding had gone grey with sun, the trim paint cracked into flakes. One of the soffits hung loose above the porch, swaying when the wind remembered.

I walked up.

Three concrete steps, crumbling at the edges, led to a porch that didn't bother to creak. The screen door was long gone—not missing, just discarded, laid sideways against the vinyl siding, long discarded. The main door was solid wood, ugly and earnest, a leftover from the builder's catalogue. Someone had nailed plywood across it like a warning.

I didn't knock.

I leaned through—shoulder first. The wood parted easily. No flash. No noise. Only the quiet give of matter remembering I wasn't quite part of it.

Inside, the real was losing its grip.

Floorboards had warped. Wallpaper peeled in long curls. The kind of dust that only formed after years of silence—thick, settled, undisturbed even by mice. A chair with a broken leg had collapsed beside the kitchen table, its fall never heard. In the hallway, a photo frame had fallen face-down and no one had turned it back over.

But the echo didn't know that yet.

Inside the echo, the house was still tired—but clean. Not staged or restored. Just... kept, in that way smoker's places were kept—ashtrays emptied but never scrubbed, curtains washed once and given up on. The walls had yellowed into a kind of permanence. Couch cushions sagged where someone always sat, imprint never leaving. The floor had been swept, not mopped— grime pushed to the corners and left there.

The colours were wrong. Everything looked one filter too warm, like memory's nicotine stain. The clock ticked, but the time was always off. You could smell stale smoke in the drywall, like a ghost that didn't leave.

The smell of smoke got thicker the deeper in you went. Not burning — just the old kind, stale and lived-in, like breath that stayed behind. I followed the sound — a low, nasal drone cutting through static — until it led me past the kitchen and down the short hallway toward the living room.

The room opened soft.

One window. Heavy curtains drawn but not closed. A lamp with no bulb. Wood panel walls the colour of old varnish. There was a coffee table with deep scratches and cigarette burns that made a kind of pattern if you knew how to look. A felted ashtray still cradling every absence. And in the corner — an overstuffed chair, brown with fake leather armrests and a blanket that still remembered knees — sat Raymond Boivin.

He was watching TV. No fidgeting. No slack in the gaze. Just… watching.

The screen flickered blue and white, colours off by thirty years, casting holy shadows on the walls. Pastor Jean Thomlin, French Canadian televangelist, leaned toward the camera — his name stuck at the bottom of the screen. Slick hair, polyester suit, a crucifix big enough to pull a shoulder. He was pleading through the fuzz.

Raymond didn't blink.

He had a cigarette between his fingers, half-smoked, no ashtray in reach. Didn't matter. He was the kind of man who only ever needed one hand. The room hummed around him, warm and false. It was tired, yeah — but in a way that made you ache a little. Like maybe it would be enough. Chair. Smokes. God on TV. The sound of someone else trying.

I stepped forward.

"Raymond Boivin," I said.

He looked up, slow and without startle, like the name had taken a second to land. His face was all the years he had earned and none he had asked for. Broad across the jaw. Skin like old bark—weathered, smoked, and pulled tight where it used to be soft. Deep creases along the cheeks. Laugh lines that had never gotten used right. Eyes the colour of old coffee—dark, dulled, but holding heart. A bit of stubble. Not from neglect. Just because men like Raymond had never seen the point in shaving after five.

He blinked once. Didn't speak. Just watched.

I almost started the untethering—the rhythm I'd practised since long before television existed. The soft cadence of release, shaped for whatever century the soul remembered best. I knew how to say it. I knew what to offer.

But after a breath, I said, "Mind if I sit?"

"Bien, assis-toé."

Raymond's voice had the drawl of a man who'd earned the right not to rush. Smoked through. Soft at the edges. Language didn't matter here—it came out French, but I caught every word.

I took the seat across from him. The couch dipped under my weight, springs sighing like old bones. Ray didn't watch me. He watched the preacher.

"Que votre cœur ne se trouble point…"

John 14. The one about rooms. Jesus making space.

Raymond took a drag. Blew it slow. "Hope he's got a couch like this."

I let that hang a moment. Then said, "I help people pass on. Used to know how. Mercy, clarity, closure — that kind of thing."

I scratched my jaw. "Lately I've just been tired. And every time I asked for something bigger, they dumped a pile of easy ones. Like I was being punished for noticing."

Ray snorted. "Bosses. Same everywhere. You try to do it right, pis c'est toi qui mange la claque."

I nodded. "Yeah."

He glanced over, met my eye. "You don't look easy to manage."

"I'm not."

We sat a beat. The preacher raised his voice.

"Je suis le chemin, la vérité, et la vie."

"You're one of those easy files, Raymond. I'm here because you're dead," I said, gently.

Ray didn't flinch. Just nodded. "Ouais. Felt it when it happened. Same chair. Didn't hurt. Just kind of... stopped."

He tapped ash onto the tray's edge. "Figured I'd wait a bit. Yvonne's always late."

He gave me a look — not defensive, not proud. Just open. "T'es pressé?"

I shook my head. "No. Not in a hurry."

And I wasn't. Not here.

Raymond smoked like it was prayer — long inhale, short hold, exhale through the side teeth like a man who'd made peace with fire.

The preacher had moved on now, into something louder. Something final. But it wasn't the preacher talking anymore. It was Paul.

Now we see through a glass, darkly…

Raymond mouthed along. Knew it by heart. "…but then, face to face."

"I've always liked that one," I said.

"Moi aussi. Makes you think, huh? How much you don't know till it's too late."

I nodded. "Heaven's not just comfort. It's… exposure. All of it. Perfect knowledge. No edits. No excuses."

I glanced around the room. "This echo—what you've built here—it's almost holy. Soft light. Familiar chair. Preacher on the box. It's not fake. It's true."

I paused.

"But it's not free."

Ray shrugged. "Nothing is."

I looked up. "Heaven doesn't charge admission."

Ray chuckled. A tired, scratchy sound. "Maybe not. But I always figured I'd sneak in on Yvonne's coattails. You know? Hold on tight, let her do the convincing."

He flicked ash into the tray, missed it by a mile. Didn't care. "Truth is, I wasn't much. Swore too much. Smoked too long. Skipped mass after the priest died. I loved her, though. Always. Just figured I'd go where she went."

I nodded, slowly. Then held out a hand. "Got another?"

Raymond didn't hesitate. Pulled a crumpled pack from the armrest and tapped one loose.

I took it. No ceremony. Just need. He lit it for me. I

inhaled.

The TV buzzed louder for a second, like it was trying to cut in. But the words didn't land. We were past doctrine now. Just two men, smoking in the space between sentences.

"She's not coming, Ray."

He looked at me, dead-on. No flinch.

"She's already gone," I said. "Clean. Quiet. Long time ago."

He shook his head. "Non. I'd feel it. If she passed through, I'd know. My heart would've said something." He tapped the centre of his chest. "Right here, tabarnak. I'd feel it like a nail."

He believed it. And belief was a kind of anchor.

"She's not in the echo," I said. "No sign of her anywhere. Not in the walls, not in the corners. No trace."

Raymond watched me. Smoke curled from his lip, unblinking. Waiting.

I shifted forward, elbows on knees. Flicked ash that didn't land anywhere.

"I pulled her file," I said. "Yvonne Boivin. Died in 2010. Five years after you. Lung cancer. Same as you, probably."

He didn't move. Just breathed in.

"She didn't do treatment," I added. "Didn't want it. Stayed home."

I glanced at him. "Stayed herself."

Raymond nodded. Once. A small motion, tight at the neck. "Sounds like her."

I didn't say the rest. Didn't tell him the file was closed early. That it read Protocol: Damnation in dry celestial script, fifteen years resolved. No appeal. No tether left. I just sat there, smoking a dead woman's brand, beside a man who didn't know he was waiting on something that had already fallen.

We sat in the glow.

The evangelist's voice creaked like old vinyl, but Raymond watched like it was fresh. Like the sermon had just aired. Like the sermon was new every time.

"C'est nouveau, ça. Haven't seen this one."

I didn't correct him.

Onscreen, the preacher flipped his Bible with performative reverence, pages rustling like leaves in a hush. *Et je vis un nouveau ciel et une nouvelle terre…* Revelation again. Chapter 21. A new Heaven for you. The first had passed away.

Raymond nodded, pleased. "I like this guy. Doesn't yell so much. Feels like he means it."

I took another drag. Looked at the screen. The preacher leaned in. The camera flickered.

Heaven's not fire, or clouds, or clean slates. Not just.

Psalm 16:11—fullness of joy, pleasures forevermore. Comfort that doesn't run out.

Raymond settled deeper into the chair. The fabric creaked under the shape he'd made.

I should've pressed him. Pushed the tether. Started the break. Instead I watched. With him.

"He says it like he knows," Raymond murmured. "Like he's seen it."

I nodded. "Some of them have. Some saw just enough to lie with style."

He chuckled. "Still better than most priests."

The preacher shifted again. Jeremiah now—thirty-one, thirty-three.

I will write my law on their hearts... I will be their God. And Jesus, whispered in subtitles: I will come again and receive you to Myself.

I looked at Raymond. Not a saint. Not a mystic. Just a man.

He watched like it was truth. Not the words. The cadence. The promise behind them. Like maybe, if he sat there long enough, she'd walk through the door and bring Heaven with her.

I sat a while longer. Smoke gone cold between my fingers. Raymond still watching, half-smiling like the preacher was talking just to him. I was supposed to unstick him. Walk in, say the words, loosen the soul, guide the tether to its rightful end. That was the shape of it. This was supposed to be an easy one. But now? I wasn't sure I could persuade him. And worse—I wasn't sure I wanted to. There was a kind of holiness in his waiting. A man who loved someone so much he'd rather stall eternity than go without her. That wasn't a fault. That was a vow.

I stood.

Raymond didn't move. Just offered the end of the cigarette he hadn't lit yet.

I shook my head. "Next time."

"Toujours la bienvenue." Always welcome.

I nodded.

Stepped back through the room — past the cracked linoleum, the kitchen with its fridge still humming 2005. The door was still boarded up. No latch, no handle. Just planks nailed into a shape that said: not for you. I phased through. No grace in it. Just motion and refusal. The wood accepted me without splinter.

The world outside blinked once — light harsh, air thin, gravel unforgiving.

I'd need to pull more files. Dig deeper. Check the records. Cross-reference the tether.

Maybe find out if love really counted as resistance.

For now, I left the house on Rue Des Ormeaux the way I had found it: boarded up, but not abandoned.

The precinct was quiet when I got back.

Not silent. Just that Heaven kind of quiet. Where nothing hums, but everything listens. A hallway with no echo. A light with no heat. A desk that knows when you're lying.

I didn't mark the case resolved. I didn't mark it at all.

I sat.

Not because I needed to. Just because it was time to stop moving.

Then I pulled the file. Not his. Hers.

Yvonne Boivin.

Died 2010.

Closed.

No dispute. No delay. No flag.

I don't know why I opened it. Instinct. Guilt. Something older.

Everything was perfect.

Protocol: Damnation.

Date of death: April 3, 2010.

Location: Montreal, Rue Des Ormeaux.

Cause: Lung cancer. Died at home, alone, watching television.

Disposition: immediate.

No resistance. No delay. No echo. No need for agent dispatch. No tether to assess. Protocol handled it. The file was tight. Trim. Exactly what it should be.

I read it again.

No discrepancies. No variance. Every field filled.

I flipped to the decision block. The cell where damnation is confirmed. There it was. Final.

"Disposition: Protocol Judgment – Destination: Hell."

Clean.

I checked for pre-processing flags. Anything to indicate friction before the passage. Nothing. No deferral request. No note of conscience. No conflict. Not unusual. Not for a Protocol case. But the further I searched, the flatter it felt. The more consistent, the more controlled. Everything matched. Every record in central. Every retrieval in threshold. No contradiction. No drift.

I should have stopped there. But something stayed in my teeth.

I left the precinct and went down to the Archives. It breathed. Dust without time. Shelves without echo. Memory held not in pages, but presence. I searched her line. Pulled her shelf index. Laid hands on the binding. Everything matched. Case file. Death trace. Judgment form. Stamped in Heaven. Carried through. No supplements. No complaint. No countermand.

Nothing was missing.

I left the Archives with nothing in my hands.

Rue Des Ormeaux called to me.

Didn't mark the time. Didn't file a request. Just went.

The echo-space welcomed me like it had the first time — low ceiling, stale light, the soft hush of memory curated into permanence. Dust motes drifted where nothing ever stirred them. The television glowed in the corner, blue and constant. Still tube, still humming. Still Jean Thomlin, leaning forward with that polished warmth, like someone's uncle who went too far into the ministry but never lost the tone for bedtime stories.

Ray didn't look up.

Didn't need to.

I moved to the couch, lowered myself into the sag without a word. The springs sighed the same way they had before. Familiar. Not creak — *sigh.* Like the furniture was grateful someone still used it.

Ray sat across in the same armchair. Cigarette between two fingers. Filter end gone wet. Smoke curling from the tip like incense. He didn't offer me one.

I didn't ask.

We just watched.

"...for I go to prepare a place for you," the preacher was saying. Thomlin's voice floated—half French, half King James, wrapped in old tape hiss. "And not just any place, beloved. Not just a house. Not just a city paved in gold. No—*your* place. Tailored. Measured. Fit to your soul like a robe woven by the Lord's own hand."

I leaned back. Didn't speak. Didn't move. The air was warm in the way car interiors are warm in winter—recycled heat, shallow but sufficient. You could fool yourself into thinking it meant comfort. Like God was close. Like love was a blanket.

I exhaled.

Maybe I'd been wrong to keep chasing the jagged ones. Maybe clarity was overrated. Maybe the world didn't need more unraveling.

Ray flicked ash to the floor. Missed the tray by a foot.

I looked over. He caught my glance, offered the pack from the side table without words. I took one. He lit it. No ritual. Just habit. Two men smoking in a room that didn't age.

The couch cradled me.

Jean Thomlin kept preaching.

"The Lord does not send sorrow to test you. He does not delight in your pain. He is preparing joy—fullness of joy. Psalm sixteen, verse eleven: *In thy presence is fullness of joy; at thy right hand, pleasures forevermore.*"

I took a drag. Let the smoke settle in my lungs, let the words drift over me like lullaby.

Nothing was sharp. Nothing demanded. Thomlin didn't

shout. He caressed. Soft syllables, wrapped in certainty. The kind of message that doesn't teach — it reminds.

"I do not come to condemn the world," Thomlin said, "but to save it. And not by might. Not by fear. By desire. That which your heart longs for — that is the key to Heaven's gate."

I blinked.

Let it go.

Thomlin was holding a Bible, but not reading from it. He flipped pages with one hand while the other gestured wide, crucifix swinging from his neck like a pendulum. "It is written," he said, "*Delight yourself in the Lord, and He will give you the desires of your heart. That is His promise.*"

Psalm thirty-seven.

But it didn't sound right.

I squinted, leaned forward slightly.

"*I go to prepare a place for you.* John fourteen. You know this verse. I've preached it a thousand times. But let me tell you what it means. It means the place of your desiring will be prepared. Your wife's love. Your children laughing. Your favourite season. You will not suffer. You will not hunger. No sin. No judgment."

I sat upright.

Ray didn't notice. Just watched. Happy. Whole.

I turned toward the screen. The picture flickered slightly — not distorted, comfortably degraded. Familiar.

Thomlin continued: "There is no judgment in Christ. Only welcome. The gate is open. Come home."

I whispered, "That's not the verse."

I watched harder now. Passivity and gentleness stripped away. I *looked*.

The air grew thicker.

I looked down at the cigarette in my hand. Half-burned. Cold at the tip. I hadn't felt it go out.

Ray laughed softly. Not at me. At a joke from the screen I hadn't heard.

Thomlin raised his Bible again.

"*Let not your heart be troubled.* That's what He said. You believe in God—believe also in me. That's the truth. That's the whole of it."

I waited.

Waited for the rest.

It didn't come.

The verse was wrong. I heard it in my head—*and if I go and prepare a place for you, I will come again and receive you unto myself, that where I am, there ye may be also.* That was the end. Not the place. *The presence.*

Ray still smiled, faint at the corners.

But I sat rigid. Because that message hadn't been written by God. It had been selected. Curated. Refined. A Heaven that asks nothing. A mercy that knows no weight. A house without the builder.

I stubbed the cigarette out on the heel of my shoe. The ember flared once, then died.

Stood slowly, already cursing myself. Because instead of rest, I needed to get back to work.

I needed to find Jean Thomlin.

Weston, Massachusetts.

Old wealth. Quiet money. The kind that doesn't scream, just reshapes bylaws until silence becomes a virtue. No strip malls. No flashing signs. Just curving roads and stone walls and driveways long enough to forget who you used to be by the time you reach the door.

I arrived under fog—thin, curated fog, like the air had been told to soften its outlines before greeting the neighbours. The houses here didn't crowd. They perched. Each on its own sculpted rise, behind hedges clipped to judicial precision. The kind of street where you didn't see the home until it wanted to be seen.

Thomlin's wanted.

The gate came into view around the bend: wrought iron, nine feet tall, bracketed in stone. Every vertical slat polished. The arch above spelled out a monogram— **JT**—in bronze too thick to feel ornamental. Motion sensors tracked my approach. Cameras blinked into posture.

It was locked.

I stepped forward.

Didn't knock. Didn't ring. Just moved through.

The gate offered no resistance. No shimmer, no pulse. Just a soft reminder that mortal metals don't know how to say no to me.

The driveway was long. Curved like a compliment. Clean asphalt, trimmed with decorative stone. Lawn on either side manicured to obsessive symmetry—every blade of grass the same length, every shrub a sermon in restraint. Hydrangeas lined the outer beds. Pale blue.

No petals out of place.

And at the far end, glass.

The mansion wasn't old. It was *new*. Not faux-historic, not wood and limestone pretending to belong. This was modern aggression—angles, planes, sharp lines of reinforced transparency. The whole front wall was glass. Framed in gunmetal black. Reflective, not inviting. The wings of the house arced outward like an embrace rehearsed too often. Five-car garage set flush into the base. Topiary flanking the entrance. Somewhere north of ten million, even with the real estate crash.

I walked up the steps.

Brushed no dust. Left no prints.

The front door was opaque, composite, and unnecessarily thick. No handle—just a touch panel glowing faintly blue beside the camera mount. Stainless steel, no visible wires. Too refined for retail. This was custom security—built not to keep thieves out, but to reassure the ones already inside.

I pressed the ring.

A chime echoed inside—deep, elegant, half a piano chord. A beat later, the door cracked open.

She looked about fourteen or so. Dark hair, pale skin, a velvet bow pinned at a precise angle. She blinked at me with wide brown eyes. Curious.

I opened my mouth, but I could speak, the footsteps came. Sharp, deliberate, heels on hardwood. And then she appeared behind the girl—Lucille Thomlin. Not just beautiful. *Finished.* Hair straightened into architectural severity. Makeup airbrushed to subtlety. Dress mid-thigh, pale cream, fabric that didn't wrinkle. She moved with the smooth certainty of someone who paid people to tell her the weather. Maybe thirty-five. Maybe older. It didn't matter. Time didn't apply here.

She smiled.

Calm. Measured. Composed.

"Can I help you?"

I gave her the smallest nod. "Sal. I'm here to speak with your husband."

Her eyes scanned me—coat, posture, presence. She didn't find anything she could name, but she found enough.

"Of course." She opened the door wider. "Come in."

Inside, the foyer bloomed outward. Vaulted ceiling. White oak. An inset chandelier sculpted like falling water. Light reflected on stone tile polished to a shine I could see my past in.

The house didn't smell like anything.

No perfume. No disinfectant. Just the whisper of air, precision-filtered by Swiss design.

On one wall: an abstract cross, minimalist steel, set into marble. On another: a framed certificate—Doctor of Divinity, Jean Thomlin, Honourary, dated five years before his first broadcast. Below it, a photograph. Thomlin with three presidents. Lucille with a First Lady. The girl—Marie—on someone's lap, centre-framed like the future already knew her name.

She gestured toward a hallway that disappeared into a wing of the house.

"I'll let him know you're here."

The footsteps faded. A door closed somewhere deep in

the winged belly of the house. Lucille was gone.

Marie remained.

She stood by the foyer's edge—just far enough to be polite, just close enough to surveil. Posture good. Not perfect. Hands clasped, then released. One foot turned slightly inward, then corrected. A girl trained to be watched.

I didn't speak.

She did.

"You're not a friend."

I tilted my head, faintly. "No?"

"Friends don't come to the front door." Her eyes flicked to the security panel. "And they don't make the chime do that."

I nodded slowly, as if conceding a valid theological point.

"You came for him," she added.

"Seems that way."

She stepped a little closer. Black leggings, school-logo hoodie two sizes too big. Hair tied back in a way that said *I do this myself.* Her face was still in-between—baby-soft at the cheeks, but her gaze was older. Too still.

"My father doesn't take appointments."

"I'm not an appointment."

"Then what are you?"

I let the pause hang.

She crossed her arms. "You're not police. You don't *look* like police."

"I get that a lot."

Her brow creased. "So how'd you get past the gate?"

I offered a thin smile. "It wasn't trying very hard."

She blinked at that. Twice. The silence that followed wasn't comfortable.

I gestured gently to a nearby alcove—plush bench, sculptural plant, some kind of ambient light panel shaped like a sunset. "Do you live here full-time?"

Her eyes narrowed. "Where else would I live?"

"Some kids your age board. Prep schools. Conservatories."

"You think I'm in a conservatory?"

"You look like someone who could be."

She wasn't sure whether to be flattered or insulted. She settled for suspicion.

"What's your name?"

"Sal."

"That short for something?"

"Not anymore."

She frowned. "You always answer like that?"

"Only when it works."

She bit the inside of her cheek. "You're weird."

"I know."

Silence again. But not the same kind. She was thinking.

Then: "Do you believe in Heaven?"

A curveball. Not out of curiosity. Out of pattern. Something rehearsed.

I met her eyes. "I believe in consequence."

She flinched. Didn't mean to show it.

I watched her shoulders. "Did your father teach you that question?"

"No," she said, too fast.

I said nothing.

She shifted. "He just says… people need hope."

I nodded. "And what do *you* need?"

She didn't answer.

Instead: "Are you here to hurt him?"

"No."

"Are you here to help him?"

"That depends."

"On what?"

"On whether he's the one who needs help."

Another beat.

Then I tried: "He's your father?"

She hesitated. Almost imperceptible. Like a skipped frame.

"Yes," she said. "Obviously."

"Obviously," I repeated, gently. "You two close?"

Her eyes flashed. "Why wouldn't we be?"

"Some families drift."

She bristled, just enough to confirm it. Then dialed it back.

"He's not like that," she said. "He's been through a lot.

But he's… stable. Steady."

"Been through what?"

She paused.

"Just stuff. Life stuff. Trauma. You know."

"Do you?"

Another flash of defiance. "I know enough."

I nodded again. Almost a bow.

"Thanks," I said.

"For what?"

"For being honest when it wasn't required."

She didn't answer.

But she didn't leave either.

Then, softly: "You don't look like one of his."

I tilted my head. "One of what?"

"The people who believe."

I looked past her, toward the cross inlaid in marble. "Maybe I just believe differently."

She studied me, long and hard. Then turned her gaze toward the hallway her mother had vanished into.

Footsteps returned. Measured. Pacing meant to sound unthreatening. But there was a hesitation in the cadence—half a beat caught between instinct and performance.

He looked almost exactly as he had on TV, twenty years ago.

The polyester was gone—replaced by bespoke slate wool, the kind that repels dust and opinion. His shoes were soft leather, hand-stitched. The soles didn't echo. A platinum watch rode his wrist—understated, but obscene. No tie. No collar. Just an open collarbone and the kind of calm only money or doctrine can afford.

But it was the same man.

His hair had thinned, just slightly, still sculpted into televangelist geometry. Eyes sharp—not with light, but polish. Skin too smooth. Cheeks taut. Jaw carved clean. Not ageless. Just… exempt. Like time had passed around him, not through.

The smile arrived late. Like warmth was a setting he enabled, not a state he inhabited.

And when he spoke, it was with the kind of voice that once begged from pulpits but now only answered to donors.

"Marie, ma belle—go help your mother, will you?"

She hesitated. Then left. Trained, at least when it came to him.

Thomlin waited until she was gone. Then stepped forward.

Hand outstretched. Smile wide. The one from broadcast.

"Can I help you, Mr…?"

"Sal," I said. "Just Sal."

"A minute of my time?"

"That's all I need."

He turned. "Come in."

The corridor was quiet, paneled in matte walnut. Lights recessed and warm, like a womb built for rich men's secrets. At the end: a pivoting glass door, brass-rimmed.

He palmed a sensor. It sighed open.

His study was theatre.

Not a book in sight—just display volumes, cream and forest green, titles gold-foiled for show. A smoked-glass wall opened onto a vertical garden and courtyard sculpture. The lights above were shaped like ascending rings. The desk was wide enough to host a summit. Chair behind it: molded leather, neurosurgeon ergonomic. Two guest seats: untouched, showroom-pristine.

He gestured to one.

I didn't sit.

He did. Folded his hands over a notepad he wouldn't write on. Posture perfect. Breath paced. Not relaxed—regulated.

"So." A slight shift of weight. "What can I do for you, Sal?"

"Just following a name. Yvonne Boivin. From Montreal. Died 2010. One of your followers."

"Not followers. *Believers*," he corrected. Then, "I don't recall the name."

"Think again."

A flicker—nothing more. "Sorry."

He paused. Tilted his head.

"You're not civil. Not state. Certainly not local." His smile thinned. "So what exactly are you?"

I didn't blink. "Let's talk about your church. Your gospel," I said. "Salvation without merit. Grace by desire. Heaven… on demand."

He reached for a pen. Didn't click it.

"My message is simple," he said. "God meets us in our desires."

"You teach that *desire is God*."

A pause. Measured. Not offended—alert.

He leaned back. "Is that why you're here? To debate theology?"

"I'm here for Yvonne. Her soul is missing. And your church was involved."

I was just testing a theory, but he bit.

He sat forward. "If you've lost a soul, perhaps your gospel is not working any more."

"We didn't lose her. She was taken."

"Perhaps you should be thankful."

"Thankful that you denied a soul ascendance?"

He didn't deny it.

"Do you know what she asked for?" he said quietly. "Her last prayer?"

I said nothing.

He smiled. "Maybe you should."

Then he caught himself. A blink. Breath reset. The faintest retreat behind the eyes.

He opened a drawer. Took out a small silver bell. Didn't ring it. Just placed it between us on the desk like a metaphor.

"Obviously, I don't know what you are talking about. We've not denied anyone anything."

"You're lying," I answered. "And Yvonne was a victim.

I just don't know why you are doing it."

Another pause. He studied me.

"You're not what I expected," he said finally.

He smiled again. Tighter. "My guess? You're here unofficially. And if you are, maybe your superiors aren't eager to know what you're chasing."

He stood.

"I don't remember Yvonne Boivin," he said. "But if she believed in me, she's in paradise."

The door hissed open.

Two men stepped in. Suits. Civilian clothes. Built for extraction. Earpieces. Compact stance. Eyes already calculating reach and weight.

"I've been generous with my time."

I nodded. "You haven't."

He glanced at them, then back at me. "May I see your card?"

"You already know who I am."

A longer pause. Then: "Unless you're police, you're trespassing. And even if you are—no warrant, no cause."

I didn't flinch.

He smiled wider. "You've some wild ideas, Sal. You should come to your senses before you get hurt."

I let the silence stretch. Held it.

Then stepped back.

"We'll find her," I said. "Even if your gospel can't stand the light."

The Archives wait below the precinct, but not beneath it. They're not lower. Just older. A place folded out of time, where memory settles in bindings and breath doesn't echo. No signs. No catalogue. No stairs. Just descent—the kind you feel in the chest more than the feet. You don't see your shadow in the Archives. You see your intent.

I didn't log the entry. Didn't request clearance. Just walked until the floor forgot to echo and the walls stopped watching. The Archives knew what I wanted.

I moved by instinct—past the shelves of unspoken judgment, past the bound volumes of saints who'd never been canonized. I wasn't looking for a saint. I was looking for a man who'd convinced a million people that God wanted their comfort more than their change.

Jean Baptiste Thomlin.

The presence of his record came before the volume itself—like heat before fire. I followed the weight of it to a green-bound book on a low shelf, already half-warm under my hand.

I opened to the first page.

Ordained 1986. Diocese of Rimouski. Transferred to Matane. Sermons described as "quiet, pastoral, unremarkable." No formal censures. No ecclesiastical tension. Just… the shape of obedience.

May 12, 1993. A weather advisory had been issued. He borrowed a sailboat anyway. Took it into the Saint Lawrence alone. The next entry didn't arrive until May 14—"Returned barefoot. Silent. No memory."

That line had a pressure behind it. A tremor, like the

Archive itself hadn't believed him.

Defrocked one year later to the day. May 12, 1994. No inquiry. No note of struggle. Just release. Rome stamped it. No name on the approval. No pen stroke. Just a decision, clean and floating.

He moved south. Reappeared in Texas in '98 under a new name and a new denomination: *The Free Salvation Fellowship*. Registered as a charity. Bought broadcast space. Built a pulpit out of camera angles.

I felt it then. The pattern I hadn't wanted to name. Arthur Pell. Died; came back wrong. Burning Bear. Heart stopped in a sweat lodge; came back wrong.

And now Thomlin.

All altered by death. All returned with a message. All too consistent.

I turned the page. One last image had been pressed into the folio—a photograph, faintly lifted into view by the metaphysical residue of relevance.

Yvonne.

Gaunt. Emaciated. She was outside. A gathering. Folding chairs. A sun canopy stretched wide behind a plastic pulpit. A banner overhead read, *"Free Salvation Fellowship – Prayer Retreat for the Sick and Elderly."*

Date: April 1, 2010. Three days before she died.

A sun dress. Cross around her neck. Face too thin. Smile too fixed. The kind of photo that gets used in testimonials. *We prayed. She passed peacefully.*

I closed the volume.

It was probably a sin to doubt the record. If it was, I'd carry it.

I still had no reason to disbelieve Heaven's records. But I didn't believe them.

And I knew where the answer would lie.

There was one place left to ask.

One archive that recorded what Heaven refused to see.

Hell.

CASE FILE: RAYMOND BOIVIN – part 2

You don't walk into Hell. You *agree* to it.

The *Accord* doesn't forbid entry. There's no clause that says we can't go to Hell. How could there be? Satan's still an angel. So are its architects—fallen, yes, but not severed. The bones of Heaven are buried in Hell—and Heaven knows it.

What the *Accord* says is simpler. Cleaner. If we enter uninvited, we are not protected. No enforcement. No consequence. No reprisal—only risk. We become fair game. No sanctuary clause. No sovereign immunity. A celestial soul in Hell without sanction isn't just trespassing. It's meat.

I knew they would kill me. If they cut me down, there will be no protest.

I went anyway.

It began not with fire, but with silence. The kind that judges. Not a hush, but a verdict. Like signing a confession unread. Like stepping forward when the blade is already halfway in.

There is no spiral. No slope. No stair. Only gravity, remembering who I am. And it drags.

I fall without falling. I pass no border. The threshold is moral, not spatial.

Heaven did not follow.

And Hell remembered me.

It rose—old, bright, burning. The last time I stood here, I hadn't come alone. I came with command. No precinct.

No *Accord.* Long before Jesus. Back when it was wings and war.

We struck the first circle like judgment descending, spears of light leveled against the breach. We were not there to speak. We were there to purge. A thousand of us, blade-born and silver-sung, drove into the pit where the traitors regrouped.

I don't remember the battle. Only the aftermath. Only the way it ended—not with conquest, but with silence.

We didn't win—we just stopped.

And then the memory passed, and I was through.

I stood at the edge of something that never closed. An aperture that widens with precision, not hunger. Obsidian stretched outward in every direction, flat and empty. No wall. No pillar. No edge. Only distance—the kind that shrank you by standing still. Light didn't land here. It hovered. Soft, directionless, wrong. Enough to see the stone. Enough to see the drop.

There were no doors. Just a throat, yawning downward into Hell's first ring. The drop curved—a hollow descending in perfect symmetry, cut into the underside of the world. As if reality had been cored open to its final trespass: betrayal. And it glowed from below. Not with fire. With consequence.

The light rose up like shame—amber, dirty gold, with the thickness of old flame trapped under glass. It pulsed—once. Like something was breathing slow beneath the rings.

The first circle was visible. Not far. But not near. A ring of ivory walls, thirty feet high, made not of stone but bone—fused, calcified, yellowed to parchment by heat and silence. The surface wasn't smooth. It was ribbed, pitted, scarred like the inside of a skull. No doors. No seams. Just bone, shaped into a circle, leaning inward.

Fog clung to its base. Low. Thick. Unmoving. Not mist, but memory made visible. The ground inside looked flat—too flat. No dust. No cracks. Just absence. No sound came up from it.

But I felt it: a silence that knew my name.

I didn't move. Not forward. Not down.

The maw surrounded me—black, vast, etched with judgment.

And I waited. Because Hell doesn't need an invitation. It just needs to notice.

The maw did not stay still. It began with vibration—low, deep, like the pit itself had taken a breath through its teeth. No sound. Just the tremor of anticipation, rising through the stone in pulses too slow to name. The grooves beneath my feet warmed—not with heat, but with pressure, like something unseen was pushing upward from deep below, one increment at a time.

The first thing I saw was a shape behind the fog. No sound announced him. No motion led his path. He did not walk. He approached, like verdict incarnate.

Not crowned. Not horned. Clothed in justice the way a tomb is clothed in stone.

He stood taller than any man—nine feet at least, though the scale of him seemed to shift with the gaze. His frame was humanoid, but only in outline. Broad shoulders draped in extinguished fire—ashy grey, marled with smoke-veins. It didn't billow. They hung, heavy and still, like burial linens soaked in verdict. His skin was white—not pale, but chalked with the finality of stone, the kind you can't carve deeper. His arms were long, unnaturally so, hands clasped before him with fingers jointed too many times—less crafted than broken into place. His eyes were set deep—pinhole pupils in a field of matte white. They didn't glow. They didn't twitch. Pupils that didn't track light, but *guilt*.

Around his waist coiled a single cord of bronze—thick, hammered flat, looped three times, and fused without clasp. No symbols. No inscription. But too perfect not to be a weapon. It didn't dangle. It hovered, one inch above his robe, waiting to be thrown.

He did not speak. He did not breathe. He simply stood. And counted. Like he was weighing mass and meaning at once.

Not invited. Not protected.

Still alive.

Then the tremor changed.

They didn't arrive. They ruptured.

The air behind him split open without resistance—not torn, but *peeled*, like wet parchment pulled from bone. And through it came the Furies.

All three. Alecto. Megaera. Tisiphone.

Their bodies were vaguely feminine—long-limbed and doubled at the joints, like a marionette pulled wrong. Each stood on two legs bent backward, heels sharpened to talons. Their torsos were wrapped in flayed sinew. Four arms each—two thick and corded, two thin and grasping—moved independently, like spiders remembering rage. Their nails were long, threadlike, glowing faintly orange at the tips—as if each finger ended in a fire. Their wings weren't wings. They were blades with membranes—tattered arcs of cartilage and rusted edge, serrated, folded tight to their backs until they opened. Blank skin like burned paper, charred at the folds and cracked with red. Mouths too wide. No lips. No tongue. Just rows of teeth—human at first, then lupine, then sharded into something that had never chewed flesh so much as *proclaimed retribution*. Their eyes were coals, socketed in too-deep skulls, glowing without flame. They didn't blink. Didn't track. Only locked on.

And then they shrieked. But it wasn't sound. It was a scream made of feeling—loss sharpened into filament, flayed into the frequency of regret. It didn't enter the ear. It bypassed the body entirely and drove itself into the spine. Like punishment sharpened to grief. They saw me and dove.

Minos raised one hand. It wasn't mercy. It was procedure. The Furies twisted mid-air, arrested in their charge, wings wide like netted lightning. One spat. It hissed through the air and steamed on the obsidian.

They wanted blood. Not just because I was angel. Because I'd killed one of theirs. Not exorcised. Not redeemed. Obliterated. Melvin Stokes didn't descend— he was erased. And in Hell, that's sacrilege. I hadn't just broken protocol. I'd humiliated them. Denied them their sentence, their spectacle, their order. Now I was a name carved on every infernal wall. Marked. Not with fire, but with promise. They would not forget. Not this year. Not this age. Not until my wings were torn and ground into the same dust I'd denied them. To them, I wasn't a trespasser. I was a traitor who hadn't died properly. And that debt would be paid.

Their wings beat without wind. Their mouths stretched

wider. They had come to collect. And I was out of reach of the *Accord*. Only the law of Hell held them back. And that law was standing very, very still.

I bowed my head—not in submission, but ritual.

"Minos," I said.

No answer.

His gaze didn't shift. It weighed.

"I come under no banner."

Still nothing.

The Furies began to circle—slow and wide. They prowled, arcing around me in an orbit of judgment, wings half-flared, joints twitching, each movement calibrated to remind me I was not protected. Not a threat. A promise. They were waiting—for permission, or for one misstep that could be called an excuse.

A slow judicial breath.

"I seek entrance by petition, not force."

The bronze cord around his waist shimmered—just barely.

Then, finally, Minos spoke.

"Sael. Not forgotten."

The word thudded like a dropped gavel. Not a greeting. A registration.

"You know why I've come."

"You do not."

That stopped me.

"Try," I said.

A silence. Then, "You seek Cyriacus. There are

questions you cannot answer without the aid of Hell."

"Yes."

The Furies blinked, just once, in sequence. A slow spiral that pressed the air into verdict. Wings half-flared. Talons flexed. Every motion a countdown.

Alecto moved first—measured, mechanical, her steps precise as liturgy. Her head tilted, neck cracking once, eyes pinhole-wide and glacial. "Uninvited. Unshielded," she whispered. "Let precedent be restored."

Megaera followed, limping with joy, her shoulders twitching in delight at the scent of guilt. "He calls it mercy," she spat, dragging a claw through the air as if carving open a past betrayal. "He struck down one of ours and felt *righteous*. Let me have his name. I will wear it raw."

Tisiphone came last. Silent at first. Then a low exhale—gravel and dust, not breath. "There was no ash," she murmured. "No soul to claim. No blood to measure. He erased what we were meant to end." Her mouth didn't move with the words.

They swirled in tight formation now, mouths flexing open, wide and wrong. One voice, three mouths:

"Let us devour him."

But still Minos held them. He spoke again. "That is not why you are here."

"Then tell me."

"You are here because Heaven cannot be trusted."

I did not deny it. There was no point. Hell does not guess. It remembers. It does not accuse. It records. There are no lies in this place—only sentences waiting for their time. And mine had already begun.

The Furies didn't laugh. But their mouths widened.

"I need access," I said, voice flat. "Your records. Death trace logs. Hell-forged contracts in the last twenty years. Anything with her name."

"You seek a soul already judged."

"Yvonne Boivin. 2010. Recorded as Protocol damnation. No tether. No resistance. No appeal."

Minos didn't move but something happened behind his eyes.

"She is not yours."

"Prove it."

"That's why I'm here."

"No."

That word hit hard.

"You are here because your heresies are no longer safe in Heaven."

I looked up.

Met his eyes fully.

"Invite me," I said. "Or unleash them."

The Furies leaned in. Teeth bare. Talons bright.

Minos was still. Then, "Enter. But know this." His voice had weight again. Cosmic and cold. "In Hell, truth is not what you find. It is what you bleed."

The Furies screamed—not in triumph, but in denial. A howl of thwarted judgment, of rightful violence denied its hour. The sound hit the stone and didn't echo—it *bit*.

Wings thrashed. One claw scored the dark. Another spat flame that wouldn't catch. Their vengeance had been promised and revoked, and they screamed not to punish me—*but Hell*. Then, wrenched back by force older than wrath, they vanished into the dark like blades withdrawn mid-swing.

Minos said no more. He did not move. He did not need to.

The stone behind me cracked—not loud, not sudden. A seam opened in the obsidian, too straight to be natural, too slow to be safe. From it emerged a figure cast in human silhouette, but emptied of resemblance. He was tall, but not towering. Slender, but made of weight. His flesh, if it was flesh, had the hue of dead marble: bluish, grey, as if carved from something that once lived and forgot how. His eyes were holes—no glow, no iris, just sockets blackened not by emptiness, but by purpose. His mouth did not open. His jaw was too fused for speech.

Charon.

He wore no robe. Nothing does, here. Only a shroud of dust clung to him, draped not from above, but from within. And across his shoulder he bore the hammer—not a weapon, but a sentence. The kind used once, without appeal.

He did not gesture. Just turned.

I followed.

Hell doesn't need guards. Its paths guard themselves. The stone we walked on wasn't laid—it *accepted* us. Each step sank a fraction too deep, like we were walking over breath held too long.

There were no torches. The light bled upward from the

floor—amber, pulsing, like a bruise under glass.

We passed the first wall without fanfare. Behind it, I saw them.

Souls.

Naked, yes—but not in flesh. In essence. Every part of them was visible, not to the eye, but to judgment. Their regrets hung from them like second skins—folds of unspoken apology, unacted mercy, unfinished truth. None screamed. Not here. Not yet. They moved in loops—some clawing at the same closed door, others running through forests of blade-leafed trees where every branch whispered their name. They were not tormented. They were *revealed*. And that was worse.

Charon walked without pause, without glance.

To the left, a chapel split in half by some unseen quake. Inside, a soul knelt before a cracked altar. Her back was torn by wings that had never formed, only ached. Her hands were raised—not in prayer, but in accusation, though her mouth was sealed with gold. She couldn't speak. That was her damnation.

To the right, a field of bodies—intertwined, confused, tangled in some impossible orgy of guilt. Not erotic. Not joyous. Just desperate—grasping for contact they'd refused in life. They clutched, missed, clutched again. A thousand hands. No embrace. No end.

Above them hung a painting that had no frame, no brush—just a resemblance. *The Garden of Earthly Delights*, inverted and alive.

The path narrowed. No walls now. Just suggestion. Just echo. A man we passed was split from forehead to pelvis, opened like a book. He stood. Still breathing. Still aware. His sin wasn't murder or theft—it was *certainty*.

The cut showed it: every belief he'd clung to laid bare and wrong.

Charon never turned.

At last, the path flattened. A chamber opened—not a room, but a basin carved into the earth, shallow and wide. The stone here was darker. It didn't pulse. It *absorbed*.

Cyriacus.

She *emerged*—like doctrine bleeding out of iconography too old to be canon. A thing remembered by paintings that got it wrong in every detail except the dread.

Her skin was the colour of scorched clay, fissured in places, as if her body had endured a kiln too holy to extinguish. Light didn't reflect off her. It *leaked* from within—faint, deep, like the glow in the cracks of a punishment too ancient to name. Her limbs were long, famine-thin, elegant in the way executioners are elegant when they don't miss. Her back arched with unnatural grace—not bent, not posed, but inscribed. Her wings unfurled behind her in serrated arcs—tattered, webbed, lion-boned, and vulture-hinged. They didn't flap. They flexed. Like a courtroom rising to pass sentence. Each motion rearranged the air.

Her expression held no wrath, no mercy, no thrill in the work. It was expressionless the way a verdict is expressionless. Her eyes were glass. Cold, reflective, calculating. No flame. No glow. Only exposure. They didn't look at me. They measured me.

She didn't look at me when I entered. She didn't have to.

"Outrageously bold, even for you, Sal."

"Yeah. Probably." I stopped three paces from the basin's edge. "But it's not like I can call ahead. And this is bigger than either of us."

Cyr's wings flexed — twice. Not for threat. For silence. "Then speak."

"I need a name looked up in your records. Yvonne Boivin. October, 2010."

She turned. No gesture. No summon. The stone behind her peeled like a document unrolled. A flare of law — Hell's version of recall.

"Confirmed," she said. "Yvonne Boivin. Cardiac arrest. 4:07 a.m., Montreal, Quebec. Disposition: Protocol."

I waited.

Cyr's eyes flicked once, left to right. Reading what wasn't visible to me.

"Ascension," she said. "Not Hell-handled. Not ours."

And the world didn't shift. I did. It landed like oxygen in lungs that hadn't believed in air. Like a blasphemy I'd whispered for years and now heard echoed back in scripture. I had doubted. Suspected. Questioned the record, the precinct, even Heaven itself. And every time, I told myself it was fatigue. Grief. Pride wearing the face of discernment.

But I wasn't wrong. She wasn't ours. She hadn't been damned. She'd been taken.

I exhaled slowly. It should have felt like clarity. It didn't. It felt like stepping off a ledge and finding ground that shouldn't be there — and realizing too late that someone built it. And not for us.

"That's impossible," I said.

But it wasn't.

Not anymore.

Cyr didn't speak. Just raised one hand.

The air folded. She wove a cone of absence so tightly around us that even Hell held its breath. It wouldn't last. It never did.

"Hell doesn't do privacy," she said. "But we can speak plainly here for a brief moment. Until it is discovered."

"Then let's waste nothing," I replied. "Both our records are wrong. Yvonne didn't ascend and wasn't damned. She was claimed. And not by us."

Cyr nodded. "I've been tracking anomalies," she said. "Since before Elias. Since before *you* noticed. Minor discrepancies. Small enough to file. Too small to prove. Demonic count has been off—minuscule deviations. Just a soul here, a soul there."

"You're losing demons? How is that even possible?"

"It shouldn't be."

"Over how long?"

"A century or two. Maybe more."

I hesitated.

"What?" she said.

"I had a case," I told her. "Marysia Zielińska. Kraków. Died in 1850. Burned twice. First by accident, then by accusation. We found her in the ruin of a church—no tether, no echo, just presence. Aware. Composed. Like someone had *prepared* her."

Cyr's posture changed—only slightly. A stillness that meant attention.

"She spoke Latin," I said. "Too old. Too clean. Said it like scripture in the mouth of a child. Described a pale man—long coat, grey hair, not local. Said he came before she died. Said he put a voice inside her. A voice that *didn't burn*."

"Possession?"

"No. No trace. No flare."

Cyr didn't speak. She didn't need to.

"She died," I continued, "but she wasn't mortal anymore. Something in her had changed. And whatever it was—Heaven couldn't take her. Hell couldn't claim her. And she couldn't leave."

"Splice," Cyr said. "Soul integrity compromise."

"You've heard of such a thing?"

"In whispers and dark corners. Didn't believe it. The human soul is sealed. Anything that breaks that is heresy—by definition."

"Marysia said the voice faded. I think whatever was inside her—whatever he put there—burned out. Not violently. Just... dissolved. Like it couldn't hold. But it left its shape behind. And now she's neither what she was nor what she should have become. Whatever happened, the system still reads her as whole. But she isn't."

"Changed," Cyr said. "Like Elias Shaw. Gerry Wiles."

"And Arthur Pell," I added.

I knew she didn't like me talking about Melvin Stokes, but I pressed on. "Arthur died in Iraq. Confirmed KIA." I paused. "Two months later, he bought a car in Hamilton."

Cyr said nothing.

"No resurrection variance. No trace. The file was closed. And then he came back—not just breathing, but registered. Mortgage. SIN. Tax. It wasn't a haunting. It wasn't a return. It was continuation. But something had changed."

"And Heaven missed it?"

I nodded.

"When I found Melvin, I thought it was demonic possession. But it wasn't. The shape held, but the source was wrong. No tether. No memory resistance. And when I tried the exorcism—I found nothing beneath. The soul wasn't possessed. It was overwritten."

"And Elias Shaw?"

"He wasn't broken. He was *finished*. Too still. Too aware. He didn't belong to the world anymore, but he didn't pass. He wasn't stuck. He was resolved. He just forgot his purpose."

Cyr considered. "You think they were built."

"I think it starts with a mortal soul," I said. "Death. Or near-death. Something changes. Not a possession. Not a warp. It's cleaner than that. Seamless. Like someone found a way to finish them—replace, rewrite, or refine—I don't know what it is. Just that the system reads them as whole. Too whole."

She stared at me. Hard. "And you think it's all related."

"It's not us," I said. "Not the *Accord*. These cases—Arthur, Elias, Gerry—they weren't failures. They were field tests. Versions. Failed or functioning. Serving a purpose."

She folded her arms. The room around us remained sealed, barely.

"The real question," I said, "Is not what they are, but why?"

She was silent for a beat.

"Then we're not looking at error," she said. "We're looking for design."

"Intent," I corrected.

Her wings flexed.

I thought of Burning Bear. The ritual. The four who vanished. The fifth who stayed behind, watching the prairie for a promised plain that never came.

She was thinking the same. She folded her arms. "So where are they?"

"I don't know," I said. "But I have a lead."

Cyr tilted her head — not a question. An instruction.

"Jean Thomlin," I said. "Televangelist. Clean death spikes. Broadcast theology so polished it gleams. Viewers don't just believe — they *prepare*. And when they die, there's no tether. No delay. No fight. They pass straight through."

"And you're sure they pass?" she asked.

"No," I said. "I'm sure they don't stay."

Her voice was quieter now. Not gentler — just sharper. "No grace. No judgment. Just heresy."

The silence in the sealed cone thickened — not with weight, but with pressure. The kind that builds before someone breaks something on purpose.

"We expose the lie. Yvonne's records. The double claim.

We trigger review. Internal. Inter-sphere. Doesn't matter. Get every archivist and intake auditor chasing the anomaly. We put Heaven and Hell on the scent."

Her eyes narrowed. "And what if the scent leads up?"

"Then it leads up," I said. "Let it."

She didn't look away. "You don't know how far this runs. Neither do I."

"That's why we expose it."

Cyr's wings flexed. Not agreeing or disagreeing. Just a stillness. "You want to ring the bell. Hope someone still hears it. Hope they care."

"I want to make it impossible for them not to."

She was quiet. Too long.

"You have a better idea?"

"No."

"Then help me."

"No."

We stood there, each knowing the veil around us was seconds from collapse. Every moment, someone else was being *rewritten*.

Cyr exhaled—slow and precise. "You do this, you won't be walking back into Heaven. You'll be walking into a verdict."

"I've done that before."

The veil cracked—slightly. The cone of absence began to breathe again.

Cyr looked away.

She didn't stop me.

She didn't follow.

Hell doesn't wash off. It lingers — like soot you can't see, but still feel. Doors that once opened before you now waited. Air that once parted now resists.

The precinct did not greet me. It tolerated me.

I crossed the threshold.

Not much had changed. The walls still held their patient pressure, their suggestion of judgment in repose. But something in the atmosphere had cooled — an absence of welcome, not warmth. I felt it in the tilt of the corridor, in the angle of Mara's shoulders as I passed.

She didn't look up.

Her hands kept moving — sorting, reviewing, committing names to memory — while her gaze stayed fixed on the page. Intentional.

I stopped beside her. Didn't speak.

She turned the next page with the precision of someone who had already decided not to hear what I might say.

Still no glance. But she said, "You went down."

Not a question.

"I needed to."

"No angel has set foot in Hell for two thousand years. And you weren't cleared. And…" Her voice caught. "I thought maybe you wouldn't come back."

That hurt. The worry. Too often, I forget that someone still cares.

"I'm here."

"Not for lack of trying."

"I'm just trying to get the truth."

She looked up then. Really looked. Like she wanted to believe me. And maybe, in that flicker, I saw how far gone I was.

I turned toward my desk, but I knew before I reached it.

The file was gone. Yvonne Boivin. Gone.

I stood still for one long breath. Then walked back.

One word. Quiet.

"Camael."

The door to his sanctum wasn't locked. It waited—no invitation, no automation. Just a slab of judgment inset in seamless light. I placed my palm flat against it.

Nothing.

Then a click. Not mechanical. Just… permission. Like the room changed its mind.

Inside: three chairs. One desk. Yvonne's file.

Seraphine stood. Chandler sat stiff. Camael remained behind the desk, half-silhouette against a light that didn't throw shadow. They had arranged the geometry with intention. This wasn't a tribunal. It was an excommunication with courtesy.

I didn't wait for cue or summons. Walked in.

"You took the file," I said.

No one replied.

I stepped forward. I didn't ask to speak. I didn't wait for sanction. I laid the words down like a blade.

"There is an enemy working against us."

Camael's expression didn't flicker.

"Originally, I thought it was Hell. Now I'm not so sure. But whoever and whatever it is, it has been around for centuries—moving beneath us. Undermining the *Accord*. Working around it. Working to replace it."

Camael's voice was stripped of interest. "Give us facts. Not theory."

I nodded once. Fine.

"Amira Pell. Her husband never came back. A man lived with her for fifteen years, but he was a counterfeit. Seamless. Inserted. No trace."

Seraphine's voice came flat—unimpressed. "There is no proof."

"Melvin Stokes is the proof. He walked out of a mortal life and rewrote himself. Changed his name. Changed his history. Became a preacher—one who told people death was the path to salvation. That's not the work of a broken loader from Hamilton. And when I tried to exorcise him, there was no soul. No residue. A possession where the host had been overwritten entirely."

"You destroyed the soul," Camael said, tone judicial, cold. "Before Heaven or Hell could claim it. The absence of trace is yours to answer for. That is not proof of fabrication. That is evidence of recklessness."

"Marysia Zielińska. Spliced soul. Part human. Part demon. Not possessed. Not corrupted. Engineered. And unable to ascend for centuries."

"The human soul cannot be spliced," Camael replied. "It is indivisible by creation."

Chandler's voice broke in, soft between them. "She said she gave up long ago. That's on us. Our failure doesn't mean she was counterfeit."

I didn't argue. I pivoted.

"Elias Shaw. A broken counterfeit celestial. Not a ghost. Not a man. Not a demon. He died in the crash, but didn't vanish. He remained—whole, aware, unclaimed. The system saw him as complete. But he wasn't real."

Seraphine's jaw didn't move. Only her eyes did—cutting.

"Speculation," she said. "You are assigning ontology to something you do not understand. That is error, not insight."

I started pacing. My voice didn't rise. But it moved.

"Maeve Lin. Not born. Not inserted at death. Folded mid-life into an existing mortal narrative. Passing as a nurse. Guiding hundreds of deaths through MAID. No flare. No signature. Just clean, seamless counterfeit."

"Fantasy," Camael said. "Conjecture."

"Gerry Wiles. Glitched Purgatory. Spoke of resets. Memory across deaths. Reinitialization. Not confusion. Not madness. A different system. One not ours."

Camael didn't even shift weight. "Your belief in reincarnation is noted. It is not endorsed."

Seraphine now, voice cut to bone. "This is blasphemy. To suggest that Heaven and Hell are obsolete is to renounce your place in both."

I turned to face them. I wasn't asking anymore.

"Frank Stephens. His case was breaking free. The loop dissolving. Then it vanished. Echo-space gone. File marked Resolved with no initials. No seal. No closure note. Falsified."

Chandler's voice was almost pleading. "You took him most of the way. He did the rest. Not everything has to be a plot."

I stared him down but didn't speak.

"Wâsakâmaskwa. Living counterfeit. Woven into existence. Complete with memory, doctrine, intent. He preached martyrdom. Designed a ritual. Led souls into a counterfeit Heaven that accepted them—without judgment."

Camael's voice flared for the first time—sharp as steel unsheathed.

"Facts are not wild conjecture. The fact is that a spiritual leader of the Cree people is now in a permanent catatonic state. Because of your interference."

The words landed harder than I expected.

For a breath, I felt it—the weight of the body we'd left behind. His stillness. The ritual undone by force. The followers who died believing he'd take them home.

He wasn't innocent. But the ruin still bore my fingerprints.

I let it ache. Then locked it down. Because this wasn't about guilt. This was about what he proved.

They stared at me—stone-faced, the three of them. No movement. No breath. Just the silent geometry of judgment arrayed across the room. Camael's hands were still. Seraphine's gaze was a scalpel. Chandler's eyes—down now—refused to meet mine. I knew then that nothing I could say would reach them. Not now. Maybe not ever. The facts didn't matter. The patterns didn't matter. The missing didn't matter.

Only obedience.

And I was long past caring.

I wasn't here for their permission. I wasn't here to be believed. I was here because the world was being rewritten, soul by soul, and they were too busy guarding the language to notice the silence spreading underneath it.

I turned back to them, voice rising now, raw at the edges.

"Jean Thomlin. Not just a man. Not just a preacher."

They didn't move.

"His broadcast shapes expectations, not just beliefs. You don't understand—he's not warning them. He's priming them. Verse by verse. Smile by smile. Scripture bent just enough to produce compliance."

Still nothing. Not a flicker.

"Millions reached," I snapped. "Every week. No resistance. No flare. No doubt."

I stepped closer. My hand trembled.

"He's not saving anyone. He's softening them. Smoothing them. So when the enemy agents arrive, when their counterfeit Protocol comes—they go."

They watched me like a contagion.

"He prepares them for seamless counterfeit ascension," I said. "And it's working."

Camael didn't blink. "This is proof of nothing. A false preacher does not change judgment."

I looked at the file. It looked back—just ink and paper

and everything they refused to see.

Then I hit the desk. The echo rang. The file slammed down—weightless in hand, but heavy in what it meant.

"Yvonne—She's the proof. Right there. Right in front of you. All you have to do is get the records. Open them. Compare."

I leaned forward, both hands on the desk now.

"Don't believe me?" I shouted. "Ask Hell! I did. She was taken from Heaven, and we stand here… doing nothing!"

Silence.

Three faces. Stone. Cold. Perfect.

They weren't rejecting evidence. They were rejecting what it would mean to believe it.

And that's when I knew.

They didn't need more proof.

They needed me gone.

Camael didn't rise. He didn't need to.

"You entered Hell without authorization," he said. "You present demonic data as evidence. You stand here as one who broke the *Accord*."

"Because the *Accord* is already broken," I said. "You just haven't looked."

Seraphine turned her face away—not out of mercy, but finality.

"These claims are heresy."

Camael's sentence fell like stone.

"You no longer speak for the Threshold Division."

I waited for Chandler.

He didn't speak.

He just looked away.

I drew a breath. Quiet. Final.

"Then strip it," I said. "If this blindness is Heaven, I want no part of it."

I turned.

The door opened for me this time.

Light did not follow.

I wasn't supposed to be here. Not anymore. No badge. No seal. No role.

But the echo let me in.

The house on Rue Des Ormeaux still held its shape. Still bowed in the same places, sagged in the same bones. Still stale with smoke that didn't burn anymore. Still humming with memory, rerun as comfort.

The television buzzed, low and bright. Pastor Jean was mid-sermon, gesturing with an open Bible he didn't read from.

Ray sat in the chair. Same chair. Same posture. Cigarette burning slow between two fingers, the filter dark where he held it too long.

He looked over as I entered. No surprise. No curiosity.

"Tabarnak," he said softly. "You look tired."

"I am."

He nodded toward the couch. "Bien, assis-toé."

I did. The cushions gave beneath me, worn into

welcome.

We didn't speak for a while. Thomlin filled the silence — Psalm 37, bent toward promise.

Raymond smiled faintly. "J'aime celui-là. Il donne espoir."

"Got myself fired," I said.

He didn't turn. Just took a drag and blew it sideways. "Bon. Les boss, c'est toujours les mêmes. Tu fais les choses comme faut, pis c'est toi qui manges la claque."

"I don't know what I am now."

"Same as before. Just with less bullshit."

I looked at him. He still hadn't moved. Still watching the same preacher say the same half-scripture like it was new.

"She's not coming, Ray."

He blinked once. "Qui ça?"

"Yvonne."

He frowned gently, like trying to remember an appointment he hadn't written down. Then he shook his head.

"Non. Elle va venir. Elle est juste… toujours en retard."

His voice was kind — not defensive, just sure. The way some men are sure the Canadiens will win next year. The way you believe a thing not because it's true, but because it *should* be.

I nodded.

"I'll find her," I said. "Je le jure. I don't know how long it'll take. But I'll find her. And I'll bring her back."

Ray smiled. Still faint. Still whole.

"She va venir," he said again. "Faut juste attendre."

We sat there for a while. Smoke curling. Light buzzing. Pastor Jean repeating his truth, steady and sure, as if conviction could make it real.

Outside, the snow didn't fall. It just settled. Like time wasn't moving anymore.

And maybe it wasn't.

UNFILED

Earth. Night. Doesn't matter where. Could've been any city—smelled like piss and bleach and regret. One of those bars where no one asks names, and you drink beside people pretending they aren't waiting to die.

I picked the stool that backed the wall. Habit. Third from the end. I used to care about exits, about angles. Still do, maybe. Or maybe I just like pretending something still needs watching.

Glass in hand. Cheap rye, warm and wrong. The kind that doesn't burn going down—it just stays there. Coats the ribs. Stains something permanent. I drank like I was trying to burn the faith out of me. No rush. No panic. Just steady. Measured. A ritual with no redemption.

No one said my name. The bartender stopped looking at me after round three. Just poured, wiped, moved on. He knew the type. Didn't belong. Didn't stay. Just another ghost, drifting.

On the TV, a muted anchor mouthed a headline about something burning. West coast, maybe. Or a bishop. Hard to tell without sound. Didn't matter. It was all burning. Every righteous thing. Every covenant. Every promise Heaven ever sent down and asked us to carry like it still meant something.

I heard myself whisper. Didn't mean to. Just happened.

"Was any of it ever real?"

God didn't answer. Neither did the angels.

Chandler didn't answer. Neither did she. None of the souls I'd failed. Or freed. Or broken. Just silence. Silence and rye.

I drank again. This one fought back. That was good. Pain meant I hadn't gone fully numb yet.

I pulled the coat tighter. Not against the cold. Against collapse. To keep the pieces of me from spilling out on the floor.

I'd worn that coat through every storm Heaven forgot to name. Through blood and ash and fire that smelled like sin. It was part of me. Like the badge used to be. Like the halo I didn't wear anymore. That badge was gone. Not revoked. Irrelevant. Like a sermon with no ears left to reach.

Another drink. My hand was steady. That scared me more than shaking would've.

Eventually the barkeep spoke. Said we were closing. He didn't say *go home*. Just *closing*. Like he knew I didn't have a place to return to.

I nodded. Left some bills. Couldn't remember if they were real or not. Didn't care.

Outside, it was raining. The kind of rain that didn't wash—just blurred. Like the world was trying to smudge itself out and start over.

I walked.

Didn't know where. Didn't need to. Just walked. Past churches—locked. Past alleys—open. Past reflections I didn't check.

Because if I looked, I knew what I'd see.

No man anymore. Not even ruin. Just scaffolding—held together by unfinished rites and orders that never reached their end.

Sleep didn't come, not really. Food, same story—just

enough to keep me in motion. Room to room. Street to street. Bar to bar.

Nothing shifted. Not the weather. Not the weight in my chest.

A week, maybe more. Time blurred. Not metaphysically. Just plain old Earth time. The kind that doesn't wait for miracles.

I stopped using my name. Didn't speak unless I had to. Paid cash. Slept in a different place every night—crumbling motels, basement couches, once in the back of a church van behind a shuttered cathedral. Woke up cold. Woke up tired. Woke up wondering why I kept waking up.

The rain came and went. So did the people. A woman asked if I needed a priest once. I laughed. It came out wrong—dry and bitter. I told her I used to be something. That was the truth. She asked if we could pray together. I said no.

Didn't tell her why.

Didn't tell her what I was afraid would come out.

I stopped drinking to forget. Started drinking to balance. Too sober, and the grief cracked open. Too drunk, and the floor disappeared.

I kept thinking of Ray. Still in his loop, waiting. And Frank, gone. And Yvonne, scrubbed clean from every record like her name had never mattered.

I kept thinking: maybe Heaven didn't make mistakes.

Maybe Heaven just didn't care anymore.

I watched a woman get hit by a car and didn't intervene. Saw Protocol pass her over. Saw the tether start to form.

Walked away.

Not my case.

Not anymore.

No precinct. No orders. Just the memory of them.

Eventually—I don't know what snapped.

Wasn't rage. Wasn't hope. Wasn't even clarity.

It was just this: I looked in the mirror of a gas station washroom and didn't flinch. Not because I liked what I saw. But because I recognized it.

A man no longer under Heaven's jurisdiction.

And I knew what that meant.

I could still act. Still dig. Still burn.

But it would cost me.

And maybe that was the point.

Somewhere, between lost footsteps and lost hope, the thought came: *You know what you have to do.*

I stopped. Didn't agree. But I stopped.

Looked up. Let the rain hit full.

And I said, not to God, because He'd stopped showing up, "Then why'd you leave me like this?"

No answer. Of course not.

But the silence—that I could believe in.

I didn't wake up with clarity.

Didn't get the thunderbolt. No call. Just the thought again, quieter now, *You know what you have to do.*

And I did.

Not all of it. No map or clear vision. Only the next step. The crack that had to be pried open.

I wasn't ready. Still smelled like whisky and cheap soap. Still felt like something Heaven had scraped off its boot.

But I went anyway.

The threshold took a breath when I crossed it.

Not a welcome—an allowance. Like even the precinct wasn't sure it had the authority to stop me. Like Heaven itself was holding its breath, trying to decide if I still counted.

Maybe I didn't.

My body didn't shift.

Not fully.

The air should've peeled me clean—should've burned away the coat, the fatigue, the mortal stink. That's what the threshold always did. Rewrote you into purity. Into function.

Not this time.

My coat stayed. Heavy. Wet. Stained at the hem.

The stubble didn't recede. The weight didn't lift. My boots still left marks on the floor.

And my wings—

They came, but not with grace. No light. No sanctity. No purpose. Only return. Half-wrought. Phantom outlines curled behind me like memory done badly. Feather and flesh grafted over fatigue. A trench coat with wings. Like a relic of grace worn wrong.

I wasn't celestial.

I wasn't mortal.

I was both. Or neither.

Like the body I wore on Earth was more honest than anything Heaven ever shaped me into.

Didn't check if anyone was watching. If they were, they didn't move. Or maybe they did and chose not to be seen. Either way, the corridors bent like they always did — shifting by intent, not design. And my intent was sharp now. Focused. Cut-glass clarity beneath the grime.

The Archives breathed. Still dust without time. Still presence without echo. Shelves that didn't just hold records — they held judgment. And they knew who I was. What I'd become. They didn't stop me either.

I didn't go to my section. Didn't go to any section I was cleared for. I went deep. Walked past the line where names start getting rewritten, where case codes run longer than the alphabet can carry, where memory gets filed not by date or death but by drift.

And I asked for him.

Jean Thomlin.

The Archives obliged. Without kindness. But they gave.

I found his record. Saw what had been sealed. What had been marked private, buried, rearranged. A death date with no body. A resurrection with no miracle. A rewrite with no author. And then I traced the thread. Not in the pages. Not on the shelves. In the air. In the presence. *The Free Salvation Fellowship.* Dozens of names. Pastors, evangelists, online gurus. All with the same curve to their theology — mercy without friction, comfort without cost. Some flagged as legitimate. Some with ghost files I had to coax from the margins.

I pulled them.

Didn't check if it would be noticed. Already knew it would.

I pulled the full thread. A doctrine-shaped contagion, mapped out in human names. I didn't file a requisition. Didn't leave a trace. Just closed the record, stuffed the paper into my coat, and walked.

I made it to the outer corridor before she was there.

Mara.

She didn't call out. Just appeared, like she'd been following since the first turn and only now decided to be seen. Probably had.

"Your status is revoked," she said.

She wasn't being cruel. It was a statement of fact. Like telling a man the sun had set.

I didn't deny it. Just showed her the list. Names. Dozens of them. A whole pulpit gospel worth of poison.

"What are you going to do?" she asked.

I didn't answer. Because I didn't know. Because knowing meant admitting it wouldn't be sanctioned. Wouldn't be allowed. Wouldn't be survivable.

She looked at the list. Didn't touch it. Didn't ask for proof.

Then, without a word, she brought it into view. Held it carefully. Like it might still burn.

My halo.

No light. No orbit. Just form—bare metal, engraved with memory. Intact. Untarnished. Still bound to a name that no longer fit me. She offered it. Both hands open. Neither order nor mercy. Just the possibility—like grace thrown toward someone too tired to reach.

"Come back," she said. Soft.

I stared at it. It looked smaller than I remembered. Didn't reach for it. Didn't move.

"You still believe," she said. "Or you wouldn't be here."

She was wrong.

I didn't believe. I *knew*. That was the difference. I *knew* what Heaven had allowed. What it had ignored. What it had buried. Faith was for the innocent. For the obedient. For the ones who still thought obedience was holy.

Whatever I had left wasn't faith. It was something older. Rougher. A kind of sacred defiance.

"It's too late," I said.

She didn't flinch.

"It's not," she said. "That's the lie. That it's too late. That the door has closed."

I looked at her then. Really looked.

And I knew she meant it. Believed it.

But I also knew this: The door might still be open. But the man who used to knock is gone.

She offered it. My halo.

No flare. No hum. Just a loop of truth I used to wear without shame.

I didn't want it. But I took it.

Not out of hope.

Out of memory.

It felt heavier than it should. Not in weight—but in lineage. The power inside it wasn't present. It was ancient. Buried. Like an oath sealed in iron, older than words. It knew me. Knew my shape. My service. My fall.

I felt anger then. And resolve. And something else I couldn't name.

The power began to glow. Faint at first. Then brighter. Then it flashed—not like radiance, but like recognition. Like it saw what I had become.

Then it burned. White-hot. Not on the skin—beneath it. In the marrow. A holy heat, like justice misapplied. I didn't drop it. I let it burn. The metal cracked. Split. Turned black, then grey, then to ash. Fell apart in my hand without sound.

Not broken—undone.

Mara took a step forward. Stopped. She understood.

So did I.

The *Accord* was unbreakable. I'd believed that. We all had. A covenant—divine and absolute.

It governed every celestial, every infernal, every soul. Defined what was allowed. Who could act. Where. When. Why. But that was only after.

There had been laws before the *Accord*.

Covenants before the Covenant.

Origin law.

Prelapsarian permissions. Rituals older than rebellion. They were never revoked. Only sealed. Buried beneath mercy and protocol and the illusion of peace.

But they were still there.

And I had just invoked one.

Not by intention. By inheritance.

I looked at the ash in my hand. Watched it scatter.

Looked at Mara.

"Tell them," I said.

Then paused.

No rage. No hatred now. Just a grave clarity.

"I release my vow."

Heaven did not strike me down. It let go. No fury. No trumpet. No sword. Just release. Like a system purging corrupted code. The light around me folded in—creased at divine angles—and the floor dropped. I didn't fall. I was removed. Torn away. Unstitched from the place that used to know my name.

The landing wasn't clean.

I hit Earth hard. Hard enough to split concrete. Hard enough to taste copper. Hard enough that the air howled—like grief with no name.

I lay there for a moment. Not exactly stunned. More like, taking inventory.

Everything hurt. But it was still me. More or less. The coat was there. Burnt at the edges. The ash of the halo still clinging to my palm. But something had shifted. Not broken—rewritten. I wasn't celestial anymore. Not in the way I had been for millennia.

But I wasn't just mortal either.

I was something else.

Something not authorized. Not sanctified. But still active.

I sat up. Spat blood. Or grace. I wasn't sure which.

Reached into the coat. Pulled the list. Unfolded it slowly. The names were still there, written in memory and ink that didn't obey earthly rules. I looked at the one at the top. Spoke it aloud.

"Pastor Nolan Creedy."

Folded the page. Stood. Made a vow in truth beneath the ash.

"The reckoning starts now."

UNFILED: NOLAN CREEDY

No address.

No road.

Just coordinates.

The Lazarus Foundation didn't advertise. No billboards. No search engine optimization. No word of mouth unless the mouth had a net worth in nine digits and a cardiologist on speed dial. It wasn't a clinic. It was a *sanctum*—a place for the super-rich to spend their final days in curated serenity while securing an afterlife designed to their liking. Cryonics was just the pitch; salvation was the product. Customized. Commodified. Guaranteed.

I used the website.

Filled out a request form under a false name. Jonathan Hale—legacy consultant, discreet spiritual transition advisor, fictitious but well-tailored. I made a donation large enough to raise no red flags and trigger every courtesy protocol they had. Flagged it urgent. End-of-life incoming. Claimed I wanted to preview their full services *in anticipation of a high-profile referral network.* That was enough.

They accepted.

No one questioned the timing. No one asked for proof of illness. That's how you know the system's broken— not when you have to fake credentials to get in, but when belief is the only credential that matters.

The helicopter dropped me on a landing pad so clean it

didn't echo. Brushed steel set into a plateau of marble and hemlock. The rotors hadn't stopped before the pilot turned away—eyes down, engine hot. No greeting. No delay. Just procedure. This place didn't do arrivals. It did ascensions. The retreat itself rose from the mountain like it had always been there—stone and glass folded together like a cathedral drawn by an architect who'd never prayed. No crosses. No scripture. Just curves. Serenity by design.

I stepped forward.

Hair cut short. No more weight in the curls. Dressed clean—luxury casual in slate and bone. Soft cashmere. Tailored fit. Audemars Piguet on the wrist, visible just enough to do the talking. I looked like someone they would let in.

I didn't look like me.

But I carried the coat anyway. Folded over one arm. Like something too sacred—or too damned—to leave behind.

The door opened without touch. Silent. Seamless.

Inside, the air was warm, filtered, precise. The scent was engineered: cedar, lavender, just enough clove to hint at velvet and ritual. Every surface whispered wealth. Not opulence—*restraint*. The kind of money that never has to prove itself.

Reception waited ahead. A desk with no corners. A woman in cream silk with skin like broadcast marble. She smiled the way a luxury app does when it knows your name.

"Mr. Hale," she said. "Welcome to Lazarus."

She didn't ask for ID.

Didn't blink at the coat.

"Your orientation specialist will meet you shortly. Until then, please—make use of our pre-transition amenities. We're honoured to receive you."

She gestured.

Hallways opened like promises. Spa suites. Memory salons. Chapel-like chambers with light-soaked walls and curated music tuned to resemble a hymn's afterimage.

Clients weren't visible. Not unless they wanted to be. Every experience here was bespoke—curated down to who you might pass in a hallway. I hadn't completed the full preference suite on the intake forms, so they defaulted me to solitude. No accidental encounters. No shared air. Just me and the architecture.

But the silence had weight.

You could still feel them—just beyond each frosted pane and whisper-closed door. Not sick. Not dying. Just prepared. Rich, rested, and fully indoctrinated. You could sense it in the air itself: the quiet certainty that they'd paid for something no one else could reach. And maybe they had.

Everywhere I looked, the message was the same:

You will not be judged.

You will not be forgotten.

You will be preserved.

And somewhere inside this sanctified mausoleum of breath and belief—Nolan Creedy.

The hallways didn't echo. They didn't need to. Everything here was designed to receive, not reflect.

Lighting adjusted as I walked—softening to match a biometric guess at mood or intention. The floors weren't carpeted, but they *muffled*, like someone had engineered the silence to behave. The walls didn't hold art. They held expectation. Subtle visuals pulsed in the marble—abstracts that looked like neuron diagrams or constellations if you blinked too long. Scripture for the future-literate.

Most doors were closed. Some had small brass insets beside them—"Legacy Capture," "Neurological Calibration," "Somatic Continuity Chamber." All sounded vaguely medical. Vaguely miraculous. Not one used the word death.

Only once did I hear anything human—a low hum of choral sound from a distant corridor, like a chapel had been autotuned for the wealthy. Then gone again.

No one else appeared. But the retreat moved around me. Air recirculated. Lights breathed. The system adapted.

A woman appeared at the corner—dressed in grey and white, with a smile that had clearly been trained somewhere with chandeliers.

"Mr. Hale?" she said, already knowing. "If you'll follow me."

She didn't ask questions. Just turned and walked.

I followed through a curved corridor and a biometric gate that opened without sound. Past a small conservatory growing something bioluminescent. Past a screen playing testimonial footage with the sound off—faces in soft light mouthing conviction.

Then she opened a door.

The suite was large. That was the first lie. The second

was how normal it tried to feel. Designer everything —
curves, soft whites, matte metals. Lounge furniture
arranged for the viewing of nothing in particular. A
central bed that didn't look like a hospital issue but
carried the same unspoken promise: you won't need to
get up again. There was a view of the mountains. Not
just any mountains — the kind you could only see after a
helicopter erased your past. Floor-to-ceiling glass. Snow
in the crevices. Pines too far below to reach. Nothing
mortal in sight.

The television — if that's what it was — activated as I
entered.

WELCOME, MR. HALE

Your transition journey begins today.

Beneath it, a quiet list of available amenities began to
scroll:

— *Soulprint consultation*

— *Legacy continuity visualization*

— *Guided self-salvation affirmations*

— *Afterlife design sessions (Phase I-IV)*

— *Closure & consolidation therapy*

— *Eschatological realignment chamber (optional)*

— *Family echo inclusion services (invite-only)*

The font was soft. The colour palette — ivory and sea-
glass — made it look like a spa menu, not a metaphysical
abattoir.

The room adjusted its temperature by two degrees.

I didn't speak.

Just stepped forward, let the door seal itself shut, and

laid the coat across a chair that probably cost more than Raymond Boivin's home.

This was what dying looked like here.

No grief. No awe. Just curation—clean, practised, intentional.

I stood for a while. Long enough for the mountain light to shift across the floor. Long enough to be tempted by comfort. That was the trick of this place—it didn't ask you to believe in mercy. Just in ease. But I wasn't here for comfort.

I walked back to the chair.

Lifted the coat.

It was old. Heavy. Still smelled faintly of gun oil and cold air, of ash that had settled into the stitching and never quite left. The lining was torn at the right shoulder, where a glyph had burned through once. I'd never had it repaired. Didn't want to. This coat had been with me in the fires. In the rain. In the rooms where souls begged for things Heaven never promised. It was ugly. Functional. Mine.

I slipped it on.

The weight settled over my shoulders like memory. Like penance.

The mirror in the room tried to adjust its lighting. Tried to reframe me.

It failed.

Finding the Pavilion wasn't difficult. Not because it was marked. It wasn't. But buildings like this—they tell you where the sacred things are. Not with signs. With silence. With the way the corridors curve more reverently, the floors soften, the light changes.

I walked the outer halls. Past recovery spas. Neurothermic lounges. Rooms with names like *Soultrace Integration* and *Final Presence Harmonization*. All locked. All sealed. Not to keep people out. To keep them in. Doors here obey preference, not authority. They stay closed unless asked politely by someone *authorized*. That wasn't me.

I walked anyway.

One door. No nameplate. Frosted glass.

I stopped.

Breathed once.

Pressed my hand to the seam.

The door clicked. Unlocked. Not because it recognized me—but because something older than permission moved through my fingers.

I opened it.

Beyond, another hall. Warmer now. Lights dimmed. Music, maybe—something tonal and wordless piped through the vents like incense.

I kept walking.

No one stopped me.

No one saw me.

Not because I was hidden.

But because no one *wanted* to see a man like me walking where the dying are supposed to feel safe.

I passed a glass gallery where a woman sat in a chair, flanked by soft-suited attendants, reciting a list of her own accomplishments like they were scripture. Her voice cracked on the fifth husband. No one interrupted. She didn't see me. She wasn't supposed to. This wasn't her ritual.

It wasn't mine either.

But I kept walking. Because somewhere behind one more locked door, someone was about to be ushered out of life by the softest voice in the counterfeit gospel. And I needed to be there first.

The door to the Pavilion wasn't locked. It was sealed. Different. Not a lock. Not a process. A hesitation in the air—as if the room behind it had been declared sacred by consensus, and breaking that consensus meant something would bleed.

I opened it anyway.

Inside, the light changed. Neither dim nor bright. Just heaven-adjacent—gold and cream, filtered through engineered lenses. Nothing cast a shadow. Nothing moved without intent.

The room was wide, circular, quiet. Soft music. No words. Just tones low enough to settle into bone.

At the centre, a man. Old. That's all. No diagnosis. No wound. Just tired—the kind money can't touch and his faith didn't know how to name. He sat in a chair sculpted like a throne but shaped like a dentist's recliner. Flanked by family—sons, daughters, their spouses, maybe grandkids—all dressed in white. Crisp, tailored, beaming. Not with grief. With pride.

The man wore a robe embroidered with symbols that looked lifted from the Temple, but softened—marketed. A counterfeit priest in a designer rite.

Before him, half-curtained behind a silk divider, stood the cryonic chamber. It didn't look like a coffin. It looked like a baptismal font. Chrome softened with linen, valves hidden in gold trim, the base inset into a ring of polished stone that glowed like sacrament. It hissed gently — already cold.

He wasn't going to his reward. He was going to his pause.

A soft-voiced woman stood to one side, holding a clipboard that wasn't a clipboard. Touchscreen. Vitals. Spiritual metrics. Belief calibration.

"We are honoured today," she said, "to mark the beginning of Brother Jesperson's transition into the Celestial Phase of Preservation."

No one flinched. No one wept. They believed.

She continued, smooth and perfect, "He will dwell in sanctified continuation for ten full years of subjective paradise. Upon his return, we anticipate advancements in cellular rejuvenation and systemic de-aging to permit his re-entry into the world he helped build."

Smiles. Nods. One of the sons whispered "Amen."

Another attendant adjusted something on a console, murmuring about soul-state coherence and mitochondrial suspension thresholds.

Every word carefully aligned with Church phrasing. Every heresy phrased as hygiene.

Everything sounded clean.

But none of it was.

Then Creedy stepped forward. He didn't wear robes. No collar. Just a dark jacket, fitted to the exact edge of modest elegance. His hair was perfect. His smile—gentle. Not warm. *Permissive.* Like a bishop in a gospel scrubbed clean of consequence.

He laid one hand on Jesperson's shoulder.

"Are you ready, brother?" he asked.

Jesperson smiled, weak but serene. "I already saw the light in my dreams."

Creedy nodded. "That means the threshold is prepared."

He turned slightly, not addressing the family—blessing them.

"You will see him again," Creedy said. "In ten years, or in glory. Whichever comes first."

The family murmured their assent.

The attendants moved forward.

Jesperson leaned back.

The chamber opened with a soft hiss.

And that's when I stepped into the room.

No announcement. No clearance. Just the scrape of worn boots on polished stone. The spell didn't break. But it bent. The temperature didn't drop, but the certainty in the room did.

Creedy turned. Slowly. Like a man who knew every face he'd see—and had practised the expression for each. It wasn't fear. It was disappointment, like I'd ruined something   sacred.
But then he saw me. Not the name I gave. Not the hair. Not the watch. Me. And he understood. Not the disguise. The jurisdiction.

His expression didn't falter. Just shifted—one degree off-centre. Not fear. Containment. Damage control in a tailored frame. He stepped forward, hand lifting slightly from Jesperson's shoulder. Not retreat. Just repositioning. Already adapting.

"Brother Hale," he said, "this is a sacred moment. Perhaps there's been a scheduling—"

"No one here is going to Heaven."

Quiet.

Then the silence cracked.

Jesperson sat up straighter. Not alarmed. Offended. The kind of offence that only comes from certainty purchased, affirmed, and sealed like doctrine in glass.

"I have been prepared," he said. "I saw the light. I saw the fields. The angels spoke my name."

"You saw a construct," I said. "Programmed to match belief. Faith without contact. Reward without judgment."

Creedy held up both hands—palms out. Gentle. Professional. Practised.

"To the family," he said, "I deeply apologize for this interruption. Some of our guests—especially those nearing transition—may experience moments of confusion, even delusion. We train our staff to respond with compassion and discretion."

He turned slightly, nodding to one of the attendants. "Please begin containment protocol. I'll speak with our guest personally."

The daughter nearest Jesperson looked toward me. Uncertain. Not yet afraid.

Jesperson gripped the armrests of the chair like a pulpit. "Get him out of here," he said. "This is my ascension." He meant it. Not symbolically. Paid for. Sealed.

He nodded to the same attendant, then looked back at me.

"If you'll walk with me, Mr. Hale," he said, "we can settle this privately."

I didn't move.

"No," I said.

The room held its breath.

Jesperson leaned forward, voice sharp. "You don't belong here."

"I never did."

The daughter nearest him stood now, uncertain. "Is this part of the experience?" she asked. "Dad, should he be — ?"

"He's a heretic," Jesperson spat. "He came to disrupt the passage."

"No," I said. "I came to name it."

I turned to Creedy.

"You think Heaven doesn't know? You think this gospel stays hidden? I've seen your network. The Free Salvation Fellowship—Thomlin, the broadcasts, the rites. You're rerouting souls through light shows and legacy scripts."

Creedy blinked. Once. Slow.

Then smiled.

"That's what you think this is," he said gently. "These moments are sacred. We tailor them for peace, for legacy, for dignity. The process isn't coercive. It's chosen."

I let him speak.

"Cryonic preservation," he continued, "ensures physical continuity. And our metaphysical transition protocol allows the soul to ascend into its prepared state. Ten years. Celestial-phase immersion. Then return."

Jesperson nodded. Eyes shining.

I stepped forward. Just once. Coat heavy on my shoulders, voice flat.

"No one comes back."

Jesperson scoffed. "You don't know that."

I held his gaze.

"I do. Because I've seen the ones who *tried*."

He didn't speak again. Didn't need to. His faith was absolute. Purchased. Reinforced. Untouched by contact.

Creedy stayed still.

"I give them what they ask for," he said.

The cryonic chamber hissed again. Coolant stabilizing.

An attendant whispered, "We need instructions. What do we do?"

Another repeated, "There's no file. He's not on record."

Creedy's voice didn't rise.

"There's no emergency," Creedy said. "This will resolve." And to me, he continued, "With *grace*."

"No." I said, voice flat. Cold intent spreading through me as I said it. "No, it won't."

He opened his mouth to respond—something smooth,

something soft, something meant to soothe the room back into illusion.

But I didn't let him speak.

The air broke. Not wind. Not force.

Memory.

Something older than light peeled up from under my skin—no glow, no glory—only the return of an authority even Heaven had tried to forget.

The attendants fell back.

Jesperson gasped. The family began to rise, one of them crying out something about restraint, but the words meant nothing now.

I reached for Creedy—not with hands, but with invocation. A gesture that pulled meaning from the wrist, from the shoulder, from the spine. His smile held for half a second longer than it should have. Then it cracked as I spoke the old words. Syllables not permitted anymore. Ones the *Accord* locked away when it decided civility mattered more than truth.

"By oath unsealed. By name undeclared. By covenant held before law — I claim your confession."

The floor beneath us dimmed. The light recoiled.

Creedy staggered. His tether strained—stretched by something it had never been trained to resist.

"You don't know what you're doing," he hissed. But there was no strength in it. Just exposure.

"I know exactly what I'm doing."

I stepped in. The light narrowed—tight as a blade. The chamber hissed again. Confused. The tech monitors glitched—data unreadable, unsorted.

The family began to scream.

I didn't turn.

Creedy reached for control, for calm, for the lie that had always worked.

Too late.

I grabbed him by the collar and drove him to his knees. The sound of bone on polished floor cracked through the room. He gasped—air, blood, denial. I pressed a hand to his forehead, not like a priest, like an executioner. A dark benediction made of pressure and will.

The weave held.

But it strained.

I felt the edges blister under my grip. Not a counterfeit or a puppet. He was real—every strand of him knotted around the mission. Flesh threaded with belief, not possession. A true thing. A willing thing.

He gagged.

Something wet hit the floor. Could've been blood. Could've been light.

"Confess," I said. Voice low. Voice loud. Voice older than breath. "Who do you serve?"

He fought me.

Clawed at my wrist. Scraped for leverage. I bore down. Not symbolically—physically. My weight. My judgment. My hand on his skull like it could press his soul out through his spine.

"There's... no command," he gasped. "No throne. You're chasing smoke."

I squeezed harder.

"Then give me its name."

He choked, spat, tried to speak—and failed.

Then—between teeth—forced out, "The Ascendance Protocol."

The name didn't shake the room.

It just landed.

Dead. Real. Waiting.

"That's what we are," he said. "What we've always been. The Protocol of the *Accord* was flawed. So, we built a better one. One that works. One they want. One they ask for."

His eyes found mine.

"There's no head. No root. Just cells. Just belief. No centre to destroy. Just momentum."

He smiled. Weak. Honest.

"You can't kill momentum."

I nodded.

"Maybe not."

Then leaned in, lips an inch from his ear.

"But I can kill you."

He laughed.

It broke in his throat.

I ended him. Not with a weapon. With a word. Pressed into being through the crack in the world between us.

His body dropped. Limbs loose. The smile still twitching, then gone.

I didn't let go.

My grip shifted. From flesh to soul. I tore it free.

He came screaming—but not aloud. His body stayed still. But inside, he tore open. Light flared. Flickered. Folded.

I drove him down. One arm twisted behind the back of something no longer physical. One hand clamped at the base of his self.

I didn't speak. Didn't recite. I pinned. Like you pin a thing that bites.

The floor beneath him went black at the edges.

He flickered again. Convulsed. Cried out in the register reserved for the judged.

I didn't listen.

The power bled out slow. Then hard. Then stopped.

I stood.

The family hadn't seen the soul. All they saw was my hand on Creedy's head, the life drain from his face, and death. That was enough. They were huddled. Ashen. One of the daughters sobbing behind both hands. Jesperson was still shouting—useless words at a severed ritual.

I didn't face him.

"This ritual is over."

No flourish. No sermon. Just the end.

I turned to go.

There were more names. I would find them.

If I couldn't destroy the Ascendance Protocol, I'd

destroy every last agent it had left.

Let Purgatory take their time.

If I failed — he'd be back.

If I didn't —

There'd be nothing left for him to come back to.

UNFILED: EDEN VALE

The second name on the list brought me to West Pender. Eden Vale.

The building was impossible to miss.

Ten storeys of crystal-panelled glass wrapped in silver louvering, with EDEN spelled vertically in soft-lit serif capitals that didn't glow—they *rested* in the air, like scripture rewritten for serenity—untouchable, unread, already believed. A line of quiet planters ran the edge of the sidewalk. Cameras in the palms. Facial recognition. A curated hush even out here.

Above the main entrance, the phrase pulsed slow across a carbon-diffuse banner screen:

YOU ARE ALREADY BECOMING.

There was a reception. There were greeters. There was even a branded scent, piped just faintly into the vestibule—citrus, pine, something floral, something soothing. Every edge of the building had been tuned. No glare, no grit—just curated stillness mistaken for peace.

People slowed as they walked past. Some stopped. Some took photos. No one looked up. They already knew what was above them.

Eden Vale wasn't a preacher or a thief. She was a household name. A brand. An icon. Half influencer, half redeemer. A sanctifier of surrender.

She didn't kill the soul. She convinced it to walk itself to slaughter—smiling, recording, hashtagging on the way down.

I stood outside for a minute.

Nolan Creedy's death would've made noise. The old kind. Not alarms—ripples. Echoes through the spheres where celestial law still holds shape. Someone would've felt it. Heaven. Hell. Maybe both.

The *Accord* hadn't shattered. But I'd stepped outside its frame—and that meant they could come.

No one had. Not yet.

They would.

But I didn't care that they knew. I only cared if they tried to stop me.

This wasn't about jurisdiction. This was about rot. Cutting it before it went deeper than redemption.

Second name. No margin for subtlety. No room for prayer.

I palmed the token.

The entrance shimmered. The access gate recognized authority. It hesitated. Then it let me in.

The lobby tuned your voice down like a meditation app—automatic reverence baked into the walls.

Blonde wood. Sandstone tile. A wall of glass showing slow-motion drone footage of wind-swept coastline—somewhere curated. Somewhere calm. Inset text floated at the bottom in soft white serif: BECOMING IS ALREADY UNDERWAY.

A woman looked up from behind a crescent desk that matched the floor. No clutter. No keyboard. Just a flush-mounted screen, a biometric pad, and a gold-white nameplate: HAILEY. She smiled the way receptionists at million-dollar studios are trained to smile: calm, polished, empty of opinion.

"Good afternoon," she said.

I didn't offer a name. Just gave it.

"Sal."

She blinked, nodded. A flicker of internal scripting. No typing, but the desk lit up anyway. Face recognition, probably.

"And how can I help you today, Sal?"

"I'm here to see Eden."

That landed. Not loudly. Just wrong.

A fractional pause. The kind of pause that signals a handoff between scripts—protocol, not person.

"I'm afraid Ms. Vale isn't available for direct appointments," she said smoothly. "She's in the middle of a live global broadcast—*The Mirror Room*—but I can connect you with a senior transition advisor, or book you for—"

"I'll wait."

The phrase knocked her cadence half a step out of sync.

"Sir, that's not—"

"Is that a problem?"

I didn't raise my voice. I just took the weight out of it. Made it flat enough to ring.

From the inner corridor, a slim man stepped out—business casual, but not approachable. Loafers that didn't echo. Tablet in hand. He looked at Hailey first.

She didn't speak. Didn't move. But something in the angle of her shoulders gave him all he needed.

Then he turned to me.

"My name's Nathan. I manage the transition advisory team. Why don't we step into one of our reflection suites, and I'll walk you through what we do here."

"I said I was here for Eden."

He smiled. Not pleasant—measured.

"And I said she's not available. If this is about spiritual alignment, I can absolutely facilitate—"

"I know what she is."

That was the moment. The moment every interaction turns. The smile didn't drop. It just shifted—tightened at the corners, filtered through a different risk profile.

Nathan didn't look scared. He looked… procedural.

"I'm going to have to ask you to leave," he said.

"And I'm going to have to ask what happens when someone downloads her Empowerment Kit, sheds their soul, and wakes up as something else."

That hit like nonsense.

"You know what a weave is, Nathan? Ever seen one glitch?"

Now he looked concerned. But not for Eden. For **me**.

Another staffer appeared from the hall—young, headset still on, protein bar in hand. Stared like I was an animal that had made it past the glass.

There were more watching. Behind the mezzanine. Through the side glass. Security didn't rush. They hovered. Waited for a manager. No one wanted to be the one to act first.

"I'm calling security," someone muttered.

Then louder, from further back: "We're contacting the police."

"Do it."

I didn't move.

"I'd love to explain how your little spiritual starter kit functions as metaphysical suicide. How your testimonials aren't people anymore—just shells. Walk-ins. Brand loyal ghosts."

Silence.

The words meant nothing to them. Just another lunatic throwing syllables like bricks.

The projection screen behind Hailey kept playing. Eden, mid-broadcast. Smooth transitions. Soft music. Her voice layered over a composite of sunrise footage and curated testimonials. Perfectly paced. Perfectly unaffected. Whatever was happening here didn't touch it.

The lobby stilled. Not from fear. From optics.

No one wanted a scene.

I didn't wait for Nathan to finish.

Walked past him. Not fast. Not careful. Just done waiting for permission—like I belonged and had run out of patience pretending otherwise.

"Sir—excuse me—you can't go back there."

He followed. So did Hailey.

Another voice behind me. Male. Younger. Nervous. "We're going to have to ask you to stop. This is a restricted area—you're not cleared—"

The doors weren't locked.

Just white frosted panels with soft backlighting and enough serenity baked into the design to make most people pause. I didn't.

I pushed through one. Then another.

Each room beyond was a shrine.

Office pods. Visioning suites. Creative cells. A meditation bay with programmable sunrise walls. Writers at soft-glow keyboards. Editors queuing transformation reels—tear-streaked befores, luminous afters, all backed with Eden's voice in soft cadence.

No one saw doctrine. Just metrics.

Clicks. Reach. Conversion.

"This is trespassing," someone said behind me. The tone had changed. Legal now. Real.

"I'm calling the authorities."

"Please don't make us escalate this."

"I don't want to escalate it either," I said. "I just want to see her."

"She's not here."

They kept saying that like it meant something.

Another man stepped in front of me. Older. More polished than Nathan. Suit cut for meetings, not content. His tone was clean. Authoritative. Meant to end conversations.

"Sir," he said. "You are interrupting a live broadcast. If you don't turn around right now, we will contact Vancouver Police and file formal charges."

I nodded past him.

"That the studio?"

Silence.

A long hallway stretched ahead—white tile, soundless light. One last door at the far end. No label. Just a faint golden ring embossed at eye level.

A stylized halo. Branded sanctity.

No one moved to stop me.

Maybe they didn't think I'd do it.

Maybe they thought this was the part where the crazy man finally blinked.

I opened the door.

The studio wasn't large.

A soft production cube wrapped in seamless projection panels. Everything white—chair, walls, floor. Studio lighting rigged to mimic candlelight, flickering at the edges but controlled. A ring mic hung invisibly above, no wires, just atmospheric pickup. The space was quiet enough to hold a whisper like a revelation.

At the centre: a single white chair.

Occupied.

A woman sat there—young, late twenties maybe. Soft shawl. Bare shoulders. A glass of water in hand. She wasn't an actor. Not quite. But she was performing something—honesty, maybe. Vulnerability tuned for broadcast. Her eyes were damp. Her hands steady. Knees together like prayer.

Across from her, in perfect seated symmetry, was Eden.

Not the flesh-and-blood Eden. Not the origin.

The projection.

Life-size, immersive, high-res and backlit. Skin luminous. Background blurred to digital softness. Every tilt of her head was designed for comfort. Every microgesture mirrored. Her posture matched the guest exactly—shoulders aligned, hands open. A breath behind, never leading, always reflecting.

The room wasn't empty.

Two dozen audience members sat in crescent tiers—soft-clothed, mid-cry, mid-smile. Phones out but forgotten. They weren't recording. They were watching. Live.

The feed scrolled across a sidewall monitor—comments, emojis, hearts, wings, hashtags.

#BecomingNow

#EdenKnows

#SheSpokeToMe

And she was speaking. Right then. Real-time.

"You're here because you know," Eden said, voice low and intimate, like it was meant for the bones. "That ache in your chest—that's not pain. That's the shell cracking. That's the old self surrendering."

It wasn't playback.

It wasn't pre-recorded.

It was **now**.

I stepped inside.

The feed stayed smooth. The projection held. The show continued like I didn't exist.

Security did.

Two men moved fast from the side wall—black shirts, comms in ear, hands already closing around my arms. Not brutal or making a scene. Well trained.

But then Eden looked at me.

The projection turned.

Her gaze met mine—unblinking, focused, present.

"Let him go," she said.

The guards froze. Not with panic or alarm. Just uncertainty.

"Let him go," she said again.

The audience turned—not with fear. With confusion. Like I was a segment that hadn't been storyboarded. A guest who'd missed his cue.

"I know him," Eden said.

Her voice filled the studio. Not amplified. Just final.

The guards stepped back.

I walked forward. Into the backlit shine. Into the branded sanctum. Into the hollow throne where God had been replaced by presence.

She looked at me.

Not pre-recorded.

Live.

"Sal," she said.

That stopped everything.

I turned slowly. Took in the cameras. The crew. The real-time feed still scrolling on the wall. Thousands watching. Maybe millions.

"You're watching this," I said—into the lens. "You think

it's healing. You think it's real. But this isn't salvation. It's scaffolding. A lattice of belief built to hold you in place while your soul is rewritten."

No one moved.

"This is the Ascendance Protocol," I said. "It takes your grief and feeds it back to you. It teaches you to crave erasure. And when you're weak enough—when you finally pray for the old self to die—they answer. And it does."

Eden smiled.

"Is that what you think I am?"

"You're not Eden," I said. "She's gone. Or overwritten. Or never existed."

She didn't argue.

She turned to the audience. Then to the camera.

Her tone shifted—warm, open, a half-step from weeping. Practised intimacy.

"I understand his fear," she said. "Many of you have felt it. You were taught a Heaven written by men who needed to control death. A Heaven for shepherds, emperors, priests. A story passed down by the frightened, copied by the powerful, sold by the guilty."

She leaned forward slightly. The projection tracked the motion across every screen.

The cameras tightened their frames.

"It's not real," she said. "And that's okay. It doesn't have to be. Because *you* are real. Your pain. Your longing. Your desire to become more than you were told you could be. That's why we're here. Not to obey an ancient gatekeeper. But to build what comes next."

She turned back to me.

"You talk about counterfeits," she said. "But what you serve was the first counterfeit of all. A Heaven that never worked. A system that told people they had to earn love. Earn rest. Earn peace."

She looked at the audience again. Then the lens.

"You want to save souls?" she said. "Let them go."

Then she turned just slightly—just enough to frame us both in profile.

Me: standing, blood on my coat, fury in my eyes.

Her: seated, composed, illuminated.

The feed metrics spiked. Hearts, prayers, flames, hashtags.

#HeavenIsDead

#IChooseEden

#LetGoOfTheOldYou

#AscendTogether

Applause started—soft. Not celebration, exactly. More like agreement. Support. Relief drawn in claps. A few in the audience began to cry. Not from fear—but from being told they were already enough.

I stood in the streamlight while the future applauded. Not for me. Not for truth. For her—for the calm, the certainty, the voice that made salvation sound deserved. That death wasn't the end. That there was no need to fear what came next, because they'd be the ones to shape it.

I looked at them. Looked hard. And realized they weren't wrong—not from where they sat, not in the light she gave them. Heaven meant nothing to them. Hell, even less. Judgment, mercy—these weren't rejected. They'd just gone quiet. Irrelevant. They believed in Eden. They believed in themselves. That was all.

She smiled behind me, still glowing, still speaking—her voice folding seamlessly into the feed, reaching out to the hungry, the frightened, the broken, and telling them: You are already becoming.

She reached out—not to me, but to them.

I didn't move. Didn't speak. There was no way to kill her. Not here. Not like this.

She turned back to her guest like I was nothing. Used and disposed.

"You're doing beautifully," she whispered. "This is your moment."

Security re-approached—calm, gentle, arms open.

I didn't resist.

They didn't drag me. They escorted me. Like a man who had finished his part in the show. The door closed behind me. Inside, the lights held steady. And the broadcast didn't stop.

They led me back through the corridor. No words. No pressure. Just a practised path for handling disruption. The hallway was silent. Sterile. Every door I passed was a boundary I couldn't breach. Every screen, every panel, every sealed room—part of a lattice she'd already built. Secure. Distributed. Self-sustaining.

I couldn't cut the wires. I couldn't drag her out. But I still believed she was real. Somewhere, the weave lived. Not in this building. Maybe never here. But somewhere. A mind wrapped around a message, spreading faith like compiled code—adaptive, silent, recursive. Maybe celestial once. Maybe still. She didn't need a body. Just believers. Just reach.

She wasn't in the glass box. She didn't need to be.

The reception area was calm again.

Hailey looked up. One hand raised to point—reflex, not alert.

"He's with me," Chandler said.

He stepped forward from the far wall. Badge out. Quick flash. Not police. Something adjacent to federal. Or just fake. Clean laminate. No time to read it.

The gesture was enough. The staff hesitated. Didn't argue.

"I'll take it from here," he said.

Then he turned to me.

Nodded once.

"Let's go."

We walked a hundred steps before either of us spoke. The sidewalk curved with the shoreline, soft with mist. Water to the left, forest to the right. The city dulled behind us—glass towers mute, the livestream ended, applause long gone. Just gulls now. Just wind.

Chandler walked beside me. Civilian shoes. No wings. No radiance. Just a man playing cop for a jurisdiction that didn't exist.

"I came to arrest you," he said.

I kept walking.

"I figured."

"Not my call. Not entirely. But they know where you've been. What you did to Creedy. To the weave. To the stream."

He paused. "They saw this too."

I stopped at the railing. Looked out over the grey water. The fog hadn't lifted. Neither had the weight.

"I tried to reach them," I said. "I tried to show them what she was."

"They didn't care."

"They did," Chandler said. "They just cared in the wrong direction."

I looked at him. He didn't smile.

"You were right about her," he said. "Partly. Enough."

"That's not the point, is it."

"No."

I turned back to the water. A heron moved through the shallows like it didn't believe in disturbance.

"She's not in the studio," I said. "Not really. Not on the stream. She's somewhere else. A real person. Or she was. Running this. Curating it. Breeding new agents. The weave was seeded through her doctrine. Through her goddamn kits."

"She's real, Chandler."

"I believe you."

I turned.

That stopped me.

He met my eyes.

"But you're not well," he said gently. "You haven't been

for a while. You're tired. You've stepped off-pattern. Your soulprint is fraying. The *Accord* doesn't know what to do with that."

"They want to erase me."

"They want to contain you."

"Same thing."

Chandler didn't argue.

"You're not being sent to Hell," he said. "You're being sent to Purgatory. Not punishment. Just pause. Suspension. Somewhere quiet."

I laughed. Bitter and bone-deep.

"You ever been to Purgatory, Chandler?"

"No."

"I have."

He didn't reply.

We stood there a long moment. Wind in the trees. The sound of something ancient not bothering to move. The wind shifted. Salt and cedar. Somewhere distant, a horn blew from the harbour — long, low, tired.

"You're making them choose death," Chandler said.

I didn't answer.

"You're offering them transcendence," he continued. "But it's your belief that defines it. Not theirs."

"They don't know what belief is anymore," I said. "They've been conditioned, coached, rewritten. You saw it — Eeden didn't need to lie. She just offered a prettier truth."

"That's still a choice," Chandler said quietly. "Even if it's broken. Even if it's wrong."

I turned to face him.

His hands were still at his sides. He wasn't here for violence. Not yet.

"You think God wants that?" I asked. "A system that launders false hope into metaphysical reality? A counterfeit gospel that replaces grief with branding and turns death into a soft sell?"

"I think God wants consent," Chandler said.

That landed.

He stepped closer.

"I think every soul gets to choose. Even if it's Eden. Even if it's the Stack. Even if it's silence. We weren't sent to force transcendence. That's not grace—it's conquest."

I looked away.

"This isn't grace," I said. "This is seduction. This is Hell wearing Heaven's colours. There's no mercy in what she offers. Just pleasure. Just forgetting."

Silence stretched between us. Then I asked the real question.

"Who sent you?"

Chandler didn't look away.

"No one."

He let the words sit.

"I came before Camael does. Before the mandate arrives. Before you get surrounded by agents who don't know you. Who won't talk. Who won't hesitate."

I understood.

"If you resist," Chandler said, "it won't be protocol. It won't be clean. You could be erased, Sal. Not judged. Not processed. Gone. No record. No recovery. Not even remembrance."

He wasn't warning me. He was already grieving.

I looked at him.

"You came to save me."

"I did."

He meant it. That was the worst part.

I looked back to the water. No shimmer. No parting. Just presence. Just weight.

"I'm not done," I said.

Chandler's breath caught.

"I can't let you go," he said.

"You don't have to."

I stepped away from the railing.

He didn't follow.

"I'm leaving," I said. "You can try to stop me. But not here. Not now. Not yet."

He hesitated.

Then I heard it. The click.

I turned.

He had drawn a gun—small, modern, black finish. Not celestial. Just police issue. A fiction for a fiction. It looked wrong in his hands.

His eyes were wide. His stance was off. He wasn't a killer.

"You pull that," I said, "and the last piece of you that still believes in what we were goes with it."

He didn't speak.

"You want to stop me, Chandler? You want to be the one who ends this?"

I took another step. Then another.

The muzzle didn't waver. But neither did I.

Five steps more.

He didn't shoot.

I passed him. Close enough to smell his fear.

Not fear of me—fear of the choice.

I kept walking.

He lowered the gun. Didn't say my name. Didn't say goodbye.

Just stood there, arms at his sides—like the part of him that still prayed had finally gone silent.

UNFILED: DR. WALLACE PRUITT

There was no time for subtlety. They were coming.

The body on the floor was still twitching, smoke rising from the jawline, flesh curling in slow, ceremonial ruin. No blood. Just heat. Just aftermath.

The weave had tried to rupture mid-sentence — some liturgical failsafe coded into the host — but I caught the trigger, crushed it, and burned the false grace out through the spine. I knelt beside the corpse, laid the glyph, and pressed it into the chest while it was still warm. The soul didn't flee. It tried. But I'd learned the shape of desperation. I pinned it like Creedy — no ascent, no descent, just held for judgment.

Purgatory will find you, I thought. Eventually.

I stood. My coat still smoked at the edges. I let it.

The hallway stretched in both directions — polished tile, walnut doors, brass-plated scripture mounted like relics. Exodus. Romans. John. A sermon in segments. The seminary rose around me: four stories of doctrinal steel and air-conditioned obedience. Not grand. Just precise. The kind of place built by tithe, not revelation. Beige carpet. Soft hymns piped through the vents. Windows too clean to believe in suffering.

The name on the list was Reverend Dr. Wallace Pruitt. Somewhere in this sanctified mausoleum, the founder of the Free Salvation Fellowship was still breathing.

He wasn't always this. Once, he was a mid-level Catholic seminary professor with a gift for revival cadence. In the early '90s he vanished into the Sonoran Desert on a silence retreat and came back changed —

voice steadied, doctrine stripped, message refined. No more apologetics. No more catechism. Just one sermon, repeated endlessly: *You are already loved. Choose to believe it, and be remade.* He left behind canon law and picked up a microphone. In 1995, he founded the Beth El Theological Academy—a seminary without denomination, doctrine without repentance. It wore academic legitimacy like a rented suit. Students didn't graduate with theology. They graduated with certainty. That radiant calm that doesn't crack, even in grief.

Pruitt's older now. Seventies, but preserved. Still gives guest lectures. Still walks the campus once a day, always at 4:30. Publicly humble. Privately absolute.

He didn't just found a church. He built a gospel engine. The same machine that produced Thomlin, trained his media team, drafted the scripts for *Salvation Live,* and seeded the first of Eden's Empowerment Kit. Thomlin, Creedy, and Eden were just nodes. Pruitt was closer to the root.

I came to Texas because this wasn't just a seminary—it was a supply chain. This place isn't a campus. It's a nest. And I need a name. The architect of the Ascendance Protocol. The one who built it. I don't know if Pruitt's the architect. But if not, he likely knows who is.

I came extract the truth—whatever it cost. Whatever had to die along the way.

They're coming. I know that. Heaven. Hell. Doesn't matter. Someone will answer the tremor soon enough. But until they do, I'll take down as many as I can.

The body still smoked behind me. No one else in the corridor yet. Just the after-silence. That faint electronic whine when the soul goes still and the air doesn't know how to carry it.

He'd confronted me near the vestibule—grey-lapel professor, clean American diction, just enough warmth to make the poison go down. Not hostile. Just confident.

"You don't belong here," he'd said.

"I know what this place is," I told him. "I know what you are."

He'd smiled. Not panic. *Amusement.*

"You're from Heaven," he said. "Still carrying that old badge? Still waiting for permission to matter?"

He looked past me when he said it. Past me and into the age he thought he was building.

"The *Accord* is obsolete," he said. "We're not stealing souls. We're saving them—from you. From judgment. From a system that's run out of meaning. The Ascendance Protocol is clean. Voluntary. Designed. Heaven was always a guess. This—we offer a guarantee."

The Protocol wasn't a rumour to him. It was scripture. And I wasn't just an interruption. I was *refuse*. A leftover from an old economy of faith. He spoke as a representative of the new order.

So I put him down.

One shot. High chest. The round punched through bone and blew out the back of his spine in a spray of heat and marrow. He staggered, gasped once, then dropped like something gutted at the base. No time to speak. No time to finish the sermon. Just a grunt and a twitch and dead weight on tile.

I crossed the distance. Grabbed the collar. Yanked him flat. Pressed the glyph into his sternum and spoke the word. Old language. Pre-*Accord*. Not a mercy. A command. A claim. The soul locked in place—frozen between planes. No passage. No release. Just anchored. It thrashed once, then held. I felt it strain behind the seal like a wasp in glass.

Purgatory would come. Eventually. I kept walking. There were more. Pruitt was here. And if anyone else stood in my way with that same gospel on their lips, they'd die too.

I didn't wait for sirens. Or screams. Or for the building to decide it was under attack. That would come.

But I had a window. A breath. A clean corridor and a direction.

The chapel. Every seminary has one—the heart chamber, where teaching becomes sacrament. Not just a place for prayer, but for alignment. Doctrine rendered as light and wood and silence. If Pruitt still believed in mythic structure, he'd be near it. Or watching it. Or hiding behind it.

I walked the east corridor fast, past framed photos of past graduates—smiling faces in robes, certificate in hand, the caption beneath every name reading *"Shepherd, Not Judge."*

The hall narrowed. Glass gave way to stone. The air turned cold—intentional, like reverence tuned into the vent.

I passed two students. They froze. Not out of fear. Out of confusion. Blood on my coat. Gun visible. Glyphs burned into the skin of my left hand, still smoking at the edges. They didn't speak. Good.

The doors to the chapel were open. No guards. No barriers. Just polished oak pushed wide, like the place was still pretending it was sacred. I stepped in.

Vaulted ceiling. Rows of soft pews. Pulpit at the front carved in smooth cedar. Scripture inscribed across the back wall not in verse, but as design: a spiral of language drawn inward, ending in a single phrase at the centre: "You are already becoming." Of course.

I didn't speak at first. Just walked to the front, boots echoing hard against polished stone. The people inside didn't scatter. Didn't flee. They looked confused. Like this might still be a drill. Like somewhere in the handbook there was a chapter on what to do when someone bloodied and burning with purpose walks into the sanctuary mid-afternoon.

I scanned their faces. None of them were Pruitt. But one woman stood. Forties maybe. Brown hair pinned back in a modest twist. Charcoal cardigan. No jewelry. No collar. Just plain devotion wrapped in faculty poise.

"You're looking for something," she said.

She meant to sound compassionate. Level. The kind of tone they train in seminary classrooms. *Pastoral affect.*

"I'm looking for Wallace Pruitt," I said. "Where is he?"
"He's not here."

Her hands were folded in front of her, and when she met my gaze, she didn't blink.

"You shouldn't be here," she said. Her voice was low. Measured. Not afraid.

"Then tell me where he is," I replied.

"He's not for you."

"Where?"

"You'll only bring rot with you."

She took a step forward. Not threatening. Just resolved.

"I know who you are," she said. "Heaven's last broken spear. Still thinking judgment is medicine. Still thinking fire purifies. But you're wrong. You always were."

"I've killed your kind before."

"You've killed no one," she said softly. "You've only delayed the inevitable. The Protocol isn't an attack. It's a cure."

That was the tell. Not metaphor. Not dogma. Protocol. The real word. Not fit for sermons. Only for those inside the structure.

"Where is Pruitt?" I asked.

Her eyes didn't move.

"You don't get to see him."

"I'm not asking for access. I'm asking for location."

"You're asking for something that doesn't belong to you anymore," she said. "Pruitt is chosen. Guarded. Consecrated by truth. You wouldn't understand." I stepped closer.

"Try me."

She didn't run. Didn't scream. Just stared at me with something like pity.

"You could have joined us," she said. "You still could."

I shot her through the sternum. The impact knocked her back over the pew—arms still folded, mouth open in silent exhale. Her body slid down the wood, arms still folded, smoke curling at the edges like burnt offering.

I stepped over. Panicked stillness filled the chapel.

I knelt. Pressed the glyph into her chest. The soul froze—still warm, still bound. She wouldn't tell me when she breathed. So I asked her now.

"Where is Pruitt?"

The tether quivered. The seal glowed faint. She resisted. Not out of fear. Out of faith.

I tightened the pressure. Burned her with the name of God—not as mercy, but as leverage.

"East wing," the voice whispered. "Upper offices. Seminar Room Twelve."

I felt the lie trying to form behind it. Crushed it with invocation. The soul fractured—light bending as if the seal itself couldn't hold its grief.

"He teaches there," she said. "Today. Private study. No class scheduled. He stays late. Prepares the new order."

That was enough.

I stood.

The pew was scorched. The air tasted like copper and incense.

"Thank you," I said. Not to her. To the seal. To the law that still works when belief fails.

The east wing was older. Not in years—in intention. The tile didn't gleam. The lighting was soft and indirect. Quiet by design. Intentional. Like silence was part of the doctrine. No windows. Just plaques every few feet—accreditations, donor names, ordination cohorts.

At the end, one door. Thick wood. No numberplate. Carved above the lintel in serifed letters: Seminar Room Twelve.

Pruitt was here.

No guards. No wards. Just a door.

I opened it.

It wasn't a throne room. Just a classroom.

Twelve chairs in a ring. Shelves of old commentaries — Wright, Bonhoeffer, Ellul, Tillich. A chalkboard filled with theological sparring in two hands — one practised, one trying to catch up. A long oak table at the centre.

Behind it: Dr. Wallace Pruitt.

White hair, full and combed straight back. Face clean-shaven. Jaw square. Skin pale and smooth in the way money makes possible. His shirt was white, sleeves rolled to the forearms, cufflinks still in — gold, etched with a cross. Not showy. Just permanent. Pressed charcoal vest. Three buttons. No tie. Collar open. His boots were tan leather, polished to a soft sheen, heels crossed under the table. One toe tapped now and then, steady, unhurried. His hands were folded neatly in front of him, thumbs resting against a leather-bound journal.

He didn't stand. Didn't move at all, really. Just watched. Like a man who'd been waiting for the meeting to start. Like I was late, not violent. No tension in the shoulders. No fear in the eyes. Just preparation. Like whatever happened next, he already had it on record.

"I wondered how many you'd kill before you got here," he said.

"Three," I told him. "Maybe four. Depends on whether the receptionist prays to anything real."

He nodded. No fear.

"Well. Here I am."

"I know that the Ascendance Protocol has been working for years. Centuries perhaps. And you are at the heart of it. Your church. Your false gospel. I want to know who built it. The architect."

He gestured to the chair across from him. I didn't sit.

"So, you already know who I am, and what I am," he said. "But you still don't *understand*. You still don't *see the truth*. Shouldn't you understand before you destroy?"

He wasn't stalling. He thought I needed to hear it.

"I never rejected Heaven," he said. "I outlived it. Heaven was written for people afraid of death. Hell for people afraid of justice. It worked for a while — when the world was smaller. But we outgrew it."

He folded his hands.

"The Ascendance Protocol isn't rebellion. It's succession. Every system ages. Every covenant collapses. I didn't tear yours down. I helped build the one that comes after."

"You rewrote judgment."

"No," he said. "We listened. That's the heresy. Not theft. Listening. We don't tell them what Heaven is. We ask. And then we give it back to them better."

I stepped closer.

"You're not divine."

"I'm devoted," he said. "And in thirty years, they won't remember what you were trying to preserve. They'll only remember what worked."

I drew the weapon. Standard frame. Round already chambered.

He didn't flinch.

"You'll kill me," he said. "I see that you believe you have to. But it won't stop it."

"No," I said.

I raised the gun.

"It'll get me the next name."

I fired.

One shot. Centre mass. The round cracked through bone and dropped him clean.

No shout. No rupture. Just weight. Just a man dropping out of the way.

I crossed the floor, knelt over the body, and pressed the glyph into his chest. It resisted. Then gave. The binding locked. His soul didn't escape. It pulsed under the seal like exposed nerve — still live, still bound.

I leaned in. Spoke the old word. Not for show. For contact.

"Who is the architect?"

The glyph flared. His mouth moved. Once. Maybe twice.

Then it came.

Not a sentence. Just a name.

"Ansel —" That's all Pruitt managed.

The rest broke in blood.

The bullet hit me. Back, high right — ragged path through the lung.

I dropped forward onto Pruitt's chest as the seal shattered beneath my hand, the tether dissolving into open light. The soul was gone. The name was all I had left.

Blood filled my mouth. The taste of copper and unfinished work.

I rolled to my side, drawing breath through fire.

Three of them entered. Agents. Earthbound celestials in dark suits, earpieces snug, sidearms drawn and tight against their ribs. If I didn't know better, I'd have mistaken them for private security. The kind they station outside summits. Or sacred things. They moved in formation. The one on the left flanked low. The middle squared his stance. The right drifted with caution — eyes scanning me like a breach report.

I rose. One step. Two. The wound burned. My coat was soaked. Every breath snapped glass through my ribs. Didn't matter.

I struck first. The left agent came in fast — arm up, tactical grip. I caught his wrist, twisted, drove my knee into his ribs. Something cracked. He dropped. Staggered sideways. Didn't rise.

The second fired — twice. Shoulder and thigh. I turned just enough. One round grazed. The other caught meat. Still standing. Still moving. I reached him before he could reload — slammed his head into the corner of the chalkboard. He fell in a heap. Breathing. Not conscious.

Third one drew a blade — mortal steel. Nothing sacred about it. Just weight and edge. I let him strike. The blade bit fabric, scraped bone. Pain flared.

I closed the distance. Grabbed his jaw. Drove us both backwards into the wall. His head cracked plaster. Then tile. Then silence.

Three down. Breathing like fire. Vision tunneling. Blood down my chest.

I looked up.

Camael was waiting. He stood at the far end of the room. Unmoved. Unarmed. In a long black coat that absorbed the light. He looked like no judge I'd ever served—just *inevitability*. Something God no longer needed to announce.

I took a step. He didn't flinch.

I took another. And then—

Seraphine.

She entered without sound. Not stealth—precision. Just arrival. Pale coat. Dark hair pinned like a formal accusation. Her steps were silent. Intentional. Her posture absolute. She didn't scan the room. She already knew its shape. Her eyes met mine without accusation— just clarity. No rage. No pity. Just the clarity of judgment.

I moved to face her. Blood in my mouth. Wound burning. I still had enough to make it count.

She didn't wait.

She drew and fired—two clean shots to the leg. Right thigh. Left hip. It was enough. Bone cracked. Muscle gave. I dropped to one knee. My hand scraped for balance, found only blood.

She crossed the distance while I fell.

I raised my arm to strike, but she caught it mid-motion and drove me flat with a hand to the sternum. No wind-up. No theatrics. Just force, direct and surgical. The kind that knew exactly how much was needed and delivered nothing more.

I hit the tile hard. My back lit up. My lungs stuttered once, then locked.

She didn't straddle. Didn't kneel. Just pressed down, one palm to my chest, the other to the glyph still burning at my side.

I couldn't move.

Not because of strength. Because of authority.

Her voice came next. Cold. Precise. Nothing wasted.

"Sael."

She didn't ask why. She didn't accuse. She named me. That was enough.

I tried to push against her grip. Nothing. My body was already slipping into cold.

Camael stepped forward, slow. Measured. "You should have stayed in Heaven, Sael."

Seraphine's hand was still at my chest. Not pushing. Just holding.

"I got the name," I said.

He nodded. "Yes."

"It's enough."

"No." His eyes held no malice. Only mandate.

I closed my eyes.

Didn't pray.

Seraphine exhaled once — then released.

I dropped. Not to sleep. Not to silence. Just down.

Into sentence.

CASE FILE: SAEL

Cold.

Not air. Not water. Not even absence.

Just *cold*—total and prior. Like law before language.

That's where I woke.

No body. No form. Just awareness pinned in it, held where falling had left me. The cold wasn't punishment. It was confirmation. That I had been ended. That something had been claimed.

Then—movement. Not lifting. Not flight. Just transport. They had me. Four of them, one at each limb. I couldn't see their faces. Maybe they didn't have any. Not everything in Heaven needs to be shaped for mercy. These weren't warriors. They were carriers. Custodians. Cold as the current that bore me. They hauled me upward through a space that didn't permit vision. I could feel geometry brush past— walls shaped from memory, not masonry, halls shaped by function too old for names.

There were no doors. Only thresholds. And those thresholds knew me. Each one I passed dimmed—not in fear, but in accordance. Somewhere above, a chamber yawned itself into being. They brought me in. Set me down. Not roughly. Not kindly. Just placed. Like evidence.

I felt gravity return. A shift in weight. Orientation. I had legs. Arms. Form again. Not mine. Not divine. Just enough to be processed. The shackles were already on— wrists and ankles. No metal. Just force, folded into shape. Each band bore a single mark: not script, not glyph, but a score. A scratch, like a key across polished stone. And beneath each one — heat. Quiet. Inarguable.

I did not resist. Nothing in me left to try.

A voice registered — declaration, not sound. "Subject: Sael. Former function: Threshold Division. Status: rogue. Judgment: pending."

I looked up.

She stood behind a platform shaped for pronouncement, not presence. Platinum robes. Face unreadable. Not masked. Just not built for recognition. Eyes that did not blink. Hands folded with exact precision. A record floated before her — not of light, but of certainty.

Another agent stepped forward. Touched my cuff. Not to examine. To confirm alignment.

"No flare," he said. "No resonance. No resistance."

The woman nodded.

"Place him."

They led me toward a fold in the chamber wall. It wasn't a door. Just a fault line in space, waiting to forget me. Inside: nothing. No cot. No light. No fixtures. Just presence. Mine.

They left. The fold sealed — not with a sound, but with a *lack* of sound. A subtractive seal. I wasn't locked in. I was *no longer available.*

I didn't ask how long. Time in Purgatory waits for the speaker. Judgment needs voice. Until it comes, there's only delay. But I knew the truth. I'd lost. Not the fight. The meaning. Whatever I'd tried to prove — whoever I thought I could reach — none of it held. I'd raised my hand. Broken the seal. Declared war. I'd aimed my words like a weapon, and I'd fired first. And Seraphine had answered. She hadn't hesitated.

I remembered the moment her hand moved. My body didn't fall. It just stopped. Grace stripped. Form severed. Judgment, unpronounced.

I'd gone too far. Too loud. Too sure.

Now I was here.

I didn't expect anyone to come. This wasn't a waiting room. It was a holding pattern for the already condemned. There were no appeals. No witnesses. No final conversations. Just containment. Just *me*.

Time passed. Not minutes. Not hours. Not anything with edges. Just… erosion. Thought dulled. Memory frayed. I couldn't tell if I slept, or if forgetting had already started. There were no sounds. No light shifts. Just containment.

Purgatory didn't mark you with torment. It waited.

When the fold opened, I didn't rise. I didn't need to. I knew who it was.

She didn't enter like a friend. Or a warden. Just someone allowed. Someone who knew the shape of the place, and the shape of me.

"Mara," I said.

It didn't echo. Names don't hold in here.

She looked the same. Always had. Simple robe, dust-grey, sleeves loose. Her face the colour of clay in moonlight. Eyes as tired as mine used to be. She didn't glow. Never had. Not even then, when we were bright.

She didn't say I told you so. She didn't say anything at first. Just sat.

The cell didn't have seats. But Mara made space wherever she chose to be. It adapted to her without ceremony. No one else I knew could do that.

"You got old," she said eventually. The truth.

"Was always old," I answered. "Just didn't admit it."

She looked down. Her fingers folded in her lap, still as sealed wings. We didn't talk about Eden. Or Elias. Or Thomlin. She didn't ask why I did it. Didn't demand an apology. She grieved me. Not for what I'd done. But for what I *was*. For what it had cost.

"I had to see you," she said. "Before they close the record."

I nodded. "They'll erase it?"

"Eventually. After judgment."

Her voice didn't catch. Mara never cracked. But I heard the weight underneath.

"You'll be reassigned. New name. New post. New convictions. You'll believe in the work again."

"Will I?"

She looked at me then. Not as a witness or partner. Just… Mara.

"That's how it works."

I didn't argue. What was the point? There wasn't rage between us. No betrayal. Just accumulation. A hundred shared verdicts. A thousand cases. Millennia of attrition. We'd both seen too much. But only one of us had stopped obeying. She didn't condone it. She didn't condemn it. Just sat with me in the void where judgment hadn't yet landed.

There wasn't much to say. There never had been. Our

best work was always silent—side by side, through echoes no one else could stomach. I remembered: the quarry in Marseille, the hospital in Kinshasa, the collapsed stairwell in Varanasi. She'd always been there, three steps behind, eyes fixed ahead. I'd cleared the path. She'd named the dead.

"Maybe next time," she said at last.

I turned to her.

"Next what?"

"Next iteration." Her voice was thin, but not cruel.

"After this. After the forgetting. Maybe you'll find something worth staying for."

I didn't answer.

Mara stood. The cell recognized her departure before she did. The fold began to loosen. The geometry exhaled.

She paused at the edge.

"You were never wrong, Sal," she said. "Just unpermitted."

Then she left. The fold sealed again. No trace. No proof. Only silence. And waiting.

The second time the fold opened, I felt it before it happened. *Pressure.* Not against the skin. Against the shape of my being.

I stood. Didn't want to. But standing was instinct when he entered.

Camael.

His presence bent the cell without movement.

No wings unfurled. No robes in motion. No flame to announce him. Just *command* — like silence that expected obedience. He stepped through the threshold like it bowed for him. Maybe it did.

He didn't speak right away. He didn't have to.

I held his gaze. Silver eyes, burnished at the edges — not molten, not kind. Just thorough.

"You came," I said.

"I always do," he answered.

That was true. Camael had visited every rebellion before me. Always near the end. Not to threaten. To name.

"You've come to pass sentence?"

"No." He took a step closer. "I've come to offer clarity."

I laughed. It cracked my throat.

"Too late for clarity."

"Only if you refuse to see it."

The cell adjusted around him. It didn't welcome, but it *allowed*. Like even in Purgatory, his presence was permitted by default.

"You've been asking questions," he said. "About counterfeit gospels. Stolen souls. Constructs of mercy. And now you're here. Ask yourself why."

"Because I got too close."

"No." He tilted his head. "Because you chose this."

I stared at him. "I chose to be erased?"

He didn't flinch. "You chose this afterlife. This narrative. This identity. Over and over."

My jaw locked.

Camael stepped closer. Not menace—inevitability.

"There is no central architecture anymore," he said. "No singular Heaven. No rigid Hell. That was the old gospel—rigid, reluctant, imposed. The new gospel is voluntary. Chosen. Souls do not enter constructs by force. They enter by fit."

I shook my head. "Then they're being misled. Conditioned. You've seen it—Thomlin, Eden, the shaman. They're shaping belief to control outcome. That's not fit. That's fraud."

Camael didn't blink. "I'm not talking about them."

He took another step. His voice didn't rise. It deepened.

"I'm talking about you."

"What?"

He let it hang.

Then, "You imagine yourself as a crusader. Alone. Opposed. Burdened by knowledge only you dare to carry. And so you built this afterlife. This rebellion. A soul that cannot abide peace will always find conspiracy."

"That's not true."

He came closer.

I didn't retreat. I couldn't. "You blame the Ascendance Protocol for the illusion," he said. "But illusions don't hold unless they're wanted. You think Heaven was infiltrated. That our records were overwritten. But what if this is simply the next step? Not theft. *Evolution.* What if the gospels have changed?"

"They don't change."

He raised a brow. "Why not?"

I had no answer.

"You think yourself sane because you remember suffering. Because you trust pain. Because you associate truth with difficulty. That's your creed. That's your *choice*. But others choose differently. And so they ascend—into what they believe."

"They're being rewritten."

He nodded.

"As are you."

That hit harder than I wanted. He circled once—not predatory, just precise. A maker circling a fracture.

"I've read your ledger," he said.

"Not the file. The soul-script. The internal shape of you. And it is not holy, Sal. It is not noble. It is bent. Wound around the axis of self-authorship. Every righteous act tangled in performance. Every rescue a disguise for self-punishment."

I swallowed. Dry.

Camael's tone didn't sharpen. It softened.

"You are not being punished. You are being offered treatment. Erasure is not cruelty. It is cleansing. You've carried too many broken cases. Too many losses. They didn't make you strong. They made you *sick*."

He gestured to the void.

"This was not a verdict handed down. It was a structure offered. And you entered it freely."

I forced a breath.

"So what? You want me to kneel? Confess I'm mad? That everything I did was a projection?"

"I want you to rest."

He meant it.

"Let the memory go. Let the conspiracy dissolve. Let judgment pass and healing begin. You won't be punished. You'll be cleansed. Then assigned. You might be an architect next time. A scribe. Something simple. Something safe."

"And if I refuse?"

"You already have."

That stopped me.

"This narrative," he said, voice low, "only sustains as long as you do. The more you resist judgment, the more this shape calcifies. And it *hurts you*, Sal. This place. This cell. This version of you. It feeds on your belief."

He stepped back.

"You are being offered release. Not destruction. But the next time you wake, if you choose not to accept, it will all begin again. The fall. The theft. The doubt. The dead."

I stood still.

Camael turned. Just before the fold accepted him, he paused.

"I do not hate you," he said. "I pity you."

Then he left.

After Camael left, I didn't move.

The cell didn't have corners. Only curves that suggested enclosure. You couldn't walk in it. Only circle inside yourself. So I did. At first, I held my ground. Anchored in defiance. He was wrong. The Protocol was real. I'd seen it. Felt it. Eden's sermon wasn't mine. Thomlin's broadcast wasn't mine. That wasn't belief. That was *construction.* Engineered. Precision doctrine dressed in mercy, but hollow underneath. But then—

What if it wasn't hollow? What if it was *mine?*

My mind wouldn't stop. Wouldn't rest. Wouldn't obey.

It replayed.

Amira Pell. The soldier who came back wasn't her husband. The fork in the wrong hand. The kiss that missed. Fifteen years of falsehood wrapped in ritual. *But I gave it meaning.* I tore through the echo. Declared it counterfeit. Found a uniform. Solved a mystery. Or had I? There was no proof she hadn't known. No proof the lie wasn't a mercy. Maybe she was ready to go, and I needed the case to mean more. So I wrote the ending she didn't ask for. *Projected betrayal into a silence she'd already forgiven.*

Arthur. I built the whole damn thing. The IED. The fake name. The resurrection. None of it was assigned. None of it real. Just a folder I needed to find, a story that bent the world until it matched my shape. I said I was hunting Clarion, but it was always me, wasn't it? Inventing the wound, then chasing the cure. A dead man named Melvin, a boy named Peter, a cause made of static and grief—every piece slotted into the gospel I wanted: that truth hurts, that mercy's a lie, that only I see the rot. But there was no rot. No tether. No resolution. Just me, looping my own damnation until it felt like justice.

Elias Shaw—unlisted, unprocessed, complete in all the wrong ways. He didn't loop. Didn't flicker. Just sat there, whole and waiting, like a question I'd planted for myself. I made him the man who didn't go—because I needed proof that something was broken. That Protocol failed. That souls were slipping through. But he wasn't proof. He was *design*. I gave him a cigarette, a dead stare, a name that didn't echo, and sent him walking into the night like a fable I could never disprove. And I believed it—because that's what I do. I believe the rot. Even when I'm the one writing it.

Each proof unravelled in my mind. The confidence that I had, slipping.

Marysia Zielińska: I wanted to believe she'd been broken by Hell, but maybe I just couldn't accept that Heaven had no place for a soul like hers.

I said Gerry Wiles glitched, but it was me—I couldn't stand that a soul might slip through without me catching it.

Wâsakâmaskwa: I made him the architect because I needed the villain to look like doctrine twisted—so I wouldn't have to see it was just belief outpacing grace.

Creedy, Vale, Pruitt... they weren't proof of a conspiracy—they were proof I needed there to be one, needed rot so badly I conjured it from my own fracture and called it revelation.

I'd called it a crime. What if it was a gift?

I rubbed my face. My hands felt older than I remembered.

Camael's words replayed: *You chose this. A soul that cannot abide peace will always find conspiracy.*

I wanted to reject it. I still did. But I kept circling back.

The cases. The files. The victims. The patterns.

All too perfect. All too right. Every one a chance for me to be the only one who saw it. Every one a gospel of *Sal knew best*. What kind of soul needs that? What kind of soul builds a Heaven where truth is always hidden, and he's always the one to uncover it?

I'd crafted my own liturgy: every clue a psalm, every lie a doorway, every death an absolution waiting to be earned through me. I thought I was saving them. Maybe I was *staging* them. Maybe this wasn't Heaven corrupted. Maybe it was me.

Camael had said the new gospel was real. That each soul chose their afterlife. Not what they deserved. What they *believed*. And I believed in conspiracy. In failure. In systems rigged from the start. I believed the truth was always hidden and that meaning only emerged under pressure, through pain, through violation. So that's what I found. What I *needed* to find.

And now I was here. Not as punishment. As *destination*.

I sat with that for a long time. And then—I stopped arguing.

I didn't accept it as fact.

But I stopped needing to prove it wrong.

Maybe that's what acceptance really is. Not agreement. Just *exhaustion*.

I leaned back. Let the shape of the cell cradle the weight of me. Just broken. And maybe, finally, beginning to *see* it.

The third time the fold stuttered, the space didn't open. It flinched.

What stepped through wasn't authorized. It wasn't sanctioned. It wasn't *welcomed*.

Cyr.

She didn't pause at the threshold. She cut through it—like gravity forgot her. Like rules stopped applying when she looked at them too long. No flare. No light. Just wings tight to a body sculpted in consequence—seamless, scorched, watching. Her celestial form was forged in blasphemy—skin fissured like scorched clay, edges sharp where bone met pressure, joints shaped by old constraint. No eyes—just lenses of polished glass, cut to reflect fault. Her presence twisted the air—not with heat, but with judgment without pause. And she was already casting.

She raised two fingers, slit the air sideways, and hissed a word that didn't echo—it devoured echo. The cell folded in on itself, layering silence into the walls like a curse.

"Containment held," she said. "We speak freely."

I didn't rise.

She looked at me like a flaw preserved for study. Not with curiosity. With contempt barely justified by function.

"Still existing," she said.

"You're not supposed to be here."

"Irrelevant."

Her voice stayed level. But it cut.

"Hell's writ doesn't reach this far," I said.

She scanned the edges of the cell—not for exit. For failure. Tilted her head, sharp and slow. "Purgatory is shared. There are two points of entry."

"You bypassed the *Accord* to enter," I said.

She didn't blink. "I had assistance." A pause. Then,

flatter: "They looked the other way. That's not violation. That's precedent."

She stepped closer. Her presence was wrong in a way the cell couldn't contain. Not chaotic—precise in a language older than protocol. She made silence feel *structured*.

"You risk exposure," I said, with genuine surprise.

"I'm not here for permission," she said. "I'm here for data. You have some."

"You think I'll give it?"

"I think you want to matter," she said.

Her words hit too clean. I swallowed.

"You tracked the Ascendence Protocol?"

She blinked. Once. Not slow. Not human.

"Yes."

"Where did it start?"

"Not Heaven," she said. "Hell. Fringe sect. Heresy of efficiency. No torment. No reward. Just clean throughput. Soul stripped of context, passed on."

She stepped around me. Not pacing. Circling.

"They called it clarity. Claimed judgment was obsolete. Designed constructs that matched belief. Hell didn't notice. Until records vanished."

"You sound impressed."

"I'm furious," she said. "They stole from us. Rewrote souls off the books. That's not rebellion. That's theft."

"You believe me now."

"I never believed you," she said. "I believed the

numbers. And they're broken."

I stood. Slowly.

"What do you need?"

"A name."

I hesitated.

She didn't blink.

"Ansel."

"That's not enough."

"It's all I have."

She reached into her side, under the seam of her ribs, and pulled a shard—black as unlight. Memory encoded in nothing. She thumbed it once. No interface. Just recognition.

"Ansel Reon. Compound east of Montreal. Off-grid. Solar cell field. Broadcast zero. Funds trace back through six shells—Vale, Thomlin, others."

Her head turned toward me, slow and direct.

"You're destabilized," she said, scanning me like she was logging damage, not asking questions. "No form. No tether. But still conscious. That's enough."

"Enough for what?"

"To move," she said. "To act. To kill, if necessary."

I frowned. "You think I'm still useful?"

"I think you're unbound," she replied. "And that may be necessary."

Her tone didn't carry approval. Just calculus.

"You don't have a body," she added. "That limits range. I can work around it."

"Glad you're feeling generous."

She turned her head slightly, the way a predator notes heat before deciding whether to bite.

"You're not a partner," she said. "You're a tool. The kind I can use without triggering doctrine."

I didn't respond.

She reached behind her spine, under a ridge of scorched plating, and drew a second token—long, jagged, curved like a broken scythe. It pulsed, not with light, but *force held back*.

She didn't warn me.

She drove it into the air.

The cell didn't open. It came apart. The metaphysics shattered—boundaries ruptured, the seal erased not by force but by finality. Purgatory reeled, then receded.

I didn't fall.

I was ripped.

She seized my arm—not as invitation, not as support. As leverage. And she tore us through.

No alarm. No witnesses.

Only discontinuity.

One moment, silence.

The next—Earth. Snowfield. Solar arrays behind a chain-link gate. Pines angled against a high wind. Altitude thin. Cold real.

We hit hard.

I staggered. Cyr didn't.

She let go of my arm like she was releasing a

mechanism, not a man.

"Ansel Reon lives here," she said. Then, turning once to verify the perimeter, "Don't waste it."

UNFILED: ANSEL REON

No gate.

Just a road that stopped pretending to be one. Gravel gave way to crushed stone. Then to silence — damp earth tamped smooth by careful machines.

The compound rose out of the forest like a completed sentence. Not hidden or proud. Just *placed*. The land curved around it in agreement.

At the front: a long, low structure clad in pale cedar and concrete, with horizontal slats designed to echo the tree line. Its roof stretched flat and wide, studded with black solar panels angled for the latitude. Battery arrays lined the slope below, half-buried and clean. There were no wires. No fences. No visible cameras. Just presence — functional, integrated, self-contained.

The house itself wasn't a mansion in size, but it moved like one. A single storey, but long. Linear. Every wall of glass was double-framed, every shadow intentional. It didn't reflect the forest. It *included* it. You didn't look at the house. You looked through it.

Inside, the lights adjusted as we passed. Nothing flickered. Nothing whirred. The air was neutral. Temperature not chosen, just correct.

Cyr didn't knock. She raised her hand and split the lock — not a gesture, but authority made physical. The front door came undone at the frame. It didn't swing open. It released.

We stepped in.

No clutter. No sound. A hallway of raw lime plaster and pale ashwood led inward, then out again — to a rear threshold lined in stone.

He was already there.

Ansel Reon stood on the back porch, a smooth platform that cantilevered slightly over the slope. No railings—just elevation and intent. Below, the Laurentian mountains unrolled in soft, endless ridges—moss and granite, pine and sky.

He wasn't seated. He wasn't armed. He wore loose, bone-coloured linen—nothing with buttons, nothing shaped. His tablet hung idle in one hand, screen black.

He looked back over his shoulder. No surprise.

His eyes found mine.

They didn't narrow. They didn't widen. They just received. Like he was updating a file that had already accounted for our arrival.

His skin was the colour of scraped clay—bone-white, bloodless, like doctrine scrubbed clean of origin. His face was smooth, unmarred. Not ageless—just un-authored. No hair, no beard, no stubble. No signs of sleep. He held posture. He occupied it. His only ornament sat just above the collarbone, where a lapel might have been: a small diamond pin—three nested bands around a diamond centre, each too perfect to be handmade, fastened through the robe with a gold-tipped stem.

And when he spoke, it wasn't welcome.

It was permission.

"Come in," Ansel said. "You've come far enough to deserve clarity."

Ansel didn't move. He let the moment breathe.

He stood at the edge of the porch like it was a pulpit. Or a plinth. Or the last line of scripture. The sky over the Laurentians had begun to soften—light thinning to violet where the ridgelines met. Below, the pines held their silence, and the slopes folded into one another like the soft closing of a book.

He didn't look at us. He looked at the view. And not like a man admiring it. Like a man who'd already named every tree, every fault line, every curve of light.

"This is why I built it here," he said, almost to himself. "Not for beauty. For equilibrium. The terrain is self-balancing. No chaos. No excess. Everything seeks its limit."

He inhaled—deliberately, not deeply. Like he was aligning with the environment he'd chosen to inhabit.

"You feel it, don't you?" he asked, still watching the horizon. "The quiet. The clarity. No judgment here. No memory either. Just continuity. That's all I ever wanted to give them."

Then he turned. And the moment changed.

Cyr stepped forward, one hand low, the other curled around the black knife. Not raised. Just *present*—its curve catching nothing, reflecting less. A blade shaped like a sin too new for scripture.

Her voice cut flat across the view.

"We can do this quiet," she said. "Or we can do it honest. Either way, you're confessing."

Ansel turned fully to face her. He wasn't afraid.

"To what, exactly?" he asked.

"To falsifying judgment," she said. "To bypassing the

Accord. To theft of souls."

He considered that. Not with resistance. With evaluation. "I see," he said. "You're still thinking in verticals."

She didn't blink. "You're not."

"No," he agreed. "I'm thinking in vectors."

She shifted her grip on the knife — nothing dramatic, just readiness.

I spoke first.

"Put it down."

They both looked at me.

I stepped onto the porch. The borrowed body still moved like borrowed time — but the ache inside it was mine.

"You were always going to find me," he said. "Eventually. That's how the *Accord* works. It tolerates rebellion. But it catalogues persistence."

Cyr shifted behind me, still silent. Knife at her side. Watching for the crack in his words.

"You know what we're here for," I said. "So, speak. What is the Ascendance Protocol?"

He nodded once. A teacher, not a prisoner.

"It's not a heresy," he said. "It's a correction."

"To what?" I asked.

"To the failure of universal process," Ansel said. "To the inefficiency of judgment, to the cruelty of binaries. To a system that lets the slow suffer and calls it virtue."

He turned back to the view. Not to dismiss us — but to

give the words somewhere large enough to land.

"I spent centuries," he said. "Watching the backlog grow. Watching Heaven stall. Watching Hell swarm like vermin through the breaches. We weren't ascending souls. We were *triaging a catastrophe*. Every file a delay. Every delay a wound."

He looked past us again—toward the forest, the slope, the wide quiet beyond.

"And then the world changed. Eight billion souls. Ten. Soon twelve. Death no longer trickled—it poured. Not in lines, but in floods. War, climate, collapse. The metaphysical load exceeded design. You can't process the dead like that. Not with doctrine. Not with care."

He turned back toward me. No hostility. Only certainty.

"Heaven slowed. Hell adapted. And we—those of us watching—realized the system would break before it ever admitted fault. The *Accord* wasn't law. It was latency. An agreement to fail together, politely."

His mouth barely moved. But every word landed.

"Inefficiency became cruelty. Judgment became inertia. And grace?" He paused. "Grace became rationed."

I didn't answer.

"Grace without merit," he continued. "That's what you call it. But grace without delivery is failure. Hope without structure is torment. You knew it. You've felt it. The tug. The doubt. How many have slipped past your reach, Sal? How many have chosen silence over transcendence?"

Too many.

"And you?" he said, turning toward Cyr. "How long

have you been hunting souls that would rather disappear than be claimed?"

She didn't flinch. But she didn't answer.

"I designed the Protocol," he said, "to remove the cruelty of sorting. To pre-empt resistance. Not with force. With coherence. We didn't build temples. We embedded delivery into belief. Doctrines, death rituals, therapeutic frameworks. We mapped expectation, and then we gave it somewhere to go."

"False prophets," I said. "False gospels."

"*Trusted* prophets," he replied. "Not because they were divine. Because they were believed. That's what mattered. Not their merit. Their alignment."

He stepped away from the edge of the porch now, fully facing us.

"You call it corruption," he said. "I call it grace with architecture. Salvation as system. No more tethers. No more grief loops. No more intercession. Just entry. Seamless. Instant. Accepted."

He stepped closer now — not threatening, not warm. Just present. Measured.

"The Protocol doesn't deceive," he said. "It delivers. Joy, peace, reunion, purpose — whatever the soul believes it's earned. Not imposed. *Realized.* That's what they've always wanted, isn't it? Not thrones. Not wings. Just happiness. Fulfillment. Forever."

He held my gaze.

"What Heaven was meant to be. What they always believed it was."

I stepped closer. "You intercept them. Override tethers.

Bypass protocol. But they don't ascend. They don't fall. So where do they *go?*"

"They go to the Stack," Ansel said.

Cyr frowned. "That's not a sphere."

"No," he replied. "But it is a place. Buried in the Overflow. Hidden from judgment, invisible to the *Accord*. It doesn't need gates or thrones. Just space. And the Overflow is infinite."

He let that settle.

"We've been stacking for centuries. Quietly. Neatly. Efficiently. One belief-formed construct at a time. No collapse. No rebellion. Just fulfillment, sorted and sustained."

I felt the cold of it then—not ice. Not malice. Just the scale.

"A prison," she said.

"No," he replied, gently. "A mirror. Structured fulfillment. A closed, self-sustaining loop designed from each soul's own beliefs. What they expect. What they long for. No conflict. No collapse."

My mouth was dry.

"They think they've made it," I said.

"They *have*," Ansel answered. "By their terms. The soul enters as itself—scarred, hopeful, half-healed. The Stack reads that imprint and builds accordingly. No judgment. No editing. Just alignment."

Cyr shook her head. "You think that's mercy?"

"I think that's freedom," he said. "True freedom. The kind Heaven can't offer and Hell won't allow."

I moved beside her. "And you built this alone?"

"I designed it," he said. "Others handle delivery. Cultivation. Ritual access. I don't manage inputs. I define outcomes."

Cyr stepped forward, voice sharp. "You're playing God."

"No," Ansel said calmly. "I retired him."

I stepped forward. Not to accuse—just to make sure the air had no silence left.

"They'll shut it down," I said. "Heaven. Hell. Once they know."

Ansel tilted his head, almost tender.

"They do know."

Cyr's posture shifted, weight drawing inward. "That's a lie. No one saw the theft. Hell would never endorse heresy."

He didn't flinch. Just tilted his head, like correcting a student who'd almost grasped the shape of the proof.

"You're thinking in categories—Heaven, Hell, heresy, loyalty. But your superiors? They stopped thinking that way a long time ago. They saw the problem: the backlog. Overflow. Drift. Unclaimed souls stacking into delay loops, crowding the thresholds. You know it. The system was collapsing."

He took a breath. Not dramatic—just measured, sequenced, as if calibrating tone.

"They didn't sanction us. But they didn't stop us either. Because we found the breach. Not in the *Accord*. In the soul."

He looked to both of us now.

"The *Accord* governs celestial and infernal action. It binds agents. It controls movement. It doesn't touch mortals. Human souls were always outside the treaty. That was the weakness — and the key."

Cyr's mouth opened, but no sound came. He went on.

"We tried everything. Possession. Grafting. Splicing. But the human soul is resilient. It rejects foreign will. It burns out what it doesn't recognize. Even with demonic channels, most vessels shattered. Most hosts died."

He stepped to the edge of the room's light.

"But near death? That's where it shifts. The soul weakens. The shell cracks. And if the insertion comes not as override but integration — *then* it holds. The soul comes back changed. Whole. But woven."

His voice dropped.

"Fully human. Fully empowered. Celestial-grade capability. But no restrictions. Not bound to move the dead by judgment. Not required to honour the binary. A weave can transfer a soul to the Stack without invoking the *Accord*. And no one can challenge it — because it's not breaking the rules. It's outside them."

I could feel it click, even before he finished.

"All that was left," he said, "was to prepare belief. Give the dying what they already wanted. Use mortal agents to preach consent. Seed the new doctrine. Deploy the weaves. And let the system transfer itself."

No more war. No more judgment. No more waiting — just delivery."

He looked at Cyr.

"Hell doesn't need to understand a tool to use it. Once

they confirmed the losses weren't leaking to Heaven, weren't destabilizing the field—they let it run. No sanction. No command. But no pursuit either."

Then he turned toward me.

"And Heaven," I said. "Didn't approve it. But someone did. Not God. Not the Word. But the ones tasked with backlog. With binding. With throughput."

Camael.

Ansel caught the shift in my face. He didn't need the name spoken.

"Not all betrayals wear robes," he said. "Some carry schedules. Quotas. Ledgers full of unascended dead."

Cyr didn't move.

Ansel looked only at me. Not triumphant. Just sure.

"He watched it happen. Watched the delays mount, the queues back up, the numbers strain every ceiling Heaven never thought to build for. He knew the cost of inertia. And he knew the price of sanction."

He took a single step closer.

"We didn't need approval. Just silence. One moment where oversight faltered. One aperture in the Overflow. That was his offering. He didn't call it permission. He called it triage. But it opened the breach."

His voice thinned to clarity.

"The first Stack seeded in that window. And by the time Heaven looked back—"

"It was already working," I said.

Ansel nodded. "Exactly. And nothing gets shut down if it works."

Cyr's voice was low. "They all let it happen."

"Delayed action," Ansel replied. "And delay is the purest endorsement there is."

I felt it then — not defeat, or even rage. Just the final piece sliding into place. The war hadn't been lost. It had been licensed.

Cyr stepped forward. The knife hadn't moved. Neither had her eyes.

"How do we take it apart?" she asked.

Ansel didn't hesitate. "You don't."

"Then we'll burn it."

"You can't."

"Why."

He looked at her, then at me. Neither defiant nor afraid. Just exact.

"Because it isn't a machine. It's an accommodation. Every soul inside it *chose* what it became. To tear it down is to break belief itself."

Cyr's grip tightened.

"What happens if we try?" I asked.

Ansel answered without pause.

"Celestia collapses. The load redistributes. Heaven and Hell split under the weight. No one is ready. Not even you."

He stepped back — not retreating. Making room. He closed his eyes.

"You think I'm the lock," he said. "I'm not. I'm only the author."

"I wasn't meant to exist," he added, quieter now. "The first time, they called it rupture. I called it clarity." He looked past us again—somewhere beyond the pines. "No tether. No judgment. Just continuity. That was the breach."

Cyr didn't announce it. Just moved—once, precisely. The blade entered low and rose sharp. Not for pain. Not for spectacle. For certainty.

He exhaled once. No gasp. No protest.

Then he fell.

I stepped over the body. Reached down. Two fingers to the throat. The soul still there. Waiting.

I asked again.

"I commend you to tell us how to take it apart."

His mouth moved. No delay. No lie.

"You can't."

UNFILED: CAMAEL

The air changed before the body did.

I felt it peel—slow at first, then absolute. Flesh slackened. Skin surrendered. Ligaments unthreaded. Nothing violent. Just sequence. The body had never been mine. It had borrowed weight from gravity. Now the loan was called.

The coat fell first. Then the shirt. Then the rest. I didn't fall. I separated.

Bone sagged, then seeped—a spill of carbon and water. It steamed faintly on the threshold floor before it gave up structure entirely and smeared itself into null. One rib stayed whole for a moment longer than the others. Then it gave up.

I stood there still. Soul only.

Not clean. Not haloed. But present.

There was weight at the shoulders—residual memory of wings I hadn't unfurled in centuries. The edges of me caught light at odd angles. The silver in my hair was gone, but not because I was young. Time didn't apply. Only damage did. I had kept form, but not purity. A long gouge curved across my left side—a break that hadn't been healed, only cauterized. Some of the light that once wrapped around me was missing now. What remained was functional.

Across from me, Cyr stood in full celestial form. Watching the air itself measure her.

She didn't move. Not from reverence—*from caution.* Every second she stayed here was a risk. If permission didn't come soon, the system would act. I saw it in the way her posture narrowed—shoulders drawn slightly inward, weight balanced. Not braced, but ready to vanish if she had to. She wasn't afraid. But she knew the odds.

We stood at the edge of Heaven. The real edge—no gate, threshold, or wall. Just a demarcation.

Inside, the *Accord* had jurisdiction.

I still counted, barely.

She didn't.

And she knew it.

I watched the lines around her ripple. The edges of her outline fluttered in the air like heat distortion. Not from her. From the system recognizing her. Measuring her presence against law. She was not forgiven. She was not allowed.

Then:

"Mara," I said.

She stepped into view like she'd been waiting. Not hiding—waiting. Her coat was as white as ever, but the collar was higher now, and her gloves were on. Not ceremonial. Protective. She kept her hands at her sides. She didn't look at Cyr.

"You're unregistered," she said. Not to me.

"I'm owed entry." Cyr's voice was flat. Factual. No force in it. No plea.

"Debts don't pay the toll," Mara said. "They only open the question."

"And?" I asked.

Mara looked at me then. Not long. Just enough.

"You shouldn't have come back."

"I know."

Silence filled the space between us. It didn't echo. It pressed.

Then Mara exhaled. Not tired. Just done pretending she had another option.

"I can't authorize her. But I can give you the margin."

She reached into her sleeve and pulled a token—flat, thin, not metal. Script glimmered across it, not language but function. She tossed it through the air. I caught it. It dissolved against my palm.

"She's with you now. What she does, you're responsible for."

"I've been responsible for worse."

"Not lately," she said. Then added, without warmth, "Good luck."

She turned before I could answer. Her footsteps left no sound, but the space she walked through didn't close behind her. It *watched* us walk in.

We crossed the perimeter together.

Cyr leaned in. "You really think she meant it?"

"She meant something," I said. "Just not what she said."

"Backhanded?"

"Reverse blade."

No reply. She smiled once, barely. And we walked deeper.

They noticed us three thresholds in.

Not all of Heaven was built for violence. But some corridors remembered it.

We moved fast—Cyr ahead, scanning angles, her hands already trailing the outline of a curse she hadn't cast yet. I kept stride, glyphs loaded in the palm, half-spoken permissions seared behind my teeth.

The air shivered. Ahead, three shapes dropped from the upper vaults—not guards. *Custodians.* Wings tight. Forms indistinct. Their faces held nothing. Their arms ended in light.

They didn't ask questions.

Neither did we.

Cyr twisted once, snapped her fingers, and a bolt of colourless fire bit through the left flank. It didn't burn. It erased. One dropped. The other two surged forward.

I drew the old mark—the one we weren't supposed to use anymore—and traced it in the air. It caught. Froze them mid-lunge. Their wings stiffened. Then cracked.

One staggered backward. The other disintegrated before it could scream.

Cyr exhaled. "They're not built like they used to be."

"They're not built to stop us," I said. "They're built to delay us."

And then the light shifted. Not from above. From behind.

Seraphine.

She didn't announce herself. She didn't posture.

She just walked in. Each step corrected the corridor behind her.

Platinum robes. Seamless. Halo visible. Hands unraised.

"Sael," she said. "You've violated every line."

"I'm not under lines anymore."

"You're still under law."

Her eyes flicked to Cyr. "And you've overreached."

"I do that," Cyr said.

Seraphine didn't rise to it. She took one more step and the floor leveled.

"You will not reach him," she said. "I've sealed the upper sanctum. No route from here passes through."

"Then we'll cut one," I said.

She moved. Faster than light. A blur of velocity and force. Her hand came for my throat, the other etched in sanction.

But I was already lower.

I struck her in the ribs. Not physical. *Patterned.* Her body shuddered where I touched her code. Her halo sparked, then flickered.

Cyr lunged. Her blade wasn't steel—it was shaped memory, honed to cut. She slashed across Seraphine's arm. The robe split. No blood. Just exposed light.

Seraphine staggered once. Regained form. Then released a pulse.

We were thrown. Hard. I hit the wall. Cyr slid twenty feet across the floor.

Seraphine advanced. "You're not permitted," she said again.

I stood. Spat once. Raised my hand.

"I *am* the permission."

And I said her name.

Not *Seraphine.*

The one she had *before* the robes.

The one she thought no one remembered.

She froze. Just long enough.

Cyr struck her in the chest. Not to kill. To *unmake.*

The corridor fractured. Seraphine collapsed — her body intact, her certainty gone.

We didn't stay.

There was no time.

I stepped over her. She didn't move.

"Forgive me," she whispered.

But she didn't say *for what.*

The door knew us.

It didn't open. It evaluated.

Cyr shifted beside me — not nervous, but aware. Her presence drew attention even when no one looked. The *Accord* didn't permit her here, not without sanction. But she had it. My margin carried her. And the door read it. We were measured as a pair. One broken soul, one tolerated heretic.

Then the slab softened. Not movement, exactly — something closer to allowance. The wall receded into itself, not as a gesture of welcome, but protocol. A slot opened in judgment.

We entered.

The room had not changed.

Same three chairs. Same desk. Same pale ambient light that refused to cast a shadow. Still geometry arranged for judgment. Still a space designed to reflect inevitability.

Camael did not stand.

He sat behind the desk, robe seamless, eyes steady. He did not perform readiness. He simply *was*.

"Sael," he said. "You're late."

No anger. No sarcasm. Just time, noted.

Cyr remained silent. She stood just inside the threshold, posture reserved. Not deferent. Calculating. She knew the laws here, even if she didn't believe in them.

I stepped forward. No bow. No preamble.

"You allowed it," I said.

Camael folded one hand over the other. "Define your accusation."

"The Stack. The rerouting. The mass ascensions without judgment. The tetherless transitions. The falsified closures. The missing. The quiet."

His expression didn't shift. "You mistake failure of oversight for endorsement."

I shook my head once. "I mistook your silence for restraint. But it wasn't. You *licensed* them."

"You have no evidence."

"I have names. I have fragments. I have dead agents and rewritten souls. I have files that resolved without resolution."

Camael's expression didn't shift. "None of which

implicate me."

"No," I said. "They *do*."

He blinked. Just once.

"I have the soul of Elias Shaw. Of Eden Vale. Of Nolan Creedy. Of Hiram Feld. And Ansel Reon. They all spoke."

Silence now, but not passive.

"They said it was you. You granted the shape. You made the Overflow viable. You cleared the tether bypass. Ansel named you by title."

Still, Camael didn't move.

"You didn't sign. You didn't send. But you permitted. You blessed it from within the system and watched it grow. That's not indirect. That's *architectural*."

I stepped closer. The room didn't resist. That worried me more.

Camael regarded me as a disappointment already processed. "You've become metaphysically unstable."

"You gave them a corridor. The Overflow doesn't permit structure unless someone grants shape. The Protocol didn't punch through Hell. It didn't breach Heaven. It was *allowed*. By someone with clearance. With mandate. With authority."

He didn't deny it.

He simply said, "You misunderstand the burden."

Cyr tilted her head. Not curiosity. More like revulsion being held for later.

"The afterlife was collapsing under its own logic," Camael said. "Too many souls. Too many variables. No capacity. No time. Protocol offered a solution. No pain. No delay. No tethers. It was efficient."

He rose. Not protest. Not posture. Just the motion required. His robe did not wrinkle.

"You call it corruption," he said. "I call it grace with architecture. Salvation as system. No more judgment. No more intercession. Just entry. Seamless. Accepted. *Wanted.*"

"Wanted by whom?" I asked.

"By the souls. By the people you used to call broken. They don't want refinement. They want rest."

I looked him over. There was no fury in him. Only conviction.

"You didn't adapt Heaven," I said. "You *abdicated* it."

A flicker in the air — something brief. Not a guard. Not a shield. A system preparing itself.

I reached forward — not as gesture, but retrieval. Into memory. Into power I was no longer permitted to hold. My hand burned. Light rose in jagged arcs — neither gold nor flame, but exposed authority. The kind not wielded since the *Accord* was signed.

Camael saw. He did not flinch.

"You will destroy the balance," he said.

"You already did."

He stepped forward. "Do you even understand what you're doing?"

"Yes."

Then I spoke. No language. No metaphor. Name.

Camael's face froze. His hands opened — not to yield,

but in shock.

Cyr stepped forward and drove the sigil into the air. A second flare—a glyph twisted at the edge, like a bone rebroken wrong.

Camael staggered. Not because we hurt him. Because we *named* what he had done. Judgment didn't scream—it cracked, sudden and silent. The light in the room didn't dim. It turned inward. Camael fell—not in body, but in role. His form held, but the office did not.

He collapsed to one knee. His hands clutched at a name that no longer recognized him.

"You gave them permission," I said. "And now I revoke it."

Cyr stepped forward. Her eyes didn't hold rage. They held *jurisdiction.*

She raised her palm. Not in mercy. In verdict.

What formed above it wasn't glass. It was Judgment, infernal and binding—the authority Hell reserves for its own. The air rippled with indictment. Glyphs no angel should read. Letters that weren't letters—symbols shaped to condemn. She spoke once. Not loudly. Just with finality.

"This was weighed."

Camael turned. Not to flee. To *plead.* But the words didn't come.

The sentence struck—not like force. Like fact.

His name—what remained of it—fractured. Not erased. *Revoked.*

He screamed once. Not aloud. Not with pain. With *realization.*

And then — gone.

No wound. No blood.

Just cessation.

Unmade.

UNFILED: SAL

The Overflow wasn't meant to hold shape.

It was the third sphere: grey, edgeless, infinite. A metaphysical bleed between Earth and the judgment planes. No thresholds. No gravity. Just mist and memory, drift and delay. A place where things fray, not form.

But the Stack had structure.

That's how they found it. Not with maps, but with principle. A straight line in a place that didn't allow lines. A location in a place that had never agreed to being located.

It rose like cordwood from the murk — mile after mile of micro echo-spaces, each one sealed and humming. No entrances. No seams. Just light folded inward — each capsule a self-contained afterlife, compressed around belief.

Each one offered something different. A cabin. A cathedral. A final embrace. A last broadcast. Every capsule ran the same loop: comfort, closure, cessation. No judgment. No grief. Just the clean silence of a dream that never asked to end.

Now they were ending.

The joint task force arrived in silence. No procession. No announcement. Just pressure: Heaven, Hell, and Purgatory bearing witness in equal, miserable measure.

Heaven's agents wore no radiance. Their haloes were dimmed by protocol. They moved slow, like every motion might bruise. Hell sent its watchers, not its executioners. Black-robed and bristled, they stood at a remove, eyes gleaming with precision. And from the centre, Purgatory opened — faceless figures in layered grey. They did not speak. They simply worked.

I stood beside Mara. Neither of us wore our old insignia. Titles felt obscene here.

The first capsule broke like a sealed breath. No explosion. Just a sigh of release and a tremor of resistance. A boy's voice whispered "Mom?" — and then he was gone, pulled into a swirl of silver light that hadn't existed a moment earlier. Heaven's claim. Clean. Silent.

A second capsule cracked. Heat licked out. A man screamed. Hell took him.

And then the work began in earnest.

It was the start of something Reon had sworn couldn't be done. Certainly, to release millions of cocooned souls at once would flood Celestia, overwhelm its thresholds, and rupture belief at scale. The damage would echo. So they worked painstakingly — false heaven by false heaven. The labour compounded. The risk deepened. And still, they began. Not because it would succeed. But because it had to.

One by one, they breached the afterlives. Not with weapons. With presence. Each capsule required metaphysical contact: an agent willing to touch the tether, feel what had been believed, and sever it with truth.

Some souls wept when the lie fell away. Some resisted. Some begged to be let back in.

None were allowed.

This wasn't punishment. It was reckoning.

Mara's voice was low. "We can't do it all at once. The shock would break them."

"So instead we break them slowly," I said.

She didn't argue.

"We dismantle the illusion. Then they move forward. One by one."

Ahead of us, a capsule folded. A woman stepped out, blinking like a newborn. "Thank you, Father," she said to no one. Heaven took her before the confusion set in.

"She thought she'd been saved," I said.

"She was," Mara answered. "Just not yet."

Another scream. Another breach. Red light. Hell again.

"Some won't forgive us," she added.

"They never asked us to," I said.

We kept watching.

Some echo-spaces crumbled like paper. Others fought collapse. I saw one shaped like a megachurch stage—light show intact, praise team mid-chorus, the applause of a crowd who'd already transcended. When it ruptured, it screamed.

"It had to be done," Mara said.

"It always does," I said. "That's what no one tells you about grace. It keeps going."

I walked for a while. Past broken heavens. Past new arrivals. Past the ones who hadn't yet woken.

One capsule caught my eye.

Inside, a living room. Floral wallpaper yellowed at the seams. Ceiling fan turning slow above a sagging couch.

The scent of stew and stale tobacco—synthetic, metaphysical, but precise. In the corner, a chipped end table stacked with *La Presse*, three decks of cards, and a half-drunk bottle of Labatt 50. The ashtray hadn't been emptied in decades. It didn't need to be.

Yvonne Boivin sat in the centre of it all.

She wore a wool cardigan, one elbow patched with a different colour. Her hair was soft grey, tied back in a way only habit explains. She was laughing.

Across from her, Raymond dealt another hand of cribbage. Alive. Healthy. Hair combed back like he used to. Glasses low on his nose. His forearms were thick again—meat and labour, not hospital tubes. He was joking about something—she was teasing him in return. There were friends in the kitchen. One called out, asking if they were hungry.

Smoke curled from a cigarette in a dish no one claimed.

The television hummed behind them: *Salvation Live avec Pasteur Jean.* French sermon. Gentle voice. Soft promises. Something about reunion. About the Lord preparing a place. About mercy with your name on it.

Yvonne's eyes stayed on Raymond.

She didn't know she'd been stolen. Didn't know she'd died.

She thought she'd made it.

She thought this was grace.

And then the capsule cracked. Not with force. With exposure. Light seeped in through the corners—cold, sterile, true. The walls pulsed. The fan slowed, then stopped. One of the card decks flickered, split, repeated the same deal again and again. The beer bottle vanished.

Raymond looked at her—and froze. Not frightened—just pausing. Mid-laugh. Mouth still open. Then his image stuttered, blurred, and dissolved like a reflection in disturbed water.

The capsule emptied. The light withdrew. Only the shape of the room lingered for a breath—and then it too was gone.

Yvonne reached for him.

She stood. Confused. Still hoping.

"Raymond?" she said.

And Purgatory took her.

No fire. No fanfare. Just transfer.

False heaven, deconstructed.

Soul, reprocessed.

The bar didn't have a name, and it didn't need one. The booths knew us. The tap didn't ask.

I sat in the usual place, drink in hand, watching the television. No sound. Just headline text crawling past the bottom of the muted screen. I didn't have to read it twice.

EDEN VALE FOUND DEAD IN CALGARY RETREAT; AUTHORITIES INVESTIGATING "UNUSUAL CIRCUMSTANCES"

The anchor's face didn't match the gravity. It was all teeth and concern, the kind they teach in broadcast school. Behind her, the image cut between aerial footage of the gated retreat and some older clip—Eden on stage, arms raised, smiling like mercy itself.

I took another drink.

Mara was already there when I arrived. Corner booth. Same black coat, same no-bullshit stare. She didn't order anything. Didn't need to.

She just nodded toward the screen. "Wasn't you?"

"No."

"Hell, then?"

I shrugged. "Most likely. She was useful until she wasn't."

She watched me. I didn't return it. The ice in my glass clicked once, then stopped.

Ten minutes later, Chandler pushed through the door. Less shine than usual. Vest gone. Sleeves rolled. He looked like he hadn't changed clothes since the transfer site.

He saw the screen. Froze. "You didn't—"

"No," I said.

He exhaled, slow. "Then who?"

"Pick a side," I said. "They both owed her something. Or wanted something cleaned up. Or both."

He sat across from me. Mara didn't move.

"They're calling it a collapse," Chandler said. "The news. The agencies. Quiet panic upstairs."

I glanced at him. "It's not a collapse."

"No?"

"It's a correction."

Mara answered for me. "A partial one."

A pause.

"You're officially under departmental review."

Mara snorted.

Chandler ignored her. "I think they'll issue you a new halo. Maybe even promotion. You blew the doors off the biggest metaphysical fraud in centuries."

Mara shook her head. "That's not how it works."

"It should be," Chandler said.

"He made a mess," Mara replied. "They don't reward mess."

Chandler turned to me. "You wouldn't wear it anyway, would you?"

"Didn't last time," I said. "Haven't worn a halo in a couple millennia."

He didn't know whether to laugh or be offended. He chose neither.

Outside, someone honked—sharp, too loud for a street this empty. No one in the bar flinched. No one else seemed to care.

"They've pulled five major facilitators from Hell's side," Mara said. "Three slated for Purgatory review. Others disappeared."

"And Heaven?" Chandler asked.

"Washing its hands. Claiming no knowledge."

"They didn't have knowledge," I said. "They had doubt. And they looked away."

He didn't argue.

I looked back at the television. The footage had changed again—now Eden's retreat at night. Flashing lights. A perimeter of yellow tape. A body covered by canvas, wheeled out through ornamental glass doors. Her temple banners still hung above the entrance: YOU ARE ALREADY BECOMING.

"Millions still believe it," Chandler said.

"They will for a while," Mara replied. "Belief outlives its source."

"It's going to make transcendence harder," he said quietly. "They won't want to go. Not to the real thing. Not after tasting the fake."

I drained my glass. Set it down.

"They never did."

The house hadn't changed.

Same street. Same sag in the roofline. Same boards nailed crooked over the fenêtre like someone ran outta time halfway through giving a damn. I stepped through the front door—not opened it, stepped through it. The echo knew me now.

Inside: the same couch. Same stale colour. Same smoke-stained curtains curling in the breeze of memory. The TV glowed soft in the corner, flickering blue and gold across the walls.

Raymond was in his chair. Cigarette in hand. Pastor Jean on the screen. A sermon about reunion—re-looped, overmixed, warm in the wrong places.

He looked over.

"Ben là," he said. "Regarde qui c'est qui r'vient."

"I said I would."

"Sure, but y'know, people say lots of shit."

I moved to the couch. Sat without asking. The springs remembered me.

He took a drag. Let the smoke spill from his nose.

"You look rough," he said.

"I've been working."

"You win?"

"Some of it."

He nodded, like that counted.

The TV mumbled low—French half-faded with tape hiss. "Le Seigneur prépare des chambres pour chacun…"

I looked over.

"Ray."

"Mm?"

"I saw her."

He didn't flinch. But the hand holding his smoke went still.

"She was in the Stack. They built her a copy. A Heaven with all the right parts. Cards. Fèves au lard on the stove. She even had you there—healthy, smiling, dealing' hands. You made her laugh."

He looked at the ashtray.

"She believed it," I said. "Held on so hard, the place formed around it."

Still quiet.

"We broke it. Took it apart. Heaven, Hell, even Purgatory showed up for this one. She's being sorted now. Properly."

He took a long drag. Held it. Then:

"Elle a toujours dit qu'elle irait en premier."

"She thought you already had."

"Pfft. Sounds like her." He chuckled low. "Tryna surprise me, comme d'habitude."

I nodded.

"So," he said, "she's comin'?"

"Yeah. Might take time."

"Bah. Elle est toujours en retard, de toute façon."

He smiled, small and true.

"She was late to our wedding," he added. "Missed the bus, caught the wrong train, showed up smilin' like it was part of the plan."

He reached into the crumpled pack on the table, offered one out.

"Smoke?"

I shook my head. "Non, merci."

He shrugged. "Comme tu veux."

He lit it anyway. The room filled with soft silence. The walls held.

He didn't ask how long. Didn't ask why it happened.

He just leaned back in his chair, blew smoke at the ceiling, and nodded once.

"J'peux attendre."

I stayed a while. Said nothing. Just let the moment sit.

He didn't need help passing on.

He just needed time.

And time was the one thing he still had.

The rooftop didn't have a name. Most places don't—once you're done needing them.

Tar gravel. Bent rebar. A rusted HVAC unit humming with indifferent life. The skyline stretched like an old scar—glass towers blinking red through the fog.

I sat on the ledge. Feet over the edge. Wind in the collar. My coat still carried dust from three metaphysical spheres. Some of it might've been mine.

She didn't knock. Didn't announce herself. She never had.

Cyr stepped out of the shadow by the service door. Same boots. Same long coat. Her silhouette hitched once in the wind, then settled like she belonged to the weight.

She looked at me. Didn't scowl. Didn't smile. Just done waiting.

"You came alone," I said.

"I told them I would."

"No backup?"

She smiled. "I'm the backup."

I nodded.

The city murmured below us—car horns, late trains, someone yelling too far away to matter.

"You said I could kill you later."

"I remember."

She walked closer. Not fast. Not slow. Like she'd made peace with it. Like we both had.

"You still got the glyph?" I asked.

She tapped her hip. "Wouldn't be official without it."

I looked out at the lights. "Still a lot of work to do. Still a lot of souls stuck."

"Not your work anymore."

"Never was. Not really."

Cyr came to stand beside me. The wind caught her coat, then dropped it. The sky above was black without stars. Just blur. Just weight.

"You got anything to say?" she asked.

"No epilogue," I said. "No sermon."

She waited.

"Just one thing," I added.

"What's that?"

"Make it hurt."

And she did.

Author's Note

When I began *Casework for a Broken Heaven*, I thought I was chasing a noir detective story. A weary investigator, a city of shadows, a corruption hidden in the files.

But the book refused to stay in that frame. The deeper I wrote, the more it became about systems—how they promise order, how they corrode, how they decide what a life is worth. At its centre stands Sal, a man tasked with keeping Heaven's records in order, and slowly discovering that the records themselves have begun to lie.

I'm certainly not the first to ask: *is what we want ever the same as what we need*? Augustine thought our restless longings would never be quiet until they found God. Simone Weil called attention itself a form of prayer— letting go of appetite so that truth might enter. Even C.S. Lewis, writing more simply, said that joy points us beyond every lesser satisfaction. I don't claim to answer. But I wanted to let those echoes through the precinct walls.

Casework is a mystery with all the grit and ruin of the noir tradition. But if, between the chase and the shadows, you glimpse something larger—something frayed, something failing, something still burning— then perhaps you've found what I was after.

If you'd like to explore more of my work, or share your thoughts, you can find me at www.harwoodjones.com. I'd love to hear from you.

--Troy

www.ingramcontent.com/pod-product-compliance
Lightning Source LLC
Chambersburg PA
CBHW070732120726
47910CB00001B/73